A CORNISH HOMECOMING

Liverpool, 1930. Reformed con-artist Leah Marshall has long yearned for the thrills of her former life. Now she has the chance to relive it all as an exciting new 'game' beckons, but she soon discovers the rules have changed. One slip-up and she could lose everything . . .

Back home in Cornwall, the Foxes are making their own difficult decisions. An old agreement has turned sour, putting the hotel at risk once more, and the children are embarking on their own, sometimes perilous, paths. Matriarch Helen Fox knows she must take charge of her own future. Should she hold on a little longer, or let go and move on?

But when a new and deadly danger steps through the revolving doors of Fox Bay Hotel, Helen finds it might not be her choice to make after all . . .

TERRI NIXON

A CORNISH HOMECOMING

Complete and Unabridged

MAGNA
Leicester

First published in Great Britain in 2021 by
Piatkus
An imprint of Little, Brown Book Group
London

First Ulverscroft Edition
published 2022
by arrangement with
Little, Brown Book Group
London

*A catalogue record for this book is available
from the British Library.*

ISBN 978-0-7505-4933-2

Published by
Ulverscroft Limited
Anstey, Leicestershire

Printed and bound in Great Britain by
TJ Books Ltd., Padstow, Cornwall

This book is printed on acid-free paper

This is for my fellow 'Bear Catz':
Shelley Clarke and Jude Singleton.

Let the good times roll . . . Again!

Dramatis Personae

Helen Fox: Part-owner, and manager, of Fox Bay Hotel in Cornwall. Helen has put all her effort into nurturing the hotel's reputation, since taking it over following the death of her husband, Harry, ten years previously; it is now one of the most highly .sought-after holiday destinations on the Cornish Riviera.

She has remained faithful to Harry's memory through the intervening years, but after learning that local farmer, **Alfie Nancarrow**'s friendship has deepened into love, she has realised she returns his feelings. However, she left it too late to tell him and he is now engaged to **Beth Nancarrow**, his brother's widow.

Leah Marshall: An honorary member of the Fox family, since befriending Helen when she first took over the hotel. Leah eventually confessed that she had lived a dangerous life in the past; she and her husband Glynn had engaged in fraud and confidence tricks, and her husband had subsequently been imprisoned. Believing her blossoming relationship with **Adam Coleridge** was over, Leah was reconciled with her newly released husband at Christmas, and she left Fox Bay, telling Helen she had rejoined her old nursing profession.

Adam Coleridge: Helen's childhood friend, and best friend of her late husband. Adam's investments had been responsible for the Fox family losing everything

1

while Harry was alive, and contributed to the financial downfall that had led to Harry's death. He remained estranged from the family for ten years, but was able to redeem himself by saving the hotel from developers, and gifting half of it to Helen. He is now part-owner, with her. Adam fell for Leah when she'd attempted to trick him out of his money, in order to help Helen save Fox Bay, but had believed Helen to be the true love of his life. He now knows what he feels for Helen is a different kind of love, and has determined to persuade Leah to come home.

Roberta Fox: Helen's eldest daughter; a keen motorcyclist, Bertie was involved in a freak accident when returning from the racetrack, and lost the lower part of her right leg. She expressed an interest in turning to aviation, when she learned that one of her best friends, **Xander Nicholls**, intended to take flying lessons. This has caused a rift between herself and her fiancé, **Jowan Nancarrow**, but they are both determined to try and overcome it.

Benjamin Fox: Helen's only son, the eldest of the Fox 'cubs', and the night-shift manager of Fox Bay. Ben had developed an early interest in the running of the hotel and become a sommelier under the tutelage of **Guy Bannacott**. He has long harboured a crush on Hollywood star **Daisy Conrad**, and when she visited at Christmas it became clear that she was attracted to him too. He attends regular poker nights at another hotel, where the assistant manager is a casual girlfriend.

Fiona Fox: The youngest Fox daughter, now sixteen years old. When they'd moved to Cornwall she'd immediately fallen in love with the beach and the sea, and is one of the shore crew at the local lifeboat station; assisting with the launching and recovery of the Trethkellis lifeboat, *The Lady Dafna.* Fiona befriended a girl named Amy, following a sea rescue, who revealed herself to be a stowaway, pregnant, and trying to re-connect with the runaway father of her child. Fiona is now becoming close to **Danny Quick**, a lifeboat crew member, son of the local constable.

The Nicholls Siblings: Xander and his sister **Lynette** are Bertie Fox's best friends, and live in Brighton. Xander has announced his intention to take flying lessons, but didn't mention, until after Bertie had also seized on the idea, that he would be taking them in Cornwall. Bertie's fiancé, Jowan Nancarrow, has always been jealous of Xander's glamour, and the easy friendship he shares with Bertie.

Guy Bannacott: The restaurant and bar manager at Fox Bay. His slightly haughty attitude masks a deep affection for the Fox family, of which the former matriarch, *Fleur*, is his best friend. Guy was recently revealed to be the father of Daisy Conrad's co-star, **Freddie Wishart**.

The Nancarrows: Farmers at Higher Valley Farm, which backs on to Fox Bay Hotel and supplies the kitchens. Beth is the widowed mother of twins, Jowan and Jory, who had inadvertently caused the accident which killed their father. Their uncle, Alfie, moved to Higher Valley to try and keep it running. Beth has long

3

been in love with Alfie, and was therefore overjoyed when he proposed to her — not realising it was a reaction to being rejected by Helen Fox. Jowan is sensible and family-orientated, while Jory is the wilder of the twins, and is prone to throwing his money away on drink and gambling. Jory had saved Daisy Conrad's life, when it was endangered by Fiona Fox's stowaway friend.

1

Empire Park Hotel, Liverpool.
February 1930

Leah Marshall didn't dare stop in the doorway, in case she changed her mind. *This is it, no going back now . . .*

The lobby of the Empire Park was like the set of a Conrad-Wishart movie. Soaring frescos, painted on the multi-levelled ceilings; glittering glass chandeliers and highly polished silver; so many mirrors it must take an army of cleaners to work on those alone; and a wide staircase, with a deep blue carpet dotted with silver stars . . . Leah half-expected Daisy Conrad herself to appear at the top of those stairs, swathed in winter-white fur and with a handsome, tuxedoed man on each arm.

The music drifting from the piano in the corner was soft but not slow, giving the atmosphere a lightly charged feeling, a sense that one must keep moving, talking, circulating, or be left behind. Unlike Fox Bay, the Empire Park was not a residents-only hotel, and the numbers were clearly swelled tonight; beautifully dressed, loudly chattering guests regularly spilled out of the main ballroom and spread to the three different bars. The party was in full swing, but where was the host?

Leah stood straighter and reminded herself that she was dressed appropriately for a huge event like this, but she still felt a little like a cabaret artiste in her figure-hugging, green halter-neck gown. Her gloves itched, and she peeled them off now that she was in the dense warmth of the hotel, feeling the rings on her wedding finger like lead weights. She forced herself not to look at them; after all, why would she do that? She was used to them. They were nothing new, and certainly nothing to twist around her finger as her nerves reached snapping point.

She gave her coat to the attendant and moved through the lobby, keeping her head up, and with a sense of purpose in her manner that she didn't feel. It wouldn't do to seem aimless, not here. Not tonight. She avoided the myriad mirrors with an effort, except to ensure her pageboy was perfectly in place after her short walk from the taxi to the front door, and to hastily adjust the silk rose at her shoulder, crushed flat by her coat.

'Mrs Scripps!'

She turned towards the voice, hiding her relief behind a mask of pleased surprise, and pulled Millicent's American accent from her wide repertoire. 'Mr Freeman, so good to see you again.'

The bearded, bespectacled man beamed and gestured her over to his group. 'I'm so glad you could make it after all,' he called out, causing heads to turn. His Cockney accent was more subdued than she'd become used to, but still distinct from most of the other voices she could hear around her.

'Thank you so much for inviting me,' she said, joining the group. 'I do hope your host won't mind?'

A man of medium height and bland, forgettable features inclined his head towards her, and she guessed him to be the man in question. Mr Freeman drew her closer, one hand at her bare back in a too-familiar gesture. She would have strong words for him later on.

6

'Here, let me introduce you,' Freeman said. 'Leonard, this is the lady I was telling you about, Mrs Millicent Scripps. I was fortunate enough to receive the point of her umbrella in the small of my back, at Ma Egerton's earlier today.'

'I'm so sorry about that,' Leah began, but he brushed it away.

'We'd never have got talking otherwise, would we? Mrs Scripps, this is Mr Leonard Neville, well known philanthropist, and the generous host of this magnificent party.'

He went on to name the others in the group, but Neville was the only one of interest. Leah kept her greeting brief, then stood silent while Mr Freeman held forth at great length about his latest investment.

'America is where the clever money's going,' he said. 'RKO, Good Boy, Paramount, you know. Since the depression hit they're desperate for overseas investors, they'll snatch our hands off.'

'Of course,' one woman broke in, 'with you being American, Mrs Scripps, you'd know a lot about the movie industry wouldn't you?'

'Oh!' Leah shook her head. 'I'm not from California. I live . . . *lived*,' she broke off, and now she allowed herself to twist the huge engagement ring, just once, 'in New York with my husband.'

'Oh . . . .' The woman looked uncomfortable. 'And now?'

'I moved away after he died late last year.'

'I'm so sorry,' the woman murmured, and when Leah only smiled sadly at her she turned back to her companion and allowed Mr Freeman to continue his story.

Eventually the others drifted away and left only

Leah, Mr Freeman and Mr Neville.

'Do please call me Leonard,' Neville invited, deftly lifting a drink from the tray of a passing waiter and handing it to her.

'Thank you. It's very gracious of you to allow me to come along tonight. I'm afraid I'm quite adrift in town. Or I was, until Mr Freeman kindly took me under his wing.'

'It's my pleasure.' Mr Freeman's hand was on her back again, this time lower, and she stepped smoothly away under the pretence of examining one of the glossy-leaved ferns in a pot nearby.

'I do hope you enjoy the party,' Mr Neville said. 'Perhaps, if you're still at a loose end tomorrow you might join me for lunch? Both of you, of course,' he added.

'Oh! That'd be so nice, thank you.'

'Well I understand from Mr Freeman here that you have a little . . . difficulty you'd like help with?'

Leah shot a scowl at Mr Freeman, who recoiled slightly. 'I spoke to you in confidence, during a difficult moment. I don't appreciate you discussing what I told you with a perfect stranger.' She turned back to Neville. 'I'm so sorry, Mr . . . Leonard, I wouldn't dream of imposing on your good will and your time.'

'It's no imposition, I assure you. I'd talk tonight, but as you can see,' he gestured with his cigar and no small amount of satisfaction, 'I have rather a lot of circulating to do.'

'Nevertheless, I'm afraid Mr Freeman here spoke out of turn, and — '

'Please, Mrs Scripps.' Neville took her hand, his eyes grazing the ring before returning to meet hers. 'I'd be delighted to help if I can. Shall we say here,

8

at twelve-thirty? If you choose not to confide in me, then we'll simply call it lunch, and an introduction to Liverpool.'

Leah hesitated, then nodded and smiled shyly. 'In that case, thank you, and I'd be delighted.'

'Ask for me at reception. Now,' Neville was already getting a faraway look on his face, 'I must mingle. Do enjoy the rest of the party, won't you?'

'I'm sure I shall.'

★ ★ ★

But ten minutes later Leah was shivering on the steps as she waited for the car to pull around. What a waste of a wonderful dress and two hours with a curling iron. Although perhaps not a waste exactly, given the lunch invitation, just a shame to have to cut the evening so short. She wondered idly if Mr Neville would be looking for her as the number of guests dwindled, and decided that even if he did he would assume she was too annoyed with 'Mr Freeman' to want to stay.

The car she was waiting for eventually pulled up, and the driver waved away the commissionaire who stepped forward to greet him. Leah pulled her coat closer and hurried down to slip into the passenger seat.

'Where were you? I'm freezing.'

'I couldn't just leave at the same time as you,' he pointed out reasonably, the East End now back in his voice in full strength. He pulled his glasses off and threw them irritably into the back seat. 'Those things were driving me mad. Home, then?'

'If you can call it that.' Leah shrank down into the seat, crossing her arms over her chest to keep warm.

9

'What's Glynn been doing while we've been wangling lunch invitations from dodgy philanthropists?'

'Sorting it from his end.' The man Neville knew as Freeman, but who Glynn had introduced to her as Wilf Stanley, negotiated the late evening traffic towards the ferry terminal. Leah neither liked nor trusted him, but Glynn had assured her he was perfect for the job. Besides, the whole thing had been his idea, conceived when the two men had shared a cell in Cardiff Prison, so she couldn't exactly refuse to work with him. But her skin crawled when his hand brushed it, as it did far too often, and she knew it wouldn't be too long before she gave him short shrift for doing so. In the meantime it was best to keep his temper sweet.

The trip back across the Mersey to Birkenhead passed in silence, and Wilf dropped her off outside the West Bank boarding house before ten o'clock. It might be hours yet before Glynn returned, and Wilf looked at her with a hopeful expression as she climbed out of the car, clearly expecting an invitation for a nightcap.

She smiled brightly, pretending not to notice. 'See you at the hotel tomorrow then. Twelve-thirty.'

He didn't reply at first, and Leah steeled herself for a firmer farewell, but eventually he nodded.

'Twelve-thirty then, darlin'. Dress smart.'

The cheek of him. 'Don't forget your glasses,' she fired back, 'they make you look clever.'

She waited for him to drive off before pushing open the door to the dingy little boarding house, and climbing the three storeys to the room she and Glynn shared. Such a far cry from the place she'd just left; she felt as if she'd been plucked out of a fairy tale and dropped straight into a Dickens novel.

She hung the dress carefully on one of the few rickety hangers in the wardrobe, and, shivering in the cold, she quickly pulled her robe over her rayon slip before going through the belongings that had come over from Fox Bay. They'd been delivered to the nurses' home at Pembroke Place, and once she'd safely intercepted them Leah had written to Helen to give West Bank as her new address, thankful her friend would never see this hovel for herself. She'd be appalled.

She carefully selected tomorrow's outfit. Lunch at the Empire Park, particularly in the company of Leonard Neville, would place her at the heart of much scrutiny and analysis, and she wanted to appear bright and personable, but not overly so, in light of her recent widowhood. It was a tricky balance, but she eventually selected a handkerchief-hemmed dress in royal blue, and laid aside the matching hat and light scarf to tone down the open neckline. She had just found the perfect watermelon tourmaline brooch to pin to her shoulder when she heard the downstairs door open, and a man's voice murmuring to the landlady. There weren't many guests at this time of year, so Leah was reasonably certain it would be Glynn, but she still tensed when she heard a heavy tread on the creaky boards outside their door; the last thing she wanted was a late-night visit from Wilf Stanley. She relaxed as the door opened and Glynn came in, looking dapper in a well-cut suit, his hat dark with rain.

'Everything go alright?' he asked, dropping his coat onto the bed.

Leah tutted and picked it up before the damp could transfer onto the sheets. 'Perfectly. Wilf's done

11

his background well, Neville seems to have accepted him as Freeman.'

'Excellent. And?'

'And we're having lunch tomorrow, at the hotel.'

'Good.' He caught her from behind, as she moved to the dressing table to begin brushing out the smooth waves she'd spent so long creating. 'You looked beautiful tonight, it's no wonder he's so keen to help.'

'We don't know that he will be, yet,' she pointed out. 'Just because he wants to hear what I have to say doesn't mean he'll fall for any of it. He's no fool, I'm sure of that.'

'He doesn't need to be a fool. Just needs to be greedy, and we know he's that at least.'

'Why him, anyway?' Leah put down her brush and turned to face him, effectively breaking his embrace. 'I half-expected some monster. What's Wilf got against him that he cooked this whole thing up even before he got out of jail?'

'No idea.' Glynn moved away to begin undressing. 'Didn't ask, doesn't matter. We'll get enough out of it to start our new life.'

'You're still keen to go to America then?'

'Aren't you? Just think how well we'd do out there. I could get a job anywhere, with a new identity, and you could teach actors how to speak with different accents, just like that producer bloke said you might.'

'Rex Kelly? Helen tells me *Dangerous Ladies* isn't going to be made after all, so my name won't be on any credit roll.'

'Still, there's work there if you want it, I'm sure of it.' Glynn pulled on his pyjamas and picked up his washbag. 'I won't be long.' His gaze drifted across her robed body, and she could tell what he was thinking, but deep down she knew it still wasn't time. They had been back together only a little over a month, and she couldn't surrender to his touch without feeling a surge of longing for that idiot Adam Coleridge.

As soon as Glynn had gone down the hall to the bathroom Leah used the bowl and ewer in their room to complete her own ablutions and climbed into the lumpy bed before he returned. She didn't bother to feign sleep, but managed to convey by her posture that tonight wasn't the night, and, to her relief, he didn't try to persuade her. Instead they talked over Leah's role for tomorrow until they both drifted off, to the comforting sound of the rain on the window.

★ ★ ★

The following morning Glynn left early, and Leah took her time dressing and, after another disappointing breakfast, readying herself for her lunch appointment. Then she put her smart shoes into her bag and walked to the ferry, once again wishing they could have stayed somewhere brighter, and closer to the Empire Park. But the cash Glynn had won from his final card game in Bude was fast disappearing, and maintaining the impression of wealth was eating into it alarmingly fast.

As always, Leah's mood lowered as she thought of that game, and how he had brushed off her questions about the bruise on his face with how it had simply 'got out of hand'. She was as certain as she could be that he had been one of those who had attacked Jory Nancarrow, and taken the money he'd been paid for pawning Bertie's engagement ring. The thought that she was even now living off those ill-acquired gains had almost made her turn tail more than once. But what would have been the use? She couldn't return to Fox Bay, not after having lied to everyone, and continuing to add to those lies with every letter she sent. A new life in America was all that was left to her now.

The ferry docked at Pier Head, and Leah turned up her coat collar against the biting cold and waved down a taxi. During the short ride to the hotel she slipped off her comfortable Mary Janes, donned a pair of low-heeled satin pumps, and went over her story yet again — this wasn't like those days at Fox Bay, when Millicent had merely been a diversion from the emptiness of her life without Daniel. The adoption of a lively, confident alter-ego had helped her, then, to suppress the memory of the man she had loved, and lost to the war, and knowing someone might rumble her little game at any moment had made it even more of a distraction. But here there could be no slip-ups; Glynn had made it perfectly clear that, despite his outward charm, Leonard Neville was not a man to be crossed. If he discovered what they were doing, things could get very sticky indeed.

The hotel was much quieter today, even for a Saturday lunchtime, and Leah, now fully immersed in her Mrs Scripps persona, marched confidently across the gold and brown carpet, and gave the reception bell a single, imperious tap.

'I'm here to see Mr Leonard Neville. Tell him it's Mrs Scripps.'

'I'll call up to his room for you now, madam.'

Wilf appeared, his hand outstretched. 'Good afternoon, Mrs Scripps. So good to see you again. Might I buy you a drink?'

'No, thank you, Mr Freeman, I'll wait for lunch.'

They didn't have to wait long. Leonard Neville came out of the lift within a few minutes, pulling at his shirt cuffs to expose square-cut silver cufflinks with an inset that might have been either ebony or onyx.

Despite the obvious wealth that draped him like a silk cloak, he still seemed as forgettable as yesterday's rice pudding, and Leah tried to put a finger on how that could be; he was distinguished-looking, with immaculate grey wings brushed back from the temple, and the smile he gave her was perfectly pleasant as he extended his hand, but his eyes were a rather ordinary mid-brown, his eyebrows neither bushy nor thin, his moustache neat but plain . . . She might have passed him four times in a day and not recognised him.

They exchanged pleasantries, and he showed them into the dining room. After Fox Bay, Leah had thought she knew what to expect, but the Empire Park had overtaken Fox Bay's quiet elegance and then covered it in glitter and gold, so much so that it actually made her wince and long for the fresh, clean decor she knew and loved. The food, however, was delicious, and since Mr Neville had not yet brought up the reason for inviting them she took the time to enjoy every mouthful. After West Bank's limp bacon and watery scrambled egg it was hard not to wolf everything down and exclaim at every bite.

But she made herself stop eating long before she had finished her main course, and pushed her plate away. 'I'm so sorry,' she said in a low, embarrassed voice. 'This is so kind of you, but my appetite . . . .' She let the words trail off, and took a sip of water. 'I hope I haven't put you to any inconvenience.'

'Not at all. Mr Freeman here said you were looking

15

for some advice. Is that the case?'

She frowned at Wilf, before returning her attention to Neville. 'I really don't want to put you to any trouble.'

'It's no trouble. Tell me what you need.'

Leah looked over her shoulder, then at the waiter, hovering nearby, and lowered her voice. 'I have a substantial sum of money to invest, and I'm looking for somewhere . . . safe.'

'Safe?'

'I can't run the risk of losing it. It's too . . . the cost was too high.'

'All investment is a risk, Mrs Scripps,' Neville pointed out gently. 'What do you mean, the cost was too high?'

'My husband, my *late* husband,' she amended with a little hitch in her voice, 'had all his money tied up in Blue Chip stocks. He was told to get out, by a, a friend who warned him the market was unstable, especially after the London crash, but he paid no attention. When Wall Street went down he thought he'd lost everything, and he couldn't stand it. He took his . . . I'm sorry!' She stifled a sob in her napkin, and felt a warm hand on her shoulder.

'Please, Mrs Scripps, don't upset yourself. Would you prefer to take this conversation somewhere quieter?'

She gave Neville a grateful look. 'Perhaps, if it's not too much trouble.'

'Not at all. The lounge has booths that offer more privacy.'

Once settled, Neville ordered drinks and prompted Leah to begin her tale again. 'You said your husband *thought* he'd lost everything,' he said. 'Can I take this

16

to mean you were in fact able to cash in his stocks without him realising? How was that possible?'

Leah didn't answer right away. She picked up her drink and took a generous slug, glad she'd at least eaten something; there was a great deal more gin in it than she'd expected. 'The friend who tried to convince him, well, it was his stockbroker.'

Neville sat forward, his expression sharpening. 'Are you talking about insider dealing?'

'I couldn't say.' But Leah made sure her lowered eyes said it for her, and heard Neville utter a little oath under his breath.

'This is extremely serious,' he said aloud. 'Mrs Scripps, this man could go to prison.'

For a moment Leah wondered if they had misjudged him, but she ploughed on regardless. 'George's entire savings, our house, everything was tied up, and our accountant tried to save it! In the end, between us we . . . .' Leah broke off again and rose. 'I'm sorry, I should never have come to you — '

'Please sit down, Mrs Scripps. Mr Freeman, did you know about this?'

'Certainly not! When Mrs Scripps and I met in Ma Egerton's she told me she had a sum of money to invest. I'd mentioned I was an investor, you see.'

'But you didn't tell her your specialism is the film industry.'

'It was just conversation, I didn't see the need.'

'I misunderstood,' Leah confessed. 'It's all so confusing to me.'

'An easy mistake, my dear,' Wilf said, taking the opportunity to pat her on the knee. She was just able to stop herself pulling her leg out of the way.

'And why aren't you interested in putting your

money into that industry?' Neville wanted to know. 'It's a flourishing business, I'm given to understand. You heard what Mr Freeman was saying last night.'

Leah lowered her face, plucking at a button on her dress. 'I would prefer to take my money out of America just now, I'm sure you understand that.'

Neville gave a short laugh. 'I do. Especially given what you've just told me.'

'Mr Freeman was kind enough to suggest that you yourself might have some advice for me.'

'Why are you here? As opposed to London.'

'Because the *Samaria* runs here from New York,' she said, sounding puzzled at the sharp question, but sending silent thanks to Glynn for his thorough research. 'I'll be moving on soon.'

Neville pursed his lips. 'How soon?'

'I don't know. I hadn't planned to stay long though, I have family back home who don't really understand why I've come away so soon after . . . you know. Obviously I couldn't tell them the truth.' Leah gave him a hopeful look. 'Do you? Have any advice, I mean.'

'About your money? Perhaps. How much is it?'

Leah took a deep breath. 'A little under fifty thousand dollars. Minus the cost of travelling here, and my hotel.'

'A not inconsiderable sum,' Neville conceded. He cast a slow glance around as much of the room as they could see from their booth. 'Leave it with me, I'll talk it through with some colleagues. In the meantime I'd very much like to meet the man who gave your husband such good advice.'

Leah's heart leapt. '*Meet* him? I, I don't think that would be possible.'

'I take it he's still in America then?'

She nodded. 'Yes, he is.'

'How soon could he travel here?'

Leah lifted her hands helplessly. 'He's so busy. It would take a real long time to organise, and then there's the voyage — '

'I agree with Mrs Scripps,' Wilf put in. 'A very bad notion, Mr Neville, if you don't mind my saying so. You'd be putting your own reputation at some risk, were it to come out later what . . . what this man has done.'

A tense silence fell over the little group, while Wilf nursed his drink and Leah's fingers went white twisting around each other.

'When did he get your husband's money out?' Neville asked mildly, after a few minutes had passed. 'The exact date, I mean.'

'October twenty-third.' It didn't seem enough, and she went on, 'When it was just coming up to close of trading, we finally accepted that George wasn't going to take his advice, and things were already starting to slip badly . . . as you'll know,' she added, 'being an investor yourself. I gave the word to go ahead and just sell everything, right there and then.' She wondered if she'd committed the liar's sin of explaining too much; he'd only asked for the date, after all.

Neville shifted on his banquette, then leaned forward and closed his hand on Leah's. She gasped as his fingers tightened, grinding her knuckles against the rings she wore. His eyes dropped to them, and his smile was thin as he released her.

'I don't believe you, Mrs Scripps.'

'I don't understand,' she whimpered, her eyes filling with tears that weren't altogether false; that had hurt, and the sudden change in his demeanour was

19

chilling. She rubbed at her hand, resisting the urge to look around to see if anyone else had seen what he'd done. But he was subtle; it would have looked like nothing more than a friendly gesture. 'You don't believe what?'

'That, risking everything for you, this man is only your husband's stockbroker. Admit it, Mrs Scripps, you and he are having an affair, aren't you?' He smiled again, though it was anything but friendly. 'And it wouldn't surprise me either, to learn that you'd realised poor old George would be unable to live with losing everything, especially after being warned. After all, you neglected to tell him his money was safe. It was deliberate, wasn't it?'

'No!' Leah breathed. 'My husband never came home, I didn't have time to tell him before the markets opened —'

'But your so-called broker is here in England.'

It wasn't a question, and there was no sense arguing further. 'Alright, yes. He was worried, with me bringing such a large sum in cash, so he escorted me here. He's not in town,' she hurried on, 'I decided to break my journey for a few days, but he travelled ahead to London, to investigate various other options.'

'Then, as I said, I'd like to meet him.'

'But —'

'Mrs Scripps.' Neville leaned forward again, his nondescript features suddenly iron-hard, and Leah instinctively jerked her hand out of his reach. 'You have freely admitted, to both myself and my friend Mr Freeman, that you have come by your wealth through nefarious means. You have broken the law, and your husband's stockbroker mightn't be the only one going to jail when, if, it becomes known how you've

20

benefited from this.'

Wilf spoke up, sounding horribly nervous too. 'Surely, Leonard old thing, we don't want to get —'

'She's played you for a fool too,' Neville reminded him, and Freeman sank back into his seat, looking admirably dismayed.

'Well now, you're probably right, at that.'

'She has her uses, at least,' Neville said. 'Arrange things please, Mrs Scripps.' Now his face relaxed into its former easy smile. 'I'm sure you'd prefer to share your lover's expertise than your own wealth, after all.'

Leah forced herself to meet those mid-brown eyes for a moment longer than was comfortable, and nodded. 'I'll try.'

'And I'll do some asking around in the meantime.'

'A . . . asking around?' Her voice trembled.

'To see what's up and coming, in the line of legitimate businesses looking for cash injections, of course.'

'Oh. Of course. When should we meet you?'

'Not you. If and when your broker friend proves himself genuine, and useful to me, I'll be back in touch. If he doesn't, or if he doesn't agree to meet me, you'd better watch your back. Before you go,' he added, as she rose, 'you'd better give me his name.'

For a heart-stopping moment her mind went blank, then she dragged a name from the shadows. 'Jacob Bitterson.'

'Have you heard of him?' Neville asked Wilf, who frowned.

'Maybe. I can ask around for you.'

'Good.' Neville turned back to Leah. 'Tell him to call the hotel as soon as he arrives in town, we'll arrange a meeting.'

'Is this really necessary?'

21

'Absolutely. If you wish to avoid a nasty court case, that is. Wait behind if you would, Mr Freeman, I'd like to talk to you.'

Wilf paused, half-standing, then sat back down again without looking at Leah. 'Of course.'

Leah left, hugely relieved to be away from him, though part of her wished she could have stayed to listen to the ensuing conversation, but there was a car waiting around the corner and she hurried to climb in.

Glynn started the Lancia and nosed out into the traffic, and when she said nothing, he glanced at her, his eyebrow raised. 'Well?'

She blew out her pent-up breath and let her head fall back against the head rest. 'Well, I hope you've been busy, because the game is afoot.' She gave him a slow, triumphant smile. 'He wants to meet you, Mr Bitterson.'

2

Truro

The office was in a side street off Lemon Quay. The area was pretty enough, but the building didn't exactly foster a sense of professionalism or success, and Adam checked the piece of paper in his hand against the mottled brass number on the wall, hoping he was wrong. On the other hand, the day was marching on, and his car headlights had developed a fault lately; they were sure to blink out on him on the way home if he didn't get back to Trethkellis before dark. It was the right building.

The door was unlatched, and he stepped into a short hall and saw a set of uneven wooden stairs ahead of him, with a paper-thin carpet tacked only to the very centre. The woodworm holes either side were mildly concerning, and Adam winced as the first stair he stepped on made a loud, groaning protest, but he climbed them swiftly until he reached the office door. The sign on the door was small and plain.

Samuel Douglas. Private Investigations Undertaken.

His knock was answered by a friendly-sounding voice, and when he went into the office he was surprised and relieved to see a stark contrast with the semi-darkness of the stairwell, and the general lack of upkeep from outside. The window offered a generous view across Lemon Quay towards the river, and let in a spill of natural, late afternoon light that illuminated the neat but sparsely furnished room and the paintings that hung on the walls. A tidy desk sat in the centre, and the man behind it rose and offered his hand.

'You'll be Mr Coleridge?'

'That's me.' He immediately felt more relaxed, hearing the Scots accent; a gentle, Highlands lilt, but it nevertheless reminded him of his Edinburgh family. 'Thank you for seeing me on a Sunday afternoon.'

'Oh, I don't keep to regular hours, Mr Coleridge, you're as likely to catch me here as not, on any given day. Take a seat.' Douglas indicated the chair opposite him. Adam put him at roughly his own age, perhaps a year or two younger, with an army officer's quick, compact movements, and that striking combination of prematurely white hair and dark eyebrows. His smile was open and friendly as he settled back in his own chair.

'What can I do for you?'

'I'm trying to trace a missing person.' Even as he spoke, Adam felt himself tighten up. A missing person? This was Leah. His mind showed him a quick succession of pictures, from the moment he'd met her as Susannah Paterson, with her sleek dark wig and tear-stained face, to the last time they'd spoken as she'd told him she was leaving.

'I see.' Douglas opened his notebook. 'Name?'

'Leah Marshall.' Adam passed the only photograph he had of her across the desk, but Douglas laid it aside without giving it more than a cursory glance.

'Missing since when?'

'New Year's Day. She said she'd taken a job in Liverpool, but I've just discovered she was never offered one.'

'So it was a voluntary move?'

24

'Yes, but — '

'Relatives?'

'An aunt, in Wales. Leah's from there originally.'

'And she went missing from there, or from Liver-pool?'

'Neither. From Fox Bay Hotel, which is where she lives now. Lived,' he corrected himself, with a little pang. 'She's been writing to us all, keeping us at arm's length, but I finally went up to find her late last week, and discovered she's not living where she said she was.'

'Which was where?'

'The nurses' home attached to the infirmary. So I went to see her aunt, who said she'd not seen her since Christmas.' Adam took a deep breath, and felt his fingers curling on his knees. 'She also said her husband had returned, and — '

'Mrs Marshall's husband?'

Adam nodded. 'I've just learned they spent Christmas together in Wales, but Leah came home on the thirtieth and said nothing about that. She left again almost immediately, a day or two before she'd planned to, and without telling anyone.'

'Didn't anyone see her go?'

'Only our receptionist, who assumed she was returning to her aunt's house. She only had a small-ish case with her, but we sent the rest of her belongings on later, to the nurses' home.'

Douglas wrote again. 'Do you think she and her husband are still together?'

'I do. And that's the problem.'

Douglas looked up. 'Why would it be a problem? They're married.'

'He's recently come out of prison.' Adam shifted in

25

his seat. 'Look, there's a reason I haven't gone to the police about this.'

'That was going to be my next question. Go on.'

'His real name is Gregory Marshall. He changed it to Glynn when he moved to Wales as a boy, and has been known by that name ever since. If you check with the police you'll see Gregory Marshall was arrested in 1915 and charged with manslaughter.'

Douglas scribbled in his book. 'Did he serve in the war?'

'No. He remained in prison for the duration, and only got out last summer.'

'That's a long stretch,' Douglas mused. 'Even for manslaughter.'

'It was a policeman.'

'Ah.'

'Glynn was under arrest for a scam he was carrying out. With Leah.'

Douglas sat back and folded his arms. 'Go on.'

Adam told him how that scam had resulted in Marshall's arrest, and the subsequent death of the arresting officer in a fall. Then he told of how he'd met Leah as Susannah, and how she'd been attempting the very same confidence trick on him as the one that had got Glynn arrested, but that she hadn't bargained on Adam falling for her to the extent that he'd tried to intervene on her behalf.

'Why aren't you writing this down?' he asked, noting Douglas still had his arms folded.

'Because I'm fairly certain you won't want this part on record, should it come to a court case.'

Adam looked at the man with fresh appreciation. 'You're right, I wouldn't. The thing is,' he sat forward earnestly, 'Leah is prone to a certain degree of . . .

26

playacting. She loves the thrill of convincing people she's someone she isn't. I'm concerned Glynn might have pulled her back into that world.'

'You think he's running some sort of scam now?'

Adam nodded. 'If Leah's involved it will only be for the thrill of it, and maybe because she and Glynn are back together now.'

Douglas's sharp green eyes were still keenly searching Adam's face. 'Would I be right in assuming you'd rather this isn't the case?'

'Yes, you would.' There was no sense denying it.

'And is this the only reason you want me to find her? Or do you want to cause whatever she's doing to fail, too?'

'I don't care whether it fails or not,' Adam said coldly. 'I have no idea what it is. I just want Leah out of Marshall's clutches.'

'Her choice, surely?' Douglas's voice was mild. 'I could understand if you were concerned for the victim of whatever game they're playing, but you can't force a woman to leave her husband just because you want her back.'

'He's putting her in danger!'

'Then you must persuade her to leave him. I can do my best to find her for you, Mr Coleridge, but after that it's up to you. I can't get involved unless someone's life is at stake, and if you believe that to be the case then you should tell the police, no matter the consequences for your . . . friend.'

Adam bit down on a frustrated retort, after all the man was being perfectly reasonable. 'How much information do you need?'

'As much as you're comfortable giving me. The more the better though, it goes without saying. And

27

remember, if anything happens to bring this to the attention of the police, I might have to tell them what I know.'

'I've already told you Leah was involved in a previous scam, would you have to disclose that?'

'Mr Marshall has served the sentence for that, and since he didn't name her then, it shouldn't come up now.' Douglas took up his pen again. 'So, I suggest you tell me what you're happy for me to write down, and then you can tell me the important stuff if we agree to work together.'

Adam stood up, sorting through all the jumbled thoughts in his mind, putting aside the little details that made Leah the first thing he thought about each morning, and his final, regretful thought before sleep took him at night. As he spoke he moved about the small room, drawn to the paintings that he had noticed on first coming in.

Each one featured a different area of a farm: the main house; a barn with the door standing open, and the barest suggestion of working figures inside; a stable with a boy mucking out; a field of hay, with a covered haystack in its corner and clouds building overhead. They might easily have appeared saccharine and sentimental, but they were so sparsely detailed that there was something ultimately peaceful about each one, and Adam found himself able to tell the rest of the story calmly, even as he described Leah's abrupt departure.

'I think I can help you,' Douglas said, when he'd gathered all the dates, addresses and facts Adam had to offer. 'At the fee we discussed on the telephone, plus expenses. That suit you?'

'Yes,' Adam said, relief pushing the word out on a

sigh. 'Thank you.' He turned to the nearest painting again, searching for the name of the artist.

'It's my home,' Douglas said helpfully. 'Or rather it was. West Glenlowrie Farm, near Fort William.'

Adam turned to him in surprise. 'Are you saying *you* painted these?'

Douglas nodded. 'Do you like them?' He seemed oddly eager, but looking at the pictures, even as a layman, and seeing the passion in the brush strokes, Adam understood he was asking about more than the quality of the artwork.

'It looks like a beautiful place, and you've clearly done it justice.'

'Aye. Beautiful.' Douglas's face held a trace of sadness now. 'It was taken over after the war and assimilated into the Glenlowrie Estate.'

'The work is superb,' Adam said. 'Look, before Leah vanished, and a lot of other stuff took over, I was talking to the co-owner of our hotel about commissioning new art. Would you consider leasing us some of your paintings? They're the perfect size and subject material for one of our smaller lounges.'

Douglas glanced at the book in front of him. 'Fox Bay? I've not been, but I've heard about it. I wouldn't have thought these paintings were your sort of thing at all.'

'They wouldn't work in the lobby, you're right about that, but they'd fit wonderfully in our first-floor sitting room. It has an altogether more countrified feel. Actually this could almost be the farm that occupies the land immediately behind the hotel. Very similar.'

Douglas considered. 'I'll be up tomorrow, to talk to the Fox family, so I'll have a look at where you intend to place them. If I agree they're suited, maybe we can talk about adding the price on to my fee.'

'No. Your fee won't come out of the hotel's money, it's me who's hiring you.'

'Understood.' Douglas closed his notebook, then stood up and put his hand out. 'Until tomorrow then, Mr Coleridge.'

*　*　*

Out on the quay once more, Adam found himself cautiously optimistic for the first time since he'd left the nurses' home. He had never employed the services of an investigator before, had never had the need, but he'd imagined a blur of action; Douglas barking questions and taking copious notes, studying the photograph, and delving into the details of their relationship. Instead he felt as if he'd sat down with a pal for a ten-minute chat, one that might soon lead to Leah being back at Fox Bay, where she belonged.

But as he passed out of the glow from the office window, and with evening creeping across the quay, he suppressed a shiver at the thought that Douglas might not find her at all, or that, if he did, it would already be too late.

*　*　*

The book wasn't holding Bertie's interest, and she glanced at the sitting room clock; almost 3 a.m., and she'd been wide awake for over an hour now, thinking about the next day and what it would be likely to bring. A trip to the hospital was nothing new, but would she return with a new lease of life this time, or with the reminder that her old one hadn't finished with her yet? Perhaps she was expecting too much.

This quietest of all hours seemed to stretch and stretch, but still the words lay flat on the page of her book, failing to instil the slightest curiosity. Eventually she heard the welcome sound of voices out in the lobby; Ben had finally returned from his card game at the Summerleaze, where he'd been taking advantage of Guy's prolonged jaunt to America, to enjoy some illicit half-nights off . . . Not that Guy would have stopped him even if he'd been here.

Ben opened the door, and she was about to greet him, but to her surprise and irritation he just switched the light off instead, and she lowered her book with a sigh. 'I'm trying to read, thank you!'

'Oh, sorry! Didn't see you there.' Light flooded the room again. 'I just thought someone had left the light on.'

'Someone did. Me!'

He came in properly. 'You can hardly blame me, the only person who ever stayed up this late was Granny, and she's a bit of a long way away. What on earth are you doing still up?'

'Not *still* up. Just up.'

'That doesn't sound good.' He crossed to the table by the window. 'Nightcap?'

She nodded. 'That might help. Just a small brandy, it's a big day tomorrow. Today, in fact.' He looked at her blankly for a moment, and she pointed at her right leg. 'Remember?'

'Of course! The prosthetic's ready. How do you feel?'

She took the tumbler and shrugged. 'One minute I can't breathe for excitement, the next I can't because

31

I'm terrified.'

'I thought you were looking a bit purple around the gills.' He grinned at the look she gave him. 'You won't know yourself,' he assured her. 'Just imagine, you'll soon be able to stop using your crutches, and especially that ugly old thing.' He gestured at the wheelchair at the end of the sofa. 'What time are you getting it fitted?'

'The appointment's at ten o'clock. I have a consultation with Mr Russell first, and after that I'll be spending time with the nurses, while they teach me to use it properly.'

'Do you want me to come?'

For a moment she desperately wanted to say yes, but in the end she shook her head. 'You need to sleep.'

'That doesn't matter. I can still come with you. I want to,' he added. 'I feel like . . . like we don't know what's going on in each other's lives anymore.'

Bertie understood, and it was good to hear him acknowledge it. She sipped her drink, and smiled. 'Of course we do. You know I'm getting this artificial leg, and that I hope to learn to fly aeroplanes. I know you're going to marry Lily Trevanion and move out.'

He stared at her. 'You . . . What are you talking about?'

'Oh, gosh!' She lowered her glass. 'You're not, are you?'

'I'm not marrying Lily,' he said quickly.

'But moving out?'

He looked away. 'It's a possibility,' he confessed. 'The manager of the Summerleaze is leaving. Lily thinks it'd be a good idea if I applied for the job.'

'Good for her perhaps.'

'And for me.'

'What's wrong with working here? You're a manager aren't you? And you know you'll never get the sack!'

He gave her a mock hurt look. 'Are you saying that's the only reason I have a job here?'

But she didn't share his humour. She felt strangely hollow, and the thought of losing him to another life, even if it were only in Bude, left her a little panicky. 'Why would you want to leave? This was Daddy's home.'

A jolt of pain showed on his face, but the words it created were angry. 'Are *you* staying here forever? No! You're going off to fly planes, start a new home with Jowan, and goodness knows what else.'

'It's not the same, Ben. This is your inheritance.'

'I'm not buying the Summerleaze,' he protested, 'just hoping to work there for a while. I'll learn tons.'

'And what about Lily?'

'What about her? We'd work well together.'

Bertie raised a cynical eyebrow. 'Is that all?'

'What else?'

'I think Lily has ideas about *what else*,' Bertie said archly. 'Does she know you're still hung up on Daisy Conrad?'

'Daisy? How could I be? She's thousands of miles away. Anyway,' he went on, clearly keen to change the subject, 'is Adam back yet?'

'He got back this morning. Yesterday, rather. He stayed just long enough for breakfast and a change of clothes, then zoomed off again. Goodness knows where.'

'Did he manage to talk to Aunt Leah while he was away?'

'I don't know, you'll have to ask him when he gets back.'

33

'Well how did he seem then? I mean, a few weeks ago he was all for dragging her back here by the hair.'

'Can you see her putting up with that?' Bertie laughed. 'Sad to say though, I'm beginning to think he should have taken the hint when she kept writing to him to stay away. What good could it possibly have done to chase after her, when she's made it clear she didn't want him to?'

'You know Adam.' Ben shook his head. 'Never one to accept defeat. So,' he said, changing the subject again, 'it's definitely still going ahead then, this aeroplane thing?'

'Of course. Why wouldn't it be?'

'Don't get defensive!' He held up a hand. 'I'm not Jowan. No, it just hits me sometimes, to think that you'll be up there, looking down on us all. D'you remember that song Dad used to sing to Fiona when she was little?'

'The one he made up?' Bertie smiled. Their father had found it uproariously funny that Fiona had refused to accept the word *cloud*, and insisted on referring to *little fluffies*, whether they were or not; often they were actually huge, purple, thunderous ones.

'How did it go?' Ben frowned as he tried to recall.

'It was actually part of that Chasing Rainbows song from the war, remember? It was recorded by someone else called Harry Fox too, so the lads in the trenches were forever teasing him with it.' Bertie's voice softened. 'I think it held some memories for him, because of that, and he used to sing it a lot after he came home.'

It had become his way of letting his youngest daughter get to know him, since Fiona had been born at the start of the war and he'd been away almost all that time. There had been a shyness between them that

34

even Harry had found hard to penetrate, but one day Bertie and Fiona had come across him sitting in the garden and looking up at the sky, humming the song under his breath.

Bertie had often wondered what had been going through his mind in that quiet, lonely spot, but Fiona's presence had forced him to smile and open his arms to her, and she had asked him to sing it again. Properly. So he had, and Fiona and Bertie had joined in.

'She corrected him when he got to the bit about clouds,' she said now, with a grin. 'Daddy! It's *little fluffies*!' But it was the thing that made him laugh the most, so of course she kept doing it.'

'I'm always chasing rainbows,' Ben sang, and Bertie joined in.

'Watching little fluffies drifting by....' They exchanged smiles.

'My schemes are just like all my dreams, ending — '

'Shining, in Dad's version,' Bertie reminded him.

'*Shining* in the sky.'

They fell silent, remembering those difficult weeks and months after their father had returned from France, and how worried they'd all been about Uncle Adam too, with his persistent cough and breathlessness; a legacy of the gas attack that had almost invalided him for the duration. Fiona's innocent joy in her father's song had helped all of them, though she'd been too young to realise it.

'Well,' Ben said at length, bringing her attention back to the original conversation, 'whatever you call them, you'll be up amongst them soon. Don't forget us mortals, will you?'

'I'll try very hard not to.' Bertie finished her drink

35

and pulled her chair closer to the sofa. 'That nightcap did the trick, I think I'll be able to sleep now.'

'Are you sure you don't want me to come with you tomorrow?'

She shook her head. 'Mum's coming, I won't be alone.' She swung from the sofa into her chair, and gave him a stern look as she stopped at the door. 'Go for that job if you must, but don't string Lily along, it's not fair.'

'Who says I'd be stringing her along? We like one another, but she's no more interested in marriage than I am.'

'And you know that, do you?' Bertie looked down at the sapphire and diamond ring on her own finger, then back at him. 'Find out what *she* wants, before you assume things,' she advised gently. 'At least do that. You never know what people are really feeling.'

'Are you and Jowan alright?' he asked, frowning.

'We're . . . .' She smiled, a little distantly, and opened the door. 'We will be.'

Ben followed her, but when she turned back he had stopped by the door and was looking at the photograph that hung there; their father's favourite, taken in the convalescent home just after the war. Dad's arm was around Adam's shoulders, and Mum was in front, looking so straight-laced that they'd always assumed she'd been a painfully prim and shy young woman. But they knew now that she'd actually been trying hard not to laugh and ruin the photograph, and now Bertie couldn't look at the picture without seeing that barely held-in mirth. She could see Ben was thinking the same. *You never know what people are really feeling . . .*

Her thoughts turned to Jowan Nancarrow, and the

36

slow realisation that had been creeping up on her since Christmas, and that she had been beating off with one hand while clinging to her dreams with the other. She had given her brother some sound advice, now it was time to follow it.

3

It was almost lunchtime before the moment arrived. For most of the morning Bertie had been talking to Mr Russell, and enduring a seemingly endless checking of her leg. Months of massage, and application of methylated spirits, had strengthened the stump and hardened it, and its tendency to leap involuntarily had long since been brought under control through careful therapy. Now came the moment for which she had been waiting. She felt her mother's hand creep into hers, and gratefully folded her fingers around it, but kept her eyes closed, instead feeling everything, and filling in the visual gaps with her mind.

One of the nurses — was it the young red-haired one, or the older lady with the kind smile? — tucked the hem of Bertie's skirt into her waistband, and after a moment Bertie felt the familiar puff of talcum powder brush her skin. A moment later firm, capable hands eased a stretchy sock over the stump, drawing it up over Bertie's knee and halfway up her thigh, before attaching the leather harness that would secure everything.

Bertie opened her eyes at last, and saw the younger nurse pick up the aluminium limb and hold it out to Mr Russell, who checked the leather straps and smiled at Bertie.

'Ready, Miss Fox?'

Bertie nodded. 'Never more so.' She closed her eyes again while the consultant slipped the straps into place and tugged and fastened, and all the time

38

her mother's hand remained firm in hers. There was no pain, but the sudden, disorientating sensation of unwieldy weight made her stomach roil and she had to open her eyes once more. She looked down.

For the first time since last August, her right leg reached the floor. A flattish boat shape splayed out from the narrow ankle of the prosthetic, and Bertie tried to tell herself that her own familiar woollen sock would soon sit over it, her own shoe would hide the plainness of it, and that it would allow her, eventually, to move about as everyone else did . . . but it looked utterly alien to her.

It hung from her knee, braced against the floor, just like her left leg, but that was where the similarity ended. She felt like crying, furious at her own ingratitude and the way she had built this up to be the miracle that returned her to a full life. How could it be? Had she expected the new limb would feel like an extension of her own flesh and blood?

'Alright, now you can stand up,' Mr Russell said, his voice brisk. She looked at him, uncomprehending for a moment, only aware of the sensation of the ground beneath one foot, and the straps on her right leg suddenly pinching the skin through the sock as she moved.

'Just a moment.' Her mother seemed to realise, and leaned forward. She slid a finger beneath one of the straps, and the stinging eased, and Bertie burst into uncontrollable and entirely unexpected sobs.

'Give her a minute,' the older nurse said gently, and put her arm around Bertie's shoulders. 'We've seen this a lot. It's a great deal to take in. She'll be alright, won't you, love?'

Bertie bowed her head, unable to speak, and felt

39

the softness of a freshly pressed handkerchief pushed into her hand. She couldn't catch her breath, and was dimly aware of the comforting hand pulling free from hers, and the bustle as the two nurses urged her mother to move back, to give Bertie space. She heard tears in her mother's voice, too, and that gave her what she needed to bring herself under some control.

She patted her eyes with the handkerchief. 'I'm sorry,' she managed. 'I don't even know why I'm crying.'

'As I said, love, it's understandable,' the nurse said. 'In your own time, we won't rush you. Will we?'

Bertie heard a sudden hardness in the voice, and looked up to see the nurse was glaring at Mr Russell, who was just pushing his watch back into his waistcoat pocket. He glared back for moment, then looked sheepish, and it made Bertie smile through her tears. She would never know if this little pantomime had been played out for her benefit, but it worked. She grasped the arms of her chair, and the younger nurse leapt forward and slid an arm around her back.

'Just take it slowly,' she murmured.

Bertie rose, and the consultant crouched beside her, studying the concoction of straps and buckles critically as she put her weight on both legs. The sensation was as strange as she'd expected; the usual hardness of the floor beneath one shoe, and now the same pressure on her other leg, but much higher up. She tilted a little, but the nurses held her with strong, practised hands as she experimented with leaning onto her right leg. She held the nurse's arm in a panicky grip, certain the straps would give way and she would be pitched to the floor, but after a moment she loosened her grasp and then finally let go altogether.

'How does it feel?' her mother asked tentatively.

'I don't know,' Bertie said honestly. 'I feel . . . safer than I thought I would, but I still want to put all my weight on my other leg.'

'That will pass,' Russell said, in his old brisk tone. 'Now, concentrate on the straps for a moment, tell me how they feel.'

For a little while everything else faded, as Bertie and the consultant discussed the leather harness, and she took comfort in the practicalities of the conversation. Russell tightened where she said it felt loose, and then he and the older nurse held her steady while she made a very slow circuit of the small room.

'You'll need your crutches for a while longer,' he said. 'And, now this is important, because I know you have plans that are going to try and persuade you to go against it . . . .' He met Bertie's innocent look with a wry smile, and shook his head. 'I mean this, Miss Fox, don't try to wear that,' he nodded downward, 'for more than two hours at a time to begin with. Once a day only. Alright?'

Her heart sank. 'For how long?'

'Come and see me next week, we'll look at it then and make sure there's no irritation. After that we'll see. Keep applying the powder, come back at the first sign of any infection, even a minor one, and make sure you wash that sock regularly. Nurse Simpson here will pack you up some spares.'

'Is that it?' Bertie looked from him to her mother and back again, hardly able to believe it. 'I'm ready to go home?'

'Unless you have any further questions?'

'No, none.' Bertie accepted her crutches from the younger nurse. 'Will I be able to switch to just one of

41

these now? While I have my leg on, I mean.'

'Soon,' the nurse said. 'Don't try to do too much at the start. For now just go on as you were, and we'll make an appointment for you to come back and see Mr Russell next week.'

She untucked Bertie's skirt, and the material fell free. When Bertie bent forward to straighten it the hem dropped, and swung against her calf, making it look almost normal. Her heart skipped in real excitement for the first time; a stocking pulled over that awful blank 'foot', a shoe, and a long coat, and no one would be able to tell.

She lifted her face to her mother's, and now the tears were a release of the almost unbearable happiness that swept through her. She was whole again.

* * *

Helen left Bertie to rest, and returned to the office and the pile of post she'd been sorting that morning. She was smiling as she closed the door behind her, thinking of Bertie's determination and how it would stand her in good stead for the future. For herself she was secretly relieved at the length of time the rehabilitation would take; the longer Bertie put off training, the better, though Helen had no illusion it would be put on a shelf forever. She also knew that her daughter was absolutely not going to be sticking to the two-hour rule.

She picked up the letter on the top of the pile, smiling to see Leah's handwriting, and set it aside to read at her leisure later on. The next one made her frown, however, and check the postmark: Exeter. Her brother, David, writing from home instead of his offices in London. Fully expecting the news that he and his tiresome wife planned to spend a week or so at Fox Bay, Helen slid the paper knife through the rich, creamy paper with absolutely no enthusiasm whatsoever. David would be a welcome guest after all this time, but Kay just couldn't seem to keep her thoughts to herself, especially when they were sour ones. Which most seemed to be.

The letter was typically short, and so to the point it might as well have been a telegram.

Dear Helen
Kay and self are separating. Hope you can accommodate me from Monday 17th. Room 8, if it's free.
Love
D.

There was no indication which of them had tried the other to breaking point, but they were almost as guilty as one another when it came to extra-marital shenanigans, so it could have been either. Or perhaps her brother had simply grown tired of Kay's sniping. Either way, Helen was as certain as she could be that it was another temporary state of affairs, so she just shook her head, knowing there was absolutely no possibility of a room on the first floor until roughly September, let alone the specific one he'd requested. All the rooms on the second floor were booked then too, so he would have to come up to the third, where Fleur's room stood empty. He was family, after all, and since he'd be alone there would be no fuss from Kay about being *tucked away in the attic*.

Martin Berry popped his head around the door. 'Mrs Fox? I have someone who'd like to speak to you.

Is it alright if I send him in?'

'Who is it?'

'A guest.'

Helen groaned. No matter how much effort the staff put in, and how much she, Ben, and Adam strived to make Fox Bay the perfect getaway, there was always someone who felt they must *consult the manager immediately*. She nodded, wondering whether perhaps the sea was the wrong temperature, or the wind smelled a bit too much of farm today, and pasted her professional hostess smile in place; welcoming, but not too familiar, and gracious without fawning.

The man Martin showed in was not at all pompous-looking, thankfully. He even appeared a little shy, and Helen began to relax.

'Sam Douglas,' the guest said, extending his hand. 'Mr Coleridge has told you to expect me, I think?'

Helen detected a faint accent, perhaps he was a member of the Scottish branch of the Coleridges. 'I don't think so. How can I help?'

The man indicated the seat opposite. 'May I?'

'Of course.' She watched him loosen his jacket before he sat down, as if he were uncomfortable in the smart clothes he wore. He reminded her a little of Alfie Nancarrow in that way, which made her smile, and he appeared friendly enough, but his eyes darted about as if he were taking mental notes about everything he saw.

'I'm sorry,' he said, 'I'd thought Mr Coleridge might have mentioned me.'

'I've been out all day, and he's been away too, but I saw his car parked outside so at least he's back.'

'I'm here about Mrs Marshall.'

Helen started, and her heart thumped. 'Leah?

What's wrong with her?'

The door opened again, and Adam came in, looking rushed. 'Sam! Good to see you again. We've had a cancellation, so I've booked you in to room fourteen, on floor two. I see you've already met Helen.'

'What's this about Leah?' Helen demanded, as Adam pulled up the third chair. Her eyes went to the letter she'd received that morning, and Mr Douglas's attention followed.

'Is that from Mrs Marshall?'

'Yes. What's going on?' Helen picked up the letter and the paper knife, then sat motionless while Adam told her briefly about what he'd found in Liverpool, or rather, what he hadn't.

'So we don't even know if that's where she went,' he finished.

'This postmark says she did.' Helen tapped the letter with the blade, then slit the envelope. 'What's she up to?'

'You don't sound concerned,' Mr Douglas observed. She'd almost forgotten he was there.

'I'm curious, of course, but the letters have been quite regular, and definitely written in Leah's hand.' Helen ran her gaze over the note, which was no different in tone from any of the others she'd received since the beginning of January. 'She says she's busy, as always, that the re-training has been going well, and that she's met some much nicer people than those at the nurses' home.'

'So we can assume she told the truth about Liverpool itself,' Mr Douglas mused, 'but why would she lie about what she's doing there?'

'Mr Douglas, I don't mean to be rude, but might I ask what this has to do with you? Are you a friend of

45

Leah's? Because she's never —'

'Sam's an investigator,' Adam broke in.

Helen stared at him then turned to Mr Douglas. 'Would you please excuse us for a moment?'

Mr Douglas looked from one to the other, then nodded. 'Of course, you two need to talk. I'll go and unpack. Room fourteen, did you say?'

'How long are you staying?' Helen asked, remembering she still hadn't booked David in.

'Just overnight. I plan to be on the road by lunchtime tomorrow, especially now we can be reasonably sure where I'm going.' Mr Douglas indicated the letter, then rose and held out his hand again. 'I'm sorry this has been a shock for you, we'll talk later.'

As soon as he'd gone, Helen threw down the letter and glared at Adam. 'What on earth possessed you to hire someone like that?'

'It's just too strange. Too many questions.'

'Because Leah's clearly put the word out that anyone fitting your description, who comes looking for her, is to be told she's not there? Did you ever consider that she simply doesn't want you chasing after her?'

'I don't believe they were lying,' Adam insisted. 'Helen, I'm fairly sure Leah's got herself involved in something dangerous this time.'

'Why? She only tried that con trick on you last year because of the way things were going with Fox Bay. She's past all that now.'

'Remember how odd we all thought it was, that she disappeared on New Year's Day without saying goodbye?'

'She explained that in her first letter,' Helen reminded him. 'She saw Glynn at the memorial ceremony, and had to leave before he tracked her here.'

46

'And you believed that?'

'Of course I did! I checked Fleur's invitation list and found a Gregory Marshall scribbled onto the end. Anyway,' she added, 'Leah only left a couple of days early, we knew she was going.'

'Listen,' Adam said, more gently, 'I spoke to her Aunt Mary, and it turns out that Glynn actually stayed with them over Christmas.'

Helen's heart sank. 'Are you saying he's talked her into going back to their old ways?'

'I think he must have done. Otherwise why the deception?'

'So there was no new job at all?'

'It would explain why she left so suddenly.'

Helen wished she felt something other than a weighty sense of the inevitable: Leah had lied yet again. 'Why are you so worried about her?' she asked. 'They were doing this for years before Glynn was arrested.'

'That's the problem. Anything Glynn's involved in now is likely to have come complete with a lot of new ideas lifted from his time in prison. I just don't think it'll have the same . . . .' he looked at a loss, then threw his hands up ' . . . the same innocence, if you like.'

'There was nothing innocent about what they did,' Helen pointed out grimly. 'A policeman was killed, remember?'

'You know what I mean. Anyway, I want her out of it, whatever it is.'

'Which is where your new friend comes in.'

He nodded. 'He seems sharp enough, and he definitely understood I didn't want Leah's name muddied in all of this. All he's going to do is try to find her, after that it's up to me.'

'Us.'

Adam looked at her, and his face finally relaxed into a faint smile. 'Us,' he repeated quietly. 'I'm going to need you, Hels. She'll listen to you.'

Helen nodded. 'Of course I'll come with you, but how's he going to find her?'

'If I knew that, I'd be doing it myself.'

Helen shrugged. 'I suppose.' She gave him a sideways look. 'Actually I can just see you as a private detective. You look the part, somehow.'

'Bulldog Drummond?' He squared his shoulders and lifted his chin, and Helen laughed.

'More Stan Laurel, in *The Sleuth*.' She ducked as he threw his pocket square at her, then her laughter faded. 'Do you really think she might be in danger?'

'I don't know.' He sighed. 'Maybe, maybe not. But I don't like the thought of her getting dragged back into that life.'

'And it's not just because it's Glynn?'

'What do you mean?'

'Well, you *were* going to tell her you'd made a mistake, that you hadn't realised how strong your feelings for her were, because they were all caught up in what you . . . what you thought you felt for me.' Helen's skin warmed, it sounded as if she were paying herself an unwarranted compliment. 'But if we try to pull her out and she chooses to stay with Glynn anyway, will that be enough for you?'

'If he agrees to leave her out of his business from now on, yes.'

But she read the lie in his face, and hoped he knew Leah better than she suspected he did.

★ ★ ★

48

Later she found Mr Douglas again, in the small sitting room on the second floor. He was looking closely at the artwork on the walls, and turning to squint out of the window. There was little to see there now; it was approaching four o'clock and the night had already painted long shadows across the landscape, hiding most of the farmland.

'Mr Douglas?'

He turned, and smiled, and it made him appear more than averagely attractive. 'Call me Sam,' he invited. 'I hope you don't mind me skulking away up here?'

'Not at all, you're a guest, and you'll be doing Adam and me a favour if you find Leah.'

'I'll be doing my job,' he corrected her, 'for which Mr Coleridge is paying my fee. I was wondering if I might ask you a few questions about her, in fact? You're her best friend, I gather?'

'Can it wait until after dinner?' Helen picked up the magazine she'd come in for, and found herself rolling it tightly in her hands as if she'd been faced with a teacher demanding information on a friend. He seemed to sense that.

'I already know she's been up to some ... interesting pastimes over the years, I only want to know anything that might help me find her.'

Helen relaxed, and nodded. 'Alright, but I really am quite busy, so perhaps you can join me in the family sitting room after dinner? I'll make sure the others are there in case they can think of anything helpful. Ben should be able to join us then, too, they've always been close.'

'Ben?'

'My son, the night manager here at the hotel.'

49

'I'm going to feel like Hercule Poirot,' he said, and he smoothed an imaginary moustache as his faint Scots faded into exaggerated Belgian. 'Thank you, *madame*, I shall see you later.' The grin he gave her was impossible not to return.

'Out of interest, do you like the artwork?' she asked. 'I saw you looking at it when I came in.'

'It's not my favourite style,' he said carefully, 'but I can see it's good. Adam was right, it doesn't really suit the room, or the view. Too . . . stark.'

'No, he's looking for a different feel now, something that matches what you can normally see when you look out there. Higher Valley Farm.' She felt a strange little tug inside as she said the name. 'Adam did mention you're a painter as well as an investigator,' she went on. 'I'm sure Mrs Nancarrow would be happy for you to immortalise her farm in watercolour, it's very pretty.' She remembered her own first view of the farm, and brought the subject back to the point of Sam's visit. 'Since you're asking about Leah, she actually saved the farmer's life when we first moved in around ten years ago.' She made herself stop at the positive part of the tragic story. 'I'll tell you about it later.'

She raised the rolled magazine in farewell, and with Higher Valley in the forefront of her mind, she stopped in at the kitchens to speak to Nicholas Gough. The head chef was with Kurt Strommer, in the tiny office where the menus were created, and since the door stood open, she knocked on the wooden jamb.

'Sorry to disturb you,' she said, as Gough looked up at her with poorly concealed impatience. 'I just wondered if Mrs Nancarrow had been by yet, to take the week's order?'

'Not yet.'

Helen ducked out of the office again and crossed the kitchen to look out of the back door. Her heart skipped unaccountably as she saw a figure in the distance, before recognising it as Beth. As she raised a hand in greeting, she acknowledged her secret disappointment that Alfie no longer found reasons to liaise with the hotel in Beth's stead, the way he used to; she could picture him now, his hat pulled low, his collar up, long legs covering the ground easily as he strode down the field path . . .

But the image made her ache inside. She had hesitated too long when he'd opened his soul to her on Christmas Eve. Instead she'd pointed out that his future was with Beth, who'd loved him for years, as if that made Beth more deserving somehow. She'd even believed it herself, and by the time Leah had helped her realise she'd been living in a bubble of denial, and that her feelings for Alfie had deepened into love since Bertie's accident, her one brief chance had passed. It wasn't even as if she'd been lonely. Quite the opposite, in fact; she was perfectly content with her lot, and not searching for someone to share her future with. Accepting Alfie's declaration, and returning it with an honest one of her own, would have been the more difficult choice. So she'd lost nothing, and saved herself a great deal of inconvenience.

She turned away from the doorway, wondering how long it would take her to believe that.

* * *

Later, Helen handed Mr Douglas a small whisky, and they waited until everyone was settled. Bertie and

51

Fiona sat side-by-side on the sofa, while Ben stood by the new French window that Adam had had put in, looking out towards the kitchen garden; he seemed restless, which made Helen more jittery than ever. Adam lounged comfortably, as always. Helen wished Guy were there; he knew Leah as well as any of them, after all, but he was still in America with his son and his son's mother.

Mr Douglas briefly outlined Adam's concerns. 'I want to make it clear,' he added, 'I'm not going to be bringing Mrs Marshall back, against her will or otherwise. I'm not even going to approach her. I'm simply going to see if I can utilise some of my former contacts, to make sure she's safe and well. I'll report back to Mr Coleridge, and from then on it's out of my hands.'

Fiona sat up straighter, her eyes gleaming. 'Former contacts? Were you a policeman then?'

'A detective, yes. I still have friends who might be able to help, given Mrs Marshall's husband's . . . activities, in the past.' He looked around the little group. 'I must say all of you, except Mr Coleridge, seem quite unconcerned. I understand Mrs Marshall is — '

'Could you call her Leah?' Helen cut in. 'It somehow feels more as if we're talking about the same person if you do that. None of us here thinks of her as Mrs Marshall.'

'Of course. And while we're on that subject, please do call me Sam.'

A murmur of assent rippled around the room, and Adam sat forward. 'The thing is, cubs, I know Leah's a, a . . . .' he shrugged ' . . . a bit of a law unto herself at times, but if she's been spending time with Glynn

52

she could be feeling under pressure to do what he asks of her. That mightn't be quite the same thing as just putting on a wig and a different accent.'

'I'm sure there's nothing to worry about,' Helen put in quickly, noting Fiona's suddenly worried look. 'But Mr . . . Sam, is just going to check up on her. And he'd like to get a bit of an insight into what we all know of her before he goes looking. Alright?'

Sam took out his notebook and asked a few questions, and Helen noted the smile that touched his lips now and again as someone related something outrageous Leah had done over the past ten years. She couldn't help once again comparing him to Alfie Nancarrow as she watched him; they shared certain similarities other than a discomfort of dressing smartly; they were both tall — although Alfie was broader in build — and with a quiet manner, and both had a way of keeping their thoughts to themselves while others spoke. She had the feeling that Sam, like Alfie, rarely said much unless he was provoked by some deep emotion.

When he had all he needed, Sam replaced the notebook in his jacket pocket, and smiled his thanks at the family. 'I'll leave you to your evening,' he said. 'I don't want to take up any more of your time. Mrs Fox, I'll be leaving first thing. What time's breakfast?'

'It starts at eight o'clock,' she said, showing him to the door. 'Would you like someone to knock?'

'Oh, I'll be leaving well before then. I like to get on the road early. No matter.'

'I can have something prepared for whatever time you like.'

'Really? At around seven o'clock?'

'Pass your requirements to Martin on reception.'

She glanced at the clock. 'No, it'll be Ian now. We'll have it delivered to your room at seven sharp.'

He shook her hand and left, and she turned back to her family, happy to see them all together for once, chattering amongst themselves in an animated fashion and speculating about what Leah might be up to. They almost never met in the same room anymore.

But it was not to last tonight, either. Bertie, predictably still wearing her leg, picked up her crutches and went upstairs to write to Lynette Nicholls; Fiona hurried away to get an early night, tomorrow was a day off and she would be at the Trethkellis lifeboat station well before daylight; and Adam pressed Helen's arm and told her he had a few telephone calls to make in the office.

Ben, however, remained by the window, and Helen remembered his fidgety behaviour at the start of the meeting. Her trepidation returned. 'What's the matter?' she asked, not at all sure she wanted to know. His next words didn't help.

'Sit down a minute, Mum.'

She did so, acutely aware of the press of the sofa, the sound of her nylons gliding over one another as she crossed her legs, and the spit and crackle of the fire in the grate. Everything seemed heightened the longer she was kept waiting. 'Well?'

He sat in the chair Adam had vacated, his fingers locked as he sat forward, looking so much like his father that she had to look briefly away. 'Come on, Ben, don't keep me waiting. You're leaving, aren't you?'

When he didn't reply, she risked a glance at him, fervently hoping to see a look of blank astonishment that she would even think such a thing. But his own

54

face was lowered, and she gave in to the crushing sense of inevitability.

'I'm sorry,' he said, his voice cracking slightly. 'I've got a chance at being sole manager. It's not definite yet, but —'

'But even if it's not this opportunity, it'll be the next one, or the one after that.' Helen forced herself to smile. 'Look, darling, we always knew this day would come, didn't we? You don't want to be working nights all your life, and I'm not ready to retire yet.'

'I do want to work days,' he agreed, relief creeping across his face. 'And it's not that I don't love Fox Bay, you know I do.'

Helen leaned forward and stretched out her hand to take his. 'You should spread your wings a bit,' she said. 'Will you go far?'

'That's the good bit.' He gave her a brief grin, and some of the tightness in her chest eased. 'If things work out for this one, it'll be the Summerleaze.'

'Oh? Mr Ellison's leaving, is he? So you'd be Lily's boss.'

'*If* I'm offered the position. I haven't even applied yet.'

'Well you must,' Helen said firmly. 'You'd be mad not to. And Bude's not so far, I was worried you might have wanted to move to London or somewhere.' *Or even abroad.* She bit down on that, in case it gave him ideas.

'That's where Ellison's going. London, I mean.'

'When will they advertise?'

'Within the week, Lily says.'

Helen squeezed and released his hand, and sat back, reminding herself she was lucky that Mr Ellison was the one moving away. 'Tell me when you're called for

55

interview,' she said. 'I know you; you'll try to sneak away and do it in secret, and I want to wish you luck.'

'I won't do that.' He stood up and bent to drop a kiss on her cheek as he passed on his way to the door. 'You do know this has nothing to do with wanting to leave here, or you?'

'I do.' She smiled up at him, then looked at her watch. 'Now go on, it's your turn to run the place.'

'What will you do when I leave?'

'In what way?'

'Will you get another night manager?'

She shook her head. 'No one could do the job as well as you. I'll give Jeremy Bickle a half-promotion, he can remain bar manager, but step up if needed. And there's Guy, of course.'

'By which I take it you mean my job was never necessary in the first place.' But there was no rancour in his voice.

'It wasn't, when I gave it to you,' Helen conceded with a little smile, 'but you soon changed that. I'm sure an awful lot of people have waited until after eight o'clock to make their complaints.'

Ben laughed outright. 'Complaints? Now I know you're talking rubbish!'

'You know you'll still inherit, don't you? My half, at least.'

'I'd assumed so, but I quite understand if you plan to change that now.'

'I won't.' Helen shifted in her seat, so she could look at him properly. 'What I want to know is, if and when you do inherit, will you come back?'

'Of course I will! What else did you think I might do?'

'Well, you'd be within your rights to sell, of course,

56

or get someone else in to run it. Even Lily Trevanion, if she'd take it — '

'Never,' Ben protested. 'No matter what I do between now and that day, which I hope won't come until I'm at least ninety,' he added with a little smile, 'I will make this my very last stop.'

'Good.' Helen relaxed, and made a little shooing motion. 'What are you hanging around for? It's time for work.'

Alone again, she pondered the shape of the hotel's future. Until now she had been surrounded by so many people she loved, and who loved her in return. True, she had often bemoaned the fact that they rarely got together anymore, but they had always *been* there. Off doing their own thing, passing one another like virtual strangers at times, but still there.

Now Fleur had gone, and Leah too. Ben was flexing his wings, and Bertie was weeks away from discovering hers. Soon only Fiona would be left, and she and Danny Quick, the constable's lad from the lifeboat station, were inseparable these days — she would be seventeen later this month, and it was only a matter of time before she too began looking for her own home and her own life. Leah might never return, and by the time Ben did, if he kept his promise, she herself would necessarily be gone.

Helen had a sudden vision of a terrifyingly empty future, and she fully understood, perhaps for the first time, why Fleur had been so desperate to welcome them back after Harry had died. She pulled her cardigan tighter across her chest and tried to push the thought away, but she knew it would come back the moment she turned out her bedroom light.

4

West Bank Boarding House
Friday 14th February

Leah's nerves were wire-tight. Wilf had been steadily building Glynn's new persona for months, and today they would find out if all that work had paid off; Glynn had left her alone all afternoon while he put it to the test in the business community at large, checking that the name of Jacob Bitterson was still alive in the minds Wilf had been able to manipulate.

Leah had bathed and put on her make-up already, and now sat in her underwear, her heart pounding, as she waited to find out whether they were staying or making another moonlight flit; by the time she heard the front door slam she had convinced herself of the latter.

There was more than one set of shoes clattering up the stairs, and male voices were raised in conversation, so Leah seized her house coat, and finished tying it just as the door opened and Glynn and Wilf came in, beaming. All the air went out of her in a rush, and she only just stopped herself from rubbing her face with her hands in relief; she didn't want to have to re-apply her make-up, and it looked as though she would need it tonight after all.

'He's in?'

'He's in!' Glynn swept her up and swung her around in a circle until she shrieked to be put down, but she was laughing. 'Well, so far so good, anyway,' he added.

58

'First step successful,' Wilf said, brandishing a bottle of something that looked hideously expensive. He must be confident, to have spent so much money.

'Tell me what happened.' Leah held out her teacup for a splash of champagne, and sat on her dressing table chair. 'All of it.' She slid a cigarette from its case, and Wilf leaned forward to light it.

'It would take too long, and Mr Freeman here has business to attend to.' Glynn took a swig of his own drink. 'I'll tell you another time, but the short version is that Leonard Neville has been asking all kinds of questions about Mr Jacob Bitterson.'

Leah blew out smoke on a short laugh. 'I told you I froze on the name, didn't I? My mind just went a complete blank.'

'I noticed that,' Wilf said, 'but Neville didn't. It wasn't for as long as you thought.'

'Good thing too,' Glynn said. 'Anyway, this is where it pays not to rush things. All the hard graft we put in setting this up has worked, and Neville still has no idea that Wilf, or rather Mr Freeman, knows me.'

'I might have spent months gaining his trust,' Wilf put in, 'but he's no fool. He won't just take my word for it.'

'He'll have checked among his usual cronies,' Glynn said. 'Fellow investors, businessmen and so on, and all of them will have told him exactly what we wanted them to remember.'

'Which is what?'

'That he's part of a small firm in the States, advising private investors. Not massive financial gains, and certainly some misses, but solid enough. Respected, that's the main thing.'

'That's the key,' Wilf agreed. 'I spoke to enough

people, independently and over time, so that by the time they met him they already vaguely recognised his name, but not as a suspiciously successful newcomer. Only as 'one of us', so to speak, but now they'll have a face to put to the name, too.'

'It doesn't take long for a name to sink into the back of the mind,' Glynn said. 'He's not someone Neville would expect to have heard of, but now you've labelled him as someone willing to exploit privileged information, he'll have no reason to doubt what he's heard from everyone else.'

'Tonight we're going to discuss what Mr Freeman himself has supposedly found out,' Wilf added. 'I'll be able to confirm what he thinks he knows from his independent enquiries.'

'What about us?'

'You'll arrive after he's talked to me, introduce Glynn, and that's when we'll find out for sure.'

'Right. So if all goes well, he'll accept your recommendation for the business deal, still in the belief you've never met before tonight.'

'Let's hope so.'

'And he'll expect me to do the same.'

'Of course, so be ready for that.'

'And then he'll give you the money to invest?'

Glynn shook his head. 'He'll pay it directly to the business Wilf's set up. Into that company's account.'

'Oh, of course.'

'He'll only invest a small amount to begin with, and we'll have to pay out on that, but it'll be small beans.'

'Not that small,' Wilf grumbled. 'It'll take everything we have left, bar nothing.'

'But it'll be worth it,' Glynn reminded him. 'Once we've earned his trust, he's ours.'

60

'Why him though?' Leah had asked before but had received no satisfactory reply. 'What's so important about him?'

Glynn shrugged and looked at his friend. 'Wilf set it up. Neville's his mark, not mine.'

Wilf waved the question away. 'Why not him? He's got money to burn, and he's about as objectionable as a man can be. You can't disagree with that.'

'I certainly can't.' Leah rubbed her hand where Neville had grabbed it; her finger still bore a faint bruise from the rings.

'I was right about the money, Lee,' Glynn said quietly, 'it'll set us up for life. Once Wilf has it in the business account he'll pay us our share, then we'll all disappear, and Neville will never see or hear from us again.'

'Won't he go to the police?'

'With what? He can't exactly tell them he's involved in insider dealing, can he?' Glynn squeezed her shoulder. 'Where's this doubt suddenly come from? You accepted all this quite happily before, without even thinking about the police.'

'I suppose I've just had all afternoon to think about it,' Leah admitted. 'And now it's so close it feels too good to be true.'

'Well, it's true enough.' Wilf finished his drink. 'Right, I'm off to meet our not-so-savvy investor, I'll see you both later. Don't arrive too early, and look out for the pocket square. Glynn, you're not to recognise me.'

'I know,' Glynn said, somewhat testily. 'I'm not new to this, and neither's Leah. Just you mind your own game.'

Wilf nodded at Leah. 'Dress up, darlin', every

night's a party night at the Empire Park.' He winked at her before he pulled the door closed behind him, and Glynn shook his head.

'He doesn't change.'

'You still trust him?'

Glynn poured himself another splash of champagne. 'You don't spend ten years or so in an eight-by-ten cell without learning who you can trust. Wilf's solid enough. Besides, we don't stand to lose anything.'

'Of course we do! We've already put up all our money.' Leah took the bottle he offered. 'It's a big risk.'

'But we haven't given any of it to Neville,' he pointed out. 'Everything he gets paid comes from Wilf.'

'And where's *he* getting the money?'

'You really have been thinking all afternoon, haven't you?'

'Yes!'

Until now she'd been carried along on the wave of Glynn's enthusiasm, propelled by Adam's indifference and the sense that she'd burned all the boats she'd still had at Fox Bay. She had taken everything Glynn had promised for granted. Today all that excitement and rebellion had coalesced into a knot of unanswered questions, and the sudden realisation that for once she wasn't in control. Far from it.

'You have to remember he's been planning this since he was sent down,' Glynn said. 'I'm as certain as I can be that this Neville character has more to do with that than Wilf's letting on, but that's his prerogative. He's using his own money as the sweetener, we've just put ours into having somewhere to stay, and making sure our wardrobe is up to scratch. Including that ridiculous engagement ring.'

'It *is* fake though?' Leah asked, suddenly worried. 'You didn't steal it?'

'Of course it is. But that quality of fake, which has to be good enough to convince someone like Neville, still costs. Speaking of which,' he said more briskly, 'what are you wearing tonight?'

Leah gave in. 'I thought it was time for the pink beaded, but I'm not sure it's appropriate for widow-hood.'

'True, but it can't hurt to remind Neville that there was a reason you and I were supposedly so close back in New York.' He plucked the cup from her fingers. 'Better not have too much of that, we need our wits about us.'

★ ★ ★

Later, Leah watched as Glynn fastened the garter on his socks. It was odd how quickly she had become comfortable once more with seeing him undressed, as if the time they'd been apart hadn't really happened at all.

'You do know what day it is?'

'Friday.' Glynn straightened, shook his leg so his trousers fell neatly, and reached for his jacket. '*The* day.'

'Not just that.' Leah rifled through her own small selection of evening wear. 'It's Valentine's Day. Remember our last one?'

Glynn laughed. 'How could I forget? I've never run so fast in my life. Thank goodness you were wearing flat shoes!'

'Not that part!' But it was remembering the thrill of that chase that had led to the memories that had surfaced now, and as her heart speeded up she wondered if they would ever be able to recapture that feeling; the fierceness with which they had clung to one another the moment they'd known they were safe; the shaky laughter that had turned to a new, charged silence, and then to a night that had put even their wedding night to shame.

Glynn turned back to the mirror, but she saw his gaze flicking to her, and she wished she hadn't said anything. Apart from giving him what would likely turn out to be a false hope, the last thing they needed now was a distraction. But as she slipped into her favourite dress, she felt her skin respond to the silky touch with a little leap of pleasure, and she wondered exactly what this adrenalin-filled night would bring.

★　★　★

The Empire Park was an even more dazzling sight this time; Leah might have only just remembered the date, but the hotel had evidently been planning the celebration from the moment last year's had ended. So much effort had gone into making the lobby a feast of romance, that it seemed to mock the distance between Leah and her husband, and force them to stand closer together; it was impossible, for instance, to enter the frothy extravagance without pressing shoulder-to-shoulder to pass under the archway made of feathers and balloons, and once inside, and their names located on the invitation list, they had champagne glasses pressed into their hands whether they wanted them or not. Leah reminded herself she'd already had plenty, and merely sipped at the drink, relieved to see Glynn doing the same.

'He's over there,' Glynn murmured, beneath the sound of the band playing in the ballroom.

She followed the discreet lifting of his finger in the direction of the stairs, and saw Wilf, bespectacled once more and dressed to the nines, in deep conversation with Leonard Neville. They had taken their conversation up the first short flight of stairs, away from the crowd.

'Haven't they finished yet?' she whispered back, frustrated. 'They could be talking about anything now.'

'No, he's still got the pocket square in place, they're still talking about me. Or rather Bitterson.'

They kept to the lobby level for a while longer, moving through the crowds, appearing utterly wrapped up in one another to avoid being approached, and every so often circling back to the stairs to check Wilf's top pocket.

'It's gone,' Glynn said, after what felt like an age. 'On you go, I'll follow.'

Leah released the tight grip she had on his arm, and drew in a deep breath and held it. As she let it out, she felt Millicent Scripps descending over her like a cool mist, and she glided across the lobby floor, her smile firmly in place.

She stood at the foot of the wide staircase, and Wilf saw her and gestured her up to join them, his eyes roving over her pink-clad form with clear appreciation.

'Mrs Scripps, you're looking beautiful tonight. Very fitting for the occasion.'

'Thank you, Mr Freeman.' Her attention moved to his companion, and her voice cooled somewhat. 'And Mr Neville, good evening.' She made a show of rubbing her hand where he had gripped it. 'How nice to see you again.'

'Mrs Scripps.' Neville nodded briefly. 'I'm glad you received my invitation. Where's your . . . *friend*?' He gave the word a sly kind of emphasis, and Leah's irritation prickled.

'He's just coming, he had someone important to talk to.' She smiled sweetly as she put her own emphasis on 'important', and was rewarded by the dull flush that stained Neville's neck.

'What does he look like?' Wilf asked, looking out over the crowd. 'Oh, is this him? He certainly looks the way I expected, after all I've heard.'

Glynn's attention to his wardrobe was as thorough as ever, and on a tight budget he'd still managed to fit himself out convincingly in the attire of a smart, well-off businessman, but without appearing ostentatious. The important thing, he'd told her, was the idea that he wasn't madly rich or even particularly clever, just that he might be persuaded to a point of view that wasn't entirely legal. To that end he had chosen a sombre-coloured suit and a double-breasted jacket, but his own pocket square was a flashy red, and his hat angled more acutely than most of the men in the room.

Leah watched him come closer, and in her heightened sense of the occasion she found herself appreciating all over again his smooth good looks, and the confident way he carried himself. 'Jacob. This is the kind gentleman I was telling you about, who helped me that first day here in the city. Mr Freeman, this is Jacob Bitterson.'

Glynn shook Wilf's hand, then turned an enquiring look towards Neville.

'This is Mr Leonard Neville,' Wilf said. 'I think the two of you might have something to discuss.'

'Of course, we spoke on the telephone.' Glynn shook Neville's hand, and his cool gaze appraised the investor. 'Thank you for the invitation tonight, Mr Neville. Millicent told me she approached you, asking for advice on the English market. Of course I'm small fry over in the States, and I don't go international, so I hope you were able to help her.'

'Small fry?' Neville gave a soft laugh. 'Not what I've heard.'

Glynn's face tightened. 'Then you've been listening to the wrong people. I'm no big shot.'

'Perhaps not, but I gather you've helped certain people make some very . . . wise choices over there.' He cast a glance at Leah, but from that moment on she was merely a decorative bystander as the three men fell into a discussion about stock value, and the benefits of splitting a portfolio across several companies. She remembered Adam talking about the same kinds of things, and fought off a sudden pang.

As the talk went on she tried to pay attention, but since Neville seemed in no hurry to broach the key matter, her attention soon wandered, and she began to watch the crowds. The couple just entering the lobby were clearly newly together; he was beaming with pride, while she made quite sure everyone knew she was no wallflower this Valentine's Day. Another couple gazed into one another's eyes as they talked, ignoring their drinks. It was a touching sight.

But it was not all hearts and flowers. One of the women in the group by the reception desk looked ready to either drag her husband away, or dump her drink over him, while the woman next to her yawned openly, and checked her jewelled watch. The balloon arch was thronged with people evidently waiting for others to arrive, and it was easy to spot those whose names weren't on the guest list; no champagne greeting for them. One of them, a little older than the young lovers surrounding him, scanned the crowd constantly; perhaps he was suspicious that the lady he was meeting was already here, and avoiding him. A sad tale of experience that hadn't yet touched the younger men.

Leah's thoughts swerved to Adam again, and she wondered what he was doing tonight, and who with. Dinner and dancing? Had he finally persuaded Helen to let him take her out? But no, no matter how much Adam thought of Helen, she did not return his feelings, Leah knew that, and would not give him false hope by accepting an invitation on a romantic night like this.

Her attention moved back to her own group. Neville was finally raising the subject around which they'd all been dancing from the moment Glynn had arrived, and she felt herself tensing all over again. A discreet hand at her elbow made her glance at Wilf, but his eyes were on Neville even as he squeezed gently. She relaxed again and listened as Neville outlined his intention to test Mr Bitterson's credentials.

'You must understand, old man, that no matter what I've heard from those I've asked about you, I need — '

'Oh yeah? Who *have* you asked about me?' Glynn sounded cross again, and Leah couldn't help admiring his audacity; pushing this man away was a risky tactic.

'People who know the business,' Neville said,

waving a dismissive hand. 'And of course Mr Freeman here.'

Glynn glared at Wilf. 'I wasn't aware Mr Freeman knew of my business deals.'

'He wasn't,' Neville soothed. 'But he's been doing his own asking around, ever since Mrs Scripps gave us your name. It seems he's also had good reports.'

'Reports of what?'

'Of your generally shrewd business sense, your discretion, and of course,' Neville lowered his voice, 'Mrs Scripps has told us how you were able to save her poor late husband's fortune, in the Great Crash.'

'Millie!' Glynn turned his glare on Leah, who almost believed it. 'What did you say?'

'Nothing! Only that you advised me just in time.'

'You're denying you had . . . helpful information, Mr Bitterson?' Neville pressed.

'Of course I'm denying it!' Glynn looked around the room, a quick, controlled glance that Leah knew was calculated to tell a different story from the agitation he'd put into his words. 'It's illegal, dammit!'

'Of course. Do accept my apologies.' The smooth tones, met by an inclination of Glynn's head, made it clear the two men were now firmly on the same page. Wilf, to his credit, was looking as baffled as he should be.

'So why did you bring me back here?' Glynn asked. 'Millie said you might have a business proposition. It'd better be damn good.'

'Well that's what I like your advice on. I have a healthy portfolio, and I'm looking to expand into something new. Something that excites me.'

'And what does he have to do with this?' Glynn gestured irritably at Wilf.

69

'Nothing, he's just someone I trust.'

'Really? How far?'

There was a pause, while Neville looked at Wilf, and Leah held her breath, thankful the men's attentions were on each other and not her. She'd rarely felt so out of her depth on a con.

'More than I'd trust my regular broker, in some circumstances,' Neville said.

Leah deliberately pulled her attention off the men and assumed a bored expression while she looked around the lobby again. The group of impatient revellers had broken up; the man who'd been scrutinising the crowd had gone, and she wondered whether he'd found his lady or given up; the adoring couple made their way to the ballroom, still hand in hand —

'There must be something you can give me,' Neville was saying. 'Granted, I've heard plenty of people sing your praises, but there must be something solid, that proves you are what you say you are.'

'I'm not trying to prove anything,' Glynn pointed out. 'You're the one making Millie here drag me back to this city, I was doing fine in London. Found some great opportunities for her there. I don't need to sell myself to you as well.'

'It *would* be to your advantage though,' Neville said. 'Your commission alone would pay for your time, not to mention a new suit,' — his disdainful gaze passed over the plain jacket — 'passage home, and more besides. We'd make a good team if this works well for me.'

Glynn exchanged a quick glance with Leah, who smiled encouragingly. 'It's something to think about, Jake,' she murmured. 'You've said before how much you'd like to explore things this side of the pond,

70

right?'

'I guess.' Glynn waited a beat, then nodded. 'Okay, so how do I prove what I can do, beyond what you've heard?'

'A trial run. Those opportunities you say you've found for Mrs Scripps? Get *her* to put her money up, and we'll see where that takes her.'

'You want to use me as a guinea pig?' Leah managed to sound suitably affronted, but felt a curl of satisfaction at the way it was going so neatly to plan.

Glynn ignored her protest. 'And will that be enough?' he asked Neville.

'It would help if you had something else to help swing my vote your way.'

Glynn was looking uncharacteristically blank, but a light went on in Leah's head, and she tried to remember exactly what had been in the letter she'd had from Helen just after the new year. 'Tell them what you told me,' she said, 'about the film company that's going under.'

'Film company?'

'Good Boy Productions.' She turned to Neville. 'Word is they're going to fold any minute.'

Neville's eyes narrowed. 'You said they're one of the safe ones,' he said to Wilf. 'You're the Hollywood man. What's she talking about?'

'I have no idea,' Wilf said, and Leah thought that, if he could, he'd have fired arrows from those eyes straight into her head. 'This is the first I've heard of it.'

Neville scowled. 'You're the expert, for crying out loud! If *you* don't — '

'Exactly,' Leah broke in. 'If even Mr Freeman doesn't know, it's obviously been hushed up for now,

71

for fear of the repercussions on Wall Street. But Jacob knows that . . . well, he told me about it.' When he didn't answer, she went on hesitantly, 'I'll tell them, Jake, shall I?'

'I don't think — '

'Just to convince them you know what you're talking about. I'm sure they'll both treat it with the utmost confidentiality, won't you, gentlemen?' She fixed both Neville and Wilf with her fiercest glare, feeling all the force of Millicent Scripps surging to the fore once more. She'd missed this feeling, and welcomed its return. 'I mean, you can't afford to let anything slip anyway, right, Mr Neville? You don't want to be accused of having privileged information, after all.'

All three of her companions were now looking at her as if she'd sprouted either horns or wings. Glynn actually looked frightened of what she was going to say next. The thought flashed into her mind that perhaps this wasn't such a good idea after all, but it was too late now.

'Alright,' she said to Neville, 'you know those movies that Good Boy is famous for?'

'The Conrad-Wishart ones?'

'Yes. Well, Daisy Conrad is quitting the business.'

Neville gave a derisive huff. 'Rubbish! Why would she? She's only young, and the films are hugely popular. She'd be mad to give it up.'

'Nevertheless. And Freddie Wishart's going with her, so their funding source is pulling out, which in turn means Good Boy's golden days are over. Anyone with shares in the company would be wise to pull their money out too, and real quick.' Leah remembered she was supposed to be telling this story second-hand, and looked at Glynn. 'Did I get that right?'

He recovered himself well, turning the last of his discomfiture to his advantage. 'I told you this was strictly between us,' he whispered harshly. 'No one knows about Daisy Conrad, and that's the way it's supposed to stay. As soon as word gets out, the share prices will fall through the floor.'

'Mrs Scripps is correct though,' Neville said, 'I certainly can't be seen to be associated with you if this gets out before its time.' For a second Leah froze, thinking she'd gone too far, but Neville shrugged. 'You're therefore assured of my complete discretion.'

'By which, of course, you mean you know people who are trading in Good Boy shares,' Leah guessed. 'I wonder how much they'll pay you for that information?'

Neville didn't respond, but his grin was a trifle shark-like and Leah shuddered inwardly, reminded that he was a dangerous man to cross.

'This is all well and good,' Wilf said, 'but it could take months to come out. We can't sit around twiddling our thumbs to find out whether or not it's true.' He shot a fierce look at Leah. 'You and Mr Bitterson will be leaving England soon.'

Glynn nodded. 'True. But I reckon that, between you, you can make some discreet enquiries in the industry to discover the veracity of my information. After all, Mr Neville knows *you* well, but I'm sure he's too shrewd a businessman to take the word of two people he just met.'

'I'll need documentary proof of your current investment success,' Neville agreed. 'And in the meantime Mr Freeman will check his industry contacts, to see if what you say about Good Boy is true. I'll also conduct some enquiries.' He raised a hand to an acquaintance, a sign that the discussion was over. 'Come and see me here on Monday morning, Mr Bitterson, we'll discuss what information you have, and analyse your recommendations. Mr Freeman, I'd be obliged if you'd join us and tell us what you've managed to find out about Good Boy, and we'll see how it tallies with my information.'

Wilf sounded almost panicked now. 'I really don't see what this has to do with —'

'You're very much involved now, wouldn't you say?' Neville pointed out. 'You've just become privy to some confidential information that's highly relevant to your specialty.'

Leah didn't dare look at Wilf. 'What about me?' she asked Neville.

He gave her a look that might have withered a more timid woman. 'You, Mrs Scripps, since you can't seem to keep your mouth shut about things you're told in confidence, probably ought to just . . . go shopping.'

74

5

Higher Valley Farm

Beth tweaked the curtain straight across the sitting room window, glad to shut out the early dark now Alfie and the boys were in; February was one of their quieter months for livestock, but they had still been out from first light, repairing and building, ready for the coming spring. Jowan and Jory had predictably vanished immediately dinner was over, and Beth had earmarked this evening for a proper talk with Alfie. What better time than Valentine's Day, to discuss the wedding?

The wedding . . . Beth still had trouble applying that notion to herself; how could she play the blushing bride, with two full-grown sons, one of whom would likely be getting married himself before the year was out?

The front door opened, letting in a gust of wind that caused the back kitchen door to slam shut, and Beth jumped and pulled the curtain aside again. Jory was hurrying across to the van, washed and changed, and eager to get off to that awful card game Bill Penneck ran from the back room at the Saltman.

'You'd think he'd have learned his lesson.'

Beth turned to see Alfie, two cups of tea in his hands, kicking the door closed behind him.

'It's boredom,' she said, moving away from the window. 'He needs something to occupy him.'

'That's no excuse. I can find him plenty to do if he

75

needs it.' Alfie put Beth's tea on the little table beside her chair. 'Ever since that American paid off Jory's debts it's as if the lad can't wait to get himself mired in them again. Like he's not comfortable unless he's struggling.'

'Don't be too hard on him.' Beth took up the fire tongs and placed more coal around the burning log. 'He's been a bit adrift since that film star left. They got on quite well, once all the drama was over.'

'He's got a girlfriend,' Alfie pointed out. 'It's about time he remembered that.'

'I didn't think you liked him seeing Sally Penneck.'

'Not a question of liking or not liking. It's a question of loyalty, and his is to Sally. Not someone he'd no chance of being with.'

Beth slid her notebook down the side of her chair, suspecting tonight was not the night to discuss their future after all. Since the dinner party at Fox Bay, when the film producer had rewarded Jory for saving Daisy Conrad's life, Alfie had been distant. He'd been reluctant to enter into any discussion, other than a brief comment, whether it was the produce, the weather, or even the contract with Fox Bay, with which he had always been keen to be involved in the past. Sometimes she felt the absence of their old, easy friendship like a chilly little place right in the centre of her chest, easily warmed in the past with a smile, or a shared memory, but lately remaining untouched for far too much of the time.

After a few minutes, when the only sound was the ticking of the clock and the spitting coal, Beth took up her teacup and warmed her hands on it. She watched Alfie surreptitiously and saw he'd not touched his own drink but was staring into the fire.

76

'It'll get cold,' she said, nodding at his cup. 'Best drink up.' She waited a moment, then, unable to bear the tension any longer, she said softly, 'Are you happy, Alfie?'

He tore his gaze away from the fire. 'Happy? Of course I am. Why, aren't you?'

'I'm not the one searing my eyeballs.'

A tiny smile touched his lips. 'It's surprisingly easy to do, but I don't recommend it.' He blinked, exaggerating to make her smile too, then picked up his tea. 'It just baffles me, how can two young men, twins, be so different?'

'You and Toby were quite different. Toby would chatter all day to a complete stranger, but you barely even speak to our nearest neighbours now.'

'The Foxes? They're more used to dealing with you. Anyway,' he went on, waving the subject away, 'we're not talking about small things like chatting to people. Jowan's about ready to settle down, with a properly nice girl, but look at Jory. Still behaving like a rebellious child, and him nearly thirty.'

'He does worry me,' she admitted. 'But I don't know that we can do anything.'

'No. Time'll have its way I suppose.' He leaned forward to prod the glowing log, sending sparks up the chimney. 'I've been thinking about our own wedding,' he said, surprising her. 'Do you want to talk about it?'

Her entire frame relaxed, and she smiled as she pulled out her notebook again. 'Of course. When were you thinking?'

'Spring seems like a good time, unless you think that's too soon?'

'Not at all. It'll only be a quiet affair anyway.'

'Of course. Just family.'

'And the Foxes,' she added, writing it down. When she looked back he was staring at the fire again. 'Alfie?'

'Hmm?'

'The Foxes should be invited, shouldn't they? They're going to be family soon.'

He frowned, then shrugged. 'If you want them there. Bertie, certainly.'

'And Helen, of course. We'd better invite them all though, so as not to seem rude.' She paused in her scribbling. 'I was thinking of asking the boys to give me away. Is that silly?'

'It's odd,' he admitted, 'my nephews giving their mother to me for a wife. What would Toby think?' Beth put her pen down, suddenly deflated, and Alfie's face fell. 'I'm sorry. I shouldn't have said that.'

'No matter,' she said dully. 'I'm going to bed early; it'll save on coal. You can have the rest of my tea.'

'Beth — '

'Maybe we'll talk tomorrow,' she said over her shoulder, and pulled the door shut behind her. Why had he felt the need to say that? Stupid man! She struck the newel post hard enough to set her palm burning, and started up the stairs, swallowing past a lump in her throat. She had only taken three steps when she heard a car in the yard, and turned back with a little flicker of hope; had Jory changed his mind about the card game?

But the voice she heard wasn't her son's, it was Bertie Fox, calling to her brother that he could go now, and that Jowan would see her home. Alfie came out of the sitting room, still looking shamefaced as he glanced at her.

'Bertie's here,' he said quietly. 'Best fetch Jo.'

'You fetch him,' she snapped. 'He's in his room.'

She pushed past him to open the front door for Bertie, who was halfway up the path, swinging her crutches easily along the uneven slate. But there was something different about her feet . . . Feet? Beth's eyes flew wide.

'You have your leg!'

'Good evening to you too.' Bertie grinned, and the hallway light reflected the pure excitement in her eyes. 'Is Jowan home?'

'Alfie's just gone to . . . oh, no need.'

'Bertie?' Jowan half-ran down the stairs. 'I didn't know you were coming over tonight. Is it still okay?' He nodded at her leg, and she reached down and knocked on it.

'It's even better now I've started doing as I'm told.'

'Good.' Jowan turned to Beth. 'She was told to only wear it for a couple of hours at a time at first, but you know Bertie.'

'I think it's wonderful.' Beth smiled. 'Come in properly, I'll make hot chocolate.'

'Never mind hot chocolate,' Alfie said, 'we have some of Ben's whisky left. A nice little nip to keep out the chill?'

Beth could see Bertie and Jowan exchange a little glance at the forced cheeriness. 'Not for me,' she said, shooting Alfie a cool look. 'We'll leave you two alone, it is Valentine's night after all. Come on, Alfie, you can help me in the kitchen.'

Alfie left them with the bottle Ben Fox had given them for Christmas, and followed Beth into the kitchen. He was still looking ashamed, and the moment he closed the door behind him he came over and took her hands.

'I'm truly sorry,' he said. 'That was unforgivable.'

He looked so miserable that her anger dissipated, and she was left with only the sense of betrayal at his flippant words, and the tired acceptance that, no matter how sorry he was, he had merely shone a light on one of their deepest problems. She was about to speak, but Bertie's voice rose, carrying clearly through the thickness of the kitchen door.

'Why can't you just accept it, Jo?'

Beth and Alfie looked at one another in surprise, especially after the young couple's happy greeting just moments before. Jowan's response was barely audible, but it was easy to tell he was making an effort to keep his voice low, and Beth moved closer to the door, ignoring Alfie's gesture to come away.

'We both knew the time would come,' Bertie went on, 'or did you think I'd give up the idea altogether?'

'Of course not.'

'Then why pull that face?'

Beth heard the rattle of a bottle against a glass, and the clunk as that bottle was replaced on the sideboard. Jo's voice was closer now, as he crossed the room.

'Because it's too soon, that's why.'

'No, it isn't. I thought you understood.'

'I do,' he protested. 'I have right from the start, when you explained how it would fill the gap left by your motorcycle racing. But you only got your leg this week!'

'I wouldn't be flying straight away,' Bertie said. 'I'm only going down there to discuss things, and Xander says there's a lot of classroom — '

'Oh, I see. I wondered how long it would be.'

Beth winced, and exchanged another quick glance with Alfie, who rolled his eyes. Sure enough, there was an ominous pause before Bertie spoke again, sounding dangerously calm.

'How long before what?'

'Before his name came up.'

'My *friend's* name, you mean?'

'He's not your friend! His sister might be, but he's just someone who enjoys flirting, and making girls like you go all soft around him!'

'Oh, Jo,' Beth breathed.

'Girls like me?' Now Bertie's voice was ice-cold. 'What do you mean by that?'

'Look, I understand,' Jowan said, after a moment's tense silence. 'He knows what to say, and how to say it so that people think he's charming, but he's never made any secret of the fact that he wants more from you than friendship.'

'Which of course means I'd run off with *him* at the drop of a hat.'

'Well, no one would blame you.' Now he sounded defeated, and Beth's eyes prickled as she fought the impulse to pull open the door and offer her son some comfort. 'He's far more dashing than a dull old farmer, wouldn't you agree?'

'Jo, why must you always do this?' Bertie sounded as if she were rising to her feet now, Beth could hear the thump of her crutches against the carpet. 'It was a mistake to tell you, I should have just gone down there on my own.'

'Did . . . did you mean you wanted me to come too?'

'Of course I did! I wanted you to see where I'll be living while I train, to see the airfield, the planes, to understand a bit of the . . . Never mind.' She sighed. 'You'd better take me home.'

'No, we can't leave things like this. Let's talk. Come on, Bertie. I'm sorry. I just worry you're trying to do

81

things too quickly, but if it's just talking then of course it's not too soon.'

There was another silence, during which Alfie once again tried, wordlessly, to persuade Beth away from the door, but she shook her head and leaned closer instead.

'You'll come, then?' Bertie pressed.

'If I can get away from the farm, of course I will. I'd be glad to drive you down.'

'And you'll come right in, see the place, talk to the recruitment officer?'

'If you really want me to.'

Beth tensed again, but Bertie didn't sound cross anymore. 'I really think it would help us. Both of us.'

'Well, February's not particularly busy,' Jowan said. 'Alright, I'll talk to Uncle Alfie about taking tomorrow off.'

Beth turned an enquiring face to Alfie, who shrugged. 'Any time he wants to go is fine with me,' he muttered. 'Now for goodness sake come away!'

Beth moved away from the door, and was safely putting plates on the rack when Jowan came in. She left him talking to Alfie and went back into the sitting room, where Bertie was once again sitting on the settee. The girl looked pale and a little tight-featured, but she smiled at Beth.

'How is it?' Beth asked, nodding at Bertie's leg. 'It must be exciting. And a bit frightening too.'

'Frightening?' Bertie looked at her with interest, but did not seem about to disagree.

Beth thought about what she was trying to say. 'I mean, people will look at you differently now. As if they expect everything to go back to normal for you. But it won't, will it?'

'No.' Bertie visibly relaxed, and appeared relieved. 'It feels odd, and a bit sore, and I don't know if I'll ever get used to the feeling.'

'No, I don't know how anyone could.'

Bertie gave her a sudden, shy smile. 'You're the first person who's come out and said that, you know. Not even Mum wanted to say it. She's all gung-ho about how wonderful it is.'

'Well, mums are a funny breed.' Beth patted her hand, smiling back. 'We want what's best for our children, and to make them feel safe and special, but we sometimes go about it all the wrong way. You'll find out, one day.'

Bertie's smile vanished briefly, and when it returned, it looked strained, and Beth's heart sank. She could read that expression all too well. Before she could say anything, and perhaps it was just as well, Alfie and Jowan came back in, and Jo bent to drop a kiss on Bertie's head.

'All set for tomorrow, I'll pick you up after breakfast. Now, what's the latest at Fox Bay? Have you told Mum and Uncle Alfie about that detective?' He turned to them with his old, carefree grin, happy again now the matter of Caernoweth was settled. 'You wait until you hear what Adam Coleridge has done now!'

* * *

After what turned out to be a pleasant evening, Jowan and Bertie set off in the van, and Beth and Alfie prepared to retire for the night, considerably later than expected, but at least the atmosphere between them had eased. Beth raked ash over the embers in the fireplace, and found her mind going back to that tight, forced smile she had seen on her future daughter-in-law's face.

'Jo's in for a rough ride with that one,' she said.

'Why? True, she knows what she wants, but — '

'And what she doesn't.'

'How do you mean?' Alfie paused as he shoved a piece of cloth more tightly into a tiny gap in the window frame.

'I mean she doesn't want children.'

Alfie frowned. 'Has she said as much?'

'No, but I could see it on her face. And you must have noticed how every time Jo brought the subject up tonight she changed it?'

'I hadn't, no.' Alfie sighed. 'I know he wants a family though. That's going to be a difficult conversation.'

'It'll be worse than that,' Beth said grimly. 'This isn't just a matter of where she ends up going to train, that kind of thing can change over time. This is their whole future.'

'But it is *their* future,' Alfie said gently. 'I know you want to stop him from getting hurt, but you have to let him work through this himself.'

'Easy for you to say, with no children of your own . . . Oh, Alfie, I'm sorry.' Now it was Beth's turn to feel shame, at her own rash choice of words, but he only shrugged.

'You're right, I was never that lucky with Sarah. But I know what it is to care about someone and wish the best for them.'

'I'm really — '

'Let's not,' he said, and started to climb the stairs to his room. He turned back once, the shadows playing cruel tricks with her eyes and changing him once again into the man they had both loved. 'Goodnight,

84

Beth,' he said softly. 'Perhaps tomorrow will make us kinder to one another.' He went to his room and closed the door, cutting off the last thin sliver of light that connected them.

* * *

Jowan dropped Bertie at the front door of the hotel. It wasn't late, and through the glass door Bertie could see there were still plenty of guests moving between lounge and lobby, and drifting up and down the stairs like brightly coloured ghosts.

Jowan kissed her cheek. 'Do you want me to come in?'

She shook her head. 'You've got an early start, if we're taking the whole day out.'

'I'm looking forward to it.'

'Are you?' She turned to study him, in the light spilling from the lobby. 'You're not just saying that because I got cross?'

Jowan put his arms around her and pulled her close. 'I do want to understand the appeal this has for you,' he said. 'It won't stop me worrying, but understanding will be enough for now.'

'I'm sure the visit will put your mind at rest,' she said as she pulled away. 'Go on, I'll be ready from around nine.'

'See you tomorrow.' He gave her one last kiss and returned to the van, but as he slid in behind the steering wheel Bertie couldn't help noticing how his smile fell away, and she gave a little grunt of renewed annoyance. At least tomorrow he would realise the military training took place in a separate area of the compound, and that the chances of seeing Xander at all were so remote as to be laughable.

As always, moving from the cold, dark evening into the brightness and warmth of the lobby gave her a feeling of instant relief, and she wondered how she would feel when it was no longer part of her life. Would she feel like a visitor whenever she returned, or would Fox Bay envelop her just as warmly when it was no longer her everyday home?

Ben came out of the office, and Bertie released her hand from the leather strap of her crutch, to give him a little wave of greeting, but rather than wave back, or smile, he stared at her with an expression she couldn't read. Then he opened the office door again, and said something to whoever was inside, before coming out from behind the reception desk, like a man approaching a terrified dog by the side of the road. She saw, over his shoulder, that her mother had emerged too, and was looking at her much the same way.

She began to feel a little ill; her mother's face reminded her too strongly of the evening she'd learned of her father's accident. She stopped walking, and waited, unable to move her crutches forward; it was as if weights had appeared on her elbows, and glue on her shoes. Was it Fiona? Had she done something characteristically reckless? Or Fleur? Or, Adam, or, or . . .

'Darling,' her mother said, 'come into the sitting room and sit down.' She spoke calmly, and Bertie understood from that, that at least her close family must be safe. And Leah too.

'What's happened?' She allowed herself to be guided to the sitting room, and to the sofa.

'Bertie, I'm so sorry,' her mother began, then looked helplessly at Ben, who sat beside Bertie and took her hand.

'We had a telephone call while you were out,' he said, his eyes fixed on the back of her hand as he clasped her fingers. 'It's Xander. He was in a terrible accident, and I'm sorry to say he was . . . he was killed.'

Bertie heard the words, but they seemed to pass over her like a chilly wind, wrapping frosty threads around her limbs and her fingers. 'Killed,' she repeated flatly, and her voice sounded like a tinny little radio, somewhere in another room.

'He was on a training flight, as a passenger. There was an engine malfunction while they were out over the water.' Ben's voice, too, sounded unreal, and his words barely made sense. 'Xander was trapped in the aeroplane.'

'He drowned?'

'I'm so sorry ——'

'When did it happen?'

From the corner of her eye she saw Ben look at their mother, who shook her head.

'I'm not sure exactly. Earlier this week, I understand. The Nicholls family are just getting around to contacting friends.'

'How did she sound?'

'Who?'

'Lynette of course.' Bertie hadn't meant to snap, but couldn't find the strength to apologise.

Ben squeezed her hand. 'It was her father who telephoned. He said Lynette has locked herself away and won't speak to anyone.'

Bertie's mind took her back to the racetrack at Bude, the day she had met the Nicholls siblings. The day she had lost her leg too, but now there were only memories of Xander: the outrageous flirting; that winning

87

smile as he'd triumphantly produced his off-colour joke about a Fox riding a squirrel; the way he'd called her 'Chum', from the very start, and insisted on calling her 'Bertram' now. Or had.

The pain in her heart blossomed then, and she doubled over it. Picture after picture flashed behind her eyes, a motion-picture mockery of the laughter, the affectionate exasperations, the understandings, and the deeper aspects of him that no one but she and Lynette shared. Oh, god, poor Lynette . . . It didn't bear thinking about, what she must be going through. She tried to imagine how it would feel to lose Ben, but with him sitting here it was impossible.

'Sweetheart . . . .' She felt her mother's arm go around her shoulders, breathed the familiar scent of comfort and home, and sank into it, hoping to lose herself in sensation instead of thought. But the memories kept coming, dragging her back to lucidity.

Somehow she drew her emotions into a tight ball that she tried to force to the back of her mind, at least for now. She sat up and accepted the handkerchief Ben pressed into her hand, and used it to pat the worst of the tears away so she could at least see again. Her mother eased away from her, but carefully, as if ready to move closer again the moment Bertie showed any sign of needing her. Ben folded his fingers around hers, and they waited for her to speak.

'When's the, the . . . .' She couldn't even say the awful word. Xander hadn't lived long enough; he shouldn't be laid under the earth before he'd had the chance to explore it. To make his mark on it.

'The eighteenth,' her mother said. 'Tuesday.'

'I have to go.'

'Of course. Would you like me to come with you?'

Bertie knew the offer was for practical reasons as well as for support, but she shook her head. 'I want Jowan to come. If Alfie will let him.'

She could sense her mother and Ben looking at one another over her head, and guessed at the silent conversation that was passing between them. 'He didn't hate Xander, you know,' she said, pressing Ben's handkerchief to her eyes again. 'He'll come, if only for me.'

'I'm sure he will.' Helen paused. 'Do you want one of us to tell him?'

'He's coming over tomorrow. We were going down to Caernoweth . . . .' Bertie broke off as the reality of Xander's death hit her all over again. 'We were going to talk to the training officer about when I might be able to start.'

'Will you still want to do that?' Helen sounded shocked, and even Ben looked at Bertie in consternation.

'Of course I will!' Bertie blew out a trembling breath. 'But not now. I have to go to Brighton instead, so I can talk to Lynette.'

'Is it fair then, to ask Jowan to come with you?' Ben asked, and he sounded hesitant. 'I mean, if you and Lynette will be talking, he'll be left alone a lot of the time, among strangers.'

Bertie had to admit the truth of that. 'Who else though? You'll both be too busy, and Ben, you have that new job to think about.'

'Fiona?' Helen suggested. 'She and Lynette got along quite well, and she adored Xander. She'd welcome a chance to say goodbye, and to help you at the same time.'

'Does she know yet?'

Ben nodded. 'She's devastated, the poor thing, she was here when we took the telephone call. She went straight up to her room.'

'I ought to go and speak to her,' Bertie murmured.

'Tomorrow,' Helen said gently. 'You both need time alone tonight. I'll telephone the Nancarrows and get a message to Jowan.' She helped Bertie to stand, while Ben passed over her crutches. 'I'll take you up now, we can sort out your travel arrangements tomorrow, and then telephone Lynette to let her know when you'll be arriving.'

Alone in her room, Bertie left the bedside light on; the darkness would feel suffocating tonight. She pulled the eiderdown up to her chin and sat bolt upright, dry-eyed now, and the throb and soreness of having worn her new leg for too long again was distant and unimportant. Her head was full of Xander's voice, calling her a 'little rocket' after she'd come second in the only motorcycle race in which she would ever take part; declaring he had no idea who Daisy Conrad was, when he met her here at Christmas; and then unknowingly telling Harry Batten that his family hotel wasn't a patch on Fox Bay. But the sound she heard most clearly was the echo of his laughter when he realised he'd committed those gaffes, and when she and Lynette had both flicked water at him for calling her prosthetic a peg leg.

Bertie slid down until she was lying flat, and stared up at the half-shadowed ceiling. A winter moth fluttered around the inside of the light shade on her bedside table; she heard the sound of its wings, battering against the glass, and couldn't bear the thought of the poor creature struggling to navigate by the false moon. It made her think of a single plane, tiny against the vastness of the sky, plunging through empty air until it struck the greedily surging sea, and taking Xander and his instructor with it.

She reached out to turn off the light. As she had feared, the darkness felt like a breathing thing, pressing in on her, and as she closed her eyes and felt fresh, hot tears slip down her temples, she gave herself over entirely to the memory of a laughing young man, who'd seized life with both hands, and drawn her along with him for its all too brief ride.

6

By late Sunday afternoon, Adam had started to eye the reception telephone with a mixture of frustration and worry. He'd expected a call from Sam Douglas long before now; the investigator had left Trethkellis on Tuesday morning and only phoned once, on Thursday, to say he had a lead on someone with whom Gregory Marshall had been in contact in prison. Since then there had been nothing.

Helen was still withdrawn and uncommunicative, worried about the girls of course, who'd left yesterday for Brighton. He himself had driven them to the station, his heart twisting in sorrow to see the lively pair reduced to a couple of black-clad wraiths. The last time he'd seen young Fiona looking so distraught was when they'd learned of Bertie's accident, and the dangerous fever and infection that had nearly killed her. She had seemed so much older than her years; he'd had to remind himself she wouldn't even turn seventeen until later this month, yet she had taken charge of the tickets and the loading of their luggage, and of ensuring Bertie had everything she needed to make their long journey comfortable.

Ben had come downstairs early, a few hours before the start of his evening shift, and Adam watched him disappear into the office after an early dinner, a determined look on his face. The interviews for the manager's role at the Summerleaze were apparently taking place over the next few days, and Ben's was tomorrow — his fond family might consider it a formality, but Adam knew better, as did Ben himself; if he didn't perform well at interview, all his years of experience, even at Fox Bay, would be useless.

'Mr Coleridge!' Martin Berry was holding up the telephone receiver. 'It's for you. A lady.'

Adam's heart leapt, and he hurried across the lobby to take the receiver from Martin. 'Leah?'

'Try again.' The voice in his ear was both amused and familiar, and he blew a harsh, frustrated breath. Jeanette Duval, his former fiancée, and the sister of his old business partner. For a moment he forgot how much he owed her, and was tempted to hang up the telephone.

'Jeanette,' he said instead, 'what can I do for you?'

'There's no need to sound so disappointed.'

'Sorry, I'm expecting an important call.'

'Charming.'

'Not that whatever you have to say isn't important, of course. I'm sure it is.'

'Only if you want to know how my little book-keeping exercise is progressing. It's almost April, and I've been putting it off for as long as possible, but Simon's getting twitchy now. We ought to discuss what I need from you in order to keep convincing him that all is on the up at Hartcliffe.'

Adam's heart sank. The comforting barrier of Christmas had passed, and Hartcliffe Developments, in whose name he had set up a false subsidiary company in order to rescue Fox Bay, would be getting ready for their annual tax audit.

Jeanette had been gradually, skilfully, manipulating her brother's books to cover the money CP Holdings had borrowed, but the deadline for paying the difference had suddenly appeared over the horizon, and there was bound to be a hefty sum involved. Adam would have to spend some time going over Fox Bay's own accounts, and he desperately hoped it wouldn't once again be a question of robbing Peter to pay Paul.

'Look, I'm in the lobby at the moment,' he said, looking around, 'I can't talk here. Give me a minute and I'll call you back from the office.'

'I'll be waiting.'

Adam could almost see her giving the little wave she'd always considered cute, and he suppressed a grunt as he hung up. That flighty exterior had turned out to conceal a mind like a guillotine, and he was doubly glad they had parted on good terms; without her help he'd have been in jail by now, and Fox Bay more than likely turned into a block of flats. But that didn't mean she wasn't as irritating as hell.

He started towards the office, but stopped with a little surge of relief as he saw Sam Douglas coming through the revolving door. 'Sam!' He gestured for the detective to follow him. 'Come in here. What have you found?'

'She's safe,' Douglas said, 'but you need to . . . Wait, let's get inside and I'll tell you everything.'

Adam closed the office door behind them. 'Well?'

Sam put down his small suitcase and loosened his tie. 'Right, well, she's in Liverpool, that much is true at least.'

'You've seen her yourself?'

'Aye. She's with her husband, as you suspected. They're staying in a dingy wee boarding house on the Birkenhead side of the Mersey.'

'And they're doing what?' Adam took a bottle of whisky from the desk drawer and raised an eyebrow, and Sam nodded.

'Again, you were right. They're involved in a con up there, set up by the bloke I told you about, a Wilfred Stanley.'

'The one Marshall was in prison with?'

'That's the one. The thing is, Mr Stanley hasn't been straight with either of them.' Sam accepted the drink, and took a big gulp before continuing. 'The con they're running involves insider dealing, something that's currently being heavily targeted by Scotland Yard.'

'Since the Great Crash, I take it?'

Sam nodded. 'Mr Stanley has been turned, by which I mean — '

'Scotland Yard have got to him.'

'Exactly. He's leading the mark, a Mr Leonard Neville, into a nice little trap that's baited by Marshall and his wife but leaves himself at a safe distance.'

'I *knew* she'd be in over her head,' Adam muttered.

'Not really.' Sam gave him a wry smile. 'Not at the moment, anyway. She's actually holding her own.'

'You mean she's safe because Neville fancies his chances with her.'

'I mean nothing of the kind. Don't get me wrong, Mrs Marshall looks the part alright. But I was watching her at a party on Friday evening, and aside from being the one who introduced Marshall to Neville, she's made herself very much a background character in this scenario.'

'Good, that'll mean — '

'But,' Sam held up a warning hand, 'she's still in danger of getting arrested alongside him and her husband.'

Adam frowned. 'But they'd soon find out she's not really engaged in insider trading, and let her go.'

'Eventually, perhaps, but she could still be charged with obtaining money by false pretences. A serious crime in itself.' Sam gave Adam a pointed look. 'As I'm sure you realise.'

Adam could feel his face colouring. 'How do we get her out without alerting her husband?'

'That's down to you, I can only tell you what I've found.'

'Helen will be able to talk her around.'

'Helen?' Sam looked appalled. 'You're surely not thinking of taking Mrs Fox with you?'

'Of course. If anyone can talk sense into Leah it's her.'

Sam shook his head. 'I'd advise against it. Strongly. You have no idea what you're walking into up there, Adam, it's not a game. You'd be putting her in real danger.'

Adam felt a chill tickle the base of his spine at the look on Sam's face. 'You're right. I'll go alone.' He put down his drink and shoved his hands into his pockets as he went to the window, staring out at the dark February evening. 'If I warn them, the scam will fall apart and then the police won't get their man.'

Sam shrugged. 'True. Though obviously I can't advise you to do anything that'll jeopardise a police operation.'

'But if you could?' Adam twisted to look at Sam, who didn't reply, and he turned back to the window. 'Right. Are they all staying at the same boarding house?'

'No. Mr and Mrs Marshall are staying at the place I mentioned, in Birkenhead, but Mr Stanley is in Liverpool, closer to the hotel where Mr Neville does his business. He's going under the name of Mr Freeman.

Very droll, as I'm sure you'll agree.'

'How?'

'Free man.' Sam smiled briefly. 'What he became, the minute he agreed to help the police, and to draw in a seasoned con artist to help him do it.'

'Of course.' Adam sighed and shook his head. 'Why wasn't Marshall offered the same deal though? He'd have been quite valuable to them on the outside too, he was even let out early for good behaviour.'

'Yes he was, and the police wouldn't have liked that one little bit.'

'Why not?'

Sam rolled his tumbler between his hands. 'Did Mrs Marshall tell you why her husband served such a long sentence to begin with? He and his wife were only running that same scam that she tried on you, after all. No arms, no violence.'

'Not intentionally, but during the arrest he pushed . . . Ah.'

'There you go,' Sam said. 'He pushed a policeman, who subsequently died from a head injury. The police have long memories, and seeing the man who killed one of their own get let out early? Well.' He finished his drink, and shook his head as Adam offered a top-up. 'This way they see him put away again where he belongs.'

'And Leah too, this time,' Adam added, his face grim.

'Which is why I came back here to let you know, as soon as I saw them together.'

'I'm going up there,' Adam decided, 'first thing tomorrow.'

'Why wait?' Sam took an envelope from his inside pocket and propped it on the desk. 'It's not even six

97

yet, you could be there before midnight if you leave now. I don't know about you, but to me Monday morning has an awful ring of, *let's get this done*, about it. Market trading will begin again, and the banks will be open. As I said though, I can't advise anything that might ruin a police operation.'

'Of course not. Does that mean you won't come with me?'

'I'm afraid I can't, no. The people I've called upon to help in this will recognise me, and if it sends an operation awry I'll be in the soup.'

'Can you at least tell me how to find this boarding house? And the hotel?'

'Absolutely not.' Sam patted the desk next to the envelope. 'Telephone me when you get back, we still have the art to discuss. Although perhaps I could take it up with Mrs Fox instead, while I'm here?'

Adam shook his head. 'Not the best time, I'm afraid. We've just had some desperately sad news about a young family friend. Helen's daughters have gone to Brighton for the funeral.'

Sam's faint smile faded. 'I'm sorry to hear it.' He picked up his case and pulled open the door. 'Good luck, and I'll see you soon, I expect.'

Adam barely waited until the door had closed, before he tore open the envelope and scanned the brief contents.

Empire Park Hotel, Liverpool: Leonard Neville

Haymarket Hotel, Liverpool: Alistair Freeman (Wilfred Stanley)

West Bank Boarding House, Birkenhead: Jacob Bitterson, and the name that first made him catch his breath, and then smile through a surprising twist of pain: *Millicent Scripps.*

There was no time to find Helen and tell her he was going without her, and she would only end up persuading him in any case, so he scribbled a note instead, and left it at reception, then hurried upstairs for his coat and wallet. He was pulling away from Fox Bay within ten minutes of Sam's good luck wishes, and had driven almost as far as Exeter before he remembered he hadn't called Jeanette back.

★ ★ ★

Higher Valley Farm

The weather always seemed to know that Monday was washday. Or the first washday of the week, at any rate. Beth checked the sky, estimating around an hour before the build-up of cloud turned into something more ominous. She seized the basket of wet laundry, and hurried out to the sloping field behind the farmhouse to begin the next task in the seemingly never-ending cycle of washing and drying, washing and drying. Her mind was, as usual these days, anywhere but on her task.

Valentine's night had been a difficult time in the Nancarrow house, and not only for the youngsters, but at least Alfie's wish that they would be kinder to one another had been granted. In fact he himself had brought up the subject of the wedding once again the following day, and they had talked, and even laughed a little, and agreed on who should be invited. They were friends again, and the more she thought about how her wishes had at last come true, the more eagerly she looked forward to becoming Alfie's wife. That he seemed to be warming even more to the idea

99

was a source of great relief after their stumbling start, and she was sure they'd be able to broach the subject of intimacy, without any further hesitation, on their wedding night.

She could feel herself blushing, even as she jammed the wooden peg down over the waistband of Alfie's trousers. 'Don't think about *that*, for goodness sake,' she said aloud, and smacked the trouser leg straight with unnecessary vigour.

'About what?'

Beth started, and looked over at the gate, to see a man leaning on it. He was holding something flat, and as she looked more closely she saw it was a large-ish sketch book. He raised his free hand, and then used the pencil clutched in it to shove his hat back on his head. She saw white hair peeking out from beneath it but could make out very little else about him.

'I'm sorry to have startled you,' he said, and his accent was clearly not local. Scottish, most likely, or Irish, it was hard to tell with those few words, and she didn't know anyone well from either country.

'Don't concern yourself,' she called back, and bent to pick up the shirt. 'You're staying at the hotel then?'

'Aye.' He tucked his pencil into his top pocket. 'Glad to meet you, I'm Sam. Sam Douglas.'

'Beth Nancarrow.' She didn't know what to say next, and was glad she had a job of work to be getting on with. She flapped the shirt straight, and pegged it in place, wishing the man would go away, but luck was not with her today.

'Mrs Fox mentioned I might like to paint your farmhouse,' he ventured after a minute.

'Did she now? Judging from the book you've got there, I assume she wasn't offering your services as a decorator.'

He laughed at that. 'If you saw my office building in Truro you'd never have to ask.' He looked a bit shy now. 'I've done some already, can I show you the sketch, so you can let me know if you approve?'

'Approve?' Beth stared, nonplussed. This wasn't anything she'd ever expected to be asked, and she didn't really know how to respond. 'Alright,' she said at length. 'You'd better come in then.'

'Thanks.' To her surprise he didn't move to unfasten the rope that secured the gate at the post, but instead put one hand on the top bar and vaulted over it like a sprightly youth. It rather spoiled the effect when he landed in the mud, and one foot shot out from under him. For a second it looked as though he'd regain his balance as his free arm wheeled madly, but he was too worried about dropping his sketch book, and his other leg buckled and he went down.

Beth couldn't stop the laughter from breaking free, but she tried to suppress it at least, as she hurried towards him. 'Are you alright?'

He pointed to the book, which thankfully had landed right-side up. 'If that is, I am.' He gave her a disarming grin from his position on the ground, and she saw he was quite attractive, clean-shaven, and not nearly as old as he'd seemed at first. Still long past a lad though, and surely should have given up leaping over gates long since. Another laugh bubbled up, and she smothered it and held out her other hand.

'Up you get,' she said, and pulled. Upright, he was taller than he'd looked bending over the gate, and of a slender build, not something she was used to seeing around the farm; all the Nancarrow men were from burly stock, with barrel chests and broad shoulders.

Mr Douglas's grip was firm though, and his movements spare and graceful as he brushed wet grass from his clothing and bent to pick up his book.

'Now that I've made a total fool of myself, would you still like to give me your verdict on my work too? Might as well go all the way.'

Beth couldn't help smiling. 'Go into the house,' she said. 'I'll just finish this, and then you can show me what you make of us. We can get that mud off you too, don't want to go trailing that back to Fox Bay.'

'Two people work faster than one,' he said, and put his book down on a stone before bending to lend a hand with the washing. 'Are you sure this is a good idea?' he said, looking at the approaching blue-black clouds.

'Not a bit,' Beth said cheerfully, 'but it'll not dry in the basket, now will it?'

He favoured her with a laugh, but her answering smile froze, and she looked on, mortified, as he pulled the next item from the basket: a pair of her oldest drawers, complete with sagging elastic, and of a questionable off-white colour. There was nothing she could do but pretend they didn't exist, and to his credit he didn't even look at her as he pegged them neatly to the line. Perhaps he assumed they belonged to some elderly woman who lived there . . .

'You're very good at this,' she said, by way of a desperate distraction.

'Comes of living alone.' He picked up the empty basket, while she shoved the pole under the line, hoisting it to catch the wind coming off the moor, and, still smarting under the embarrassment, she led the way back up to the house. It occurred to her that he had been gracious enough in his acceptance of

102

humiliation, but then again it was humiliation of an entirely different kind, and her face flamed again as she pushed open the porch door and kicked off her boots.

She left him in the bathroom sponging the worst of the mud off his trousers, while she busied herself setting out teacups and what was left of the weekend's fruit cake. But he'd left his sketch book on the sideboard and she couldn't resist peeking at it before he came back.

The outline was unmistakeably Higher Valley, despite the sparseness of the detail. He'd captured the broken fence post that Alfie kept forgetting to replace, and the peculiar bend of the apple tree by the barn, even the loose brick in the chimney hadn't escaped his attention. The suggestion of a dog was sniffing at a clump of greenery by the gatepost.

'I do the little bits before the big bits,' he said, appearing in the kitchen doorway. 'You'll see I've not filled in much else, beyond the outline.'

She nodded. 'You've done a grand job, Mr Douglas, you've even caught Reynard there.'

'Please do call me Sam,' he said, and looked at her a little shyly. 'Are you sure you don't mind me doing it? I've a fondness for farmhouses, and they make such wonderful, individual subjects. But I'm more than happy to stop, if you —'

'Oh no, please don't!' Beth picked up the pad and studied the drawing, now that she could do so openly. 'I like it very much indeed. What will you do with it, once you've painted it?'

'Nothing much,' he admitted. 'I've got a roomful of them at home. I just love seeing beautiful places like this come to life in front of me.'

'But you must do something!' Beth could imagine how it would look when it was finished, and the thought of Higher Valley joining a stack of others, nameless, unseen, unappreciated, was a surprisingly sad one.

'Well I could make a gift of it,' Sam mused. 'Would you like it, Mrs Nancarrow?'

Beth had thought she couldn't have been any more embarrassed, but she'd been wrong. 'I wasn't asking,' she mumbled.

'But would you?'

'I couldn't possibly.'

Sam nodded, and stowed the book by the side of his chair. 'That's alright, it's not to everyone's taste.'

'No! I mean, it must be worth something. It's going to be beautiful, anyone can see that, and you can't go giving your work away.'

Sam looked at her for a moment, and she noticed how his dark eyebrows contrasted with his white hair. She'd never seen such a combination before; it gave him a youthful look, though he must have been around the same age as herself.

'That cake looks wonderful,' he said, making her blink at the swift change of subject. 'It must have taken hours.'

'Oh, not long,' she said dismissively. 'I soak the fruit overnight though, so it's not something I can knock up in an hour. Would you like cheese with it?'

'If you can spare a slice, I'd love some. Thanks'

Sam poured the tea, while Beth fetched the cheese from the cold pantry, and while they ate he told her about the farm he'd loved up in Scotland.

'West Glenlowrie,' he said. 'Or it was, before it was assimilated into the big estate. Oddly enough it can

104

translate roughly as *valley of the fox*. Seems fitting I should find myself here at Fox Bay.'

'It does sound lovely,' she said, picturing glens and mountains, and the massive waterfall he described so vividly.

'Hard work though, just like it is here. You must be at it from dawn until nightfall, just the same. My mother never stopped either, doing all the little things the rest of us thought happened by magic.'

Beth couldn't help laughing at that; it was true the boys tended to forget that when their work was done for the day, hers still had hours to go. Toby had been just the same. She glanced out of the window. 'Shower's starting,' she observed.

'Want help bringing in the clothes?' Sam settled his cup back in its saucer, but Beth couldn't face that again and she shook her head quickly.

'I'll leave the washing out for a bit, it'll blow over.'

'Aye, it's just a quick one.' Sam pressed a finger into the crumbs on his plate. 'I was right, the cake was delicious. I don't know how you find time to bake.'

'I make time,' Beth said, pleased. 'I love doing it.'

'And watching people enjoy the result, I expect.' Something about his tone made her look at him suspiciously, and he smiled and pointed to his feet, where the sketch book lay. 'A gift,' he repeated. 'From someone who makes time for it and loves doing it.'

'And seeing others enjoy the result.' Beth relaxed and smiled back. 'I'd be honoured, thank you.' An idea occurred to her. 'If you see Alfie about, don't tell him. It'll make a lovely wedding present.'

'Is Alfie your son?'

'Alfie's my intended,' she said, feeling a sweep of pride.

'Oh, *your* wedding present!' He tapped the side of his nose. 'Mum's the word.'

'About what?'

Beth turned in surprise; she'd been so engrossed in her conversation she hadn't even heard the front door open. Jowan shucked off his oilskin and hung it on the back of the door.

'A wedding present for Alfie,' Beth said. 'This gentleman's staying at Fox Bay, and he's an artist. He's going to paint the farm.'

Jowan's eyes widened. 'You're the detective!'

Beth shook her head. 'No, I just told you, he's an artist.'

'Yes, but don't you remember I told you about him on Friday? Adam Coleridge has hired him to find Leah Marshall.'

'You told me about that, but you didn't say he was also an artist.' Beth turned to Sam, who looked sheepish. 'And you didn't tell me you were a detective.'

'It wasn't a deliberate attempt to mislead,' he said. 'I've done the work I was hired to do, so I'm on my own time until someone else hires me. This area's got everything a landscape artist could ever want.'

'You should join the Trethkellis group,' Jowan said. 'They stay here every year.'

'At the hotel,' Beth clarified, 'not here. Bit rowdy, but they work up a good appetite being out and about all day, so the hotel's always got a big order for us when they're staying.'

'You supply the hotel? Well that would explain the eggs I had this morning.' Sam patted his stomach appreciatively. 'Freshest I've ever tasted.'

Beth nodded her thanks, but she could tell Jowan was home early for a reason, and as much as he was

106

fascinated by their visitor, he was clearly glad when Sam took the faintly awkward silence as a hint and stood up.

'Thank you for the elevenses. I'll send the painting when it's done.'

'Actually, would you mind sending it to Fox Bay, so we don't spoil the surprise?'

'I will.' Sam tugged on his shoes, grimacing slightly as the wet mud soaked into his socks again. 'When's the wedding?'

'We thought Easter weekend. That's the nineteenth of April this year.'

'That'll be a lovely time for it.'

'You'll come, won't you?' she blurted, out of politeness.

'Oh.' Sam looked flattered, but also a little discomfited, and Beth realised how odd it sounded. She wondered what Alfie would think, since he'd never even met the man.

'Easter weekend, you say?' Sam nodded, and Beth recognised the same politeness in his response. 'I'll make sure I'm free. Thank you, I'd be delighted.'

After he'd left, Jowan grinned at her. 'He's never going to come, of course.'

'Well no, but what was I supposed to say? He knows he won't really be expected.'

'What happened to him anyway? He was covered in mud.'

'He did try to wash most of it off, but the water's not hot yet.' Beth told him about the fall by the gate, as she cleared Sam's cup away and replaced it with a clean one for her son, and was glad to see some of the tension fade from Jo's face as he laughed. 'Now, what brought you back here before the others?'

Jowan's laughter faded. 'I just wanted to know what you and Bertie talked about the other day, while I was out of the room.'

Beth's movements slowed, while her thoughts turned faster. 'How do you mean?'

'When Alfie and I were talking about me taking time off so I could take Bertie down to Caernoweth. You two were alone in the sitting room, and when you saw me you had a . . . .' he shrugged ' . . . a *look* about you.'

'I'm sure I don't know what you mean.'

'Mum!' Jowan pushed his cup away, sloshing tea into the saucer, and now she could see the tension was back, tightening his mouth, and making a muscle jump in his jaw. 'I'm not an idiot. There's something up with Bertie and I know you know what it is.'

'Her friend's just died!' Beth brushed imaginary crumbs off the table into her hand, so she didn't have to look at him. 'You might not have liked Xander, Jo, but he was —'

'This was before she found out about that,' Jowan pointed out, but his manner softened. 'I don't want to put you in an awkward position, but, well, I'm fairly sure Bertie will be changing her mind about flying now, and I need to be sure there's nothing else that might threaten our future together.'

'Why would she change her mind?' Beth seized on the one thing that might distract him from pursuing his questions about other issues. 'You know she wasn't going because of him.'

'She wouldn't even have thought about it if he hadn't mentioned he was doing it.'

'But it was different for her,' Beth reminded him. 'He was joining the military, she's not. And she didn't

108

even know he'd be training in Cornwall. Now she has her new leg fitted, why would she give it up?'

'Because of what happened to Xander!' Jowan stared at her, incredulous. 'You can't think she would want to carry on with that idea now, surely? She's bound to change her mind, anyone would!'

'You know her better than me.' But even Beth knew the chances of that young woman giving up her ambitions lay somewhere between minuscule and non-existent. Jowan was deliberately deluding himself, but if it helped him cope she couldn't begrudge him that.

She attempted to deflect the subject again. 'It's the funeral tomorrow, isn't it? I hope she'll be alright. At least she's got Fiona with her.'

He nodded. 'I'm ready to be with her when she gets back though. I know Xander and I had our differences, but he was quite the character. She'll miss him a lot.' He looked up at her earnestly. 'I do understand how difficult it will be.'

'Of course you do. She knows you do.'

'I won't put any pressure on her to change her plans though. I know better than to even try.' Jowan smiled a little ruefully. 'But maybe I won't have to, once we're wed and things take their natural course.'

Beth smiled back, but she knew that, even if Bertie were to take her ambitions in a different direction after all, Jowan was going to find a future with her anything but straightforward. If they even had one.

7

Empire Park Hotel

The sticky warmth of the over-heated lobby fused Leah's silk blouse to her skin as she removed her coat, and she plucked the light blue material away from her body in case it looked like the heat of guilt. Glynn and Wilf should already be here, and she wished she could have been privy to their conversation with Neville, but their parts in this were out of her control.

She looked around her with increasing distaste. The hotel had been a vision of sophistication and a source of deep interest for a while, but it was now irrevocably tied up with the memories she had created here in just a few days: the sight of the bland, yet oddly menacing, Leonard Neville around every corner; the panic that she, Glynn, and Wilf would be discovered for what they were; and the relief whenever she stepped outside onto the wintry street, feeling the air on her face like a granted wish for freedom.

Something about the air today felt prickly, too. Understandable enough, given the importance of the meeting that was taking place, but still . . . She wandered through the lobby and allowed her gaze to wander, with apparent enjoyment, over the pillars and the greenery, the elaborate lighting, and the flower displays on the tables. But as she made her way towards the stairs her attention was on the reception desk, where Wilf was talking to the concierge.

'Mr Freeman?'

He turned, and she thought she saw a tightening of his features. 'Mrs Scripps. How nice to see you again so soon.'

They moved away, and she lowered her voice, reverting to her own accent. 'Why aren't you in the meeting?'

'I couldn't really arrive at the same time as Glynn, could I?'

Leah conceded that much, but couldn't shake her own uneasiness. 'Did you manage to slip those documents to him?'

He nodded. 'The finest selection of share certificates you could wish for, and the stock market figures to back them up.' He grinned. 'Never let it be said I didn't make good use of my time in prison. Or my ability to make friends there. Come on, let's go up.'

★ ★ ★

Glynn and Neville were poring over a large mahogany table strewn with papers, mostly green and brown and with ornate edging and beautifully crafted texts. Neville was comparing one to a sheet of paper he held in his other hand, squinting at them both in turn. He only looked up briefly, as Leah and Wilf came in, and Glynn not at all.

'What have you found out?' Neville asked, apparently satisfied with what he was looking at. 'True about the divine Miss Conrad, is it? All I've learned is that there's definitely some unrest in the industry, and that it *might* be connected with mob activity.'

Wilf shrugged. 'It took some digging, and no one knows of any trouble at Good Boy itself. In fact, if Freddie Wishart wasn't engaged to some mobster's

111

niece there wouldn't have been anything on them at all. But, when you go deeper, certain people have been seen to be making life difficult for Rex Kelly, who's the studio head. It seems to fit.'

'Difficult how?'

'A small fire here and there, a vandalised set. The kind of thing that smacks of coercion at best, protection at worst.'

Leah couldn't help admiring the quick thinking in that detail, but it made her a little queasy to think he was probably drawing on experience.

'You think they're trying to get the starlet to stay then?' Neville asked, picking up another certificate.

'Sounds like it.'

'And what if she does?'

'That makes no difference to us,' Wilf pointed out. 'You're not *actually* thinking of investing in Good Boy anyway, or selling this information on to others. I mean, you just wanted to know if I genuinely found out something useful, to confirm Mr Bitterson's credentials. Didn't you?'

'Of course,' Neville said, and Leah didn't have to look at Glynn to know he'd heard the evasive tone too.

'Well then,' Wilf said. 'The Falciones are making trouble for the studio head. That's what matters.'

'And how *did* you find out about it?' There was a sudden wariness in Neville's manner, presumably it was the mention of the notorious Falciones that had done it.

'That's my business,' Wilf said, but with a respectful edge to his voice. 'Come on, Leonard, you know better than to ask.'

'So, Mr Neville.' Glynn finally looked up. 'Now you've seen all this, and we've established that I have

112

access to useful information, shall we go ahead and start talking turkey?'

While the three men checked Glynn's list of companies, and he pointed out which ones he recommended for a fast return, Leah tried to analyse the uneasiness she could still feel niggling at the back of her mind.

It had begun the moment Glynn had left the boarding house, and she had started dressing for the most important meeting of the entire operation. She had felt the old tension creeping up on her, stronger with each passing moment; there was always that sense that they were poised on the edge of a precipice, that there was still time to back away, but that if they did they would return to the dull inevitability of a life less lived. Accompanying that, of course, was the undeniable thrill when an unexpected shove took the decision from them. That free-falling exhilaration, not knowing whether there would be a safe landing, but unable to do anything now to change it.

This meeting was the leap. There was no going back now, not without risking reprisals; should Leonard Neville suspect he was being duped he would unquestionably want his revenge . . . She prodded gently at her bruised fingers, and returned her attention to the conversation as she realised they were talking about her now.

'Mrs Scripps has put approximately half her savings into a company from Manchester,' Glynn was saying, 'which has just floated sixty per cent of its stock.' He pointed to a name on the list. 'They're a clothing company.'

'So what makes them a good investment?'

'I've learned that they're about to purchase land for two new factories: one in London, one right here in Liverpool. Both sites were difficult acquisitions, and neither seemed likely to get the green light. But it turns out that your so-called 'proud English heritage' doesn't mean a lot, when you compare it to the value of retail these days.'

'So the share prices are low now, but they'll go up,' Neville said, making a note against the name.

'Considerably, the moment the announcement is made. Mrs Scripps is very sensibly buying now, before that happens. By the time she sells she should make roughly three times what she paid.'

Neville eyed him. 'And how do you know about this land sale?'

'Doesn't matter. Are you in?'

'Maybe. If you can get me proof.'

'That's going to be . . . .' Glynn shook his head. 'It means risking my contact's job, and putting myself in the firing line. It's not worth the pathetic amount you're going to put in for your little *trial run*.'

'I'm quite happy to take his word for it, Mr Neville,' Leah put in. 'You have to admit, his record speaks for itself.'

Neville was staring out of the window and seemed to be wrestling with a decision, so Leah fell silent so as not to sound desperate. She caught Wilf's eye, and silently urged him to say something instead.

He cleared his throat. 'When will they make the announcement, Mr Bitterson?'

'They won't get official confirmation until Friday morning, then negotiations will take the rest of the day and maybe even the weekend. I'm guessing that next Monday at the latest is when they'll go to press. Demand will go up, and there you go.'

'You don't have to explain to me how it works,'

Neville said waspishly, but he still looked uncertain.

Glynn shrugged. 'Okay, here's what I'll do. I can get you the proof, by tomorrow afternoon, that the transfer's been signed. But you have to go all in. No pussy-footing around with trials, it's just not worth it to me, and time is short.'

Neville shoved his hands into his pockets and chewed at his lower lip. 'And what's the fee?' he said at length.

'A hundred-dollar flat fee for facilitating it, and a two per cent commission on assets.'

'I don't need you to facilitate it,' Neville pointed out, with a faintly amused smile. 'I know what I'm doing.'

'No, you don't.'

'I'm sure I don't have to remind you — '

'This is risky, Mr Neville, you know it is, that's why the return is so good. So, do you want people to come to *you* with questions? Or do you just want to say you left your portfolio in the hands of a reputable broker, and to give them my details?'

There was a tense pause, and finally Neville nodded. 'Alright. Tomorrow afternoon. Come straight up.'

'If you gentlemen don't need me after all,' Leah said in a bored voice, 'I have some very important *shopping* to do.' She directed this at Neville, who grinned and offered her a conciliatory hand.

'You've played your part, Mrs Scripps. It was good of you to introduce me to Mr Bitterson, and I wish you well with your investments.'

'Likewise, I'm sure.' Leah nodded at the other two men. 'Jacob, will I see you again before you leave?'

'We'll have dinner,' Glynn said. 'I'll call your hotel.'

Hotel? That's pushing things. Leah pictured the dingy

115

little backstreet boarding house, as she closed Neville's door behind her, and decided they'd spent their last night there; they deserved an actual hotel after this. It was done! Her part in it, at least, and now all they had to hope for was that Wilf's forger friend would come up with the requisite Land Registry documents before tomorrow. Though, if she'd learned anything about the long con in these past weeks, he'd likely already done those sometime last year.

She declined the taxi offered by the concierge, choosing to let the February wind blow away the last of her niggling unease. As she walked to the ferry terminal she thought back over everything, the perfectionist in her certain it had all gone too smoothly, and that they must have missed something important.

But the worst that could happen now, even if Neville realised he'd been tricked before handing over his money, was that they'd lose their savings. They had done nothing illegal; Wilf had been the one to provide forged documents and accept the money, and he'd been the one to set up the fake business, and the bank accounts to go with it. What she and Glynn had done had been little more than playacting, only this time it hadn't felt like their game, and the rules had felt too flimsy.

Yet they had jumped, and a safe landing was in sight. On Monday, when the fictitious factories didn't appear in the newspapers, she, Glynn, and Wilf would be gone, and Neville would find every avenue to tracking them down blocked. Wilf would pay them their share in cash, as agreed, and they'd buy their passage to America, free to explore whatever their life together might become now; Glynn already had false documents ready, with new names for them both. She wondered again what the connection might possibly have been between shabby little Wilf Stanley and debonair Leonard Neville, that had driven Wilf to concoct this trap, but she'd never know now. Perhaps that was a good thing after all.

Back at the boarding house she pulled her suitcase from beneath the bed and began folding her clothes into it, and when Glynn arrived home in the late afternoon he needed no persuading to do the same with his own belongings.

'You're right, we've earned a night of luxury.' He gave her a little smile. 'Why don't we stay at the Empire Park itself?'

'Too risky!' she reprimanded with a laugh. 'There's a perfectly decent place behind St George's Hall, called the Haymarket. There's parking there, too, so we can be away the minute Wilf pays us.'

'Speaking of which, I'll be glad to get rid of that Lancia now, and get myself something decent,' Glynn mused. 'Neville drives an Armstrong Siddeley. Much more my style.'

'They probably have even nicer cars in California,' Leah said, and threw his pyjamas across to him. 'We'd better go to the Haymarket separately, Neville's still around, and the two hotels are quite close to one another. You drive, and take our things, I'll walk down to the ferry in a bit, after I've paid the rent.'

'Alright. I'm meeting Wilf in just under an hour, he's collecting the Land Registry documents.' Glynn pulled back the curtain and looked out at the gathering dark. 'I don't feel very gentlemanly though, letting you walk around alone at this time of day.'

'Walk? I'll be running, just to keep warm!' She was touched, despite the joke, and came over to kiss him goodbye. 'I'll get a taxi from the ferry to the hotel, don't worry.'

'Good.' He pressed some change into her hand. 'This will cover it.' He picked up their cases, and Leah brought the small, extra bag, and went with him to the car, where he loaded it all into the back. She waved as he drove away, then stepped back into the hallway, hoping the landlady wouldn't be too late home; every moment felt as if it were drawing out forever now, and she couldn't wait to just —

A tall shadow fell between her and the streetlight, plunging her into sudden darkness, and she drew a breath to cry out, but as she instinctively stepped back into the hallway, her heel caught in the carpet and she stumbled back against the newel post at the foot of the staircase. The back of her head connected with the wood, and for a second she saw lights flashing against the blackness of the shadow that pressed down on her.

Her first coherent thought was, *Neville ... Who told him?*

* * *

Fox Bay Hotel

Helen picked up the note she'd screwed up and left on the sitting room table last night, and smoothed it out to read again. Not that she needed to, it had been easy to memorise.

Helen,

Couldn't find you. Gone to L'pool, v. urgent. Sam will explain.

A.

He'd left yesterday afternoon, while Helen had been overseeing the menus, and could easily have found her if he'd tried. Fear had quickly followed disbelief, but Sam's calm explanation had helped with that at least. The feeling of helplessness, however, hadn't been so easily dismissed. First there was Bertie and Fiona, whose joint grief she had been unable to soothe, and now Leah was possibly in danger hundreds of miles away, and what was *she* doing? Discussing menus and drawing up staff rotas.

A brief tap at the door made her sigh and screw up Adam's note again. 'Come in.'

'Adam said I shouldn't bother you with this,' Sam said, 'but since you asked?'

'Oh of course, yes. Bring it in.'

Sam passed her the small painting she'd asked to see, and Helen drew the cloth away, conscious that her reaction was being closely observed, and hoping she would be able to suppress any unfavourable reaction.

She carefully composed her features, just in case, but she needn't have worried; the picture was simple but elegant, and had a real sense of the wide open countryside about it. When she looked at the farmhouse, and at the brown and green hills in the distance with the hint of a winding road leading away into them, she found herself wanting to follow that road, especially now, with her mind such a tangled mess. It seemed to promise both escape and adventure, and for now it would be enough just to disappear into those hills, away from everything that was happening here.

She looked more closely and saw, all but hidden in the clouds, the faint outline of lumpen mountains in the distance, and in the bottom right, the words *West*

Glenlowrie. She looked up to see Sam looking at her, not anxiously, but with curiosity. Of course, he hadn't come to them asking to have his work displayed, so for him it wasn't a matter of whether she approved, as a potential client.

'It's beautiful,' she said at last, having searched for something cleverer to say. 'I'm afraid I'm no connoisseur of art, but it does make me feel . . . peaceful.'

He smiled. 'Good. That's the way the place made me feel, too, when I lived there.'

'It was your home?'

'It was, aye. Now I spend most of my free time painting it, and places like it. That's what Adam saw hanging in my office.'

'Well he was right about it being perfect for the upstairs sitting room,' Helen said. 'Have you had a chance to look at Higher Valley Farm?'

'I have, yes. Lovely lady, Mrs Nancarrow, isn't she? I'm painting the farm as a surprise for her husband.'

'Her husband?' Helen tried not to show her shock. Surely they hadn't married in secret already?

'Husband-to-be, I should say. A wedding gift.' Sam took the painting back and wrapped the cloth over it. 'I know you and Adam are equal partners, but it was important that you both agree on this.'

'So what made you move down here to Cornwall anyway?' she asked, as they left the sitting room. 'It's very different from your life in London.'

'And that's precisely why. When I left New Scotland Yard I was looking for something a little more peaceful.'

'But you didn't want to return to Scotland?'

'The farm was gone by then.' Sam's voice dropped. 'And I was . . . well, I had hopes of a relationship

120

becoming something more permanent.'

'Ah.' There wasn't anything she could say to that, so she just gave him a sympathetic smile.

They'd reached the reception desk now, and Sam put the painting down. 'I'll leave this with you, then, and fetch the others from my room. You can decide which ones you'd be interested in leasing.'

'How many did you bring?'

'Just four others. Three the same size, but one's a little bigger, so you might not be interested in that one.'

'Well it'll be hard to choose if they're all as good as this one.' Helen was momentarily distracted by a familiar figure coming through the front door. 'That's my brother. I need to speak to him, but do put the other paintings in the sitting room, and I'll look at them later.'

Sam nodded and started up the stairs while Helen turned to greet her brother. He looked less harried than he usually appeared, but she reflected that he was usually with his rather tiresome wife, and they were *usually* in the midst of some disagreement or other by the time they arrived at Fox Bay.

Tall and narrow-shouldered, with the perpetual stoop that reflected his tendency to bow to the demands of a difficult marriage, David nevertheless gave her a glimpse of the brilliant smile that had no doubt drawn Kay to him in the first place. She'd rarely seen that smile since the wedding . . . the day she had met Harry. The little stab of pain faded as David folded her into the first brotherly embrace she could remember since those days.

'It's good to see you, old thing. You're looking lovely, as always.'

121

'And you're looking surprisingly chipper,' Helen observed. 'Adam will be pleased to see you.'

'It'll be nice to catch up,' he agreed. 'Been a while. Too long.'

Although he and Adam had been the original friends at boarding school, Harry Fox had soon swelled the friendship to three, but it hadn't taken long for him to have become the light that had inadvertently out-shone poor, quiet David. A situation for which Kay had never forgiven Harry.

'He's away in Liverpool at the moment,' Helen said, feeling her heart give a little shiver as she thought about the reason, and how he and Leah might be faring. 'He should be back by the end of the week, though.'

'Splendid. Was I in time for room eight then?'

'Sorry, no. I've had to put you in Fleur's old room, which is at least free, in both senses of the word.' Helen gestured to the hovering bell boy. 'I'll show you up there myself.'

'No need,' he said, 'I know the way.'

'I know you do,' she said, and gave him a little smile. 'But you can tell me everything on the way. Your letter wasn't exactly crammed with explanations.'

David sighed and picked up his hat. 'Come on then, let's get this over and done with. Who was the fellow you were talking to?'

'What fellow? Oh, the one who gave me this?' She decided David only needed to know part of the truth. 'He's an artist we're commissioning for upstairs. Very soothing, a lot like Edward Hopper.' She handed the covered painting to Martin. 'Pop this into the office, would you?'

She accompanied her brother to the third floor, and

waited until the bell boy had put down the bags and gone, before turning back to David. 'Come on then, what's happened this time?'

'This time?'

'I know you and Kay have been on a bit of a rocky path,' she said. 'Which one of you has been caught out this time?'

'I only did it the once,' he pointed out, rather crossly. 'Clare and I were indiscreet, it's true, but Kay has a string of — '

'Yes, well.' Helen didn't want to hear those kinds of details. 'I just mean, which of you is going to be doing the grovelling this time?'

'You know she had an affair with Adam, don't you?'

The statement brought Helen up short. She remembered, some time ago, Kay telling her about a soldier who'd been home on convalescent leave during the war. Helen had asked if she'd been in love, and Kay's self-satisfied smile had faded even as she'd denied it.

'I can see it doesn't come as a complete surprise,' David said now, 'so I can only assume she told you. Adam certainly wouldn't have.'

'She didn't, exactly,' Helen said. She also recalled the day when they'd all been gathered in the sitting room, during that awful time when they thought they'd lost the hotel. Helen had sensed something unspoken between Kay and Adam, and had fully intended to investigate, but with everything that had happened afterwards it had slipped her mind.

'It was after he'd been gassed,' David went on, and Helen nodded.

'Yes, I realise now. But you and Adam stayed friends.'

'We were never the same as we were when we were

123

children, especially after his involvement in that Blue Ensign thing that wrecked Harry. But he does have a way of winning people around, as you'll know. Anyway,' he went on, with a dismissive wave, 'of all the men she's been unfaithful with, I blame him the least.'

'Why?'

He paused, then shrugged. 'He was going through something terrible. He wasn't himself. He was a mess, we all saw it.'

'Yes, he was. He still suffers from it, you'll see that. Thank goodness he and Harry both came through it. I can't imagine what they must have seen, neither of them ever really talked about it.'

'They were both always braver than I was. Always quicker to climb the tree, jump off the wall, wade into the river.'

Helen smiled. 'Joining up wasn't bravery at the start though, was it? I mean they both went at it as if it were some kind of adventure.' Her voice dropped. 'But it took unbelievable courage to go back, once they knew what they were returning to.'

'No one could accuse *them* of cowardice, could they?' David turned away. 'I had my share of white feathers, but you know I'd have — '

'I know,' Helen said gently. 'And so does everyone who matters. You had a vital job to do, David, and you did it brilliantly.'

'Don't patronise me, you're as bad as Kay!' He turned back, and his face was flushed. 'Look, I've been proud to serve my country in whatever way I've been needed. Might not have been glamorous, like your Harry and his friends, but . . . .' He sighed. 'I'm sorry. That came out wrong.'

'It was years and years ago. Let's not drag it all up again.'

And there was nothing glamorous about waking at three in the morning to feel your husband shaking and weeping beside you, or about seeing your best friend coughing himself to pieces when he thought he was alone in the garden of the convalescent house. But she said none of this. The war was over, and they could only hope they would never have to live through anything so terrible again.

Helen lifted a jacket from David's case and shook it out. 'Why don't you tell me what happened between you and Kay?'

David stood looking out of the window. She knew him well enough to know he wasn't ignoring her, just thinking of his reply, and she patiently began to hang his shirts beside the jacket.

'I've been let go,' he said at length.

Helen froze, one hand on a clothes hanger. 'What?'

'Sacked. My services are no longer required by the War Office.' David sank down onto the bed, and looked at her with an expression as close to helplessness as she'd ever seen. 'They've cut back on funding, been doing it for years but I've always escaped the axe. Now though?' He threw up his hands. 'It's my turn.'

'Is *that* why you're here?' Helen sat down at the dressing table. 'Did you and Kay fight over it?'

'She doesn't know. We fought, yes, but it wasn't about that. Nor was it about anyone else,' he went on, pre-empting a question Helen hadn't intended to ask. 'I suppose it was connected with both though, in a way. She's constantly buying new clothes, presumably to impress some bloke, and I don't know how to

125

tell her we can't afford them.'

It was dangerous to keep such a secret; Helen knew better than anyone how such a thing could destroy someone. 'Why haven't you told her?'

'I will,' he promised, 'just . . . not yet. I need to find something else first. I thought maybe there might be something down here. Plymouth, perhaps. Great naval town . . . well, city now, isn't it? Place like that ought to have something for someone with my experience.'

'You're welcome to stay here while you search, but won't she come after you?'

'She thinks I've gone back to the city. She's positive it's an excuse of course, and that Clare and I are back on, and I thought it best not to disabuse her of that notion, in the circs.'

'David, think about it! On past experience, where's the first place Kay always comes when you and she are having difficulties? Fox Bay is her bolthole! You know she's always wanted to move down here.'

'Really? Still? I mean I know she felt that way years ago, but I thought she'd given all that up.'

'Well she hasn't. Only last year she told me that she'd hoped Fleur would sell her half of the hotel to the two of you.' Helen stood up and crossed to the door. 'It was why she came down here when she found out about you and Clare. She would have done anything to get you out of the city, including buying Fleur out. She loves this hotel as much as she ever did that first time you brought her down here.'

'Oh, lord.' David rose too. 'Well, if she turns up, she turns up. We'll worry about it if and when it happens.'

'Good, because I hate lying. To anyone. But your wife reminds me of our old headmistress. Remember

126

Miss Treadaway?'

David barked a sudden laugh. 'Gosh, do I ever! She could needle a secret out of anyone.'

'And Kay could still give her lessons.' Helen smiled. 'Shall I see you at dinner then?'

'I'd like that.' David surprised her by dropping a peck on her cheek, and she went back downstairs feeling a little pocket of warmth inside her that brought back sweet memories of simpler times, when they'd been friends as well as brother and sister.

8

West Bank Boarding House

Leah's heart hammered painfully in shock, and her mind scrambled for ways to convince Neville he'd been misled. But there was no time, and the tall figure leaned in close to hiss in her ear.

'Don't scream!'

Leah's eyes adjusted to the bright light of the hallway, and a huge wash of relief swept over her and she found her voice. 'Adam!'

He closed the front door behind him. 'Which is your room? Quick!'

Leah tore her incredulous gaze away, and led him up to the room she shared with Glynn. Once inside, she turned to look at him again; he seemed tired, but almost as relieved to see her, as she was that he wasn't Leonard Neville.

'Thank god,' he murmured, sinking down onto the bed as if all the energy had drained out of him. 'I didn't think I'd be in time.'

'For what?' She rubbed the back of her head, and he winced in sympathetic apology, but pressed on.

'You have to come with me.'

'Where?'

'Back to Fox Bay. Your aunt's house. Anywhere!'

'Why?' What she'd really meant to say was, *absolutely not!* but those words were drowned in the confusion he'd caused by his evident agitation. Her fear rose again. '*Does* Neville know what we're doing?'

128

'No, at least I don't think so. But Neville's not your enemy, Lee, Wilf Stanley is.'

'Wilf?' Leah sat down next to him, bemused. 'But he's the one taking all the risks. It's his set-up.'

'Yes it is, but he's not taking any risks. Glynn, on the other hand, is going to be the one who goes down, and he's taking you with him.'

'Wait!' Leah shook her head. 'How can you say that? Wilf is providing the forged documents, and he's the one who's going to be taking Neville's money. Glynn and I are just — '

'Engaged in fraud,' Adam said grimly. 'You stand to be charged the minute that money is passed into your possession. And Wilf will be the one who damns you both.'

Leah's head felt light. Part of her still stood in the doorway downstairs, watching Glynn drive off towards the ferry . . . Everything that had happened since was too strange and distant-feeling to be real. Had she fallen asleep waiting for Glynn to get back from the hotel? Or knocked herself out on the newel post?

She glanced sideways, noting Adam's uncharacteristically rumpled suit, the blond shadow stubbling his jaw, and the smudge of oil on his temple, as if he'd shoved his hair away from his eyes with dirty fingers. She dropped her gaze to his hand and saw that it was indeed grimy. It was all too detailed to be a dream. He turned to look at her, and she noted the dark bags beneath his eyes, and the way his brow was furrowed with worry.

'I can't believe you're here,' she muttered, not knowing what else to say.

'You have to come away,' he repeated, and his grubby hand covered hers. 'No matter what you think of me, you have to believe me when I tell you you're in danger if you stay.'

'How do you know all this?'

'Never mind now, I'll tell you later. But for now my car's in the street, and I've even had a go at fixing the bloody lights, so we can leave the city tonight. I'd have been here last night if I'd bothered to do that before. Come on.' He stood up, tugging at her hand, but Leah remained where she was.

'I can't go without warning Glynn.'

'Of course you can!' He pulled again, and she slipped her hand away from his.

'No! I'm not leaving him to face this alone. I'll come with you, but you have to let me find Glynn first, and tell him, so he can leave too.'

Adam looked at her, exasperated. 'Alright! I'll drive you to wherever he's taking your things, and I'll give you ten minutes to talk to him, but then we're going.'

'I have to pay the landlady — '

'Damn the landlady, just push it under her door!' Adam pulled out his wallet and took out a handful of ten-shilling notes. 'I'm surprised you're even bothering. Will that be enough?'

'Put it away, I have the money here.' Leah showed him, wondering why she and Glynn hadn't left it behind, or even just left; some residual sense of politeness perhaps, as if doing right by their landlady somehow took the edge off using her rooms as a base for crime. She left the notes on the bed, then picked up her coat. 'Come on then.'

She locked the door behind Adam, still feeling that sense of the surreal that he was standing close behind her, and posted the key through the landlady's own room door. Then she followed Adam out to his car, letting the familiar scent and feel of it envelop her as he closed the door and ran around to the driver's side.

'Tell me everything,' she said, as he drove towards the ferry terminal. 'How do you know about all this?'

'I came looking for you,' he said, his eyes fixed on the road ahead. 'I wanted . . . .' He fell silent.

'Wanted what?' she prompted. Her heart had leapt at his words, but she didn't want to read into them what might not be there. Wanted to return some belongings? Wanted to give her a piece of his mind for leaving without saying goodbye? Wanted *what*?

'I wanted you back,' he said at length, and the pent-up breath left her body on a long, silent sigh. 'I was worried,' he went on. 'You weren't at the hospital; they'd never heard of you. Then, when your aunt told me you and Glynn had spent Christmas together at her house, I had a nasty feeling he'd pulled you into something. And I was right, wasn't I?'

He took his gaze off the road, and now she was the one who avoided looking at him.

'How did you find out where we were?'

'I hired someone to find you.'

She blinked in astonishment. 'Hired someone? Who?'

'A bloke from Truro, name of Sam Douglas. He's an investigator.'

They had reached the ferry now, and as Adam manoeuvred the car into position Leah tried her hardest to envisage him demanding to see her, at the hospital where she'd never worked, but all she could picture was that tired, worried face he'd turned on her in the boarding house, and the oil-grimed fingers that had closed on hers as he sat next to her on the bed. Her breath stuck in her chest as that same hand

131

crept across the gap between them now, and brushed gently across her fingers.

'I love you, Leah,' he said softly. 'I've learned a very hard lesson since New Year's Day.'

'I'm married,' she reminded him, but the quiet, painful words were swallowed up in the sound of the motor, and she tried again. 'There's Glynn to think of now.'

'There's always been Glynn,' he pointed out. 'Just because I never knew about him doesn't mean he wasn't there.'

'But he's out now.'

'And do you love him?'

'I . . . I care about him.'

'Of course you do.'

'He didn't *pull me into this*, as you put it. I agreed. It sounded . . . .' She shook her head.

'Let me guess.' He gave a soft laugh. 'Fun?'

She couldn't help smiling. 'You know me too well. Look, Glynn turning up at Christmas wasn't something I'd planned. Then he came to the memorial, but couldn't stay at the guest house so he came to Fox Bay. He was as surprised to see me there as I was to see him.'

'You didn't have to run away with him,' Adam pointed out.

'I didn't plan to. He realised about Daniel and me, and I wanted him to blow up at me, to tell me how disgusted he was, but he still forgave me.'

'And *that* was enough?'

'It wouldn't have been,' she said, 'but you didn't seem too bothered whether I left or not.'

'But Fox Bay was your home before mine, so why should that matter?'

132

Leah looked at him, half-amused, half-exasperated. 'Are you fishing for compliments, Mr Coleridge?'

'I just want to know what pushed you away,' he said, for once not matching her humour.

'You being in love with Helen.' The words came out flat, so she tried to give them some shape, to help him to understand. 'I know she's not in love with you, though for a while I thought she was. But watching you watching her was becoming . . . .' She shrugged. 'It hurt, that's all. And whatever else Glynn does or doesn't do, he loves me. It's intoxicating after months of indifference.'

'Indifference?' Adam looked genuinely shocked. 'How can you say that? We had a wonderful time!'

'*Friends* have a wonderful time, but when someone has your heart it's different. And Helen has yours.' Leah was dismayed to find her voice catching on the last word, and turned away to look out of the window.

Adam's voice was soft. 'This mightn't be the time for a discussion, but I can just say that you're right, she does. But not in the way that you mean. Will you at least believe that much?'

Leah looked back at him, and read honesty in the reflected light and shadow on his face. There was no way of knowing if she were seeing it because she wanted to, or because he genuinely believed he no longer loved Helen, but he was right; this wasn't the time to discuss it.

The ferry bumped slightly as it reached the Liverpool side of the Mersey. Leah's stomach gave a lurch as she realised she hadn't given the first thought to how she was going to convince Glynn to abandon this enterprise. Especially now they were so close to the end. Months and months of preparation and

133

planning, and they were days away from the biggest pay-out of their lives.

'Will you go to this Wilf bloke?' Adam asked, as they nosed their way off the ferry.

'No, just to Glynn. I want to get him away without Wilf knowing.'

'Where are we going then?'

'There's a hotel called the Haymarket, just around the corner from the Empire Park. I'll direct you.'

'The Haymarket?' Adam dug around in the breast pocket of his jacket and handed her a tattered piece of paper. She squinted at it by the intermittent light of the street lamps, and saw a neatly printed list of familiar names and hotels.

'Wilf's staying there?' Leah groaned. 'I knew it wasn't far from the Empire, but I didn't realise it was the same place. Glynn didn't mention it either, when I told him.'

'Are you sure you don't want me to come in?'

'Quite sure. He'll never believe me if he thinks you're the one trying to get me away . . . .' Leah paused, and looked hard at him, and he clearly sensed it although his eyes remained firmly on the road.

'I promise you, it's true,' he said. 'I'm acting on intelligence given to me by the man I hired.'

'Alright. I believe you.'

They drove in silence for a short while, then Leah straightened up. 'Right, there's Ma Egerton's, and there's the Empire Theatre, look.' She pointed. 'The big hotel is just up there, and if you go left at the top you'll see the Haymarket just around the corner.'

'And Glynn's booking you in there?'

'He was seeing Wilf to pick up some Land Registry documents to show Neville, but he should have them

134

by now.'

'Well I'm waiting in the lobby,' Adam said. 'You can go in by yourself, if you like, but you can't convince me I should wait in the car.'

'There's no need,' Leah said, with a little sigh of relief, and pointed again. 'See that man just leaving? That's Wilf.' She put a hand on the door ready to push it open, but Adam leaned across to stop her.

'Wait. Let's see where he goes, first.'

Leah subsided, and watched as Wilf hesitantly approached a Daimler idling several yards away. The lights flashed once, and Wilf's pace picked up. He leaned in through the open window for a moment and then walked around and climbed in beside the driver. The car drove slowly away, and Adam looked at Leah grimly.

'Did you say Glynn has the documents already?'

'Yes.'

'Then that's probably the police Wilf's gone off with. Nice and safe and away from any suggestion of fraud, until the money appears in his bank account.'

'Then that will paint him with the same brush as Glynn.'

'Not if it's the police who've done the setting up,' Adam muttered. 'Didn't you wonder how Wilf had the resources to do all this?'

'Glynn said it was all done through people he's known for years.'

'Tosh. I'll bet the police set up the business, provided the documents, and even put the money up for the sweetener.'

'What are you doing?' she asked, as he opened his door.

'I'm coming in with you, remember?'

135

Leah shook her head. 'I'll be safe with Glynn, now Wilf's gone, and we've already discussed that Glynn won't — '

'Still,' Adam said firmly, 'I'll be in the lobby, as I said.'

Leah hurried in, immediately feeling a growl of hunger at the smells wafting from the dining room. She glanced at the clock and realised it was now dinnertime; she hadn't eaten since breakfast, and her nerves had used up a lot of energy today. After a quick word with the receptionist she took the lift up to the second floor and found the room Glynn had booked. She knocked quickly and, noting the number of guests coming and going from their rooms to dress for dinner, she leaned down to hiss through the lock.

'It's me! Let me in!'

'Why all the secrecy?' Glynn smiled as she pushed past him into the room. She didn't even glance around, but dragged the curtain across the window, glad to see Glynn had left her case on the bed, thankfully unpacked. She picked it up.

'We have to leave, now.'

'What?' His smiled faltered but didn't disappear entirely. He looked bemused rather than alarmed. 'Look, I've got the documents from Wilf. You'd never — '

'I mean it!' Leah moved towards the door again, but he caught her arm as she passed him.

'Wait! What are you saying? Has someone tipped Neville off?'

'No, not yet. But Wilf isn't who you think he is.'

Glynn frowned. 'What are you talking about?'

Leah briefly outlined what Adam had told her, which was admittedly very little. 'The minute we

136

accept any money from him, we're going to be arrested and charged,' she finished.

'You don't know what you're talking about,' Glynn said after a moment's pause. 'I *know* Wilf, we served time together, and you don't — '

'I know. You said! You don't spend that sort of time with someone without knowing you can trust them. But this time you've got it wrong. Come away, I'll explain more on the way.'

'On the way where? Leah, you're going to have to give me more to go on than, *Wilf's going to turn you in.*'

'It's all I've got! Adam just said . . . .' But it was too late to bite back the words now, and Glynn's expression said all she needed to know.

'Adam,' he repeated. 'How the hell does he know about this? Have you been blabbing to him all along?'

'No! He was . . . worried about me. He sent someone to find me, and that someone has found out that Wilf's set this up with the help of the police. They turned him when he was in prison!'

'Why?' Glynn's voice was tight, his face a mask of anger. 'Why would they pick someone like Wilf when they have their pick of anyone?'

'Presumably because of what he does, and because he was getting out of prison. And because he let them.'

'*Presumably* isn't enough for me,' Glynn said. Then he softened. 'Look, I understand you getting cold feet, you've been twitchy about this for days now, but there is no way I'd believe that smarmy bastard Coleridge over someone I've known for years.' He sighed. 'Go on then, Lee, you've done your bit. Brilliantly, as always. But don't go back to him, go to your aunt's instead. I'll come and find you after it's over. We can

137

talk then. There'll be no hard feelings.'

'You won't come with me?'

His expression darkened again. 'Coleridge is just trying to get you away from me, don't you understand that?'

'Why on earth would he go to all this trouble to ruin this, if that's all he wanted?' she fired back. 'Why not wait until it's over, when I have some money to show for it too?'

'He's a nobody. A low-grade crook. Maybe he's just jealous that I can give you this life for real, while all he can do is pretend. Maybe he knows that once this is over you'll realise that! If he can convince you to leave now, he can say it would never have worked, and . . . Where are you going? Leah!'

'Stay here then, if you insist,' Leah said, fury choking the words off before she could finish. She pulled open the door, and had slammed it behind her before he could grab her again. She heard him give a grunt of frustrated anger, but knew his pride would prevent him following her. That, and the knowledge that he wouldn't be able to change her mind, any more than she could change his. He was right; she'd served her purpose, and her role was now over.

In the corridor she took a few steps towards the lift, but stopped. Yes, anger had driven her from the room, and Adam waited for her downstairs, but she didn't want anything to happen to Glynn either. There was only one way to make sure Wilf had no ammunition to use against them, and it was a dangerous game to play . . . But this time the rules were hers.

She ignored the lift, hefted her suitcase, and ran down the corridor, ignoring the curious looks of the other guests and focusing only on the door at the end.

She pushed through and clattered down the uncarpeted back stairs, emerging into the night around the corner from the Haymarket's grand entrance into the loading bay, where vehicles of different sizes rumbled constantly in and out with produce, laundry, and cleaning supplies. She picked her way carefully between vans and out into the street, and within five minutes of making her decision she was walking up the steps of the Empire Park Hotel.

9

Fox Bay Hotel

Dinner with David had been both fun and heart-warming. Helen couldn't remember the last time she'd had a chance to reminisce so freely, and he'd coaxed memories of their childhood out of her that she'd had no idea she still retained; from before David and Adam had left for boarding school, and the three of them had been inseparable. She'd laughed at those memories, which had temporarily banished her worries for the future, and sensed that was David's intention.

'Kay says Harry ruined your chances of staying friends with Adam,' she said, as they moved from the dining room into the lounge. 'She swears you'd have made something of Adam's investment choices, and not thrown everything away like Harry did.'

'You can't blame Harry,' David said, 'not for any of it. Kay's always looked for a reason for something that was only ever a problem in her own eyes. I liked working for the War Office. I *liked* being in the city during the week, and at home at the weekends.'

'Well I suppose it worked well for long enough,' she conceded. 'And you're certain you don't blame Adam for ... for what they did? He'll be home in a day or two, you know.'

'I know. And no, I don't. It's all water under a very distant bridge.' David settled himself into a chair and lifted a finger to catch the bar steward's attention. 'What about you?'

'What about me?'

'Any chaps on the horizon for you? That fellow who was talking to you earlier, for instance?' He gave her an exaggerated wink. 'You looked rather good together, I thought.'

Helen had to pause for a moment to think, then she gave a short laugh. 'Sam Douglas? I told you, he's a friend of Adam's, and an artist.'

'Good-looking chap though.'

'Better not let Kay see him then.' Helen gave him a mortified look. 'I'm sorry, that was completely uncalled for.'

He gave her a faint smile. 'Don't give it a thought. You're quite right of course. Poor bloke wouldn't stand a chance.'

'I don't know how you can be so sanguine about it,' Helen said, accepting the drink the staff had already prepared for her, while he ordered his. 'Doesn't it hurt just a little?'

'Massively,' he said, and now she could see the smile wasn't quite reflected in his eyes, although a certain wry humour lingered. 'But if I didn't laugh, I'd go mad, I think. The ironic thing is, if she'd been successful in buying half this place, I think we'd have been fine.'

'Even though she was the one having the affairs?'

He shrugged. 'I think if she had somewhere like Fox Bay to keep her mind occupied, she wouldn't care that our marriage isn't all it could be. Anyway, change of subject, why's Adam scuttled off to Liverpool in the middle of the week?'

Helen hesitated, then decided to tell him everything after all. It took a while, and by the time she'd finished explaining about Leah and Adam, and what they'd

141

learned of Leah's husband, he seemed to have forgotten all about his own problems.

'So that chap's actually a private detective?' He whistled. 'Who'd ever have believed in such things, in little country backwaters like this?'

'Thank you. We do have our fair share of drama you know, it's not all confined to the city.'

'Anyway, you didn't answer my question,' David said, signalling for a refill. 'The detective artist might not be in the *picture*, so to speak,' he gave a little laugh at his own joke, which Helen dutifully returned, 'but it's been ten years, Hels. Isn't there another man in your life yet? You're still a looker, you know.'

'I've never been one of those,' Helen protested, 'we both know that.'

'Well,' he studied her in the frank way that only a brother could get away with, 'you're a handsome woman, and you've got buckets of intelligence — '

'Not to mention an hotel.'

'Quite,' he said cheerfully. 'Any chap would be glad to snap you up. Anyone on the horizon?'

Helen tried to keep her easy smile in place, but she knew it had slipped. A picture of Alfie Nancarrow rose behind her eyelids as she closed them to hide the truth, a refuge masquerading as a slow blink. Image-Alfie was smiling, a little helplessly, and snow was fluttering down to land on his hat as he told her he was doomed.

They both were, as it turned out, and not in the half-joking way he had meant it. She knew, from the thin wire of pain that went through her, that the passing of days would not make it easier after all, and that once he and Beth were married it was only going to become worse. With that, and the sudden and rapid dispersal of her friends and family, Helen found herself wondering, for the first time in ten years, if her future lay somewhere other than Fox Bay after all. The thought was sudden, and startling, but this was no time to explore it.

'Well?'

She refocused, and saw David looking at her all too shrewdly. 'Sorry,' she said, and smiled. 'I was miles away.' *Or a few hundred yards away at least, in the churchyard at St Adhwynn's.* 'Oh! I haven't told you about what happened when we had Hollywood to stay at Christmas, have I?'

'It was in the papers.' He waved a dismissive hand. 'That film star fell into a hole or something. Anyway, about — '

'There was a bit more to it,' Helen said. 'Just wait until you hear *this*.'

'Stop it, you annoying wretch! Just tell me who you've got your eye on!'

'Helen?'

She looked around, grateful for the interruption, but the gratitude drowned in a rush of astonishment. 'Jeanette?'

The woman, still tiny, and as pretty as Helen remembered, leaned down before Helen could stand, and hugged her with unexpected warmth. 'It's so lovely to see you after all this time!'

'Gracious, it's Miss Duval, isn't it?' David said, rising to his feet. He held out his hand. 'We met once or twice when we came up to Bristol. I'm David, Helen's brother.'

'Of course!' Jeanette allowed him to raise her hand to his lips, and laughed. 'Chivalry, no less! I must come to Cornwall more often.'

143

'Alas, if you do we shall never see each other, since my home is in Devon. But I've only just arrived, so I do hope our paths will cross again.'

'This is a very nice surprise, Jeanette,' Helen said, breaking in before he forgot he was still married. 'What brings you down to Fox Bay?'

'I always felt bad about the way our correspondence just sort of, faded out.' Jeanette sat down, her expression earnest, but Helen wasn't fooled.

'Presumably you're here to see Adam though?' She twisted in her seat to catch Jeremy Bickle's attention, but the bar manager already had one eye on them, anticipating the summons. When he'd melted away again with their drinks orders, Helen repeated her question, and Jeanette nodded.

'Yes, I do have something to discuss with him. Something Simon's brought up from Adam's time at Hartcliffe.'

'Oh? I thought everything was wrapped up there now. Adam never mentions it.'

'It is.' Jeanette smiled easily. 'But I told Simon I was coming down to Bude to see our grandparents, so he asked me to drop in and have a word. You know my brother; he can't pick up a telephone and ask a simple question. Such a pity you're full, I had to take a room at that place in the village. Sandy-something.' She looked around. 'Is Adam here, then?'

'He's away at the moment,' Helen said. 'I'm not sure how long it'll be. Sorry we're not able to accommodate you though. We're not very big, and since we appeared in the newspapers, thanks to Daisy Conrad's accident, we've found ourselves very much in demand.'

'Yes, I'd have liked to have stayed. I thought it odd

144

that I'd never actually been, considering how close we were. Before . . . You know.'

'Before Harry died,' Helen said. 'Yes. We did drift rather, after that.'

'Adam and I were still engaged at that point,' Jeanette said confidentially to David, 'but of course things changed.'

Helen bit down on the urge to point out that 'things' had changed because Adam had lost his entire fortune at the same time, and that no one had been the least bit surprised that the engagement had ended fairly swiftly after that.

'That was before Simon's business really took off, wasn't it?' she said instead. 'I gather he's doing terribly well.'

'I work alongside him now, you know,' Jeanette said, with unmistakeable pride in her voice. Helen remembered Adam saying how his former fiancée had shown a remarkably astute business brain, surprising those who'd known her only as a society hanger-on.

'Yes, so I've heard.'

'Oh?' Jeanette shot a quick glance at David, before lowering her voice. 'And did he explain how I . . . helped him? In the matter of CP Holdings?'

'He did. I know he's extremely grateful, we all are.' Helen hoped her voice was firm enough to put an end to that conversation, but not too obviously secretive. 'David, I never finished telling you about our Christmas guests, did I?'

'No, and nor have you come clean about whoever it is who's managed to capture your attention romantically at last.' David grinned at Jeanette. 'I believe my sister here has a secret yen for someone, but she's determined not to say who it is.'

'Maybe it's Adam?' Jeanette said, and her laugh was unconvincing as she put a hand on Helen's arm. 'I'm joking, darling! Everyone knows he's batty about you, but that it only goes one way.'

'Do they?' Helen couldn't hide her surprise. 'Who's 'everyone'?'

'Well of course it's a long time ago now, and I was talking about our social circle back in Bristol.' Jeanette accepted her drink from the steward and took a sip. 'Gosh, I wish I'd come sooner. This place is utter bliss, isn't it?'

Helen thought back to the party in Bristol, when she'd convinced herself that Harry and Jeanette had been having an affair. She had built the woman up in her memory to have been some grasping, scheming social climber, when the reality had simply been Jeanette's envy of the Fox marriage, and her desire for Adam to make her just as happy. Despite everything, she and Helen had been quite friendly for a year or so, although never close in the way Helen and Leah were. The thought of Leah sent a little shiver down her spine, but she felt it only fair to let Jeanette know that Adam was no longer free.

'Adam's in Liverpool,' she said. 'He's gone to pick up his girlfriend, my best friend Leah.'

'Jolly good,' Jeanette said, and her lack of any curiosity or pique seemed genuine enough. 'I'm sure I can amuse myself for a day or two, while I'm waiting. Lots of bracing walks, I imagine, and I gather you have some scintillating evening entertainment too.'

'And you'll have your grandparents to visit, of course.' Helen was amused and interested to see a faint flush touch Jeanette's fair skin. Why was she lying about why she was here, if she really wasn't

146

trying to get Adam back?

'I'll ask your chap on reception to arrange a taxi back to my guest house in an hour or so,' Jeanette said. 'Now what was it David was saying about a new man?'

'He was surmising,' Helen said firmly, 'there isn't one. Look, are you going to let me tell you about our Christmas guests, or not?'

Even David acquiesced, evidently realising he was beaten in the matter of Helen's romantic ambitions. By the time she'd told them all about the Hollywood visit they were both wide-eyed and fascinated, and any further probing questions were successfully banished to the backs of their minds. For now, at least.

★ ★ ★

Empire Park Hotel

Adam had watched Leah until she'd rounded the first bend in the stairs, before following her at the same careful distance he'd maintained since she'd left her husband at the Haymarket. She'd left that room at such a pace, even lugging that suitcase, that he'd only just managed to draw back out of sight in time, and by the look on her face he'd done the right thing in following her. For a split second he'd even considered bursting in on Marshall himself, *low-grade crook*, indeed. But there was no time; Leah had made for the back stairs, and disappeared through the door before he'd had time to think twice.

Now, having put her case down by the Empire Park's reception desk, she had marched up the stairs to yet another hotel room, and this time it could only be Leonard Neville she was going to see. It made sense; if she couldn't persuade her husband to come with her, the next best way to make sure he couldn't get caught up in the backlash of this business was by scuppering the whole thing herself.

Adam still wasn't sure whether to try and apprehend her before she reached the room, or to wait and see how it played out. He had absolute faith in her ability to handle things, but none whatsoever in this Neville character. And worse, Leah was unarmed. He felt the old tightening in his gas-weakened chest, that signalled a coughing jag was on its way, and he suppressed a groan. Now was not the time.

When she reached the correct floor, Adam hung back until she had been called in. Then, praying the imminent coughing fit would pass, he crept forward and leaned against the wall beside the door, and brought his pipe out of his top pocket. He hoped it would appear to the other guests as if he were just waiting for someone, and as he tamped down the tobacco he strained to hear Leah's voice; she was still in character.

'Thank you for seeing me like this, Mr Neville, I have to talk urgently with you.'

Her flawless American accent made Adam want to smile, and he had to remind himself to remain alert to the very real danger of the situation, instead of just appreciating the performance. He also realised his need to cough had eased off, and breathed more easily in relief.

'Where's Bitterson?' That rather pompous, nasal tone could only be Neville himself.

'He split the scene,' Leah said. 'And that's what you should do, too.'

'Really? And why would I want to do that?' Neville

sounded amused. Indulgent.

'Because,' Leah said, slowly and clearly, 'your friend has betrayed us all.'

'What friend?'

'Freeman! He's taken everything we've told him, and he's gone to the cops with it. You're the patsy here, Leonard.'

There was a pause, and Adam held his breath, hearing the clink of a glass decanter stopper.

'You're lying,' Neville said at last.

'I wish I was. I'm telling you, I saw him not ten minutes ago, getting into a car right outside his hotel.'

'Describe the car to me.'

'It was a black Daimler, with a horn right there by the door. And a uniformed cop at the wheel,' she added pointedly. 'I know a cop car when I see one.'

'We call them policemen here.'

'Call them what you want, I call Freeman a snitch! He's clearly made some kind of deal, and Jacob found out about it, so we're splitting. I'm risking everything by coming here to warn you about it first. Take it or leave it.'

Adam could imagine her whirling ready to leave, and stopping as Neville barked out, 'Wait!'

'What?'

'Where does that leave me?'

Leah sighed so loudly Adam could hear it. 'This deal's off, but there'll be others. If you still want in?'

'Of course I do!'

'Then sit tight. One of us will be in touch.'

'When?'

'When it's safe! Which isn't right now, not until the heat's off. Don't try to contact us, you won't be able to.'

Adam felt a smile flicker on his face, and his respect

for her took another leap higher.

'What about the money you've lost?' Neville wanted to know. 'Do you trust Bitterson to get it back?'

'I trust Jake about a million times more than I trust that little weasel you're hooked up with.'

'Freeman's no weasel.'

'No? Why don't you head down to the police department, and tell them they've made a deal with the wrong guy?' Her voice was coming closer now, and Adam prepared to move out of sight the moment he heard the door handle turn.

'Mrs Scripps?'

'What?'

'Did you get yourself invited to my party on purpose?'

'Why would you ask that?'

'It seems to me you're a lot smarter than you wanted me to believe.'

There was a long pause, and Adam felt the tension like a crank, twisting tighter and tighter. Now what?

He heard real amusement in Leah's voice. 'Why would I do such a thing?'

'Because you knew I'd never take you seriously if you'd just come up to me out of the blue, but you know I trust . . . trust*ed*, Mr Freeman. So you engineered that little scene in Ma Egerton's because you knew he'd invite you to the party that night.'

'How could I possibly know that?'

'Because you're a beautiful woman, and a man like Freeman likes to show off beautiful things.'

Leah gave a low, throaty laugh. 'What can I tell you? A wealthy woman, alone in the city, she has to use what she has at her disposal. I'm sure you realise that.'

150

'I really underestimated you, didn't I?'

'What we all did was overestimate our value to Mr Freeman. He's been playing us all.' The playful tone was gone now. 'This is your one warning. Get out, Mr Neville, before he takes you down.'

Adam leapt away from the door and flattened himself against the wall. As soon as she'd pulled the door closed behind her he seized her arm. She barely jumped, and he stared at her in growing amazement.

'My god, you're a courageous idiot! I'll give you that much.'

'You *followed* me?' She looked a little shaken, but livelier and brighter than he'd seen her since long before she'd left Fox Bay. She was even smiling. 'Never mind. Come on!' She seized his hand and dragged him to the top of the stairs. 'Go and get your car. Hurry!' She glanced back at Neville's suite door, and when she turned back to Adam her smile had turned into a laugh, and her eyes were wide and excited.

'Where am I taking you,' he asked, 'Cornwall or Wales?' Suddenly the answer was more important than anything. Even more than the immediate danger they were in.

She looked at him incredulously, and he remembered Glynn's dismissive words: *Maybe he's just jealous that I can give you this life for real, while all he can do is pretend* . . . 'It's alright, that was a silly question.' He started down the stairs, but stopped when he heard her ask, hesitantly now.

'Will you, and Helen and the cubs, still have me?'

He raised his eyes to hers but seeing the sudden vulnerability there, he couldn't answer; he just nodded and held out his hand. She spared one last glance over her shoulder at Neville's room, and turned back

151

to Adam.

'Fox Bay it is, then.'

152

10

St Joseph's Church, Brighton

Bertie reached out blindly and felt Fiona's fingers grip hers. The service had left everyone shaken, and not at all comforted by the words of the priest who had conducted it, and now the mourners emerged, red-eyed and wordless, and barely looking at one another.

The cars stood waiting to return them to the Nichollses' home, and Bertie looked around for Lynette and her parents, who were standing beneath the shelter of the stone church doorway with the priest. Lynette stood back a little, her head bowed, and once again Bertie's heart tore to see her; she had lost every last scrap of life and light, all the more noticeable because of her former abundance of it.

Beyond Lynette's expression of gladness that Bertie had her leg now, there had been no tearful reunion, no embrace that might have allowed them to share some comfort; Xander's death had ripped through his family with cold, impersonal savagery, leaving every member stunned and deeply hurt.

The wake was an equally bleak affair. Bertie had only ever been to her father's funeral, but even then, as the day went on, his friends and family had felt able to share humorous stories and learn new things about him; many of his mourners had even been able to smile. Not so here. Low murmurs passed from person to person, unbroken by laughter even of the saddest, most reflective kind, and the pain on every

153

face looked as if it might never fade into acceptance.

'I have to go,' Bertie said in a low voice to Fiona. 'I can't bear it.'

'You ought to try and talk to Lynette first,' Fiona whispered back. 'You can't leave it like this.'

'She's made it quite clear she doesn't want to talk to me. I can't blame her; I must remind her all the time of . . . of Xander.'

'She needs you though,' Fiona insisted. 'Just try once more. You'll hate yourself if you don't.'

Bertie waited until Lynette had moved away from the group who had been pressing their condolences upon her, and saw, with a flicker of hope, that she was moving towards the hallway. She exchanged a quick glance with Fiona, who silently urged her to follow.

'Lynette,' she called out in a soft voice, as her friend's hand reached for the front door handle.

Lynette turned, her face swollen from crying. 'I need some air,' she managed.

'I'll come with you.'

'No, you'll catch your . . . You'll freeze,' she finished lamely.

'Please?'

Lynette shrugged and tugged open the door, letting in a cold February wind that flattened Bertie's skirt against her legs. Bertie settled her hand more comfortably on her single crutch and followed her out into the grey afternoon. They were less than a mile from the coast, and the wind carried the sharp tang of salt; Bertie felt the swell of homesickness for Cornwall.

'Will you come to Fox Bay sometime, so we can talk properly?' she ventured. 'Not now of course, but soon?'

Lynette stared out over the rooftops of the houses

in her street, and didn't respond beyond a brief shake of her head. Her arms were folded, but Bertie didn't think it was in an attempt to keep the wind from blowing her coat open; she wanted to wrap her own arms across her chest too, and press hard enough to numb the pain. Just for a moment.

'I miss you,' she said again, her voice lower. 'And so do the others.'

'I won't be good company.'

'You don't have to be.'

'Oh yes I do!' Now Lynette spun around, and her eyes were fierce. 'Everyone loves the Nicholls kids because we're such *fun*. Isn't that right? Xander's such an ass, but a loveable one, and Lynette keeps him in line, and flutters her eyelashes at men . . . Xander puts his foot in it, Lynette rolls her eyes and pretends he's just too silly for words.' She broke off and took a deep breath. 'Bertie, he was my *soul*. I can't think without him. I don't know what I am anymore. What I'm for.'

'You're still the same person.' Bertie took a tentative step towards her.

'I've never *been* a person in a world that didn't have Xander in it.' Lynette turned away again. 'I'm never coming back down to Cornwall, Bertie. I can't bear it. I've written to Harry Batten to explain it's all over between us.'

'Then may I at least come and see you again soon?'

'No.'

Bertie wasn't sure she'd heard correctly; she hadn't expected such bluntness. 'What?'

'I said no. I don't want to be rude, today of all days, but I don't think I can be your friend anymore.'

Bertie couldn't think of a thing to say. Her sorrow

155

was momentarily eclipsed by a sense of unfairness; she hadn't had anything to do with Xander's choice of career, or even of the place where he chose to pursue it. She'd lost one of her best friends, and now Lynette was robbing her of the other, as if she'd personally caused Xander's death. She hadn't changed, so why would Lynette withdraw like this?

'I know what you're thinking,' Lynette said.

'Do you?'

'Of course. But it's *because* I love you so much that I can't stay friends with you.'

'I don't — '

'You're still going to fly, aren't you.' It wasn't a question, and Lynette's voice was flat.

Bertie nodded. 'I have to.'

'And that's why.' Lynette brushed past her on the path as she made her way back to the house, and her hand rested briefly on Bertie's. 'I can't go through this again, darling. I'm sorry.'

Bertie watched her step reluctantly over the threshold, returning to the awful reality of a home without her beloved brother in it, and the tears she wept alone in the garden did nothing to ease the burning in her eyes. Still she let them come.

Why so glum, chum? Xander's first words to her, at the side of the track. She thought she felt them brush her cheek now, but it was only the wind after all. That's all there was left.

★ ★ ★

The train moved slowly out of the station a scant two hours later. Hurriedly packed bags were safely stowed away, and the only two occupants of the carriage sat

156

opposite one another and stared wordlessly out of the window, as the view of the city gave way once more to open countryside.

'I'm certain she didn't mean it,' Fiona said at last. 'She loves you too much. She's just — '

'She meant it. You didn't see her.'

Fiona fell silent again, and Bertie was sorry she'd spoken so harshly. Her sister had adored Xander too, and the funeral had taken just as much of a toll on her.

'Thank you for coming with me,' she said, and tried on a smile. It faltered, but it was real at least, and Fiona returned it with a tired one of her own.

'Of course I'd have come. Not just because it meant you had company, though that would have been enough. I was glad to be able to say goodbye, but you couldn't have done this by yourself.'

'You've been wonderful.'

'It's a pity Jowan couldn't come.' Fiona looked a little nervous, as if she wasn't sure how Bertie would respond to that.

'I wouldn't have put him through it,' Bertie said. 'He's never been a friend of Xander's, I can still remember the fight they got into at the racetrack that day.'

Fiona's smile returned, and now it held a trace of real affection. 'He was a bit of a rogue, wasn't he? He always knew when he was winding Jo up.'

'Jo understood, eventually, and learned to ignore it. Except . . . .'

'Except what?'

'When he found out Xander was also training at Caernoweth. Things got quite touchy, and it took a while to convince him we'd be in completely separate

157

areas of the camp, training at different hours, with different living arrangements and social circles too. I'd probably have seen Jo more often than I saw Xander. Particularly if Jo had come to live there too, as he'd planned.'

They swayed along in silence for a few minutes, then Fiona looked at her, frowning. '*Had* planned?'

'What do you mean?'

'Well, have you changed your mind about the engagement?'

'No, but I think he will, and soon.' Bertie's heart tightened again as she accepted what she'd been holding at arm's length for days.

'Well don't just say that and not explain.' Fiona leaned forward. 'What are you talking about?'

'I believe Jo and I have reached a fork in the road, and we can't both go the same way. He wants children,' she clarified, seeing Fiona's puzzlement turning to exasperation, 'and I very much do not.'

She couldn't look at her sister for a moment. Having spoken her choice out loud she realised for the first time that it was the unshakeable truth. Jowan loved her, she was as certain of that as she could be about anything, but she had also recognised in him the need to father children and to raise a family of his own. It wasn't just something he'd *quite like one day*. It had been, she realised, at the forefront of any and every serious discussion they'd ever had about their future together.

'It's not fair of me to lie to him,' she said. 'He has the right to make his choices based on the truth. And the truth is that I will never give him a child.'

'But surely one day,' Fiona said, 'when you've done your training, and learned all you want to about flying.

158

And anyway you can always go back to that after — '

'No! It's not that I want to fly more than I want children.' Bertie tried not to sound impatient. 'It's that I just don't want children. Ever. Flying or no flying. I can't be responsible for something so precious and so fragile, something that needs me, when . . . when I might not always be there.'

'Like Dad, you mean?' Fiona's voice was soft now.

'Like Dad, like Jo's dad, like Xander, like everyone. I can't do it.'

'And it's not just because of this?' Fiona gestured at Bertie's leg.

'I thought it was, at first,' Bertie admitted. 'I saw Kitty Buchanan at the station, trying to juggle her baby, her luggage, and climbing off the train, all at once, and I wondered how I'd have managed it with one leg. I knew I'd have dropped something, and who could guarantee it'd only be a bag?' She shrugged. 'But after that I just couldn't stop thinking about how terrifying it must be, even for someone without any added difficulty.'

'And you're certain Jowan wants children more than he wants you?'

Bertie raised an eyebrow, acknowledging her sister's deliberately blunt choice of words. 'I think that with him it's the same thing. Just as I'm not prioritising flying over children, he wouldn't be prioritising children over me. It's just the way we both are. You have to remember how close the Nancarrows are as a family.'

'We're close too.'

'But we've all got our own different ambitions. You with your lifeboats, me with my flying, and Ben's off to the Summerleaze — '

'What?' Fiona's eyes shot wide. 'When?'

'It's not definite, but it's likely. Anyway, my point is, the Nancarrows are close in a different way. They share everything, even their work. Beth's family are all so focused on the children, and Jo wants, no, he *needs*, to build the same kind of life. He won't have that with me.'

'Does he know you feel like this?'

Bertie shook her head. 'Not yet.' She twisted her engagement ring around her finger, her eyes following the flash of reflected light in the tiny diamonds. 'But I'll have to tell him soon.'

★ ★ ★

Fox Bay

'I'm sorry again,' Adam said, switching off the engine at last. 'I spent ages fixing those lights, I'd have expected them to get us a bit further down the road than Ellesmere Port.'

'Not to worry.' Leah stretched, as far as the cramped interior of the car allowed. She looked out of the window at the comforting familiarity of the austere-looking hotel, and enjoyed a swell of quiet happiness. 'We're here now.'

'A whole day later than we needed to be.'

'I don't care about that, I've slept in worse lodging houses than that one in Ellesmere Port, remember?' Leah pushed open the car door and leaned out to take a deep breath of the fresh Cornish air, feeling it spread through her like life. 'We're home, and I can't wait to see everyone.'

'Wait a moment.' Adam sighed. 'There's something I haven't told you, and it's important for you to know

160

before you go inside.'

'Has that artist you've hired covered the walls with a mural?' Leah's smile faded when he didn't return it. 'What is it?'

'There's been an accident. A bad one. Not one of the family,' he hurried on, as Leah felt the blood drain from her face, 'it's young Xander Nicholls. I'm afraid he was killed.'

Leah's scalp tightened. 'Oh god, poor Bertie. How?'

'An aeroplane accident,' Adam said. 'He wasn't even doing the flying though.' He explained about the accident off the coast of Porthstennack, his eyes unusually grave. 'Bertie's broken-hearted, we're all still shocked.'

'How awful,' Leah breathed. 'I can't even imagine. And his sister must be . . . oh, that poor girl.' She couldn't take it all in. 'Has the funeral happened yet?'

'What day is it?'

'Tuesday.'

'Then it's today. Bertie and Fiona went up, they're expected back tomorrow.'

'Devastating for them both. I imagine that's put an end to Bertie wanting to take up flying.'

'That's probably the only half-hopeful thing to come out of all this.' Adam went to the back of the car. 'Go on in and find Helen, I'll bring the bags.'

Leah climbed the steps slowly. She pictured Xander's laughing face, and Bertie and Lynette exchanging long-suffering looks mingled with deep affection. The lad and his sister had exploded like excitable puppies into Bertie's life, and Leah had no doubt it was the two of them who'd pulled her out of the worst of her darkness. The thought of that exasperating but cheerful young man having his future snuffed out so

161

suddenly brought a wave of cold reality to her home-coming.

She found Helen in the office, on the telephone. She knew she had no right to expect a warm reception, after all she'd done, but Helen looked up as the door opened, and to Leah's immense relief her eyes shot wide in happy surprise. Leah sat down, feeling quite tearful, and waited for Helen to finish the call. The moment she had, Helen came around and Leah rose again to return her friend's embrace.

'I'm so glad to see you!' Helen said, her voice muffled in Leah's scarf. 'You have to tell me everything!'

'I will,' Leah promised, 'but I'm so grimy and mucky from travelling. Let me go and have a bath and change, and I'll meet you in the lounge.'

'Are you starving? Shall I get something sent up to your room?'

'No. I'm just glad to be back.' Now the tears did come, a delayed reaction to everything that had happened, to the news about Xander, and to the sounds, smells and familiarity of this place she still called home, no matter what her head tried to tell her.

★ ★ ★

Later, in the lounge, she took Helen through everything, from Glynn picking her up unexpectedly at the railway station in Wales, to her real reason for leaving Fox Bay so suddenly after the memorial dedication, and then to Liverpool. She went on to explain how the con was to work, and how much preparation had gone into it during the months before, and Helen's eyes widened again.

'So this Wilf chap had been working his way around

the business district all that time? Just dropping the name so people would recognise it again?'

'More or less.' Leah realised she'd been talking so much she'd not even touched her drink, and now she took a sip and closed her eyes briefly in bliss. 'Oh, I've missed this.'

Helen looked confused. 'Gin?'

'No! Sitting with you, somewhere warm, safe and comfortable, and enjoying a drink without worrying I'll say something indiscreet, or to the wrong person, and bring the world crashing down around our ears.'

'I thought you liked that. The excitement, I mean.'

'I do, but it's nice to be able to relax, and just . . . floomph.'

Helen coughed her laughter, having taken a sip of her own drink at that moment. 'Floomph?'

'You know.' Leah flopped back into her cushions and assumed an air of exaggerated relaxation. 'Floomph!'

'Mind your drink!' Helen nodded at the splashes on Leah's blouse. 'That's our best stuff. So what happened after you met this Neville man?'

Leah described the Valentine's night party, and as she went into some detail about the decorations at the Empire Park she could see Helen making mental notes. 'Don't,' she begged, 'they were actually awful! Not right for Fox Bay at all.'

'But the place was packed?' Helen pursed her lips. 'Alright, if people really do think that much of Valentine's Day we ought to make a much bigger fuss of it next year.'

'Please, no balloon archways!'

'Perhaps not *that* much of a fuss,' Helen agreed. She said something else, but Leah's attention had wandered to a guest who had just come in. There was

163

something familiar about him, but she couldn't quite grasp what it was, and it didn't feel like the easily dismissed familiarity that came with seeing the same guests year after year. In fact something about him gave her a flicker of associated unease, as if the last time she'd seen him she'd been tense, or worried.

'Mrs Fox?' Martin Berry appeared at their favourite alcove. 'There's a telephone call for you at reception.'

'Who is it?'

'It's Mr Bannacott.'

'Calling from *America*?' Helen jumped up. 'I want to hear the rest of this the moment I get back,' she called over her shoulder, as she hurried out after the receptionist.

Leah's attention turned once more to the newcomer, who was now chatting comfortably to Jeremy Bickle as if they were well acquainted. A known guest, then. She relaxed a little, without knowing precisely why, before the memory clicked into place and she caught her breath. It was something about the way he turned his head to scan the room. He'd been at the Empire Park on Valentine's night, standing alone by the desk. She'd even felt sorry for him, and the story she'd invented for his missing lady.

Her heart beat uncomfortably fast; the coincidence was too much, he must have followed her here. But who was he working for, Wilf or Neville? Both of them had reason to seek revenge . . . Her thoughts flew to Adam, out there in the hotel somewhere, oblivious.

The man hadn't yet seen her, and for a second she considered trying to slip out of the lounge to warn Adam; there were enough people milling about to make that possible without being noticed. But, before she'd even had time to consider her own reasons for

164

not doing that, she was halfway across the floor and calling a greeting to the bar manager. 'Jeremy! So nice to be back! Please excuse me for interrupting.' She turned to the guest, and realised her assumption of advanced age was wrong and that, despite the thick white hair, his features were surprisingly youthful. In fact he was likely not much older than Adam.

'Are you following me?' she demanded.

'Not anymore,' he said, and extended a hand. 'My name's Sam Douglas.'

'*Not anymore?* Who sent you?'

He blinked. 'Has Adam not told you my name then? I assume you know he hired an investigator, at least?'

Leah subsided, not sure whether she felt more embarrassed or relieved. 'I see,' she said, taking the proffered hand. 'No, he didn't give me your name, and nor did he tell me you'd still be here. I'm so sorry.'

He patted her hand consolingly. 'Don't worry, my dear, it was very sensible of him, you're probably not the discreet type. Based on the fact that you suspected I was up to no good,' he added, 'yet you've just marched up and made yourself known to me.'

Leah's lips parted to say something blistering back, but she caught the gleam of humour in his eyes just in time. 'If you've really been following me,' she pointed out, 'you know that's not true.'

'I do.' He grinned then, disarming her. 'In fact I've been very impressed. I've clearly just caught you on an off day.'

Behind them, Jeremy had melted away to continue his work, and Sam indicated the alcove where Leah and Helen had been sitting. 'May I join you both?'

'So you already knew I was here?'

'Of course. You might have noticed I'm quite good

at my job.'

'You certainly found me quickly enough. Adam says he only hired you a week ago.'

'I can't claim all the credit, I used to be on the force, and still have contacts.' Sam lowered his voice. 'Did you tell your husband the truth about this so-called friend of his? He's how I tracked you down.'

'I told him,' Leah assured him, 'but whether he'll do anything about it, I can't say.'

'You've done all you can, then.' Sam sat back, and smiled a greeting as Helen returned. 'Mrs Fox, I won't disturb your reunion long, just wanted to see that Mrs Marshall is alright.' He looked at Leah with one dark eyebrow raised, and she nodded.

'I am now. Thank you.'

'Then I'll speak to you another time.'

'Adam's in the lobby,' Helen said to him, 'perhaps you could talk to him about the arrangement we're considering, with the paintings?'

'I'll do that.' He withdrew, and Helen sat back down. 'Sam's going to produce three new pieces for the upstairs lounge.'

'Very nice. How's Guy?'

'He's hoping to be back in time for Fiona's birthday next Wednesday, and he promises to bring a surprise.'

'How long's he been in America?'

'He went not long after Freddie and the others left. He wanted to talk to Freddie's mother, and his adoptive father.'

Leah shook her head. 'Somehow reading about all that in a letter made it seem a bit like it was all happening to strangers. Like you were describing a film. But sitting here, hearing you say it out loud?' She laughed. 'I'm still stunned, to be truthful. More than anything, I find it impossible to believe he kept it a secret that he's Freddie Wishart's father. All the years we've known him.'

'We can talk about that later.' Helen picked up her drink again and settled back in her seat. 'Right, I've floomphed, so carry on. I want to hear all about what happened in Liverpool. Leave absolutely nothing out.'

★ ★ ★

Adam's chat with Sam was comfortable, as if they'd been friends for years. Now the job was over Sam had relaxed into an easy familiarity with Fox Bay, and had much praise for the way it was run, and Helen in particular.

'A very accomplished woman,' he said, looking around at the lobby decor. 'A widow, you say?'

'Ten years, almost eleven.' Adam felt a private smile forming, and tried to picture Helen and Sam as a couple. He couldn't do it, despite the man's easy charm; she'd never liked it when Harry went away, and Sam's job took him all over the country, at the drop of a hat. 'When do you go back to Truro?'

'I'll only stay for a couple more days.' Sam settled into one of the lobby chairs. 'Though of course I'll pay for my own accommodation now. I have a project to finish, and I need to make a few more illustrations before I go back to my studio.'

Adam sat down opposite. 'Painting the hotel?'

'No, the farm up the road. A wedding gift, apparently, for the groom. So if you know him,' Sam tapped the side of his nose, 'under the hat, alright?'

'Understood. He's a good chap, that farmer, helped Helen out no end when my goddaughter had her accident.'

'Ah yes, she's the one going off to learn to fly, isn't she?'

'She is,' Adam said proudly, but then, remembering Xander, his smile faded. 'I'm going to be as twitchy as I ever was when she began racing her motorbikes, that's for sure.'

'You're very close to this family, aren't you?'

But Adam was facing the front door of the hotel, and Sam's next words faded into a vague hum as, for a moment, he felt sure his eyes were playing tricks. But no; Jeanette Duval was breezing through the lobby, passing by the reception desk on her way to the bar. This was likely not her first visit then.

'Excuse me,' he murmured to Sam, and hurried across to meet her before she went into the bar. 'Jeanette!'

'Hello, darling!' She stretched up to kiss his cheek, and he glanced reflexively around in case Leah had come out of the bar. 'Don't worry,' Jeanette grinned, wiping lipstick off his face, 'I'm sure your lady friend knows you and I are long over.'

'What are you doing here?'

'You said you'd call me back.' She gave him a mock pout. 'I was hanging around the telephone for hours, you rotten thing. Then I decided you'd forgotten, so I came down instead. I've been in and out of here like an absolute idiot waiting for you.'

'I've been in — '

'Liverpool, I know. Picking up your girlfriend.'

'Why are you here?' he repeated, aware that Sam would be watching and making mental notes about every nuance of their actions. He stepped away.

'We have to talk, Adam.' Jeanette sounded serious

168

now. 'In private. It's hugely important, or I wouldn't have come, you know that.'

He nodded. 'Go into the office, Martin will let you in. I'll join you in just a minute, after I've explained to Sam.'

He guided her to the reception desk and instructed Martin to unlock the office. 'I'll be joining Miss Duval shortly,' he added. 'Fetch a tray of tea in, please.'

He went back to Sam. 'That's my old business partner's sister, she has something to discuss. Look, I really just wanted to thank you for everything you've done.'

Sam nodded and stood to shake Adam's hand. 'I'm glad it all worked out for you and Mrs Marshall,' he said. 'It was a pleasure working with you.'

'Likewise. And thank you for leaving those addresses — '

'Uhp.' Sam held up a hand. 'I did no such thing.'

'Of course.' Adam smiled. 'Well, I hope to catch up with you again before you leave. In the meantime, enjoy your stay, and let us know if there's anything you need that we haven't catered for.'

★ ★ ★

Jeanette was waiting with an impatient look on her face, having dropped the warm, friendly façade she had presented out in the lobby. 'This conversation is long overdue,' she said, without preamble.

Adam took the seat behind the desk, in an attempt to regain some of the control he could feel slipping away; for her to have come all this way, things had to be serious. 'You'd better get on with it then,' he said calmly.

169

'For a start you can drop that superior tone.' Jeanette sat down opposite him. 'Look, Adam, we both knew this was coming, the embezzlement was too — '

'Ssh!' Adam looked instinctively at the door; of course it was still firmly shut, and Martin was the soul of discretion, but the sudden appearance of a woman like Jeanette was bound to stretch even his professionalism if curiosity took over. 'Let's just refer to it as . . . our previous transaction.'

'Our *previous transaction*,' Jeanette said, 'was so audacious it was bound to take longer than this to smooth out. I've had to be careful not to make things too obvious, so the money you're paying back has had to be put through other accounts.'

'And there's a shortfall,' Adam guessed.

'Oh yes, there's a shortfall alright.'

'Simon's put you in charge though, hasn't he?'

'Yes, but — '

'Well then, you'll have to step up the overpayments on your projects,' Adam said irritably. 'Simon trusts you, and while he's got no reason to think there's a problem, there isn't one.'

'That's alright for you to say! If Hartcliffe is brought under suspicion it'd mean prison for Simon, who's completely innocent, let's not forget, and maybe even — '

'Why should it be though?'

'Stop interrupting!' Jeanette gave him a glare that would have floored someone who didn't know her as well as he did. 'The point is, we're coming up to the new tax year. After that business with Brent Forest Holdings . . . You did hear about that, I take it?'

Adam shook his head. 'I've been preoccupied lately.'

'Brent Forest was caught under-declaring for tax

170

last year, and they've been clobbered with a massive fine. They'll be lucky to avoid bankruptcy. Simon's been hopping around like a cat on hot bricks ever since word got out, and has hired an independent accountant to make sure I've been doing my job properly. He's had his head pulled out of the clouds, and he's bound to start asking questions.'

'But he knows you're a dab hand,' Adam said, uneasy now, 'that's why he started leaving it to you. And the invoices and receipts match the payments, I presume?'

'Of course they do! But they won't all match the returns those companies are making.'

'Any of them noticeable enough to raise suspicion?'

'Hopefully not, but —'

'Then you'll just have to find one that you can inflate to cover the shortfall, and do it before April.'

'That's why I'm here.'

'I don't see what I can do now,' Adam protested. 'Even if I were able to give you a lump sum, which I can't, you'd still have to square it all somehow on paper.'

'I know that.' Jeanette stood up and went to the door, as if she too were nervous about Martin now. She pulled it open a fraction, then closed it again and came back to face Adam across the desk. 'Look, I originally only agreed to help you because you promised me a cut of that reward money you were trying to steal from your girlfriend.'

'Quiet, for goodness sake!' He lowered his own voice. 'You make it sound awful. Besides, she wasn't my girlfriend then.'

'No. As far as you knew, she was a woman in deep despair who was trusting you.'

'She was a con artist,' Adam reminded her firmly, almost adding, *she still is*, before stopping himself. The last thing Jeanette needed was ammunition, especially now. 'I know, it doesn't make any difference to you why it didn't go ahead. That's why I was surprised you were still willing to help me.'

'It was all in place before I found out there was no reward,' she reminded him. 'But I hadn't lost anything at that point. It was a challenge for me, quite exciting, and . . . well, you know I still have a fondness for you, even if it's just for old times' sake.'

'Well then — '

'A fondness for an old friend isn't enough when the Inland Revenue comes calling.' Lynette's voice hardened. 'I can't risk sending my brother to prison, even if I somehow manage to avoid it myself. Which, incidentally, I doubt I would, now it's gone this far. It's all looking too much like my idea, and less as if I'm just incompetent.' She cleared her throat. 'Which is why Hartcliffe is going to buy your half of this hotel.'

Adam stared at her, stunned. 'Are you mad?'

'Well, I say 'buy', but of course there will be no *actual* money changing hands.' Jeanette was back to her old, brisk self now.

Adam wanted to stand up and argue, but his whole body felt weighted to his chair. 'Who would believe I'd sell to a company like Hartcliffe?' he managed.

Jeanette shrugged. 'Perhaps you're moving away, so you're in a hurry to sell. You feel you owe Hartcliffe, and your old friend Simon, a debt of apology for the mess you made of the farm acquisition last year. Naturally we're given first refusal, and at a very competitive price.'

Adam felt ill. 'Presumably this won't just be a paper

transaction this time.'

'Of course not. Once the title deeds are updated it's as official as it can ever be.' Jeanette sat back down, as if able to relax now that her message had been delivered. 'This is your only way of paying off the rest of what you owe in time for the audit.'

'All because of Brent Forest, and Simon's paranoia.' Adam's voice was hollow. 'How far along this little story trail are you? What have you told Simon about why you're here?'

'I told him you'd called and asked me to come down, but that I had no idea why. I'll go back and explain you've made your more than generous offer, but that we have to take it up quickly or it'll go wider, and the price will go up.'

'And what is Hartcliffe likely to do with the hotel?'

'Nothing. I'll make sure of that.' She sounded sincere enough, and even looked slightly regretful. 'Look, I know you and Helen love this place,' she said, more gently, 'and I'm not trying to break you. It's nothing personal. I just want Simon to go back to trusting me to do his books, and for the three of us to avoid prosecution.'

'What if I find the money to buy back later?'

'Then you can make an offer later. *After* the audit, or it'll raise alarms all over the place. Of course, I can't guarantee the price won't have gone up substantially.'

Adam nodded, his heart heavy. 'So much for not breaking me. How long do I have, before I sign it over to you?'

'I'll get the transfer drafted as soon as I get back, and when it's approved I'll post it to you. You and Helen need to sign it right away; we can't have it looking too last-minute, that'll only prompt an investigation. I'll

173

make sure to claim expenses for my trip down here this week too, so that'll add to the evidence that we've done business.'

'And what do I tell Helen?'

Jeanette shook her head. 'That's your department, I've done my part. It's no easy job, filtering money through so many other transactions and praying I haven't overplayed my hand on any of them.'

'How on earth do you live with the constant worry?' Adam rubbed his forehead. 'I've been tight as a wire this entire time, waiting for something to blow up in my face.'

'How do you think I've felt?' she snapped. 'This has been a *huge* risk for me!'

'And yet . . . .' Adam gave her a quizzical look. 'You're very much like Leah, you know.'

'How so?'

'She thrives on excitement and danger too. I don't know how either of you would cope if you weren't constantly looking over your shoulders.'

'She's not a bit like cosy old Helen either, then?'

Adam tensed again. 'There was no call for that.'

'No.' Jeanette sighed. 'I'm sorry. I do like her, I could just never understand what you saw in her.'

'It doesn't matter anyway, does it?' Adam stood up, wondering how on earth he was going to break the news. 'When are you going back?'

'I'll leave tomorrow, no point in hanging around. And that guest house in the village is run by the *nosiest* woman, you wouldn't believe it!'

'Is it now?' Adam almost managed a smile, despite everything, as he remembered his own stay there when he'd first met Leah. 'What do I say if Simon telephones?'

'You can tell him exactly what we've said. You and Leah are leaving Fox Bay in the early summer, and so forth.' Jeanette held out her hand. 'I can't pretend it's not been very nice to see you again, but I wish the circumstances had been more pleasant.'

'Don't say anything to anyone here, leave that to me. Agreed?'

'Agreed.' Jeanette lingered by the door for a moment, then turned back. 'I really won't interfere with the hotel itself,' she repeated. 'I promise it will all be as it was. Except you won't own it.'

'And you won't sell your half on to someone who *would* want to change things?'

Jeanette hesitated. 'All I can promise is that I'll do my best to make sure Simon doesn't.'

Adam sank back into his seat again. 'That's not enough.'

'But it's all I can do.' She gave him an apologetic look, and he heard her speaking warmly to Martin on her way out, her light laugh drifting back into the office.

Just as it had eleven years ago, when he'd convinced Harry to buy into Blue Ensign, Adam's world was secretly sliding out of control and, just like eleven years ago, he didn't think there was anything he could do to stop it.

11

'Have you spoken to Jowan yet?'

Bertie jumped as Fiona's voice broke through her reverie, and she almost dropped the tumbler she was holding. 'Do you want this table to look nice for your birthday, or would you prefer it covered in broken glass?'

'No need to snap,' Fiona said mildly. 'Well, have you?'

'No.' Bertie sighed and gave her sister an apologetic look. 'I haven't seen him alone since we got back from Brighton.'

'That was a week ago!'

'I did go to see him, but Jory was home, and Jo didn't want to come outside to talk.' Bertie braced herself on the stick she now used, and moved forward, still stiff on her right leg, but at least now the movement came more naturally. And best of all, when she wore a longer-length skirt and thick stockings it was impossible to tell that there was anything different about her at all, unless she was walking. 'I think he's avoiding being alone with me,' she added.

'Because he doesn't know what to say about Xander?'

'Partly. And because I think his mum knows something about what I'm feeling. Maybe she's said something.'

'She wouldn't, would she?'

176

'I have no idea. They're a very close family, and if she thought she were protecting him . . . .' Bertie shrugged. 'She might, yes.'

'Is he coming for dinner?'

'No, it's just us. And Guy, of course.'

Fiona eyed the table with a mournful look. 'Do we really have to have a special dinner? It's not even an important birthday. I just want to go to — '

'The Saltman with Danny Quick,' Bertie joined in, and grinned as her sister blushed. 'I know, but between Ben leaving, Guy coming home, and your birthday, Mum says it's time we all sat down together. We haven't properly welcomed Leah back yet, either.'

'What do you make of all that?' Fiona asked, absently straightening a fork. 'I mean, it's wonderful to have her home, but she and Uncle Adam have been awfully close-mouthed about the whole thing. And Adam's been even stranger lately than Leah has, have you noticed? Not at all his usual self.'

'They'll tell us in their own time.'

Maybe.' But Fiona looked sceptical. 'I knew there was something up, you know, at the New Year's Eve party.'

'You did not!'

'I did! There was something about the way Leah was determined to get Amy to teach her all those dance steps. As if she *had* to get it right, not just wanted to. I thought then that she had something brewing.'

'Well it seems you were right,' Bertie conceded. She looked at the glass clock on the wall. 'What time is Guy due back?'

'The train gets in at four, so he shouldn't be too long after that. Ben was supposed to go in and pick him up, but he's gone out.'

'Let me guess,' Bertie said, 'the Summerleaze?'

'I think he's been called in about the job. I hope he doesn't get it.' Fiona looked sheepish as Bertie turned to her, surprised. 'I mean, I know that sounds awful, but with you going too, I'll soon be the only one of us left.'

'Cheer up, you'll soon be able to leave too. You and Danny are getting along very well.'

'Not that well,' Fiona protested, flushing. 'We're not exactly ready to talk about marriage!'

'It won't be long, you're a young woman now. At least Mum's stopped assuming I'd be ready to give up the idea of training.'

'She wasn't the only one who thought you would.' Fiona tugged a final wrinkle out of the tablecloth and looked around the room with satisfaction. 'Well, as the birthday girl I don't have to do anything else today, so I'm going to the station for an hour or so.'

'You'd better not be late, Guy took the Saturday sailing especially, just so he'd be home in time for your birthday dinner.'

'Oh, I'll be in ages before he gets back,' Fiona said airily. 'I'll even have time to wash and change.'

'Of course you will.' Bertie smiled, it felt good to let some light back into her thoughts and she pushed away the niggling guilt that she was being disrespectful to Xander; he'd have been the first to tell her to stop moping, and to grab life with both hands and enjoy it. She hoped he was finding a way to tell Lynette the same thing.

★ ★ ★

By five o'clock the lobby was all but cleared of guests, most of whom were either in their rooms changing for dinner, or in the lounge. Bertie was passing the time waiting for Guy, by writing yet again to Lynette, when Fiona came hurtling through the door, predictably just as Guy's taxi rolled up outside. She skidded to a halt beside Bertie, who looked down at her sister's wet boots and then at the trail of footprints on the marble floor.

'Mum's going to skin you,' she remarked. 'And worse, who's going to come through that door any minute now?'

'Oh, don't be stuffy! Guy won't mind.'

'He'll think the place has gone to rack and ruin without him,' Bertie pointed out, then she grinned and admitted, 'which will actually please him no end.'

The office door opened, and their mother came out, alerted to Guy's return by Martin Berry. She too looked at the floor, then at Fiona, and shook her head in resignation. 'Take your coat off, love, at least.'

'There's someone with him,' Bertie said, straining to see through the mizzly grey mist on the other side of the glass door. 'It's a woman.'

'Perhaps he's offered a lift to a guest?' Helen moved closer to the door, and then turned back with a huge smile lighting her face. 'It's Daisy! So *that* was the surprise!'

Fiona gave an excited squeak. 'I wonder how long she's here for this time?'

Bertie grabbed at Fiona's arm and pulled herself to her feet, fumbling at the same time for her stick. 'Ben's going to be so furious he went to Bude, instead of picking Guy up at the station!'

'Martin,' Helen called, 'go and find Leah!'

179

Guy held back and allowed Daisy to come through the revolving door first, wearing the same deep green coat and ribboned bucket hat, and the sensible brown Oxfords she had worn the last time she had arrived. So much had happened in the short time since then, but the dazzling smile and the easy charm had not changed at all, and Daisy stood still for a moment, staring in surprise and delight as Bertie walked across to her.

'Your leg!'

'My leg,' Bertie agreed, and found herself enveloped in a damp woollen hug, and breathing in Daisy's favourite Shalimar scent. 'It's lovely to see you again so soon!' She pulled back. 'How long are you here for this time?'

Daisy transferred her embrace to Fiona, with whom she'd shared such a terrifying ordeal up at the golf resort site just a couple of months before. 'I'm only here for a few days — '

The chorus of disappointment made her laugh, and she seemed about to explain, but Guy had made his own entrance and he too was greeted like a much-missed family member. Helen ushered them all back into the seating area of the lobby, and Bertie saw how she only had to lift a finger to the bell boy for him to draw one of the ornate birdcages forward and begin loading cases onto it.

She smiled to herself, wondering if her mother ever stopped to think about how the hotel staff were alive to her every movement, just waiting for a wordless command or even a glance. Now, for instance, when she looked at Martin he sensed it immediately, and reluctantly tore his stunned gaze from Daisy and focused on his boss, then disappeared into the

180

kitchen to arrange a tea tray. Fiona's footprints had already gone from the marble, and Bertie saw Miss Tremar hurrying out of sight as discreetly as she had arrived, broom in hand. Leah appeared, and took a seat, squeezing Bertie's shoulder on her way past.

'So hey,' Daisy said to Bertie, the minute they'd all settled, 'tell me about your leg. It's so wonderful to see you walking! You look like you've been doing that for months.'

'Just over two weeks,' Bertie said. 'I can't tell you how thrilled I am with it. But that can wait, I want to hear all about what Guy got up to in America, and what's brought you back!'

Guy didn't have much to tell them about his trip, but that was understandable; it had been a very private affair, during which he had spent much of his time closeted with Gabrielle Wishart and her husband, while they discussed his role as Freddie's father.

'The papers will be hunting for stories when the Conrad-Wishart partnership breaks up,' he said. 'And if my private life came to light, which it would the minute they found out about me, Freddie would be lucky to find another acting job anywhere at all. I can't risk it, but we're all agreed at least.'

'Doesn't that make you sad?' Fiona asked. 'After all these years of keeping it to yourself, it must be so wonderful to know he knows, and so hard not to tell the world.'

'It's only for Freddie's sake,' Guy said, 'it always has been. Now he knows, and we can at least write to one another, it's actually easier.'

Daisy, who also looked tired from travelling, nevertheless had an intriguing new light about her. She had draped her coat over the back of her chair and removed her hat, and now she seemed more the down-to-earth girl they had all come to know by the time she'd left.

'What have you done about Good Boy, Daisy?' Helen wanted to know. 'Have you officially left yet?'

'Not yet.' Daisy accepted a cup of coffee gratefully from the waiter, who was staring at her as if he'd never seen her in the flesh before. She did have that effect though, Bertie thought, once you'd been with her for five minutes you felt like her best friend, but every time you saw her anew it was another glimpse of the kind of glamour and excitement you could only dream of being associated with.

'The thing is,' Daisy said now, with a secretive little gleam in her eyes, 'I've heard a whisper that Stagehand Sally is being considered for two Academy Awards of Merit this year!'

'What wonderful news!' Bertie squeezed her hand. 'Two?'

'What are those?' Fiona was the only one of them who didn't read the papers, and evidently hadn't kept up with the latest Hollywood news.

'They started last year,' Bertie told her. 'There are lots of award categories, not just for the film itself, but almost everyone involved in making it.'

'Because they're chosen by the Academy,' Daisy added, 'only the very best films get nominated. Last year everyone who'd won knew about it months before, but there's no official list this year, so all of this is just hearsay. It's very hush-hush though,' she went on quickly. 'Please don't tell anyone. It's not definite, and we're not even supposed to know about the nomination. The only other actress who knows she has a chance is Mary Pickford, but Rex hoped it would make me consider staying with Good Boy if I

182

knew *Stagehand Sally* was being evaluated too.'

'And has it?' Helen asked.

'Not for a minute.' Daisy grinned. 'But what a way to bow out, if it wins!'

'It might help the studio though, mightn't it?' Bertie said. 'Surely they'd get someone to replace the funding they're losing, if they've won awards.'

'I hope so. I don't wish anything bad on the studio, or Rex, but I'm so glad to be out of it all now.'

'When's the ceremony?'

'Early next month. I won't be there for it though, I'll still be here.'

Fiona looked puzzled. 'I thought you said you weren't staying long?'

'I'm not. Not in the hotel, at least.' Daisy looked at them all a little nervously. 'I'm renting a cottage near the village, and I'm going to live there and write.'

'You're staying for good?' Fiona voiced everyone's excitement at this news.

'Well, I've had to jump through some hoops, but I've proved I can support myself financially, so . . . I guess I'm staying for as long as I still love it.'

'What will you write?' Bertie asked.

'Remember *Dangerous Ladies*, that film we were talking about when I was here before? I'm going to develop it for Stone Valley Pictures, my dad's studio. And then . . . Well, I guess I'll just see what I feel like writing next. It's so exciting!'

'Will you still write under that anagram of your own name?' Bertie asked. 'What was it? Andy Discaro?'

'I will for this one, since it's Dad's studio and it's better if it's an unknown. But if that's a success I'll write the next one under my real name. Hey,' she reached out and gripped Fiona's hand, her green eyes alight, 'maybe I'll write an adventure story about what happened to us up there at the construction site!'

Fiona was clearly delighted to be at the centre of Daisy's plans. 'I'd love that!'

Bertie smiled; it would be good for Fiona to have a friend nearby, and would take her mind off that misfit Amy. Her smile broadened as she imagined how Ben would react when he found out. 'Have you found a cottage already then?'

'I have. It's just this side of Trethkellis, before you reach the village itself.'

'Oh, the one near Stan Houghton's yard, with the little apple orchard overhanging the road?'

'That's the one. Guy made some calls for me since he knows the owner.'

'A friend of mine was renting it last year,' Guy said, and Bertie noted a touch of pink on his smoothly shaven cheeks, and recalled Philip Rose, the architect. 'That's how I know it's nicely appointed inside, apart from a small leak in the roof. All that rain we had over Christmas hasn't helped.'

'It's being fixed up,' Daisy said, 'but it'll take a few more weeks until it's just right. When I learned Guy was travelling back now, I decided to come over early, move into the rooms that are done, in a few days, and have my things sent over when the rest is ready. I mean, what better place to stay in the meantime than Fox Bay?' Her eyes widened suddenly, and she looked at Helen. 'I didn't even think to ask! I hope you have a room?'

'Well,' Helen raised an amused eyebrow, 'since a certain pair of film stars stayed here at Christmas we've been booked almost solid, right through the summer at least. But,' she added, as Daisy's face fell,

'Mr Douglas has checked out early, so we do have a second-floor room just for a few more nights, if that's acceptable?'

'It's all acceptable!' Daisy smiled. 'I'd honestly sleep on the floor tonight, anyway!'

'Yes, you must be exhausted,' Helen said, standing up. 'I'll see your things are taken up immediately. Come over to the desk, and I'll get you the key.'

'Well,' Guy braced his hands on the arms of his seat, 'I'm off to give young Benjamin a piece of my mind for not picking us up. Is he awake yet?'

'He's out, actually.' It occurred to Bertie that Guy didn't yet know Ben was almost certain to be leaving Fox Bay, and she avoided his eyes by rubbing at a non-existent smudge on her skirt.

Guy was fond of all the Fox children, but Ben had had a special place in his heart from their very first day here, when he'd sensed the boy's instinctive interest in fine wines; he'd encouraged him to train as a sommelier, and even, eventually, bowed to Ben's insistence on adopting the sabrage method of opening Champagne on special occasions. His leaving would upset Guy greatly, and Bertie knew no one would want to be the one to break that news, so she didn't know whether to be relieved or dismayed when Fiona tapped her arm.

'Jowan's here, hovering by the door as usual.'

Bertie gave Fiona and the others a quick, apologetic smile, and left them. Jowan was, indeed, hovering, looking at her as if unsure of his reception, as well he might after a week with no contact.

'Shall we go out into the cloisters?' he asked, their usual place to talk when he wasn't staying for more than a few minutes. Bertie sighed inwardly. Was he

185

rushing off again because he sensed an argument, or because he didn't want to intrude on Fiona's birthday?

'Come into the sitting room,' she said instead, testing him. 'I think we need to talk properly, and we'll be left alone there too.'

He assented, though with evident reluctance, but as they made their way across the lobby, waving to the little group as they passed, he watched her with open admiration. 'You're doing brilliantly on that leg. How's it feeling now?'

'Still a bit sore,' she admitted, 'but that's my own fault.' She could sense him holding back the blunt agreement he would normally have voiced, and it saddened her further; if he'd just say it, she could respond in her usual acerbic way too, and some kind of honest normality would be re-established between them. As it was, they were almost strangers again, as they had been when she'd come home from hospital, and before she had pushed him away with her deliberately cruel barbs designed to make him dislike her.

She closed the sitting room door behind them and sat down with a little hiss of relief; she'd definitely been wearing the prosthetic for too long today, though she was delighted she'd been wearing it when Daisy arrived. The minute Jo was gone she'd take it off.

'Has Fiona had a nice birthday?' Jowan began, unbuttoning his jacket and sitting opposite her. 'Been down at the station for most of it though, I reckon.'

'What did you come here to say?' Bertie asked, suddenly very tired. 'This is the first time we've been alone since Xander died, I'm sure you're not here to discuss Fiona's birthday.'

'I told you I was sorry to hear about him,' Jowan

said. 'You know I didn't like the way he behaved around you.' *Or the way you responded*, was the unspoken addition, once again halted by that awful, distant politeness. 'He was a decent enough bloke though,' Jowan went on, 'what happened was . . . just horrible. Wouldn't wish it on the devil.' He shifted in his seat, and Bertie sensed they were coming to the reason for his visit at last.

She decided to spare him. 'I'm still going to train as a pilot,' she said. 'I've already talked to the training officer.'

Jowan looked at her steadily for a moment, then nodded. 'I see.'

'Did you really think it would change things? Even knowing me as you do?'

Jowan shrugged. 'If you're looking for a row, you won't get one from me.'

'Why would I be looking for a row?'

'Because you're right, I do know you. And I know that tone in your voice.'

'What tone? Knowing my own mind?' Bertie wondered for a moment if she were being unfair, but he'd sounded too patronising for words. 'If you expected me to give up this dream just because — '

'You had no notion of this so-called *dream* before that . . . before Xander put it into your head!'

'And that stops me wanting to pursue it, does it?' Bertie wished her leg wasn't so sore, she could feel the tension tightening her muscles, and needed to jump up and walk some of it off. 'I told you, I'm not doing it because of him. I thought, if anything could convince you I was serious, this would.'

'But it only proves how dangerous it is!' Jowan did stand up now, and because Bertie felt at a disadvantage she rose too, and managed not to wince as the raw flesh of her leg burned where it rubbed against the sock that covered it.

'I can't win, can I?' she retorted. 'First you don't want me to do it because Xander would be there, now you don't want me to because he isn't!'

'Stop twisting things!' Jowan turned a despairing face to her, and she bit back the denial that she was doing any such thing; of course she was twisting it. If she could force him to break off their engagement, she would be spared admitting the real reason they had no future; their break-up would fall onto his shoulders, the intolerant and dominating Jowan Nancarrow, who had put his foot down and demanded his woman stay at home and give up her ambitions. But the description was so far from his true nature that Bertie knew she couldn't sustain that myth.

'You said you wouldn't argue,' she pointed out, tight-voiced. 'You've avoided talking to me alone for over a week, the least you can do is listen while I explain what my plans are.'

'I thought . . . .' The sentence trailed away, and he shrugged. 'I thought you'd see sense, now you've seen what can happen.'

'*You've* seen what can happen when someone falls from a motorcycle going at a walking pace,' Bertie countered, slapping her leg, 'but I've still seen you riding down the lane like Syd Crabtree!'

'That's hardly the same thing.'

'Of course it is!' Bertie made her way to the window so she could lean on the sill. 'My father died racing a bike, and *your* father died because of his sons tinkering with one. And look at us!'

Jowan's face paled, and Bertie wished she hadn't

reminded him so bluntly of his part in Toby's death. She adopted a gentler tone. 'You know it's the truth, Jo. If either of us had turned away from what we wanted, just because of what happened to our fathers, we'd never have become friends, let alone anything else.'

'And this is what you want? Still?'

'Yes. Look, when I've finished my training we can talk about what comes next, and . . . well, whether you think it's something you can still live with.'

'What do you mean?' Jowan had grown very still. 'What are you likely to want to do next?'

Bertie held his gaze, knowing the time had come. There was no avoiding it now. 'It's more what I don't want to do.'

'And what's that?' Jowan frowned suddenly. 'Are you telling me you don't want to marry me?'

'No! I do want that, but it's . . . I don't . . . .' Bertie closed her eyes. 'I don't want children.'

There was a brief pause, and he nodded. 'Well of course not right away, but —'

'Not ever.' Bertie blew out a short, harsh breath. She'd said it. Now it was all down to Jowan. 'I've thought about this,' she said carefully. 'You have to realise there's no point in trying to convince me I'll change my mind.'

He gave her a strange look, part-puzzled, part-angry at the low opinion she clearly had of him. 'I wouldn't want to try. That wouldn't be fair.'

'I mean I don't want you to think I'm going to change my mind someday. I don't want you to waste your time waiting for that.'

Jowan's face was unreadable now. She stared back, defiant, but conversely hopeful, and as the emptiness between them stretched unbearably, she wanted to blurt out that, actually, she *might* one day think again. And she could see that, for his part, he was fighting the impulse to tell her the same thing. But after a minute she accepted that the silence had gone on too long; it didn't matter which one of them spoke now, whatever they said would be a lie.

She twisted the ring off her finger, and as she placed it on the little table that stood between them she could see all the tiny moments that had gone into making it such a special one. The midnight church service where he had first shown it to her, and it hadn't fitted; the way he and Jory had fought, when Jory had pawned it using Jowan's name; the way they had finally been able to retrieve it from Charlie Templeton . . . all of that joy, violence, and redemption, encompassed in the slim gold band with its three tiny diamonds and two sapphires.

Jowan barely glanced at it. He bent and picked up his hat, and, with his eyes fixed on hers he backed away as far as the door, perhaps waiting for her to smile and claim it had all been a joke, or a test. But of course she couldn't.

When he'd left, Bertie crossed to the closest chair and sank into it. Maybe he would take a deep breath out there, away from her, and realise they were worth fighting for. But as she looked at the door, solid and unmoving in its frame, she accepted that all he had done was afford her the respect she had demanded. How could she fault him for that?

12

Just as Friday evenings were livelier in the lounge, the Saturday changeover always resulted in a more pronounced sense of occasion at dinner. Dresses were usually a little more elaborate, suits more neatly pressed, laughter louder, and, as guests greeted one another and introduced themselves, the talk between tables flowed more freely.

It was the perfect night to set up a family table to celebrate Ben's final night as a manager at Fox Bay Hotel, and Helen made her way through to her seat, nodding at those guests she knew personally. At the same time she was giving herself a stern talking to; tonight was all about sending her eldest child off into his future, and, while she couldn't deny the sadness that went with it, she ought to be grateful that he was only going a few miles away, and, unlike Bertie, to a safe, calm environment.

Her mind kept taking her back to the last party they'd had at Burleigh Mansions in Bristol, that New Year's Eve party when Ben had been sixteen. His first society party, and one that had resulted in him sitting on the floor surrounded by broken crockery and food, howling with laughter, and then being escorted from the room by his furious and embarrassed mother. Now he was a sophisticated young man, and the image of his father; a trained sommelier, and natural manager, but it didn't take much to reveal that sixteen-year-old boy, not yet buried too deeply beneath the layers of responsibility.

He and Lily Trevanion were all but engaged, if Lily were to be believed. Ben had seemed content enough to let people believe it, until now, and had even seemed likely to accept it himself at some point, but Helen had seen the look on his face when he'd returned on Wednesday to learn that Daisy Conrad was not only back, but back to stay. He'd expressed surprised interest, smiled at Bertie — who'd delivered the news with great relish — and been in a perfect daze for the rest of the evening. When he'd seen Daisy himself he'd been distantly polite, but Helen could see his thoughts scrambling, and the confused boy behind his eyes, and she understood the conflict only too well.

It was hard, she knew, living so close to someone for whom you'd finally acknowledged you had deep feelings, especially when you knew you'd left it too late to express them, and now Ben had done the same thing, by accepting Lily's suggestion and the unspoken agreement that went with it. Helen couldn't be sure, but she suspected that, as much as he wanted a change and more responsibility, he might not have taken the Summerleaze job at all had he known Daisy would be living so close to Fox Bay.

Once again, as she thought of his imminent departure, Helen was horribly aware of the gradual diminishing of the previously full, rich world she inhabited; it felt as if everything were fraying at the edges, and she was barely holding the core together against the inevitable march of erosion.

She slipped her hand into the pocket of her jacket, and felt the piece of paper she'd folded and unfolded a dozen times since she'd torn it from her copy of today's newspaper:

Vacancy: manager wanted for new commercial premises, details to be confirmed upon successful application.

Must have at least five years' managerial experience in a hospitality role. Salary to be discussed upon acceptance. Interviews to take place in Truro during March.

The telephone number to call was a Truro one too, which wasn't to say the premises definitely would be, but it was likely it would at least be in Cornwall. Helen hadn't been sure, when she'd torn out the advertisement, exactly why she'd done it, or if she were really thinking of calling the number, but more and more often lately she'd felt certain that living so close to the newly wed Nancarrows would be the last straw, once the distraction of her own family was gone.

There was nothing to say she had to live and work at Fox Bay, as well as owning it, and if this advertisement was for a new hotel, she'd have living quarters there . . . She looked over at Guy, fussily straightening serving spoons and piles of napkins on the sideboards that ran around the edge of the room; the hotel would be in safe hands until Ben came into his inheritance. Adam's idea to create a new concierge position had been perfect for Guy; it drew on every inch of his suave manner, his local knowledge, and his love of this hotel in particular. He'd been given a smart new uniform, and took visible delight in being the face of Fox Bay as guests arrived — he'd make an admirable replacement for Helen if she did decide to explore a life further afield. It was a comforting thought.

The family began to arrive. Fiona first, closely

193

followed by Bertie, who would have her own farewell dinner in a little over a month's time. Leah and Adam came in soon afterwards; Adam had been looking odd since the day he'd come back, but today he looked even more distracted. Helen hoped Jeanette's presence hadn't caused friction between him and Leah, but she was reasonably certain Adam had ensured their paths had never crossed. He was disturbingly good at that.

Daisy, keen not to take the shine off Ben's evening by eclipsing him, slipped in at the last moment and took her seat at the far end of the table, nearest the wall. A few people noticed, and nudged one another in delight, Helen noted, but thankfully behaved with decorum. Guy didn't join them for the meal, since he was working, but as their coffee was served Helen rose to her feet and tapped a glass to catch the diners' attention.

'Ladies and gentlemen, for those who don't know me, my name is Helen Fox, and I'd like to welcome you to our hotel. I won't keep you for long, but you happen to be having your evening meal as we celebrate good news for my son Benjamin, who some of you will know has been our night manager here for several years now. He's off to a new position in Bude, where they have been lucky enough to secure his expertise as hotel manager at the Summerleaze. Before I say my goodbyes, I believe our bar and restaurant manager, Guy Bannacott, who trained Ben, has a few words he'd like to say.'

She led the polite applause, and took her seat again while Guy made the speech he'd been preparing. Ben looked both pleased and embarrassed, but above all deeply touched, as the famously taciturn Guy

194

launched into a litany of praise, and regret that Ben would no longer work alongside him.

While he spoke, the waiting staff moved around the room with glasses of champagne for each guest, and when he'd finished, Guy reached behind the piano and brought out a cloth-covered object around a foot long. Fiona stood up and whipped off the cloth to reveal a polished wooden stand, upon which sat a sabrage sword complete with silk tassel.

'A token of our esteem, and a good luck wish for your new position.' Guy handed the gift to Ben, who obliged the room by taking the bottle of champagne from the bucket on their table, and wielding the short, ceremonial sabre with a flourish. He slid it along the bottle until cork and collar flew off beneath the pressure of the blade, tumbling harmlessly against the heavy curtain behind him. A small amount of champagne frothed over the neatly sliced neck, and the room erupted into cheers as Ben twirled the sabre and replaced it carefully on its stand.

He made his own short, oddly emotional speech, and Helen kept a careful eye on Daisy while he did so; the girl's eyes shone as she looked up at Ben, and Helen felt a mixture of pride and misgiving; she didn't know Lily very well, but well enough to sense she wouldn't take kindly to the arrival of a Hollywood star, particularly one to whom she knew Ben had absolutely surrendered his heart at Christmas. To see there was clearly a reciprocal affection was uplifting, and Helen could only hope there wouldn't be a backlash from Lily that would hurt either of them.

The small party broke up soon after, with the young ones gathering in the family sitting room, while Helen, Adam and Leah went to the lounge. When

Leah slipped away for a moment, Adam turned to Helen.

'Can I have a word? It's important.'

'Of course.' She peered closer. 'Though from the look of you, you'd rather not.'

Adam gave her a flicker of a smile. 'I was always an open book to you, wasn't I?'

'What is it?'

'Not here.' Adam looked around. 'This all looks a bit . . . celebratory.'

Helen's unease grew. 'In the office then. Guy?' she called. 'I'll be in the office if anyone needs me for anything.'

'I'm sure we won't,' Guy assured her, and although it was intended to release her from any concerns she might have, it felt like another chilly little reminder that she was surplus to requirements today.

Her mood was, therefore, even lower when Adam faced her across the desk and dropped his devastating piece of news. 'So that's why Jeanette was really here.' She felt sick, furious, and, to her dismay, even tearful. Everything was happening at once, it was too much. 'Have you signed your share over yet?'

'Not yet.' Adam leaned across to lay his hand over hers, but she jerked it away, and he sat back. 'I'm sorry, I honestly thought Jeanette had it all covered.'

'Do you think she's done it on purpose?'

Adam looked genuinely startled at that thought. 'I'm sure not,' he said. 'I mean, she wouldn't, would she?'

'Think about it. She only set it all up to begin with because you promised her enough of the reward money to start her own business. It was a risk worth taking until — '

196

'We talked about that.'

'And what was her response?'

Adam looked as if he didn't want to answer. His face coloured as if he were embarrassed to say it, but he shrugged. 'She said it was challenging, and that she had a, well, a fondness for me.'

'Oh, you idiot!' Helen breathed, and couldn't help the sharp little laugh that came with it. 'She's getting her revenge.'

'I honestly don't think she is. You weren't in the room, Hels, you didn't see her.'

'No, but I know her. She could have gone to Simon at the start and told him you'd swindled her, and together they'd have put an end to it. Or she could even have convinced him he didn't need to go to an independent accountant. But this way was too much fun. This way, she's got you dangling by your loyalties, to me and to her, and guess which one's going to get the chop?'

'It's not like that! I would never betray you or the hotel.'

'But you're going to give her your half, just like that, because she says that'll pay off your debt?'

'And close the gap in the Hartcliffe books.'

'So she says. Tell me something though, have you had your share valued?'

Adam stared for a moment, then shook his head. 'Why?'

'Have you seen our bookings for this year?' Helen got up and went to the door. 'Martin! Bring in the ledger a moment, will you?' She returned to her seat, aware of Adam's face as he went through a series of realisations; she didn't need the book now, to prove her point, but it was satisfying to flick through the pages and pages of solid bookings, right through this year and into the next, and then to the long list at the back, from which the rare cancellations were filled.

'This hotel must be worth twice as much as it was when you bought it,' she said. '*Look* at this, Adam.'

'We've always had a full book, more or less,' he pointed out, but they both knew he was ignoring the obvious.

'And the prices? Have people always paid as much as they're happy to now, just to be able to stand in the same spot as Daisy Conrad and Freddie Wishart? To eat at the same tables? And more to the point, to stay in the same rooms? That one visit has made Fox Bay *the* place for the London elite, and some of these names are from Hollywood too, look.' She turned the ledger around and pushed it towards him, tapping the page. 'Alfred Hitchcock next Christmas! And others too. Word has already spread, just as we hoped.'

Adam's grim expression cleared. 'I hadn't even thought.'

'Speaking of which, we should re-name those rooms, don't you think? And Mr Hitchcock's, once he's been. Much better than just a number.'

Adam gave her an admiring smile. 'I shouldn't have underestimated you. I'm sorry.'

'And you'll tell Jeanette Duval, sorry, *Jean Hill*, that she can have a fraction of your share and be thankful?'

'I'll get someone out here to value the place first thing on Monday, and get the official estimate sent over to her.'

'Do you think she'll accept it, or will she demand more because of what she knows?'

'She'd be mad to; it'd drop her off the same cliff she'd be pushing me from.'

198

'Well that's something, at least, though I'd pay good money to see it. I take it you haven't told Leah yet?'

'How did you know?'

'Because this is the first I've heard of it.'

Adam smiled. 'And if I tried to convince you I'd asked her to keep it under her hat?' He shook his head. 'Never mind, you don't need to answer that. No, I wanted to tell you first, and now I've done that, I can tell her what you said. It'll take the sting out a bit.'

Helen watched him leave, a much happier man than when he'd come in, and knew her own decision should have changed too. She should be facing Fox Bay's future with renewed energy and excitement, but knowing she would have to share the decision-making with Jeanette, even on a reduced basis, sealed it for her. She would telephone that number on Monday morning and arrange an interview.

★ ★ ★

The morning after the party, a subdued Leah knocked on Daisy's door. 'All set? Ben's got the car running.'

'Ready!' Daisy beamed. 'I can't believe it's finally happening. Do you know this is the first time I'll have ever lived alone?'

'Well you're young yet.' But Leah felt her own years heavily today; she had never had her own home either, not even when she and Glynn had married, and she hadn't the excuse of youth on her side now. 'There might be unexpected little things you'll need help with,' she cautioned, 'but don't worry, the telephone's connected, and you can call us at any time. Now, are your bags downstairs yet?'

Daisy nodded. 'The bell boys took them down about a half hour ago.' She picked up her handbag from the dresser. 'Let's go! It's so good of you to offer your help like this,' she went on, following Leah down the stairs. 'I can't thank you enough.'

'Happy to,' Leah assured her. She made sure to keep her smile in place as they crossed the lobby, with Daisy giving discreet, happy little waves to the admiring guests who had been so excited to discover she'd been staying, but every now and again the memory intruded of the conversation she'd had with Adam last night.

Jeanette Duval, coming here, to steal Adam's future . . . How dare she even think it? Adam had been quick to point out what Helen had said, about the hotel being worth so much more than Jeanette was owed, but Leah had a sneaking suspicion that the woman wouldn't let that lie, not for a minute.

Leah had found Helen directly she'd left Adam that morning, and they'd both agreed that Jeanette's aim was to do more than balance her firm's books, and that Adam was putting far too much trust in the 'fondness' she'd had for him ten years ago. The only trouble was how to convince him he was being a fool.

For today though, there was nothing she could do, so she'd offered to help Ben and Daisy move Daisy into her new cottage. There were only a few bags, since Daisy's things would be sent over from America once the cottage was completely ready, but for now the basics were in place, and there was electricity, water and a telephone, and Daisy was too eager to begin work as a writer to wait any longer. She sat in the front of the car next to Ben, and Leah was able to watch them from the back seat as they set off on the short drive from Fox Bay to Orchard Cottage. She smiled to see Daisy's eyes graze the side of Ben's face, as he negotiated the tight turns; never had she been happier to be the gooseberry.

The Bugatti drew up outside Orchard Cottage, a compact little stone-built dwelling just outside Treth-kellis, with a walled orchard, and a small garden with untidy borders and overgrown patches of nettles in the corners. Daisy didn't wait for Ben to come around and open her door, she was out and running up the path before he'd even crossed in front of the car, and Leah couldn't help grinning, despite the pang of envy.

'She's like a child at Christmas,' she said to Ben, who was looking after the excited film star with a hopeless little smile on his face. 'She likes you, you know,' she said, in a lower voice. 'Just remember she has a lot of new things to get used to.'

'And so do I,' Ben added. He reached back into the car and removed a leather box. 'Tomorrow I'll have an entire hotel to take care of.'

It had the sound of someone firmly changing the subject, but Leah wasn't going to put up with that. 'You're used to that,' she pointed out. 'But about Daisy — '

'We know how it is from my side, Aunt Leah, but come off it, she's not going to be interested in someone like me when she has the world to choose from! Never mind that now, anyway. Look.' He opened the box. 'This is what Adam gave me for Christmas.'

'Oh, yes, he said he was getting you a camera, I'd forgotten.'

Ben drew the instrument out with great care. 'It's a Leica. There's even a rangefinder I can add on, so I shouldn't get blurred pictures once I've had some

201

practice.'

'Have you used it much?'

'I've not taken many pictures yet, but I've been getting to know it, and reading a lot about how to develop the negatives. Lily says I'll be able to rearrange one of the storerooms at the Summerleaze to make a studio.'

'That's very obliging of her,' Leah observed. They'd reached the front door of the cottage, and she put a hand on Ben's arm. 'Just before we go in, tell me. Are you and Lily an item? Properly, I mean, not just in her head?'

Ben didn't answer right away, but Leah got the impression it was because he genuinely didn't know the answer, rather than that he just didn't want to say, with Daisy so close. Then he shook his head firmly. 'No. We're just colleagues, and now I'll be her boss. There's no room for anything more when you work together like that. We do get along alright though.'

'Good,' Leah said, and pointed to the little hallway beyond the front door, 'because no matter what you say, that young lady is just dying for you to ask her to dinner, and if you don't do it soon you'll have young Mr Nancarrow snapping at your heels.'

'Jowan?' Ben looked startled.

'No, you idiot, Jory! Don't forget he saved her life, and that's quite a good basis for a chat over a meal, wouldn't you say?'

Ben tried deflection once more. 'He's supposed to be marrying Sally Penneck, so everyone says.'

'And, so everyone says, *you're* practically engaged to Lily Trevanion.' Leah gave him an arch look. 'But you say that's not true, so . . . .' She shrugged, and slipped past him into the house. 'Daisy? Where are you? You're not a film star anymore, and there are bags to bring in, you know!'

She and Daisy made up the bedroom, and then went downstairs to unload some boxes of dried food and cleaning supplies that the hotel had provided to see Daisy through her first few days. Leah felt the return of that twinge of envy as she watched the girl proudly straightening antimacassars and looking around with deep satisfaction every time she added something new. Perhaps her own restlessness on returning to Cornwall wasn't due to a hankering for excitement and danger after all? Perhaps it was simply that she needed a home.

Ben prowled around the cottage with his camera, capturing the transformation from merely functional to cosy. Leah caught Daisy glancing uneasily at him as he snapped her putting a clock on the mantlepiece, but the girl was too polite to say anything, so she stepped in.

'Some help you're being, Benjamin Fox! Put that blasted thing away and start making yourself useful!'

'Just practising,' Ben said. 'I'll give you some copies, Daisy, if you like them when they're developed.'

'That'd be nice, thank you.' Daisy blew a lock of sweaty red hair out of her eyes and pulled a face. 'But don't you dare show them to anyone else, I have a reputation to protect! Until after the awards at least.'

'Don't worry.' Ben clicked once more. 'That'll be a nice one of the two of you. Alright!' He held up a hand as Leah opened her mouth to berate him again. 'I'll get cracking on bringing those logs in.'

He picked up the wicker basket, and went out to begin ferrying in the logs they'd arranged to have cut over the past few days. Leah glanced out of the window to make sure he was busy, then sat down and indicated the settee next to her.

'What is it?' Daisy asked, accepting the invitation.

'Do you still like him?'

Daisy flushed. 'Ben? Sure, he's nice. Sweet. And handsome,' she added, her flush deepening. 'Why, has he said anything?'

'No, but I think one of you ought to,' Leah said, 'or you'll be dancing around each other until next Christmas.'

'I thought he and this girl at his new hotel were an item?'

'No, I checked.' Leah patted the famous hand, now soot-streaked where Daisy had wiped down the mantle before putting her clock there. 'If your new life really begins today, *cariad*, then I think it's time you let the young cub know you're not ridiculously unattainable after all.'

'Surely he doesn't think that?' Daisy laughed, and gestured to her messy hair and unmade-up face. 'How could he?'

'Because, my sweet girl, you're still *Daisy bloody Conrad*!' Leah shook her head. 'Just spill some food down your front, or drop a log on his foot, or something!'

Daisy laughed harder at that. 'That'll sure help. Put the poor guy in a cast to begin his new job!'

Leah stood up, smiling down at her. 'I'm going to walk back now,' she said. 'And by the time Ben comes home to get his own stuff, I want him to be talking about you like a person instead of a saint. So use your wits and break the spell before it's too late!'

★ ★ ★

204

By Monday morning, Leah had made up her mind. All the way home yesterday she had been turning over the notion of her own home; how she would afford it, whether Adam would be part of it or whether she would go it alone; how Helen would feel when she told her that was what she wanted . . . Although, if the first consideration had no solution then it was pointless even thinking about the rest. How *would* she afford it?

She wanted to discuss it with Adam, but he was out today arranging for the valuation of the hotel, and there was no knowing how long he would be. She picked up a newspaper from the stack on the end of the reception desk, and was about to take it over to one of the more secluded parts of the lobby when she saw Helen going into the office. Now was as good a time as any.

She went through the reception desk and knocked at the door. 'Helen? It's me.'

'Give me five minutes,' Helen called back, 'I'm making a telephone call.'

Leah withdrew, puzzled and a little stung. She'd never been excluded from hotel business before, and in the light of all that was going on she found it disturbing that Helen was looking for privacy in the office now, or worse: secrecy. Not that she had any room for complaints on that score, she reminded herself, but it was so unlike the open, and sometimes painfully honest, Helen, that it sowed further seeds of unease.

She waited for Helen to come to her, telling herself it was to avoid rushing her friend, but in the deepest part of her heart she knew there was a peevish element to it. She hated herself for that, but there was no denying it.

'I'm so sorry,' Helen said, when she came out. 'I wasn't trying to be secretive.'

Leah flushed, feeling caught out, and Helen saw it and gave a little laugh. 'Well I never. A dose of your own medicine not going down too well, eh?'

'Horrible,' Leah admitted, allowing herself a smile in return. 'But I deserved it.'

'You absolutely did.'

'What are you up to then? Since it's not a secret?'

Helen sat down. 'I've been thinking about my future. And that of the hotel.'

'In what way?' Leah couldn't quite place Helen's mood, which seemed tense and a little distracted, but oddly light. 'You're not thinking of leaving, are you?'

'That's exactly what I'm thinking of, yes.' Helen sat back. 'Do you know, that's the first time I've said it aloud.'

'Even to Harry?' Leah felt safe saying it; Helen made no secret of the fact that she often still talked to him, in the privacy of her room.

'Even to him.'

'So . . . you're selling?' Leah wasn't sure how she felt now, things seemed to be moving at such a speed.

Helen shook her head. 'It's not mine to sell, and I wouldn't want to cut all my ties here. I'm just not sure I can live here anymore.'

'But what about Fiona?'

'She'll have a home here as long as she needs one, as will all of us. But . . . .' Helen looked around at the bustling lobby, and Leah couldn't help a smile, despite the sadness that moved within her.

'You're thinking this place doesn't need you day-to-day, since it's running so smoothly, aren't you?'

'Well, yes.'

'And, as ever, you're not stopping to think that you're the reason it is.'

Helen gave her a little smile. 'I'm not under-selling my worth,' she said. 'I know I've helped to make this place what it is. But above all it was a home for me and the children, and now two of them are going, and with Adam giving half his share to Hartcliffe it just won't feel the same.'

'But that's not everything, is it?'

'Isn't it enough?'

'It's not the reason you haven't spoken to Harry about it,' Leah pressed. 'It's the Nancarrows, isn't it?'

There was an odd, stiff little silence, then Helen's eyes met hers, and the usually bright sherry colour was a little duller now. 'I can't live so close to them anymore. Not now I've let him in.'

'Oh, Hels.' Leah reached across the space between them and folded her fingers around Helen's. 'I understand, I truly do.' It was pointless to say it wouldn't matter, that Helen could go on being a friend to Alfie and be glad he was happy; it had only been a few short months ago that she had made the same vow about living with Adam and Helen, believing what she had. But it hadn't taken her long to realise she couldn't do it, and nor could she expect Helen to.

'You mustn't tell anyone,' Helen said, 'not even Adam, but the telephone call I made was to a number in Truro, about a managerial position in what I assume is a new hotel.'

'You assume?'

'They're asking for experience in this trade,' Helen said, 'and I can offer that, if little else. We've proved I can build a reputation, which is what they'll need. It's going to be my chance to strike out on my own,

207

now that the children no longer need me, and neither does the hotel. Just think, I can come back and be treated like a guest of honour, whenever I like.' Her face broke into a grin then. 'I'll be like you!'

'The cheek of you!' Leah sat back, laughing. 'I believe I've paid my dues, one way or another!'

'You've certainly kept Adam under control. Or as much as you could, at least. What idiots we were, believing Jeanette was the least bit sentimental. She's a climber, she always has been, and now she has the tools to climb over everyone else on her way to the top.'

'Do you think she'll push for changes? It'd be hard, living up in Bristol.'

'She won't need to, she'll convince Adam to do things her way, and with their combined shares I'd rather not be the one in the firing line. It'll be easier not to care, from a distance.' Helen sighed. 'I'm going to miss being able to talk to Ben about things.'

'Sorry to make things worse, but Adam and I will be away for a few days too, we're going to stay with Aunt Mary. We thought it was time they met properly, rather than last time's debacle.'

'Punch-ups with your husband probably didn't get him off to a good start,' Helen agreed. 'It'll be nice for all of you.'

It was time to take the plunge, and Leah's voice lowered. 'And then I've decided I'm going to . . . Well, helping Daisy yesterday, it made me realise . . . she was so excited — '

'You want your own home,' Helen said, matter-of-factly. 'Of course you do. I've thought this was coming, it's only natural.'

'Even Glynn and I never had our own place,' Leah

went on. 'I went from living with Mum, then her and Glynn, then the nurses' home, then France of course. Back to Mum, and then Aunt Mary . . . then here.' She shook her head quickly. 'And please, don't think I haven't loved every moment I've spent here with you and the cubs, and Fleur of course. I do miss her.'

'So do I,' Helen said. 'We didn't get off to the best of starts either, and she could be a tartar when she wanted to be, but she was a wonderful presence here. The children adore her. But this is about you, and I understand why you're looking to settle properly.'

'It wasn't until I talked to Daisy today, and saw the pleasure she took in getting things just so, in her little house, that I realised what I'd been missing. I'd thought it was excitement, and adventure, but it seems I was wrong.'

'It's still both those things, starting a new life,' Helen pointed out, 'just of a different kind. And will you be setting up your new home with Adam?'

'I don't know,' Leah said honestly. 'I wanted to talk to him about it today, but he's still out.'

'Well, let me know what you two decide,' Helen said. She stood up and smoothed her skirt. 'It's going to be a strange time, though I do think it's quite perfect that we're both thinking the same thing.'

'It's your pesky children who've done it,' Leah said, feeling the sting of tears through her smile. 'If they hadn't decided to grow up and become all independent and strong-willed, we might have carried on just like this forever.' She chose not to mention that her striking out alone would rely entirely on her finding an income; Helen would only insist on helping out, and that would defeat the purpose entirely.

'Oh, I forgot to ask,' she said, as they walked back

across the lobby, 'what did they say, when you made the call?'

'I'm to travel to Truro on Friday afternoon for an interview.' Now when Helen looked at Leah, her eyes had their old shine back. 'I've held lots of interviews before, but never had one myself. I can't decide whether I'm delighted or terrified.'

'Well we have a few days yet,' Leah said, and she turned Helen towards the office and gave her a gentle shove. 'I'm going to teach you everything I know, which will take *ages*, of course. Martin? Plenty of strong tea please, and after that, do not disturb unless the ceiling's falling in.'

13

Bertie watched as Jowan closed the door to what they'd always referred to as the barn. She idly wondered why she'd named it that; this wasn't a farm, it was a hotel, and that was the machine shed ... but still, it had always felt more romantic to call it the barn, as if it gave her a link to Jowan. Now, with his final visit, and the Squirrel back behind its solid wooden doors, it was a machine shed again. No need for romance, or links, or a pretence that their lives might follow the same path together.

'Thank you for bringing her back,' she said. 'She was a gift, you needn't have.'

Jowan shrugged. 'She was never mine, not really. What will you do with her?'

'I'll sell her back to Stan Houghton, and send the money over to Granny, to help pay her back for the flight training.'

'She won't want it.'

'She won't have a choice,' Bertie said firmly.

'When do you leave?'

'Next Friday. Training begins the next day, on the fifteenth.'

Jowan shook his head. 'I can't believe you're ready for this. You've not been on that leg a month, do they know that?'

'I've spoken to them a lot,' she said, immediately defensive. 'They're aware. Besides, there's a lot of

211

classroom stuff to do before anything physical, and it seemed best to start with the new intake instead of halfway through. I'd have had to wait until May, otherwise.'

Jowan held up a hand. 'I was only asking.' He spoke more gently. 'How are you getting down to Caernoweth?'

'Ben's driving me.'

'Ah. Good.' There was a difficult pause, and Bertie wondered if she ought to begin making her way back indoors, but he seemed keen to keep talking. 'How's he getting on at the Summerleaze, anyway?'

'Quite well, I gather. We haven't seen him a lot, since he and Daisy have been getting very chummy.' Xander's word again, chum. She waited for the flicker of pain to pass. 'How's Jory?'

'Alright. He threw Sally Penneck over for about a week, when he heard Daisy was back, but he soon realised he was pis . . . whistling in the wind.'

Bertie felt a smile pulling at her lips. 'I liked the first version better,' she said, and Jowan relaxed and grinned back. 'And here's me trying to behave.'

'Don't,' she said, 'it doesn't suit you. How about your mum and Alfie? Getting all prepared for their wedding?'

He nodded. 'Are you going to be there?'

'No, only Mum and Leah were invited, since they're old friends of Alfie's.'

'That's a bit rude, I'll talk — '

'No,' Bertie said quickly, 'you mustn't. It's their wedding, and it's a very small church. Mum will be too busy that weekend to come anyway, so I'll just feel awkward.'

There was a long pause, and then Jowan put a hand

on Bertie's arm. 'I'm glad we're friends. We under-stand one another now, don't we?'

'We always have, Jo. We just didn't know there was something else *to* understand, or that it would be the thing that meant we couldn't be together.'

'Not without one of us giving up what we want the most.'

'And neither one of us would allow the other to do that.'

'No.' He squeezed her hand. 'You won't forget about me, will you, when you're up there exploring the sky?'

'Quite the opposite.' Bertie linked her arm through his as they began to walk back across the yard. 'Whenever you see a plane flying over, look up and wave, just in case it's me.'

He snorted. 'You must be joking!'

Bertie laughed. 'Well anyway, I hope you'll let me tell you all about it when I come back for a visit.'

'Planning a break already?' Jowan shook his head in mock disappointment. 'And I thought you were dedicated.'

She aimed a punch at his arm, and his chuckle warmed her. He would always be her first real friend, and her first lover, and that would have to be enough, but she wondered how she would feel when the inevitable happened, and he met someone who wanted children as much as he did.

Watching him walk away, back to the farm, she thanked her stars that she'd be living a long way away by then and wouldn't have to find out.

★ ★ ★

213

Higher Valley Farm

Beth stopped kneading the dough for tomorrow's bread as she heard Jowan return from the hotel, where he'd finally taken that motorcycle back to its rightful owner. Hearing his feet heavy on the stairs, she put the dough back in the bowl and draped a damp towel over it.

'I won't be a minute,' she told Alfie, and went upstairs to find Jowan sitting on his bed looking bleak. 'How did it go?'

'Alright. We're friends, at least.' He looked up at her helplessly. 'I should have told her children didn't matter, shouldn't I?'

'No!' Beth sat down next to him. 'You certainly shouldn't have done that. Anyway, there was hesitation on both sides, wasn't there?' He nodded. 'Then you telling her you didn't mind, or her telling you she might change her thinking one day, that would have been the worst sort of start to your life together.' As she spoke, Beth felt the cold hand of truth on her heart. Building a marriage on a lie, even a well-intentioned one, was something she would do anything to talk her sons out of, so why was she even contemplating it for herself?

'We've talked about your need to build a family,' she said softly, to take the harshness from her earlier words, 'and you can't just push that aside as if it doesn't matter. If it were the other way about, she couldn't expect you to be a good father if your heart wasn't in it.'

'I know.' He sighed. 'The bugger of it is, I know she'd be a good mother.'

Beth frowned. 'No, you don't. And I'm not saying

214

this because *I* don't think she would,' she added quickly, as Jowan opened his mouth to argue. 'I'm saying that no one knows that kind of thing until it happens. If it ever does. And it's fair to say we all only learn it for ourselves then, too.'

'You sound as if you know a bit about it.'

'Your dad wasn't keen, at the start,' she confessed. 'He'd put off any conversations I tried to have, and just . . . wave them away as if we'd talk about it later. But when you two came along, well,' she smiled in remembrance, 'I've never seen anyone so smitten.'

'But that's exactly what I — '

'No, Jowan,' Beth said gently. 'It's different for mothers. You can't expect a woman to sit by during her own pregnancy, and just grumble about it, taking no part in it, in the hopes she'll 'come to her senses' when she sees her baby. If a woman's heart isn't in it right from the start, it can be too big a wall to get over. A father can just go about his ways and leave his wife to it, but a mother isn't granted the same free-dom. And it's the little ones who suffer.'

She left him to absorb her words, and went into her own room, where she sat thinking over how her own advice applied to her and Alfie. He only had to mention Toby's name to throw icy water over any hint of intimacy between them, and, for the first time, she wondered if he did it on purpose without even real-ising it. Likewise, her own jibe about the twins not being his own had struck him deeply, so had she done that deliberately? Were they both, deep down, trying to sabotage their own relationship?

She looked up as she heard Alfie's feet on the stairs, a sound as familiar and distinct to her as his voice, and a moment later he appeared in her bedroom doorway.

215

'Jo alright?'

She nodded and told him what had happened. Alfie listened gravely, and when she reached the part where they'd agreed they had no future, she saw a shadow cross his face.

'Seems we can learn as much from the kids as they do from us,' he said.

'What does that mean?' But she couldn't look at him, and her heart was beating too fast. 'I thought we'd got past that little . . . those cruelties.'

'We have.' Alfie smiled, and she felt the usual tightening inside when his eyes rested on hers. 'I just meant that when I was younger I would never have spoken my mind like they have. Sarah and I limped on for so long because she wouldn't either, and we both danced around the important things.'

'Like having children?'

'She was like Bertie, knew she didn't want them, only she never told me that's what she truly felt, and instead she just put on a big, sad performance each month.'

'But she never fell pregnant anyway? That was lucky for her.'

He gave her a wry look. 'Queen Anne's Lace, they call it.'

'Wild carrot?'

'That's the stuff, grows everywhere along the coast, and one of the best ways to prevent an unwanted pregnancy. Or so Nancy Gilbert told me later on, and she'd know.' Alfie sounded bitter now. 'Funny what you learn when it's too late. I had no idea, and spent days every month consoling Sarah when her so-called passionate wish for a child didn't come true.'

'But she surely had no need to be sly about it,' Beth

216

said, frowning. 'She must have known you wouldn't try to force things.'

'That's what I meant about Jo and Bertie being honest with each other. Better that way, even if it means they have to part ways. Sarah and I wasted so many years lying to one another, and now look at me.'

'You're a father to those boys, no matter what I said in that moment,' Beth said, feeling the end of everything rushing towards her, as unstoppable as the sunset.

'You'd tell me if you thought I hadn't been fair and open with you, wouldn't you?' he asked, his voice very quiet now.

'You've always been fair and open.'

He had offered marriage on transparent terms, and she had accepted. Now she had to find a way to see past Toby when she looked at him, and perhaps it was time to find out, before it was too late and they were locked into a marriage made of dust.

'I'm going to bed,' she said carefully, giving him what she hoped was a direct and inviting look.

His eyes widened slightly, the question clear on his face as he came to stand before her. She deliberately lowered her gaze, so she was looking at his chest instead of his face, and slipped her hand into his. He returned the pressure of her fingers, then closed the bedroom door and came back to stand behind her, his hands on her shoulders, those hands she had longed for years to feel on her bare skin.

She pictured the familiar long fingers, the light hairs on his wrists, the strength in his forearms, and she leaned back into him, feeling the solid height of him at her back, and the brush of his breath on her neck as he bent to touch his lips to the back of it. She closed her eyes, chanting his name over and over in her head, and felt his hands slip down her arms to gently cup her elbows, and turn her to face him.

She looked up. Alfie's eyes were a darker blue than Toby's, and his jaw leaner, but if she half-closed her eyes, the cruelty of that long-ago accident had never happened and she still had the man she'd married in her arms . . . *Stop, Beth!*

But it was too late. Alfie grew still, then stepped back. 'I understand.' His voice was quiet, but not surprised.

'I wish you weren't his brother,' Beth blurted, her own voice thickening with tears. 'Oh, Alfie, I wish it with all my heart. I've loved you so much, I always will, but — '

'I feel it too, and it's only getting worse, the longer we're without him.' His manner changed, as if he were forcing himself to remain in the room and talk this through. 'It feels like . . . I don't know. Like I'm biding my time and stealing everything that was his. And the lads must think it too, though they never say it.'

Beth looked helplessly up at him. 'We never meant to make you feel like a substitute.'

'I know, but that's what I've been. The farm has no need of me now, and neither have they.' His face softened again. 'Thing is, I've grown as fond of those boys as if they were mine. And of you, too.'

Beth studied him, as she had so often in the past, seeing the differences now as much as the similarities, but it was too late. 'I've always known you didn't love me in the way I wanted you to.'

He looked startled, then ashamed. 'Did you? I'm sorry. Why did you accept me if you knew that?'

'Because it didn't matter to me.'

'But it should. You deserve someone who loves you as completely as Toby did.'

'We're not children, Alfie. We're not star-gazing young lovers, who feel it can't be love unless it makes our hearts fall over themselves.'

'I know. And two people can be happy without the poetry, can't they?'

She noticed his eyes had taken on a faraway look, despite the prosaic words. 'Yet you wish that poetry for me,' she said. 'What about you? Don't you deserve it too?'

Alfie lifted his shoulders in a faint shrug. 'I'm not sure I do, no. I had my chance, and I let it go. You had yours stolen, that's not the same.'

'I *could* love again though,' Beth said, 'I felt the possibility of it, and you showed me I still feel the . . . the romance of it.'

'Poetry and all?' he asked, smiling slightly.

'Poetry and all. I know it won't be with you, there's too much between us, but I'm not giving up on it. And you shouldn't either.'

His eyes narrowed slightly as he met the challenge in her gaze. 'I think I'll write to Keir,' he said, turning away. 'Maybe see if he needs some help down at Priddy Farm, now spring's here and he's got no Ellen by his side.'

Beth nodded, swallowing her disappointment. 'I understand. The boys will be able to cope here, especially now we're so much smaller. I can call on Michael Sherborne to help out for a while if needs be.'

'I won't leave you high and dry, Beth, you know that. I just think perhaps it's best if I . . . step away for a while.'

'Of course. And I'll call on Father Trevelyan in the

219

morning.' Beth was hardly able to believe she was saying the words. In the space of five minutes it was all over; Alfie was leaving Higher Valley Farm.

As she went back downstairs she couldn't help wondering at that distant look she had seen in his eyes as he denied his own need for romantic love. He might still hold the same physical appeal for her that Toby always had, but his heart and soul were his own, and she had no claim over them. Though someone clearly did. Beth wondered if whoever Alfie had been thinking about in that moment knew what they held in the palms of their hands.

★ ★ ★

The following morning she sat in Father Trevelyan's study, her bag clasped on her lap to disguise her shaking hands, and told him the wedding was cancelled. He was kindness itself, but it gave her a jolt to see him make a discreet note on his jotter to cease reading the banns in church on Sunday; she'd soon be answering a dozen questions from her neighbours, and she wondered how on earth she would explain it to them.

She returned to the farm, still despondent, and had just changed back into her working clothes when she heard a car pull up in the yard. It was too early for Alfie and the boys to be looking for their lunch, and besides, it hadn't sounded like the farm van, but something smaller. Reynard was barking, but more in greeting than in warning, and Beth frowned, wondering if she'd forgotten someone was coming. She stepped outside the door to see someone manhandling a large, flat object out of the back seat of a car.

'Oh, my word, the painting!' She'd completely

220

forgotten about the artist and his promise to paint the farm. Alfie's wedding gift. Of all the days . . .

'Mrs Nancarrow!' Sam Douglas was smiling as he came towards her, but the smile faltered. 'You were still expecting this, weren't you?'

'Of course, but I thought we agreed you'd send it to Fox Bay.'

'I didn't like to entrust it to the Royal Mail,' he admitted. 'And I assumed your intended would be out at this time of day. Is it alright here, or shall I take it to the hotel anyway?'

'It's fine, come in.' Beth forced a smile onto her own face, but knew it wasn't quite doing the job, by the way his brow creased as he hefted the covered painting. She should have just told him she no longer wanted it, but after all the work he'd put in, she could at least offer him a cup of tea and an explanation.

In the kitchen, his smile had returned and it was oddly infectious. He looked such a serious man usually, with that distinguished white hair and intense gaze, but now, as he carefully withdrew the material covering his canvas, he looked as nervously excited as a youth at his first dance.

'What do you think? Have I captured it?' he asked anxiously. 'I had only my sketches to work from, and I always question my own memories when I'm back in my studio.'

'It's . . . .' Beth had polite words of appreciation ready to say while the rest of her mind picked over the best way to tell him his work had been for nothing, but as she looked at the painting she felt an unexpected swell of emotion. It was her home, hers and Toby's and the boys', and here it was captured on a piece of cloth by a stranger. All her memories and

221

hopes seemed gathered behind those painted walls; she felt that if she'd been able to peer through the windows she would see her life play out in the rooms.

'It's beautiful,' she managed at last, her voice hoarse.

Sam propped it against the window and sat down without being invited. 'What's the matter?'

'Nothing!' Beth cleared her throat. 'You've done a truly remarkable job. It's so strange, it's not like a photograph, yet it's Higher Valley to the last stroke.'

'But you do have something to tell me,' he guessed. 'Don't worry,' he hurried on, 'I won't be taking you up on your kind wedding invitation, so you mustn't feel you have to make room for me.'

'There's no wedding,' she said. 'Not anymore.'

For the second time that day she found herself explaining the situation. She didn't add that Alfie's proposal had been driven more by chivalry than by want, because then she'd have to admit that she'd been prepared to wed a man who wasn't in love with her. It was irrelevant in any case; all Sam needed to know was that the wedding was off.

'Would you like me to ask Mrs Fox if she'd like the painting for the hotel?' Sam asked.

Beth started to shake her head, then nodded. 'She'd pay you for it, at least.'

'But is that what you want me to do?' he pressed. 'Put aside the question of money for a moment, this painting was done for you as a gift.'

Beth looked over at it again. As much as she hadn't wanted the picture of her farm to be left nameless and forgotten in an attic, having now seen it she wasn't certain she liked the idea of something so personal being displayed at the hotel either. It should be viewed by someone with affection for it, someone who would understand the broken fence post, the crooked chimney brick, the puddle by the gate that never seemed to dry up, no matter what the weather.

'I'd still like it, please,' she said. 'If it can't be a wedding gift, it can at least be a farewell one.'

'He's leaving?'

'He's planning to go back to Porthstennack, to the farm where he used to work.'

'Ah, I see.'

'This was his boyhood home, so it'll make a nice memento for him.'

An awkward silence fell over them, and just as it looked as if Sam was about to leave, Beth remembered she hadn't offered refreshment.

'Can I get you a cup of tea?' She gave him a rueful smile. 'Though hardly payment, is it?'

'We've had this conversation before,' he reminded her. 'As I recall, it centred on fruit cake?' The questioning tone was accompanied by a hopeful glance towards the larder, and Beth laughed, for what felt like the first time in weeks.

'I'm sure I can find something.'

She glanced at the picture once more, as she passed by to investigate the contents of the larder, and could almost believe she saw herself peering out of the window, waiting for Alfie to come in from a day's work. All dreams had to end, and at least this one had ended without rancour, just like Jowan's . . . She gave a bitter little smile. The Nancarrows clearly had a knack for that.

14

Caernoweth
14th March

Bertie hoisted her case onto the bed and went to the window. It looked over the airfield from this side, while their position on the hill above the town gave onto a view of the sea from the other. She had a moment to wonder if she'd made the right choice in taking one of these holiday flats, instead of a place in a dorm with the other two female trainees, but as she turned away from the window she knocked her metal foot against the leg of the bed, and knew she'd done the right thing; this way she might miss out on the camaraderie, but at least she wouldn't stand out for the wrong reasons.

'I can't believe this place has no working lift!' Ben grumbled, shoving the trunk he'd carried against the wall. 'Shall we go across to the hotel for dinner before I go? I must say, it's good to be able to say that, now I'm not working nights anymore.'

'That'd be nice.' Bertie picked up her coat. 'We can pass on the news to Harry Batten that there'll be a vacancy in the kitchen at home.'

'It's true then, Nicholas Gough is definitely moving on?'

Bertie nodded. 'The advert's going in the paper next week. Harry will be glad of advance notice though.'

'Good idea.' Ben held the door open for Bertie, who eyed her stick for a moment, but left it propped against the bedstead. 'Don't you want that?'

'No, I'm going to see how I get on without it, so tonight will be good practice. You can always carry me back,' she added with a grin.

Ben snorted. 'After you've put away half a roast chicken and a mountain of potatoes? I think not!'

Bertie switched off the light, laughing. 'Come on then, I'm starved.'

★ ★ ★

Harry Batten was indeed pleased to hear that Fox Bay was already looking for another chef. He was also keen for news of Lynette, and how she was coping with the loss of her brother, and as soon as the chance arose he joined them at their table.

'It was awful when the news broke,' he said. 'It's all anyone could talk about for ages, around here. I know you were close to him, Bertie, I'm that sorry.'

She accepted his condolences with a little nod, but the stab of anguish she felt was as sharp as ever, and she changed the subject. 'I've never worked out why you're so keen to leave this wonderful place,' she said, looking around the dining room. 'Especially since your family own it.' She gestured at his grubby chef's whites. 'You wouldn't be allowed to sit here like this at Fox Bay, you know.'

He grinned. 'I know, but the simple thing is, I'm bored. I've been here all my life. You must know what it's like,' he added to Ben. 'You've moved on, even though your family owns the most gorgeous hotel on the coast. Do you regret it yet?'

'Nope.' Ben shook his head firmly. 'I love Fox Bay, but it's so good to be doing something different. You

225

must get that too, Bertie.'

Harry turned to her. 'What are you doing that's different, then?'

'I'm joining the flying school,' Bertie said, feeling a tingle of excitement even as she said it. 'I begin training tomorrow.'

'Bravo! A friend of mine's doing the same.'

'What's his name? I'll look out for him.'

'He's a she. Her name's Tory Gilbert. Bit of a tomboy, you can't miss her.'

'Have you known her long?'

'Since we were tackers.' Harry grinned. 'She was part of my little gang. Her, my best pal Bobby Gale, and one or two others.'

'Is she staying in the dorm?'

He nodded. 'You?'

'I've taken one of the holiday flats at the top of town.'

'Ah, the old hotel conversion.' Harry looked around as they heard raised voices from the kitchen. 'They're playing my song,' he sighed, 'I'd better go.'

'I'll call in and let you know if I hear anything from Lynette,' Bertie said, and Harry lifted a hand in thanks as he hurried away.

When he'd gone, she finished her drink and looked around for the bill. 'It's going to be a long day tomorrow; I'd better get an early night.'

Ben clicked his fingers for the waiter's attention, and finished his own coffee. 'How's the leg holding up? It's a lot of stairs up to your flat.'

'It's fine, just rubbing a bit,' Bertie said, although her good leg was starting to ache a little now, from constantly re-adjusting her balance. 'I'll get used to it.'

226

He helped her into the car for the short drive back. 'Do you wish you'd opted for the dorm instead?'

'No, I'm not ready for that yet.' Bertie settled herself into her seat. 'You will come and visit me though, won't you?'

'Of course.'

'Will you bring Lily?'

'Why on earth would I?'

'So it's true then, she's getting ahead of herself with talk of engagement?'

'So far ahead, she'll meet herself coming back.' Ben sighed and sat back in his seat. 'I'm sure she's still under the impression that me accepting this job was me accepting her.'

'You haven't come out and said it's not?' Bertie shook her head. 'Ben, you can't assume she knows, you have to tell her.'

'She should have realised by now. And it's a bit tricky coming out and saying something like *I don't want to marry you* to a girl, when they haven't mentioned it themselves. I'll feel a proper ass.'

'Which is why you have to talk! Find out if she really does still believe that, and then you can be more up front about Daisy.'

'The trouble is, Daisy doesn't really want it known that we're getting close, either. Something to do with it getting back to her studio, and her having to appear 'available', if you can believe that.'

'I do believe it,' Bertie said, 'especially until after the awards. A holiday is one thing, no one would begrudge her that, but any word about her actually setting down roots somewhere so far away is bound to cause ripples.'

'Well the sooner she's out of their clutches, the

227

better. Anyway, it means that whatever I do tell Lily, I can't tell her it's because of Daisy.' They were turning in at the entrance to the holiday flats now, and it was obvious he was relieved the conversation had come to an end. 'Right,' he said, as the car rolled to a stop by the door, 'are you going to let me see you up to your room, or are you going to go all Bertie on me?'

'I think you've already guessed the answer to that, since you haven't even stopped the engine.'

'Are you sure?' Ben's face grew serious again. 'You should have brought your stick, at least, even just to leave in the car. Will you be alright on those stairs?'

'They might have fixed the lift by now,' Bertie said, pushing open her door. 'But even if they haven't, I'll be quite alright. You ought to get back, it's a long-ish way to Bude.'

'I keep forgetting I'm not going back to Fox Bay.' Ben gave her a sad little smile. 'I miss everyone, but you most of all.'

'Don't.' Bertie felt the familiar sting in the back of her eyes. 'I don't want to go in there looking as if I've just been jilted at the altar.'

'Don't mention altars!' Ben's mock horrified expression had the desired effect, and Bertie smiled.

'Watch out for white dresses in her wardrobe, don't say, *I do*, no matter what the context, and if you see a vicar, run!'

He wouldn't drive away until she'd passed through the front door, so she waved and closed it firmly behind her, listening to the familiar sound of the Bugatti's powerful engine as Ben returned to what already felt like another world.

She wondered what this lobby had looked like before, when it had been the Caernoweth Hotel. Had it been huge and open, like Fox Bay? Or smaller and neater, like the purpose-built Summerleaze? Whatever it had been, it was now little more than a wide hallway, with bland white doors leading off it, labelled with neat stencils to indicate the accommodation office, the first-aid station, and, somewhere down there in the distance, the communal laundry. The lift still had the hastily written 'sorry out of order' sign taped to it, and the stairs rose like a personal challenge in front of her.

She eyed them nervously, took a firm grip of the stair rail and moved forward, trying not to think about anything other than each step taking her closer to the privacy of her room, where she could gather herself and prepare for tomorrow. When she reached her second-floor room, she bolted the door with a sigh of relief, and sat down to remove the prosthetic.

She massaged cold cream into the inflamed stump, and lay back on her bed, thinking about everything that had brought her to this point and, naturally enough, though she tried to avoid it, her thoughts went to Jowan. His face flickered behind her closed eyelids, reproachful, sad, but resigned to the truth; it was over. Bertie had no doubt there were plenty of women ready to step into the vacancy she had left, but would any of them bring him to life the way she had? She determinedly turned that thought on its head: was there anyone else out there who would do that for her? And if so, would they be just as unwilling as Jo to accept her choice when it came to children? Perhaps it was time to accept that extending the family line was going to be Ben's and Fiona's privilege, while Bertie forged ahead through life on her own. There were bleaker prospects, after all, and Bertie closed her eyes, feeling a new and exhilarating acceptance in her own destiny.

★ ★ ★

Fox Bay Hotel

Changeover day again, they seemed to come around so quickly these days. Helen helped Martin at reception, as usual, summoning and despatching bell boys with a look, answering queries, bidding farewell to regulars and greeting others, but her mind was almost entirely on the interview she'd had. Here they were, a week on from that frankly terrifying experience, and she hadn't heard anything yet.

She'd not been surprised to find the company she was applying to was Pagetts; the man had hotels all over the South West, after all. Judging by some paperwork she could see on the desk, the job she'd applied for was managership of the new build, currently going up on the outskirts of Truro: The Pearson, named after the architect of Truro Cathedral. She'd walked back that way after her interview, and spent some time before her train was due studying the work that was going on there. It was odd to think that this wood and stone skeleton would be home to thousands of people over the years to come, and that, if she were successful, she too would soon be cocooned behind walls that did not yet exist.

A clear, familiar voice cut through her thoughts. 'Helen, darling!'

She looked around to see her sister-in-law crossing the lobby, her arms outstretched for a perfunctory embrace and the usual kiss on each cheek. Helen

230

swallowed a groan, and wondered if David knew his wife was here; it had been almost a month since he'd arrived, and she didn't even know if he'd told Kay the truth yet about losing his job. She masked her guilt quite well, she thought, as she summoned a welcoming smile.

'How nice! What brings you down here on a Saturday? I thought you hated changeover day.'

'You needn't look so shifty,' Kay said briskly. 'I know he's here and not in the city, I checked. I was all but certain he was back with that Clare woman, so it was actually a relief to find that wasn't the case, even though he lied about where he was.'

'How did you know he was here though?' Helen moved Kay aside, out of the path of a bell boy with a teetering birdcage. 'Has he spoken to you?'

Kay shook her head. 'I guessed, as soon as I realised he wasn't in London. I have been reading his post though, and I know about his job.'

'Ah.'

'Why on earth didn't he *tell* me, Helen?' Kay looked and sounded unusually subdued now, and it gave Helen a bit of hope that things could be mended between her brother and his wife. She opened her mouth to say as much, but her attention was distracted by raised voices at the reception desk.

'I'm sorry, sir. We *are* fully booked, but we have a cancellation for Friday the twenty-first, if you'd like to reserve that room?' Martin had evidently said this several times already, judging by the strained patience in his voice, and Helen gave Kay an apologetic look and went to help.

'I'm sorry,' she said to the gentleman at the desk, who was glaring at poor Martin as if he'd personally

231

taken up every spare room in the place. 'We do get booked up very quickly I'm afraid.'

'And you are?' He looked away again, uninterested. 'Never mind. I'd like to speak to the manager.'

'That's me,' Helen said smoothly, used to this easy dismissal; he had the look of someone used to getting what he asked for. 'Our head receptionist is quite correct, but I can highly recommend the Summerleaze, in Bude. I have it on good authority from the manager there that they're not yet full.'

'And what makes this place so special anyway?'

Helen bit back the retort that he himself had been keen enough to stay. 'We had some illustrious guests recently,' she said instead, 'who have been kind enough to recommend us. Would you like me to call ahead to the Summerleaze for you?'

'Don't trouble yourself,' he said. 'I'm sure your man here can do that much, at least.'

'That man was on the same train as me,' Kay said, when Helen returned to her. 'Such a nice gentleman.' Her voice was low, and Helen sighed to see her looking at the man almost reverently. 'Quite handsome too, don't you think?'

'Not in the least.'

'I suppose your idea of handsome is all wrapped up in what Harry looked like,' Kay allowed. 'He was rather film star-ish, wasn't he?'

'He was, but film stars aren't my only *idea of handsome*, as you put it.' Helen blinked away the image of Alfie that rose in her mind. 'Anyway, about David.'

'Yes.' Kay glanced around. 'I'm sorry to see you're fully booked. I mean,' she added quickly, 'only for selfish reasons, of course. I suppose I shall have to go to the Summerleaze too, shall I?'

232

'Don't be silly. You must stay with David.' Helen raised her hand and a harried-looking bell boy appeared. 'Take Mrs Marlowe's bag to Mrs Fleur Fox's old room please.'

'I don't want to stay with —'

'Then yes, you'll have to go elsewhere,' Helen broke in. She would find out now, how serious this rift was. The boy hovered, one hand outstretched ready to pick up the bag, his eyes going from her to Kay and back again.

Kay looked over at the desk. 'I wonder if that gentleman would mind sharing a taxi?'

'Really?'

'I told you, David lied to me.'

'But if you didn't want to talk to him, why did you come down?'

'I do want to talk! I just don't . . . .' Kay dropped her voice to a harsh whisper as she saw heads turn towards them ' . . . I just don't want to share a room. Why is that so difficult to understand?'

Helen held up a hand. 'Alright! Let me think.' Kay drummed her fingers impatiently on her folded arms, and eventually Helen nodded. 'You can have Bertie's room for a few nights.'

'Oh! Has she started training already?'

'She left yesterday. You can have it until you sort out this nonsense with David.'

Kay nodded. 'That would be fine, I suppose. Though generally I don't like to be locked away —'

'In the attic,' Helen finished for her, suppressing a sigh at the familiar refrain, 'I know. Let me speak to the housekeeper then. Go through to the sitting room, and I'll send some tea in, I'll be there in a few minutes.' She turned to the hovering bell boy. 'Take

233

the bag to the sitting room for now, please.'

Kay followed the boy across the lobby, and Helen went back to the desk, where Martin had just completed the telephone call to the Summerleaze.

'They have a room waiting for you, sir,' he said to the waiting guest. 'Would you still like to take the cancellation here for the twenty-first?'

He admirably avoided pulling a face as Helen passed by, and she smiled at him and went through to the housekeeper's office. She'd normally be more than happy to help him and his reception staff on days like this, but she needed to find out what Kay intended to do. And, just as importantly, how long she planned to stay.

★ ★ ★

By the time she joined Kay in the sitting room, David had also found her. Helen walked in to see them standing at opposite ends of the room, glaring at one another like cornered cats, and she turned to leave again, but Kay stopped her.

'I gather you've offered to put him up until he's found a job in Plymouth?'

'If that's what he wants, yes.'

'And if he changes his mind?'

Helen raised an eyebrow. 'Or has it changed for him, you mean? In which direction might he do that?'

'Excuse me,' David interjected crossly, 'I'm over here, you know!'

'In the direction of . . . part-owning this place.' Kay raised her chin. 'We're going to offer to buy Adam's half.'

Helen sighed. 'We've had this conversation before.

234

Besides, the value of the hotel has gone up, so if you couldn't do it then, how could — '

'Compensation pay.'

David and Helen looked at one another, then back at Kay, and Helen could see her brother was bristling. This conversation was bound to end badly. 'Compensation for what?' Helen asked.

Kay ignored her husband's furious look. 'I told you, I've been reading his post.' She turned to David. 'It seems the War Office has offered you a sum of money for dispensing with your services. A compensation for losing your income through no fault of your own. It's a generous sum.'

'It won't be generous enough to buy half an hotel!' David pointed out. 'Anyway, how dare you open letters addressed to me? Particularly from the War Office!'

'And how dare you keep all this from *me*?' Kay's eyes were flashing now. Neither she nor David seemed to remember Helen was there, so she left them to it. Besides, she wasn't ready yet to try and explain that Adam was on the verge of signing over half his share to Hartcliffe, and she hadn't had time to come up with an excuse as to why. That was Adam's job, and he'd be back from Wales on Monday, to explain it himself.

She went back to her own office and picked up the pile of post on the end of her desk. Flipping through the envelopes, she recognised various postmarks and handwriting, and put them aside for attending to tomorrow, when things were less hectic, but she stopped as she found one with a Truro postmark. Considering she had a perfectly good job, and was still happy living at Fox Bay for now, the sudden lurch came as a surprise as she turned over the envelope

235

and slid her paper knife into the fold.

Dear Mrs Fox
Following your interview conducted
in our Truro offices on the 7th
inst, Pagetts are pleased to
confirm you were successful in your
application. The position will be
available to take up on Monday 1st
September.
Details and contract will follow.
Please sign and return one copy
before 31st March.

Helen stared at the few typed lines, feeling the foundations shifting beneath what had, until this moment, been a solid, settled life. She closed her eyes and pictured The Pearson, going up brick by brick, becoming something real even as she sat here wondering what life would be like working there. She blinked herself back to clarity; she would have to contact Pagetts and ask if accommodation was included, and how much rent she would have to pay, or if it would be included in her pay, or deducted from it . . . Or maybe all that would be set out in the contract. Should she wait and see? Should she tell the family before she knew the details? So much to think about.

She gave a little shiver as she pushed the letter back into the envelope. For the first time in her life she was considering leaving everything to do with her family behind; even the huge change moving here from Bristol hadn't been like this; she'd been moving to Harry's family home, and she'd had her children and Fleur with her. This was completely new, and she wondered if she was finally experiencing the same sense of excitement Leah felt when she set out to do something different.

The thought of no longer living minutes away from Alfie was both a relief and a source of sadness, even without his Christmas confession, and her belated realisation that he was the one man she knew she could be happy with. They'd shared so much together, and a warm friendship was the least of it. She closed her eyes, reliving the terrifying, heart-breaking, and physically exhausting morning they'd found Bertie by the river.

He hadn't flinched from the job, or from the screams that had echoed through the valley, both hers and Bertie's; later his unexpected appearance at the hospital, covered in Bertie's blood, had given her somewhere to weep out her fears away from the gazes of those who waited with her. He hadn't flinched at that, either. She should have realised then that he was special.

Lucky Beth. To have that smile turned on her, those arms around her, and that rare, but rich, laughter rolling around her home . . . Helen shook her head, and the image scattered; she'd had her allotted share of happiness, with Harry, and she shouldn't begrudge anyone else the same. But that didn't mean she wanted to be here to see it.

15

Mountain Ash, Wales
17th March

'Glad to be going home, by any chance?' Adam asked, amused, as Leah set her suitcase on the hall floor with a satisfied grunt. 'Or just glad to be finished packing?'

'Are you trying to say I brought too much with me?' Leah grinned and shoved the case towards him with her foot. 'Go and put that in the car before I change my mind.'

'As if you would!' Adam hefted the case and groaned. 'Dear god, woman, what have you got in here?'

'Stop griping!' Leah went to say goodbye to her aunt, and Adam picked up the case, which was actually quite light, and took it out to the car. It had been a surprisingly pleasant stay, and even sitting through an evening of parlour games with Bethan and Dewi Carter from next door hadn't been so bad; Leah had made it all much more bearable than he'd feared. But she was clearly beyond relieved to be setting off for Fox Bay this morning, and he knew she was already anticipating a nice long chat, over a couple of gin fizzes, with Helen this evening.

'We'll be off in a few minutes,' she called to her aunt, who he could see sitting at the kitchen table with her newspaper. 'Is there anything we can do for you before we go?'

Mary shook her head. 'It's a pity you couldn't stay longer,' she said, although Adam was quite sure it was

238

only politeness; Mary Clough made no bones about the fact that she preferred her own company, and, knowing Leah's restless spirit, Adam sometimes wondered how the three of them had lived together in harmony while Leah's mother had been alive.

'Well,' Leah said to her now, avoiding looking at Adam, 'that's nice of you to say, and we'd have liked to stay longer. Adam's got a lot to sort out at the hotel though, especially now Ben's left. And Helen could do with the help, too.'

Adam had successfully avoided thinking about Hartcliffe for a few hours, but Leah's words reminded him that time was running short; he'd need to get the paperwork signed over soon or Jeanette would begin pressuring him, and there was no knowing where that might lead.

'I'll come and see you off.' Mary closed the newspaper and followed Leah to the front door. 'Mind you don't — ' She stopped abruptly, and Adam followed her gaze to where a policeman was leaning his bicycle on the lamp post a few feet up the road. He looked terribly young, and clearly not sure which of the women he should be addressing, so he spoke to both of them at the same time, his nervous gaze flicking between them.

'Am I at the home of Mrs Gregory Marshall?' he asked.

'Yes,' Mary said, gesturing to Leah, who had gone white. 'My niece.'

'How can I help you?' Leah asked in a thin voice. 'I haven't seen Gly . . . Gregory, for a while now.'

Adam closed the car door and moved closer, his own blood running a little chilly. If Marshall had been arrested after all, and dragged Leah's name into it . . .

239

'I'm sorry to say, Mrs Marshall, that we have reason to believe your husband has been killed.'

Leah flinched, and, through his own shock, Adam saw her sway. Her aunt's hand curled firmly around her forearm, keeping her steady.

'Killed?' Mary said, when it was clear Leah couldn't speak. 'What do you mean? By a car? Or by . . . other means?'

'A train accident.' The policeman seemed on more familiar ground now he was able to concentrate on the details, instead of the woman to whom he was delivering the worst possible news. 'A body was recovered from the track just outside Cardiff. We think he'd fallen asleep drunk, under the bridge, and rolled onto the track. We have the driving licence from his jacket, and that's how we found your address, but . . . .' He faltered again, and looked at the ground. 'We need you to come and formally identify him if you can.'

'Christ!' Adam stepped forward now, pushing past him to stand at Leah's other side. 'You can't ask her to do that, it's inhuman!'

'Mrs Marshall?' the constable prompted, ignoring Adam's outburst. 'Would you be able to spare the time?'

'What happens if I don't want to?' she asked in a thin voice.

'Then we'd have to track down another family member, which might take a while.'

'There isn't anyone,' Leah said. 'His parents are dead, and his brother was killed in the war. He hasn't seen any of his other family since he moved up here when he was fourteen.'

'You still shouldn't have to,' Adam said, 'it might be truly awful.'

240

'I've seen some truly awful things as a nurse,' she reminded him gently. 'I was at clearing stations as well as in nice clean hospitals.'

'That's different, and you know it. This is your husband.' Adam wanted to bite the words back, as she flinched again. 'I'm sorry, but you're not thinking straight.'

'The injury that killed him was to his legs, if that helps,' the constable said. 'Mr Marshall's face is a bit bruised, but anyone who knew him would be able to identify him. So, will you do it?' He sounded a little impatient now. 'I can arrange for someone to take you down.'

'Can't she do it by just telling you about some marking on the body?' Adam asked. 'We're just about to leave for —'

'I'll do it,' Leah said quickly, drawing herself upright, and he understood what had pushed the decision; the last thing they wanted was for any of Glynn's dealings to be linked to either her or Fox Bay. 'Where do I go?'

'Cardiff Royal Infirmary, on Glossop Road,' the policeman said. 'Shall I arrange a car for you?'

'I'll take her.' Adam was still angry and didn't try to hide it. 'Who do we ask for?'

'Go to reception and give your name, there'll be someone waiting for you.' The constable shuffled his feet. 'I'm sorry for your loss, Mrs Marshall, and to be asking this of you on top of it all.'

Leah blindly groped for Adam's hand, and nodded. She didn't speak until the policeman had retrieved his bicycle, then she turned to her aunt. 'I'll come back after. We can travel down tonight instead, can't we, Adam?'

His heart sank, but he nodded. 'Of course.' He

guided Leah to the car, and helped her in, then raised his hand to Mary. 'We'll telephone the Carters if we're delayed too long.'

'I wish she'd get a telephone,' Leah said, as they set off. 'I'd rather not have Dewi or Bethan hovering over her while we share our business. Especially this.'

'I suppose they knew Glynn quite well too.'

She shook her head. 'I can't understand it,' she said. 'Why would he be sheltering under a railway bridge? And drunk? That's not like him. At all,' she added, in a suspicious voice.

He gave her a sidelong look, and noticed she was sitting very upright, still pale, but focused now. 'Do you think someone killed him, and made it look like an accident?'

'I don't know.' Leah closed her eyes, and Adam shifted his attention back to the road.

'It's possible,' he said hesitantly, 'given the circles he moves in.'

'Yes.' A silence fell over them, and they had gone as far as Pontypridd before Leah spoke again. 'Maybe Wilf named Neville to the police, and blamed Glynn for it, and Neville has taken his revenge. God, poor Glynn.'

'Darling, I'm so, so sorry. He didn't deserve this.'

'He was a rogue, but he never deliberately hurt anyone.' Leah took out her handkerchief and dabbed at the mascara streaked beneath her eyes. 'I never liked Wilf, but this? Hateful.'

'We don't know for sure that's what happened.'

'No, but he was the one who dragged Glynn into all this, and then left him to fight his way out.'

'Glynn had you to help him,' Adam said softly. 'He was lucky.'

242

'Only because you and Sam found out what a lying beast Wilf is, and then came all that way to tell me.'

'We did it for you, not him, I can't pretend otherwise.'

'Well you still helped him.' She pushed the handkerchief up her sleeve. 'Can we go any faster? I just want this over with. I feel sick.'

★ ★ ★

Inside the hospital Adam watched Leah carefully as she gave her name at the desk, noting the pinched expression and haunted eyes. She might have been separated from Glynn, and horrified at the thought that he was out of prison early, but he wasn't foolish enough to believe they hadn't become close again during the time they'd spent together. How close he didn't know, and never intended to ask.

'Mrs Marshall?' A police officer approached them, looking professionally sympathetic. 'Are you ready to follow me?'

'Should I come too?' Adam was looking at Leah as he asked, but the officer answered.

'If you like, but you'll have to wait outside the . . . the room.' Adam was glad he hadn't said the word *mortuary*, but knew they had both heard it, nevertheless.

Leah slipped her hand into his. It felt cold, so he covered it with his other hand and gave her a faint smile of encouragement. 'I'm here,' he murmured, not at all sure it was the right thing to say, but he felt he should say something at least. It seemed to work, and she walked steadily at his side as they followed the officer down the corridor.

The mortuary attendant who met them was distantly polite as he gestured for Adam to take a seat, then led Leah into the room adjacent. Adam couldn't sit still, however, and stood near the door with his arms folded.

'She and the deceased still close, then?' the police officer asked, seemingly only out of the wish to make conversation, but Adam was on his guard just in case.

'They've been separated for years,' he said, 'but they do have a lot of history together.'

'Ex-con, so I gather?'

'That's why they separated, yes.'

'And you are . . . . ?'

'A friend,' Adam said firmly. 'Can you tell me a bit more about how this happened?'

'Sorry, sir, I think you know more than I do anyway. I was just asked to come here to meet Mrs Marshall and record the identification.'

'Is she going to find it difficult in there?'

Before the officer could reply, the door opened and Leah came out, red-eyed and with the back of her hand pressed to her mouth. She cast a distraught look at Adam, and he moved quickly to put his arms around her.

'Mrs Marshall?' the policeman said, after a moment. 'Have you positively identified the body as that of Mr Gregory Marshall?'

Adam felt her nodding against his shoulder, and his heart ached for her. She pulled away from him and wiped a finger beneath her eyes, making an effort to sound clear and calm.

'Yes, that's my estranged husband.' She looked at Adam, her eyes brimming again. 'I didn't think it would affect me like this,' she confessed, 'not the way things were. But — '

'It's understandable,' the officer said. He looked unsure what to say next, but the mortuary attendant, clearly used to moments like this, passed Leah a facial tissue from a silver dispenser on the table. She pressed it to her eyes, and Adam saw her fingers were shaking.

'Am I allowed to leave now?' she asked at length, wiping her eyes again.

'Of course.' The officer noted the time in his book, and passed it to Leah, who signed it. 'Thank you for coming all this way, Mrs Marshall. Oh, before you go, these are his effects. Not that there's much there.' He handed Leah a small cardboard box, and she gave him a distracted, watery smile, then turned to Adam.

'Can we go? I hate the smell here.'

They walked back to his car in silence, Leah clutching the box tightly, and Adam wished he could think of something to say but he sensed she didn't want to talk. It was understandable, she had a lot to think about, and a lot of old memories to sift through, both good and bad. The long drive back to Cornwall would be a good time for her to do that, and he was glad they were returning tonight; she would be able to talk to Helen in a way she might not be able to with him. Helen had experienced the loss of her husband, after all, even if the circumstances were nothing alike.

He helped Leah into her seat, and was crossing the front of the car to climb into the driver's side, when he realised he hadn't checked the faulty headlights recently. He looked up at the sky, and had only just begun to mentally check off the hours before he accepted, with weary annoyance, that it would be dark long before they arrived back at Fox Bay.

'I think it might be a bit of a risk driving back

tonight,' he said, settling into his seat. 'I'm so sorry, would you mind spending one more night at your aunt's house? I hadn't reckoned on coming to Cardiff today, and even if we start back now we won't make it before it gets dark. I just don't trust these lights.'

Leah sighed. 'I can't believe you've not taken it to be properly fixed. It's been ages.'

'I know, I'm sorry. I just keep putting it off, and then they'll be okay for a while so I don't even think about it. But I'd rather make the drive in full daylight, just to be on the safe side.'

'Alright.'

'It will give you a chance to talk to your aunt about Glynn,' he added. 'That might help you both.'

'I don't really need to talk to her about him.'

'Oh? From what you say, she and Glynn rubbed along quite well.'

'So they did.' Leah turned to him, and now there was no sign of tears. 'But that wasn't him.'

For a moment Adam just looked at her, uncomprehending. 'What?' he managed at last.

'The man they pulled off the tracks wasn't Glynn,' she repeated. 'I knew it even before I saw his face. They leave a hand out of the covers, see, so people can at least hold it even if they oughtn't to look, so I knew before they pulled back the sheet. No scar.' She indicated her right wrist. 'When we met, it was because he'd nearly torn his hand off on a swinging chain at the Alexandra docks, and I was the one who bandaged him up. It was just lucky they left his right hand out. It meant there was no surprise when I saw him, so I was all ready to put on the act.'

'Act?'

'I made them pass me a tissue too, when I already

246

had a handkerchief up my sleeve,' she reminded him. 'They'll remember my reaction a little bit better for that, if they ever have cause to.'

He let out a bellow of laughter. 'You absolute fraud! You had me well and truly fooled!' He was momentarily lost in admiration, then frowned. 'But . . . why pretend it was him anyway?'

A tiny smile finally touched Leah's lips, but there was no humour in it, just relief. 'If Gregory Marshall's officially dead, he's as safe as he could possibly be. The police won't be looking for him, and he can go to America, just like he wanted.'

He nodded, feeling silly for not realising, then studied her more closely. 'There's something else, isn't there? Come on.'

'It was Wilf Stanley on that table,' she said. 'Otherwise known as the snitch, Mr Freeman.'

'So . . . you think Neville tracked him down and killed him, after you told him that?'

Leah's smile faded. 'I couldn't have known that would happen. He was supposed to be being protected by the police.'

'I'm sorry, that was crass,' Adam said, putting his hand over hers. 'No one could blame this on you. You had to do whatever you could to protect yourself and Glynn, and this Wilf character was playing a game even more dangerous than you two.'

Leah opened the box and peered into it, and her eyes narrowed. 'This pocket watch,' she said, drawing it out by the chain. 'I think it belongs to Jory Nancarrow.'

Adam blinked. 'How on earth did Wilf get *that*?'

'He must have stolen it from Glynn, when he took Glynn's driving licence.'

247

'And how did Glynn . . . Ah, he stole it from Jory, when he mugged him after that card game.' Adam shook his head. 'What a mess.'

'Another good thing's come of that mess though, we can return Jory's property.' Leah looked back towards the hospital, where Wilf's body lay awaiting the mortician's blades. 'All I have to do now is make sure Glynn stays dead.'

★ ★ ★

The Summerleaze Hotel, Bude

Helen had been to this hotel before, several times, but today she looked at it with different eyes, comparing Ben's new home to the one he'd left. In contrast with Fox Bay's ecclesiastical high ceilings and arched doorways, the Summerleaze was purpose-built, with economy of space very much the architect's watchwords. But still there was no denying the expensive atmosphere and air of exclusivity as she walked in.

The lobby was large, but the ceiling was noticeably low, the windows were small too, and uplighters reflecting off the many mirrored surfaces provided most of the light. There were none of the intriguing little corridors leading away to rooms where monks had once stood for hours at a time, illuminating countless texts throughout the centuries. Taking a wrong turn at this hotel could never be mistaken for wanting to explore a building rich in history and tradition; you'd just end up looking silly. Helen stopped that train of thought; it was hardly the right time to be thinking about Fox Bay with fondness, now she was planning to move away from it, and in any case The Pearson, as a new build, was likely to be as featureless as this place. She'd better start liking it.

She crossed to the reception desk, which was small, round and high, and topped with black marble, and where a tall young man was skimming down the pages of a ledger. 'Good morning, I'm here to see the manager.'

'Is he expecting you?'

'No, I just wanted to — '

'He's a very busy man, Mrs . . . .?'

'Fox,' Helen supplied, amused by the flush that touched the young man's cheeks, but feeling a little sorry for him all the same. 'Ben is my son.'

'Of course, Mrs Fox. Would you like to take a seat while you wait?'

Helen looked around at the few elegant, but uncomfortable-looking seats, and nodded. 'Thank you.'

The seats weren't as hard as they looked, but weren't a patch on Fox Bay's deep, luxurious chairs . . . Helen gave herself another mental shake, and allowed maternal pride to overtake her personal taste. Square and modern it might be, but the Summerleaze had already built a reputation as one of the finest in North Cornwall. Ben had done well.

'Mrs Fox?' The receptionist appeared at her side, almost putting Guy to shame with his ability to materialise from nowhere. 'The manager's office is just on the right, there.'

Helen thanked him, and presented herself at the door labelled, *Mr. B. Fox. General Manager.* Unable to decide whether to knock or go straight in, she did both, and her heart lifted to see her boy, sitting behind his desk as if he'd been born there.

'I hope you don't mind me dropping in,' she began,

feeling an odd kind of hesitancy for the first time, but it disappeared as he rose and came around to draw her into a tight hug.

'Never! It's so good to see you.' It had only been two weeks, but he already seemed separate from her now, and although she ached a little, she told herself it was altogether right that he should. But when they drew apart he was Ben again, youthful and smiling.

'How are things going?' Helen asked sitting down. 'All settled?'

'Brilliantly, thanks. Are you staying long enough for a cuppa?'

'If you've got time.'

'Stop it! I'll make time.' Ben picked up his telephone and called for a tea tray, and sat back in his chair, eyeing Helen with a quizzical look. 'You've got something to tell me.'

'Have I?'

'You know you have.' Ben frowned. 'Are you ill?'

'No!' Helen gave a little laugh. 'Why are you so sure it's something bad?'

'Because you don't look particularly happy.'

'Don't I?'

'Enough questions!' Ben smiled faintly. 'You're going to make me drag it out of you, aren't you?'

'No.' Helen sighed. 'You're right. The thing is, I have to tell you something about when you come into your inheritance.'

Ben's smile froze. 'Is the hotel in trouble again?'

'Far from it. Daisy and Freddie did us an enormous favour there.'

'Then what?' Ben broke off, as a uniformed maid brought in a tray and left it on the desk with a curious glance at Helen. When she'd gone he leaned forward, but didn't pour the tea. 'What's happened?'

'It's Adam.' Helen told him what had happened with Jeanette and Hartcliffe. 'Your uncle David and Aunt Kay are talking about buying his remaining share,' she finished. 'They don't know yet that it's only a quarter, but he'll probably sell it to them anyway and move somewhere with Leah.'

'Trust Adam!' Ben groaned. 'What on earth is it about him? How does he manage to get himself into this kind of mess?'

'Well he's getting himself out of it now, at least. I'm just glad it hasn't affected my share too, so your inheritance is still safe.'

'It would have been fun sharing ownership with him . . . though not for ages yet,' Ben added hurriedly.

'Ages,' Helen agreed, and smiled, keeping the other news to herself; she didn't want to burden him with another choice just yet, he was too fresh in this new job. She was still certain that Guy would fill the manager's role admirably until Ben was ready. If he ever was, now things had changed this much. He might choose to sell his half too, when the time came. 'Anyway,' she said, reaching forward to lift the teapot, 'I just thought you ought to know, and now you do. Let's change the subject, shall we? Tell me about Daisy.'

Ben's face softened. 'She's absolutely wonderful,' he said, taking the cup she passed him. 'Just the sweetest thing.'

Helen laughed. 'We know that! Tell me how you and she are getting along. Does she visit you here?'

'No fear,' Ben said, automatically lowering his voice, and looking at the door. 'Lily would go absolutely off her head if she did.'

'Oh dear, does she still think you and she are an

item? You ought not —'

'Don't you start,' Ben grumbled, stirring sugar into his tea far too vigorously. 'Bertie gave me a proper talking to about that. It's just hard when we work together and I'm so new. I need her to be on my side for the time being.'

'That's a dangerous game,' Helen observed, and held up a hand as he gave her a look. 'Alright, to change the subject again, are you managing to take lots of photographs for your hotel magazine?'

Ben's smile returned. 'Loads. I've got a special room set up for developing them. Would you like to see?'

'I'd love to!'

Helen followed him up a flight of stairs to where a small room at the end of one of the identical corridors had been fitted with a padlock. Ben produced a key and let them in.

'This used to be a storeroom for soaps and suchlike, but they've got a much bigger one now, so Lily says this one's fine for me to use. It's not huge, but big enough for what I need.'

He proudly showed her the trays in which he'd suspended the negatives. 'The gelatine silver process,' he said, 'and if I use glossy paper I can get some lovely clear images. Look.'

He unclipped one from the row hanging above the trays and tilted it so she could see it more clearly. A laughing duo, Leah and Daisy looked like best friends as they posed together in front of the fireplace at Orchard Cottage. Both messy, but somehow still glamorous, Helen couldn't help the little twinge of envy at the effortless elegance of them both.

'This is wonderful,' she enthused, hiding it well, as always. 'If you took some like this of Lily she'd be very

252

happy, I'm sure. Is she keen on the idea of a magazine?'

'She already has a name for it,' Ben said. '*The Summerleaze Siren.*'

'Is that her, or the magazine?' Helen quipped, surprising Ben into a laugh as he pegged the picture back up.

'I can tell Leah's back again, you're always different when she's around.'

'Well she's still in Wales at the moment,' Helen said, 'so I've no one to blame but myself for that one.'

'Shame on you then,' Ben said, still grinning. 'Anyway, not a word to Lily about Daisy, alright? At least until after the awards, when the studio's in a better financial state. She knows Daisy's around, but just assumes she's on holiday.'

'I was going to suggest you ask her to write something for this magazine,' Helen said. 'Lily can't object to that, surely? It would be quite a coup for the hotel, and Daisy can still keep up the pretence of being here temporarily.'

'That's an idea.' Ben led the way back to his office. 'In the meantime, how's everything at home?'

'You still think of it as home then?'

'It'll always be home,' Ben said, to Helen's relief. 'This is just live-in accommodation. How's Fi doing?'

'Delighted to have Daisy nearby of course, and getting along very well with Constable Quick's son. The lad from the lifeboat.'

'Good. I know she misses that Amy girl, though goodness only knows why, the little wretch.'

'Don't be mean, love. Amy was devastated about what happened to Daisy. She was in a difficult situation.'

253

'And she put everyone else in a worse one,' Ben pointed out. 'I don't think Danny Quick likes her much either.'

'No, he doesn't, but you know Fiona, she won't let him stop her spending time with Amy when she comes back.' Helen finished her tea, sensing Ben's attention wandering back to the paperwork on his desk. She knew how that felt. 'Right, Guy will be waiting with the car, so I'd better hurry along. It's so good to see you, darling. Come over when you have a day off.'

After securing his promise to do so, Helen left him to his work and as she passed through reception on her way to the door she looked back to see Lily Trevanion already walking towards Ben's office. She had clearly been waiting for Helen to leave, and she raised a hand and smiled, but there was something lurking beneath that smile, something proprietorial that called the silent warning: *you had your time with him, now he's mine.*

Helen returned the wave, and gave Lily her most dazzling smile, before pushing her way out through the hotel door. *Good luck with that one, Benjamin.*

16

Caernoweth Air Base

Bertie pushed open the door of the classroom, feeling very much the new girl despite it being everyone's first day of training. It had taken her longer than she'd anticipated to get from the flats to the airfield, which had seemed so close when she'd looked out of the window, and the others, who were presumably all sleeping in the dorms, were already at their desks. Bertie avoided looking at anyone directly, and slipped into a seat at the back.

'Miss Fox, I presume?' The instructor, a beefy man who looked to be in his mid-fifties or so, checked the list in front of him. 'Session began ten minutes ago.'

'I'm sorry,' Bertie stammered, 'I'm not staying on the base, and — '

'You're paying for this,' he said dismissively, 'so you're only cheating yourself.'

Bertie's face flamed, and she looked down at the clean sheet of paper on her desk. But the instructor was right; it would be one thing if she'd been part of the military school, but she *was* paying for this course, thanks to Stan Houghton finally agreeing to buy back the Squirrel, and paying handsomely for it. All the more reason to ensure she got her money's worth.

'Now the introductions are over,' the instructor said, 'it's time for a lesson in what you're not.'

With all eyes safely on the instructor again, Bertie raised her own to look around the room. There

255

were around fifteen trainees, and the only other two women had, naturally enough, already gravitated to one another, and sat three rows in front. One had dead straight strawberry-blonde hair, the other's was dark as jet, but that was as much as Bertie could see, and since she had missed the introductions, she would have to wait until later to find out which one was Harry Batten's childhood friend.

Most of the other trainees were little more than boys. The eldest looked around her own age, thin, intense, his eyes never leaving the instructor, who was getting back into his stride.

'You look out of the window today, and you see your planes waiting for you. You will learn to maintain them, and to care for them. They are yours while you are here, starting from today. However, you are *not* pilots.' He turned to the chalk board, and Bertie noticed the name already printed there, and underlined twice, as if he had emphasised it as he'd introduced himself. There was even a thick, crumbling full stop beside the underline. Flt. Lt. Bowden. So he was from the military school, then. She should have guessed.

'You are, what I like to call,' Bowden said, printing the word in capitals, and sending a cloud of chalk dust flying with every tap on the board, 'ostriches.'

A murmur ran around the room as the trainees looked at one another, eyebrows raised. Bowden seemed to expect this, and enjoyed his moment before pronouncing, with evident satisfaction, 'You have wings, but you cannot fly.'

The murmur turned into a faintly sycophantic chuckle, and Bertie couldn't help smiling too. Bowden began writing on the board the things they would learn, and in which order. Flying came low on a dauntingly long list, and as the flight lieutenant kept writing, Bertie's gaze wandered to the window and to the sky beyond it. The clouds were light today, drifting along in a fairly snappy late spring breeze, and she found herself wishing she could step outside this stuffy room, just for a moment, and feel that breeze on her skin.

'Take down the list,' Bowden ordered, and as the trainees obediently picked up their pens and began to write, Bertie noted that the second lesson was cloud recognition, and had to suppress a grin as she wondered what the instructor would make of her calling them *little fluffies*.

'Some of you will be taking up your military flight training in due course,' Bowden said, when most of the scratching of pens on paper had stopped, and faces were once more turned expectantly to him. 'A handful,' his gaze flickered over the three women, 'will be going down the civilian route. For now though, you'll all undertake the same ground training. I'm going to introduce you to your flight instructors this afternoon, as a courtesy, but I've no doubt some of you won't even get off the ground. As you've seen, there is much with which you must familiarise yourselves first, and you must pass *all* the tests before you'll be permitted to begin flight training.'

The lesson progressed, a litany of housekeeping and warnings, no doubt designed to weed out those without the necessary ambition to take their training seriously. Soon Bertie's paper was full of scribbled notes as she tried to take absolutely everything down, certain she'd miss the one bit of information that would prove vital at some point. Before she realised it, lunchtime had crept up on them, and they were directed to the canteen in the main building.

With her tray of soup in hand, Bertie was glad to see her fellow female trainees sitting at a four-seater table with two spare seats. She approached them a little warily; although she had been around other people almost constantly, this was the first time she had actively tried to befriend anyone since joining the telephone exchange three years ago. She would have given anything to have had Lynette at her side.

'May I sit here?' she asked, hoping the pleading sound was only in her head.

'Oh, hello. Yes, of course.' The blonde girl moved her cup out of the way and patted the table. 'There you go.'

She had a strong Cornish accent, and a round, friendly face with wide blue eyes and a squashy-looking nose. Something about her was instantly appealing, and Bertie gave her a grateful smile and sat down.

'I'm Bertie Fox. Roberta,' she clarified, seeing the girls' surprised looks.

'I'm Tory Gilbert,' the girl said, thrusting her hand across the table. 'This here's Gwenna . . . what was it again?'

'Rosdew.'

'Nice to meet you, Tory.' Bertie shook the hand, then turned to Gwenna beside her. 'You too.'

The girl nodded. 'Likewise.' Her tone was cooler than Tory's, but Bertie persisted.

'Gwenna's a nice name. Cornish or Welsh?'

Gwenna looked as if she'd asked the question in Greek, then blinked slowly. 'I was born in St Austell, what do you think?'

258

'Oh, I'm sorry,' Bertie fired back, nettled, 'I must have dozed off at the bit where you told me where you were born.' She met Tory's eye across the table and saw the girl was struggling to hold in her laughter, and forced a conciliatory note into her voice. 'I do like St Austell.'

'It's nice enough. What about you?' Gwenna asked, though she couldn't have sounded less interested.

'Bristol, originally,' Bertie said. 'But I've lived at Trethkellis for ten years now. My family owns Fox Bay Hotel.' She'd hoped for a sign of recognition at that, but there was no response at all from Gwenna, so she turned to the friendlier girl again. 'I understand we have a mutual friend. The chef at the Cliffside Fort.'

'Oh, Harry!' Tory beamed. 'Yes, we've been friends since school. Real name's Henry. He was a proper tearaway, considering who his family is.'

'What family?' Gwenna asked, looking interested at last.

'The Battens, from Pencarrack House.'

'The place that caught fire?' Gwenna looked impressed for the first time. 'Lucy Kempton's family?'

'That's them. They built that hotel out of the ruins of the fort. Harry's bored though, wants to move on.'

'He said you had a little gang,' Bertie said. 'Sounds fun.'

Tory helped herself to more bread. 'He was always winning marbles off me and Bobby Gale, the sly little weasel.' She sounded more affectionate than disapproving, and Bertie felt a pang of envy for their easy friendship. She began to understand Fiona's keenness to keep on the good side of the stowaway Amy, and it occurred to her, with a sort of vague regret, that none of the Fox siblings had really belonged to a group of friends since Bristol.

'We used to knock about all the time,' Tory went on, 'though his mum didn't approve. Once, we actually thought we'd killed someone.' Encouraged by Bertie's wide-eyed look she continued, 'Bloke was riding his horse along the path at the back of Pencarrack, and us lot were messing about in the gardens. We jumped out at him, his horse went up, and he went flying. Blimey, we were all convinced he was a goner! If he'd gone into the valley he'd have — '

'Why do you want to learn to fly?' Gwenna asked Bertie, clearly bored by Tory's chatter.

Bertie hesitated. 'That's rather hard to answer, just like that.'

'No it's not.'

'It is for me.' Bertie found her exasperation mounting again. 'What about you, then?'

'I want to fly fighter planes.'

Tory snorted. 'The war's finished. Besides, the WRAF's been disbanded for years now.'

Gwenna shrugged and poured water from the jug into her glass. 'Anyone else?' she offered, and both Bertie and Tory pushed their glasses forward; the heat from the classroom was clinging to them all, it seemed.

'Does your fiancé know you want to fly fighters?' Tory directed the question at Gwenna, a reminder that the two of them had already had the chance to talk in some depth while staying in the dorm together.

'Of course not. You know what men are like.' Gwenna looked at Bertie, one eyebrow raised. 'How about you, do you have a boyfriend?'

'I was engaged, but we've broken it off.' It was a surprisingly difficult thing to say, despite having had

260

more than two weeks to get used to the idea. 'He wasn't keen on me doing this,' she confessed, 'but I think he'd have got used to it. We actually broke up because of something else.'

'Eat up,' Tory urged her. 'You missed it at the start, where Bowden said that anyone who's late back from lunch will be refused admission to the afternoon session.'

'Well he might have reiterated that!' Bertie spooned her soup up faster, and fell to listening to the rumble of conversation around her instead of talking. The overwhelming tone was excitement and laughter, and Bertie began to relax for the first time since her arrival. Everyone was in the same situation here, all learning together from the start, and she had as much chance of making it through the training as any of them. It wasn't until she rose to leave, with the others, that she remembered she was different, after all.

'Leg gone to sleep?' Tory joked, as Bertie's right side suddenly dipped and she caught the back of her chair. 'Guarantee our bums will do the same before they let us out again!'

It was on the tip of Bertie's tongue to correct her, but she clamped her lips over the words before they could escape. This feeling of equality and acceptance was too precious to throw away just yet, and despite discovering the advantages of taking a dorm bed, she was glad now that she had chosen not to.

'Pins and needles,' she agreed instead, and focused hard on making her walk as smooth and natural as she could, as she fell in with the others on their way back to the classroom. It was easier in a crowd, and she knew she could stave off the inevitable for a while longer, at least.

261

This time she took a seat next to Tory, and the afternoon passed in an intense but pleasant blur of diagrams and equations, and grainy photographs of altimeters, pulsometers and inclinometers.

'You'll have plenty of hours dedicated to learning these instruments,' Bowden told them, 'but it can't hurt to get a picture of them in your heads in the meantime, so feast your eyes, ostriches.'

Mid-afternoon, Bowden told them all to rise to greet their instructors, who, he was at pains to point out, would be treated with the utmost respect at all times, and woe betide anyone who failed to pay attention to their lessons. To Bertie's disappointment the seven experienced pilots merely entered in a line and were introduced by name, but no one found out who would be assigned to whom. Gwenna made a small sound of frustration, presumably she'd hoped for the same.

She found herself hoping she would draw the oldest-looking man at the tail end of the line; he looked calm and friendly, and more likely to have the most hours under his belt. The other six men eyed the room with frank curiosity, but he just smiled at the floor as if he were ready to take anyone Bowden cared to throw his way.

'You may sit,' Bowden said, once the instructors had trooped out again. 'Some of you are already paired with your instructors, the rest will be assigned at the end of your first week, when I have the measure of you all.'

By five o'clock Bertie was wilting in the heat, and, as Tory had predicted, her behind and lower back twinged and ached. The scrape of chairs was almost drowned out by the groans of relief as everyone rose to leave, and Bertie couldn't help grinning in sympathy at their shared misery.

'Come for a drink?' Tory asked, appearing at her side. 'Be nice to stretch our muscles after all that sitting.'

'Where is there to go?' Bertie hadn't seen a pub nearby, but the idea of having a drink and cementing a possible friendship was certainly appealing. 'Not the Fort, surely?'

'God no! Far too pricey. The Tinner's, in town, is small but really nice.'

'It's a bit of a long way, isn't it?' Gwenna said doubtfully.

'Only twenty minutes there, though bit longer back as it's mostly uphill.' Tory turned to Bertie. 'A bit less for you, though, since you're at the flats. What do you say?'

Bertie was at a loss; she didn't want to look stand-offish, but she knew she'd never manage to walk all the way into town without alerting them to her prosthetic leg. She'd planned on seeing them off with a friendly wave, and making her own solitary, stiff-legged way back to the flats — at least she'd have had one day of relative normality.

'I'm going to have a look around,' she said at length, 'I'll catch you up later.' She could always claim a headache had descended and forced her to return home instead.

'A look around?' Tory shook her head. 'I have the feeling we're all going to be sick of the sight of this place before too long, why spend your first evening poking around it?'

'I . . . I had a good friend who trained here during the last intake,' Bertie said. 'He only died a few weeks

263

ago, and I think I'd like to be alone here for a while.' As she spoke she recognised the truth of it; remembering that last day she had spent here with Xander might go some way towards helping her say goodbye to him properly.

'Last intake?' Tory frowned suddenly. 'You don't mean that poor lad who went into the sea on his first flight?'

Bertie knew the rush of raw pain was showing on her face, because Tory paled. 'I'm so sorry, Bertie! I didn't mean to say it so harshly. We were all shocked, it was so sad.'

'Xander was one of my best friends,' Bertie said. 'Look, I don't want to bring down the mood. You go on. I might . . . I might just go to bed early after all, if that's alright.' It wasn't an excuse anymore, she no longer felt like celebrating the end of her first day, and both her legs were aching for different reasons.

'Of course. What about you?' Tory looked at Gwenna, who looked uncomfortable, but shrugged.

'I'll come.'

Bertie watched them go, torn between envy that the two girls would have even more time to build their friendship, and relief that she wouldn't have to lie about her plans after all, but neither would her secret need to come to light today. When the new recruits and trainees had melted away, to the hotel or the pub, or maybe to the canteen, she made her way out to the airfield.

Most of the aircraft were housed in the hangars, and she remembered her first sight of those huge buildings with the arched roofs. She looked over at one of them now, recognising the Type 76 Jupiter she'd been told Xander would be flying. The outlines of the planes

264

suddenly seemed daunting rather than fascinating, as she wondered what it would be like to lose control of one, and to know there was no way of getting it back. She closed her eyes, imagining the stuttering throb of the engine, almost hearing it, and feeling the tip and tilt of an aircraft caught in a spiral.

'Can I help you?'

She opened her eyes and turned to see a familiar face at her shoulder. She couldn't put a name to it, but the young man's serious face broke into a smile and he stuck out his hand. 'Hello again. Bertie, isn't it? Tommy Ash. We met when . . . .' He trailed away, and his smile faded. 'Xander talked about you all the time, you know.'

'Tommy,' Bertie repeated, shaking his hand. 'Of course.'

'So, your training started then?' Tommy asked. His gaze dropped to her boots, and he smiled again. 'Look at that! You'd never know.'

'Not until I walk,' Bertie allowed. 'I'm a bit worried about using the rudder pedal bar, if I'm honest. I gave up riding because of the lack of sensation, but now I'm not so sure this is going to be any better.'

'No comparison,' Tommy said cheerfully. 'You'll be fine. You don't need anything like the level of feeling to use the bar as you do to support yourself in a slide.'

'You sound as if you know a bit about it.'

He grinned. 'I've done my share of sliding,' he confessed.

'What can you tell me about . . . what happened to him?'

Tommy walked with her into the hangar. 'He wasn't even supposed to be flying,' he said, and when Bertie looked startled, he gave a short laugh. 'Come on,

265

you've been told how long the ground training is, didn't you think it was a bit soon?'

'I do now, but back then I didn't know how long it all takes.'

'You saw Xander race, didn't you?'

'Only once.'

'Then you'll know he was competent, but that what got him through more than anything was his total lack of fear. It was the same here. Still, it'd only been a month or so, and Singleton, his instructor, said it was too soon to take the Camel out since it can be a bit of a bugger for new pilots.'

'I'm surprised Xander wasn't able to talk his way into it anyway,' Bertie said, with a wry little smile. 'Go on.'

'Singleton had to go back to Leeds for a family emergency, so Dennis Haydock took over Xander's lessons for the week, and you were right, Xander persuaded Den to take him out. He told Haydock that Singleton had been planning it.'

Bertie found the words, *typical Xander*, trying to get out, but bit them back, feeling disloyal.

Tommy seemed to hear them anyway, and his faint smile made her feel a bit better. 'Word is, the plane developed a fuel blockage,' he said, 'and they couldn't get back to shore to make a forced landing. It's dual control, and we can assume Haydock took them back at the first sign of danger, but we'll never know who was actually flying the plane at the time.'

'It's awful,' Bertie murmured. 'Not just because he was such a good friend, but the whole tragic thing. Poor Xander, and poor Haydock.'

'And poor Singleton,' Tommy added. 'The guilt was the least of it.'

266

'Why guilt?'

'Xander's impatience was what led to this whole thing, and Flight Trainer Singleton is the strictest instructor we have. Most of the other lads were at least taken up for a taster, but Singleton wouldn't allow even that.'

'It must be awful to shoulder the blame like that when it's not your fault,' Bertie said. 'We were introduced to the instructors this afternoon, but only as a group. We didn't find out who was who.'

'Well you could do a lot worse than draw Jude Singleton as your instructor,' Tommy said. 'Xander was lucky in that respect, despite not being allowed near the sky. Singleton's the real thing.'

Bertie wondered if he was the solid-looking older man on the end of the row. 'But if that was what pushed Xander to lie to this Haydock bloke,' she said, 'I'm not sure I'd want the same instructor.'

'Ah. The impatient type, is it?' Tommy's face broke into a grin. 'Don't worry, the time will pass quickly enough, and you'll be in one of these before you know it.' He patted the fuselage and stepped back. 'Right, I've still got a prop to take off before I go home. See you tomorrow, I expect.'

Bertie stayed a while longer, staring up at the aircraft and listening to the shouts of the men working on them echoing around the hangar. Bowden had put maintenance high on the list of lessons, so she knew that fairly soon she too would be levering off props, and cowlings, and be shoulders deep in an engine bay. It was an exciting thought, and would certainly help ease the frustration of seeing others taking off from the airfield every day while she and her fellow new trainees just watched.

267

'Would have to have been one of you three, I suppose.'

Bertie peered around the nose of the Jupiter to see a woman of around sixty, leaning on the lower wing of a biplane several feet away. She was dressed in overalls, belted tightly at her slender waist, and her blonde hair was pulled back, emphasising narrow, intelligent features. She eyed Bertie shrewdly, then put out her hand, and it was no surprise to Bertie to find her grip firm, dry, and offering nothing more than a quick, single-pump handshake. 'Jude Singleton.'

'*You're* Jude? I thought you were a man.'

Jude snorted. 'This from a girl calling herself Bertie.'

Bertie couldn't help smiling at that. 'Short for Roberta.'

'Obviously. And I'm Judy, to my family at least. Never here.'

'You were Xander's instructor.'

There was a flash of pain in the blue eyes, then Jude nodded. 'I was. Him and a hundred others.' Her voice was low-pitched, and carried a clear northern accent; Leeds, Tommy had said.

'What did you mean, you knew you'd get one of us three?' Bertie asked.

Jude shrugged. 'I only ever take on one new trainee at a time, and every time a woman comes through here they pair us up. Which means I don't usually get to fly my own plane. They told me this year it was because I wasn't at the introduction to your class, but — '

'Wait, it's a *punishment* to get a female trainee?' Bertie glowered at the instructor. 'I'd have expected different from you, of all people.'

'Get down off your high horse, Miss Fox.' Jude

268

waved a grimy, oil-streaked hand. 'I didn't say I agree with them. Come outside, I want to smoke.'

Bertie followed her out into the open air but declined a cigarette. 'When will you know which of us it will be?'

'Actually I already know it's you.' Jude flicked her lighter and drew deeply on her cigarette. 'Xander told me about you, and what happened to your leg, and he said you'd be here soon, so I check the lists regularly.'

'Why?'

'I was curious.' Jude eyed her. 'Still am.'

'But Xander was doing the military training, not civilian.'

'So are you.'

Bertie shook her head. 'No, I'm not.'

Jude gave her a tiny smile through the smoke as she exhaled. 'If you say so, but I'm still going to insist I use my plane this time.' She stepped back and her voice took on a dismissive tone. 'Anyway, you don't get split away for ages yet, and in the meantime you need to get off home, rest that leg. I can see it's bothering you.'

'It's not,' Bertie said quickly. 'I can do anything the others can do.'

Jude held up a hand. 'Don't get defensive, lass.' She took another pull on her cigarette. 'Give yourself a fighting chance, at least.'

'Where's your plane?' Bertie asked, refusing to be dismissed. 'If I'm going to be flying it, I'd like to at least see it.'

'Not now,' Jude insisted. 'I've got work to do.' She threw down her cigarette and stubbed it out with the toe of her heavy boot. 'Come and find me after training Monday though, and I'll introduce you to Joey.'

'Joey? I thought planes were always female. Like ships.'

'And we all used to think pilots were male,' Jude pointed out. 'Besides, what was I saying about girls called Bertie and Jude?'

Bertie grinned, her liking for Jude already growing. 'After training on Monday then. Here?'

'I'll be expecting you.'

17

Higher Valley Farm

Beth placed the post beside Alfie's plate, as always. It was a mechanical gesture, but looking at the postmark on the topmost envelope, she realised it was something that would very soon come to an end; Alfie must have written to Keir Garvey more or less right away. Sure enough, when Alfie opened it, he glanced at her, skimmed it once more, then tucked it wordlessly away in his pocket.

She put down her spoon, sick of dancing around the subject and pretending all was well. 'It's time we told the boys,' she said to Alfie.

Jowan and Jory had been applying themselves to their rich, warming stew with the ravenous appetites expected from two hard-working young men, and now they looked up in surprise and interest.

'Told us what, Uncle Alfie?' Jory asked around a mouthful of dumpling. 'Mum's pregnant?'

'Jory!' Beth glared at him, but he winked and continued eating, unabashed.

Alfie didn't look at anyone, but chased a piece of carrot around his bowl, one elbow on the table ostensibly propping up his chin, but effectively blocking his expression from Beth. On his other side though, Jowan must have seen something that told him the news wasn't good.

'What's happening then?'

'Wedding plans got stuck?' Jory put in, grinning.

'I told you, I'm not wearing any fancy hired suit, my good Sunday one's fine for the job.'

Alfie sighed and lowered his own spoon. 'There won't be a wedding. I'm going back to Priddy Farm.'

'What?' Jowan looked from one to the other. 'Why would you do that to Mum?'

'He hasn't done it to anyone,' Beth said quickly. 'It's something we both talked about and agreed. Alfie came here to help us, and he has done. Now he's got his old life to go back to.'

'With Aunt Sarah?' Jory looked puzzled. 'I thought you two were divorced.'

'We are,' Alfie said. 'You know Keir Garvey lost his wife before Christmas, and then the lad who was helping him out turned out to be . . . Well, he left in the night with no explanation.'

'He was the father of that girl's baby, wasn't he?' Jory said with a scowl. 'Fiona Fox's runaway friend, her that nearly killed Daisy.'

'I believe so,' Beth broke in quickly. 'But that's by the by, Jory, nothing to do with us. Uncle Alfie's going back to help Keir like he helped us.'

Alfie nodded, giving her a grateful look. 'This farm's so much smaller now, since we sold that land. You lads can manage, and there's Micky Sherborne, and the others, for busy times like harvest.'

'So I'm assuming that letter's from Keir,' Jowan said, nodding at Alfie's pocket.

Alfie took it out and read it aloud, clearly leaving out certain parts. 'He says, *I'd be glad of your help if you can spare it, and if Beth can spare you so close to your . . .* Well.' He cleared his throat. 'He goes on, *The boy leaving like that left me high and dry . . .* and so forth. And he finishes with, *Please tell your family I'm grateful to them for releasing you while I get things properly organised.'* He folded the letter. 'So you see, I haven't told him anything about the wedding being off.'

'Why not?'

Alfie shrugged. 'Some things just don't look right on paper. Our situation was too complicated to reduce to just words on a page, don't you think?'

Beth gave him a small smile. 'I can't even do it justice in spoken words,' she admitted. 'Even now. It's just . . . barriers. Too many of them.'

'I know that feeling,' Jowan said in a low voice.

Jory dropped his spoon and sat back, looking at the three of them in turn. 'Honest, you lot! After all the hard times you've given me about the way I do things, it turns out *I'm* the only one out of the four of us with his life in order!'

Beth felt an unexpected chuckle bubbling up. 'You've got a point there, love. So the rest of us will take our lessons from you from now on, shall we?'

'Christ, don't do that,' Alfie said in mock horror, and ducked to avoid the half-heel of bread that his nephew lobbed across the table at him.

Jory grinned, clearly relieved he had managed to lighten the grim atmosphere that had pervaded the farmhouse for the past week. 'Me and Sally Penneck are setting the date,' he said, 'so you'd all better get over your little doldrums, and get ready for the *actual* wedding of the year.'

'Decided not to marry the film star then?' Jowan asked innocently, and received the other half of the crust in his stew. The gravy splashed onto the tablecloth, but for once Beth didn't admonish them for the horseplay; that one little comment from Jory had been like someone pulling the curtains open in a gloomy room, to show its self-absorbed occupants that light and life existed beyond.

When the men had gone back out for their afternoon's work, she went upstairs to look at Sam's painting again. Propped on the bed, against her pillows, it seemed to grow until it took up her entire field of vision, and she became part of the simple, familiar scene.

But of course she was part of it. *Her* farm, *her* future. She still hadn't told Alfie about the painting, and now she was glad; she didn't think she wanted to give it away after all. She remembered the day Sam had brought it into the house, and thinking she could almost see herself at the kitchen window, waiting for Alfie's return. She had worried then how her life would be, once that comforting, loving presence was gone, but she was growing surer by the minute that the woman in the window was going to be absolutely fine.

* * *

Leah fixed her hair in the vanity mirror, as Adam pulled up to the door of the hotel. 'Why don't you go and see Stan Houghton now, about the lights?' she suggested. 'I don't want to waste any more evenings sitting around waiting for daylight just so we can go anywhere.'

'There's plenty of time yet,' Adam began, but fell silent as Leah gave him a look and pushed open her door.

'There always is.' She got out and went to the back for her case. 'Poor Aunt Mary wasn't expecting overnight guests again though. Go on, I'll unpack my things and meet you for dinner when you get back.' He opened his mouth to protest, then rolled his eyes and closed it again, making her smile. 'Good lad.'

She blew him a kiss and bent to pick up her case, but was beaten to it by a bell boy, no doubt despatched by the ever-vigilant Guy Bannacott. She followed him inside, as Adam drove back towards the village.

'Is Helen about?' she asked Guy, watching the boy hurry across to the lift. 'I need a drink and a chat.'

'She's in the office with her brother at present. Shall I tell her you're here?'

Leah shook her head. 'No, don't trouble them. I'll get unpacked and changed, and see her later.' She gave a little stretch and looked around with pleasure. 'It's so lovely to be back.'

Even as she spoke she wondered at the thought; hadn't she just convinced herself she wanted to leave for good? But there was something about Fox Bay that felt more like home every time she returned from somewhere. She climbed the stairs slowly, knowing it would all change if Helen got that job.

Passing Bertie's door on the way to her own, she thought she heard movement behind it, and stopped; Bertie was supposed to have left on Friday. What if she had lost the courage to do it? If *that* girl had wavered, something must be horribly wrong.

'Bertie?'

The door wasn't latched, and eased open under her knock. She went in without thinking; after the months she had spent nursing Bertie in this very room it was a purely reflexive action. 'Are you alright, love?'

'Who the . . . You!'

The woman who stepped out of the *en suite*, wrapped in a huge towel, was only vaguely familiar, and Leah stared at her in surprise. 'Where's Bertie? And who are you?' She peered closer, and almost laughed. 'Oh, it's David's wife, isn't it? I didn't recognise you without all the . . . .' she circled her own face ' . . . you know.'

The woman stared, incredulous. 'How dare you? Get out of my room!'

'I heard a noise, and thought it was Bertie,' Leah explained, more politely. Much as it galled her to admit, she *was* actually in the wrong. 'I'm sorry. I didn't know you were staying.'

'Well now you do. So you can leave.'

'Don't worry, I'm going.' Leah stopped at the doorway. 'How long will you be here? Just so I know how long I have to keep out of your way for.'

'Don't be facile,' Kay snapped. 'I'm here in my sister-in-law's home, to discuss private matters with my husband, none of which has anything to do with a spiteful little hanger-on like you.'

'Half the hotel currently belongs to my fiancé, so your being here is as much my business as anyone's.'

'You and Adam are actually engaged?'

'As good as!' Leah realised she'd overstepped a mark, and went on quickly, 'The point being, I live here, you don't.'

'Yet.'

Leah slowly closed the door, ignoring Kay's scowl. 'You're moving in, then.'

Kay drew herself up and reached for her house coat. 'Better than that. David and I are planning to buy Adam's share, so we'll own half with Helen. Family, just as it should be. As it always used to be.'

Leah was stung into her response. 'You'll have to be quick then, he's expecting the final papers any day now.'

'Papers?' Kay pulled the house coat on over her towel. 'What papers?'

'Oh, I thought, seeing as the hotel was so much your business, you'd know. Adam is selling half his share to Hartcliffe. His *ex*-fiancée in fact.' Leah stopped; anger was making her careless, though after the couple of days she'd had it was a wonder she hadn't blurted out the whole nasty affair.

'Oh, really? I believe I've heard a similar tale from you before,' Kay said, a thin smile on her face. 'I think you were calling yourself Grace Gardner at that time though. Fictitious wife of the *actual* owner, and threatening to have me barred.'

Leah saw her chance to lessen the trouble she might have just caused; at least she wouldn't be called upon to expand on the information. 'Well you can't blame a girl for trying,' she muttered. 'What makes you so sure he'd sell to you, anyway?'

'By which I assume he hasn't discussed his plans with you?'

'He loves it here,' Leah said evasively.

'He loves *Helen*,' Kay pointed out. 'And now he knows he can't have her, he'll be ready to move on.'

'You couldn't afford this place even if he'd sell to you,' Leah said, this time refusing to rise to the bait. 'Ever since the Americans came, the value of Fox Bay has shot up. And David has no job . . . Or didn't you know that either?'

'Of course I knew.' Kay drew herself upright. 'We have no secrets from one another. Unlike you two, clearly.' There was the faint flicker of a triumphant smile, then it was gone. 'Now, I have no wish to discuss this any further with you, it's between my family and Adam. I'm sure we can at least be civil to one

277

another, but that doesn't include you marching in here as if you own the place.'

Leah gave her the benefit of her most shark-like smile as she left, but it fell away as soon as she was on the other side of the door. The comment about Helen had been a low attack, and although Leah knew now that Adam understood his true feelings for both of them, it had still hurt. It had made Leah want to snap back that Kay knew nothing about them, but that would only have been playing into her hands and feeding what seemed to be an innate need for drama.

But, if Kay wanted drama, she was going to get it by the bucketload, she didn't need Leah to provide it.

* * *

Downstairs later on, she was about to go into the office to find Helen, but Martin handed her a yellow envelope as she passed behind the desk. 'This came for you, not ten minutes since.'

Leah wondered if the sight of a telegram would ever give her anything other than a hollow, sick feeling in the pit of her stomach. She took it, and, remembering Helen might still be with David, she retraced her steps into the lobby and sat down. She tapped the envelope against her fingers, her thoughts racing down ever-darker paths; had Glynn gone back to Aunt Mary's to find her? Been followed there by police, even, and her aunt was now writing to warn her? The sick feeling persisted; she'd be arrested, imprisoned even ... She spared the busy lobby a quick glance, already wondering if her days here were numbered, and how it would feel to find herself dragged away from all this. But it was no use putting it off, there was only one way to find out.

278

Caernoweth Air Base

By the end of Tuesday Bertie's mind was falling over itself with everything that had been pushed into it since the first real day of training. Two full days of measurements, physics, weight-to-lift ratios, and diagrams with hard-to-decipher labels; barely five minutes to think of anything else. Even their day off had, for the most part, been taken up with writing up scribbled notes into something readable.

She, Tory and Gwenna had met for lunch at the hotel on Sunday, but there had been no sign of Harry, and as she'd watched Tory and Gwenna going off together to walk off their lunch, Bertie had fought down a dismaying resurgence of envy at the casual ease with which they'd climbed over the crumbling little wall separating the old fort from the cliff path. It wasn't their fault, and she still hadn't told them about her leg, so they could hardly be blamed for simply waving goodbye and going on their merry way. She had instead returned to her room alone to continue her reading and note-taking, determined to be prepared for Monday's lessons.

She'd waited for Jude yesterday after training, as agreed, but had only seen a few of Tommy Ash's fellow mechanics; no sign of Tommy himself, or the dryly humorous woman who seemingly had many stories to tell. And, more disappointingly, no sign of her Camel either. Bertie had waited, eyed curiously by those working in the hangar, until almost eight o'clock when the mechanics' curiosity had melted into irritation as she kept wandering into their

279

working spaces. Then she'd returned to the flats, feeling let down and far too much like a silly girl who apparently couldn't stay away from men.

Today she had made up her mind to apply herself entirely to learning. She concentrated on the calculations on the board that would enable her to make tiny adjustments to the carburettor in flight, and tried to imagine how it would feel to be making those calculations high above the ground, when getting them wrong would result in worse things than a glare from Flight Lieutenant Bowden.

'The Avro 504,' he was saying, meandering with deceptive aimlessness up and down the rows of attentive trainees, 'was released onto the civil registers after the war, but that doesn't make them less of a fighting machine. Should the far distant day come that you actually evolve from ostrich to eagle, we have four of them here at the base. The rest are Jupiter 76s, and we still have a few 1½ strutters.'

'And a Camel,' Bertie put in, without thinking.

'And, as you rightly point out, Miss Fox, a Sopwith Camel.' He swung back to the front. 'There are differences in the operations of all these craft, of course, so be sure to listen to your instructors if and when you're finally deemed competent enough to attempt your first solo flight.' He looked back at Bertie. 'As you're going to be assigned the Camel, you'd do well to pay especially close attention, since the controls are notably lighter, and their response quicker, than the Avro.'

'*You?*' Gwenna's whispered voice cut across the rest of Bowden's words, and Bertie looked at her in surprise.

'Why not me?'

'But *I* wanted . . . .' Gwenna frowned. 'I wanted Singleton as my instructor.'

'It wasn't up to me,' Bertie pointed out. 'It's all on a list, apparently.'

'When you two have finished chattering?' Bowden said, and Bertie realised the class had fallen silent and was waiting. She held up an apologetic hand, and Bowden continued pointing out the differences in various craft, comparing fuel controls, with a speed that had everyone scribbling frantically to keep up.

★ ★ ★

Now they had jotted their last note for the day, and were permitted out into the gathering dusk, Bertie glimpsed the slender, overalled figure of Jude Singleton, ducking beneath the wing of a Jupiter and marching into one of the hangars at the edge of the field.

Gwenna followed her line of vision and gripped her arm in sudden excitement. 'That's her, isn't it? The fighter pilot?'

'Fighter?' Bertie looked at her, startled. 'I didn't know that, I thought she just owned the plane. Assumed it had belonged to a brother or something.'

'My father told me about her. He was a fighter too, though he never met her.'

'What did she do?' Tory asked, round-eyed. 'She doesn't look the type to fight a pillow, never mind fly in combat!'

'Evidently she flew dirigibles before the war, then she signed up to the RFC, incognito. Dad says she actually ended up shooting down Zeppelins over the west coast.'

The other two stared after the woman, in awe. 'So that's why you wanted her as your instructor,' Tory guessed.

Gwenna nodded. 'I expected to see her on our first day, when they all came in.'

'Ah, I thought you sounded a bit disgruntled,' Bertie said. 'Look, I'm sorry you didn't get drawn the way you wanted, but I really didn't — '

'Well of course you didn't,' Tory said crossly, giving Gwenna a look. Clearly their friendship had progressed to that comfortable point now. 'Don't be rotten, Gwen.'

'Gwen-*na*,' the girl retorted, but she shrugged. 'I know it wasn't your fault. But it's obvious whoever gets Jude will go on to do the military training, not just civilian.'

'It doesn't work like that,' Tory pointed out. 'They can't just tell us which one we're doing, it depends what we've signed up for, and we're all civilian.'

'For now,' Gwenna said. 'I fully intend to switch the first chance I get. As soon as I've proved I'm descended from good fighter pilot stock.'

'And I'm civilian,' Bertie said firmly. 'That's what I signed up for, and that's what I've paid for.'

Gwenna gave her an odd look. 'For now,' she repeated, and Bertie remembered Jude's comment to the same effect.

She turned to look over the planes dotted around the field, and at the bustle of activity around the hangars, and felt a little shiver run down her back; it felt rather as if machinery were turning beneath her, shifting her into the position fate wanted her in, and preparing everything around her, seen and unseen. She began to wonder how in control of her life she really was.

'Are you coming?' Tory asked her, as she did every day. But the two were already pulling away from her, anticipating the usual response. Bertie felt a flash of panic; this might be the last time they asked. The last chance she had of becoming one of them.

'Can I come to your dorm?' she asked. 'I need to talk to you both about something.'

'Is it about your leg?' Tory asked, and Bertie blinked. 'What?'

'We wondered when you were going to tell us,' Gwenna added. 'It's alright, honestly. We worked it out on Sunday, when you didn't want to come on our walk.'

'How?' Bertie stammered. She didn't know whether to be relieved or horrified. How many others had been talking behind her back?

'Is it your whole leg?' Tory asked, with childlike curiosity. She bent to peer at Bertie's foot, clad in sturdy boots and just peeking out from her trousers. 'You can't tell, you know.'

'How did you know?' Bertie insisted, and the other two looked surprised at the tension in her voice.

'Well we didn't think it was a secret,' Tory said. 'I just thought you looked as if you didn't really want to go back and work on your notes, and were just using it as an excuse.'

'We couldn't work out why,' Gwenna went on. 'I mean, you work hard, but you don't strike us as a swot, or a bore. Then we realised we'd never seen you more than a few hundred yards from the training room.'

Tory nodded. 'I remembered your so-called pins and needles thing, from our first day. Harry Batten's Uncle Hugh came back from the war with a false leg,

283

and it sounded familiar so we just started putting two and two together. We went to see Bowden after class yesterday, to ask him.'

'And you don't think I'm mad to be doing this?'

'Oh, completely,' Tory said with her usual candour. 'But aren't we all? Look, we'll come to yours instead, it'll be easier for you. It's about time we all had a good chat, away from this place.'

'How did it happen?' Gwenna asked.

'A motorbike accident.' Bertie started to tell them, beginning with Xander's promise to put her in his team, but she had only reached the part where he and Jowan had come to blows, and she'd started away from the racetrack in a temper with them both, before a voice called from the hangar.

'Fox! Singleton wants a word!'

'You'd better go,' Gwenna said, her newly opened expression closing down slightly again. 'This can wait. Tell us the rest tomorrow.'

'See you do,' Tory warned, as Bertie nodded. 'I want it in far more detail than this, too. Buying that motorbike with the adorable name, first meeting with Xander, and everything else. Alright?'

'Alright,' Bertie promised. Her heart was lighter now, as she waved and started back across towards the hangar where Jude had vanished earlier.

'Sorry about yesterday,' Jude said, meeting her at the doorway and wiping her hands on a rag. 'And about summoning you back like that just now. I didn't want you to go home before I had a chance to speak to you, but I was up to my eyes in it so had to get someone else to shout.'

'That's alright,' Bertie said. She was too relieved now to make an issue of it, and Jude evidently noticed.

284

'You look like a weight's been lifted,' she observed. 'Told them about that at last, have you?' She nodded at Bertie's leg.

'It seems I didn't need to. Are you going to introduce me to Joey now?'

'I'd better, since I've deprived you of your other company. She's behind the hangar.' Jude beckoned to her to follow. 'Here we are then, F6302, also known as Joey.' Jude approached the modified two-seater and looked up at the darkening sky. 'We've just got time for a quick orientation. Hop in.'

Bertie hesitated. 'Was that a joke?' she ventured, and Jude stared at her blankly for a moment before letting out a husky bellow of a laugh.

'Would it bother you if it was?' she asked, still chuckling.

Bertie honestly didn't know, until she saw that Jude was looking at her kindly. 'No,' she said, and found her own smile. 'I don't think it would.'

'Good, but it wasn't.' Jude shook her head. 'I'm sorry, it's just a habit to say that. Do you want help, or will you manage?'

'I'll manage.' Bertie was aware she sounded a little sharper than she'd intended, but Jude just raised her hands and stepped back.

Bertie went around to where the wing was lower, at the back, and reached out to grasp the wing strut. She was able to steady herself in this way, as she climbed on to the wing and slid her right leg into the cockpit. Her foot knocked loudly against the seat.

'Watch you don't kick the mixture lever, down there on the left,' Jude called, 'or the fuel gauge.' She appeared on the other wing, watching anxiously as Bertie slid her leg forwards and down, bringing herself fully into the cockpit with a small grunt of triumph.

'Good.' Jude leaned in to point out some of the features. 'Right, you've seen these in the classroom: the tachometer, the oil flow, magnetos and so on? Air pressure down here on the right.'

Bertie looked at the instrument panel, thinking how different it was seeing the dials in front of her, accompanied by the stench of fuel and leather, and then the creak of the cane seat as she leaned over for a closer look. She felt a sudden revulsion at the sound, as unexpected as it was swiftly passing, and it took a second for her to realise it was because she was reminded of the cane wheelchair she had hated so vehemently. Then Jude's voice banished all thoughts of that awful time; she was here in the cockpit of a plane that had flown countless miles, in the service of its country and at the hands of a wholly extraordinary woman.

'You'll notice there are no brakes,' Jude was saying, 'but there, on your control column, is the blip switch. That cuts the ignition to the cylinders, which slows the engine.'

Bertie reached out and brushed a thumb over the little button in the middle of the control column; it would be strange to transfer control over braking from her foot to her hand, but she had the feeling it would be one of the fastest lessons she'd learn once she was up there.

'Now,' Jude said, settling into the seat behind, 'I just want you to get used to the way the nose looks above the horizon, the angle of it while the plane's on the ground. Fix it in your mind, 'cause that's what you'll be looking for when you come in to do your three-point landings.'

286

'Just . . . sit here?' Bertie said, trying not to sound too disappointed.

'Just sit there. You need to be familiar with it.'

They sat in silence for a while, and Bertie stared out at the front, studying the rising angle of the nose, and trying to imagine the blur of the propeller cutting the horizon ahead of her, and the sharp, staccato noise of the engine. How much louder would it be here, right next to it, and how different would it feel, with the rocking motion of the plane as she waited for the chocks to be pulled away from beneath the wheels? But the overwhelming sense she had was one of fierce triumph; in this seat, she was the physical equal of everyone else.

The evening was drawing down now, the chilly March wind was tugging at Bertie's hair, and she remembered the relief and joy she'd felt when, on Christmas Eve, Jo had presented her with his gift and his blessing: the white silk flyer's scarf . . .

A sharp finger between the shoulder blades made her jump. 'Are you concentrating, or daydreaming?' Jude demanded. 'The cockpit light's just above the compass there if you need it.'

'I don't,' Bertie said, 'I can see well enough.'

'Well I think you've had enough looking at the inside for now, tomorrow I'll take you through how this machine differs from the Avros that Bowden's so keen on telling you all about. There's a lever in this model that switches the supply over, you'll probably not get told about that in your classes.'

'Thank you.' Bertie twisted in her seat, to see Jude looking at her as if suspecting sarcasm at worst, politeness at best. She hoped she sounded as sincere as she felt. 'I mean it, the lessons are one thing, but sitting here like this, even if I don't touch anything . . . It's made it all feel that bit more real.'

'Oh, it's real, alright,' Jude said, shades of grim lurking behind her smile.

'I didn't realise you'd actually been a fighter pilot.'

'Who told you then?'

'Gwenna. Her father told her about you, and she wants to do the same.'

'If she's got it in her, she'll do it.' Jude hoisted herself out of her seat and swung her legs over the side with the agility of someone half her age. 'And so will you.'

There it was again. 'I'm not sure I want to.'

'That's an improvement from I don't want to,' Jude observed as she jumped off the back of the wing. 'Come on, you'll be needing to get back before it gets proper dark.'

Climbing down was harder than getting up; Bertie lacked the confidence to jump, the way Jude had, and sat down to slide off the wing instead, but the minute her boots touched the grass she felt an odd, vague sort of resentment at the solidity of the ground beneath her. She blinked at the unexpected feeling, frowning downwards, and then looked up to see Jude's eyes on her, and the slow smile that spread across the instructor's face told her she knew exactly what had just passed through Bertie's mind.

'Welcome to the world of aviation,' Jude said, her voice lower than usual, but rough with feeling. 'She's a tough mistress, but kind to her own when she finds them.' She put her hands deep into her overall pockets and leaned forwards, and her eyes narrowed as she studied Bertie for a moment. 'Aye, I think you've found each other at just the right time.'

288

18

Helen re-read the Pagetts letter once more before she finished for the day. It was all very well telling her she had to sign and return the contract before the end of the month, but how long would it be before they drew that up and sent it? She was probably going to need someone else to look over it first, and since that was likely to fall to David, she needed time to get him used to the idea that she was leaving for The Pearson in the first place.

She pushed the letter back into the envelope as a knock sounded at the door.

'Helen?' Leah said, 'Have you got a minute?'

'Of course, come in.'

Leah entered, looking distracted and pale. 'Is Adam's whisky still in the desk?'

Helen checked the drawer, but there was only a dribble left. 'Shall we go into the lounge?'

'No, this has to be kept between us. Can I come to your room instead? But I do need a drink to steady myself.'

Helen decided not to question the fact that even Adam was excluded; Leah had rarely looked quite so serious. 'I'll bring something,' she said, more troubled now. 'Go on up. I'll make sure Guy knows not to disturb us, I'm sure he'll be able to deal with anything that comes up.'

'You should never have let your night manager go,' Leah said, with a weak smile. 'He was a good one.'

Helen spoke briefly to Guy, then seized a bottle of

gin and two glasses from the bar and followed Leah to her room, where she made sure the door was firmly shut.

'What on earth's happened?'

Leah took her drink and gulped half of it, and gasped at the neat spirit running down her throat. 'Right,' she said, when she could speak again, 'pay attention, this is a big one.'

Helen listened in rising disbelief as Leah told her about the visit from the policeman, just as they'd been leaving her aunt's house, and then went on to describe how she'd lied about the identity of the man on the table.

'So your husband isn't dead?'

Leah shook her head. 'Which brings me on to this.' She pulled out the yellow telegram envelope and passed it across to Helen, who took it with a sudden sense of fear.

'Have the police found you out?'

'No, just read it.'

Helen did so, glad it was short; the handwriting of the post office clerk left much to be desired, and he could have done with a sharper pencil too.

Millicent — Staying at Summerleaze, Bude. Be there 6pm Weds — Jacob B.

'Jacob who?'

'Bitterson,' Leah reminded her. 'Glynn's assumed name for this thing in Liverpool.'

'So this is from Glynn.'

'Yes.' Leah's relief was visibly tempered with worry. 'But what if someone's seen him? What on earth is he thinking, coming down here? He could have led

290

anyone to me.'

'And why the Summerleaze?' Helen frowned. 'That's a huge coincidence, isn't it?'

'I probably mentioned Ben's girlfriend at some point, while we were together. There was an awful lot of waiting around, we talked a lot.'

'And we are full,' Helen mused, 'or he'd probably have tried to . . . Wait, what does he look like?' she asked.

'Tall-ish. Slender-ish. Quite attractive I suppose. I always thought so anyway.'

'I wonder if that was him?' Helen mused. In response to Leah's raised eyebrow she explained how she'd recommended the Summerleaze to a tall-ish gentleman, who Kay had also found quite handsome. It seemed they had similar taste, given Kay's history with Adam, but she kept that to herself. 'It was on Saturday,' she remembered, 'but you were away then. He'd have known that, presumably, if he knew he needed to use his pseudonym.'

'Wilf must have spoken to him before Neville found him,' Leah said. 'Or . . . what if he was there, himself, and got away?'

'It doesn't bear thinking about,' Helen said with a little shudder. That this kind of thing can just happen to anyone and the murderer gets away with it.'

Leah took back the telegram. 'I can't tell Adam; he'll swing for Glynn for getting me mixed up in this. He didn't even want me to waste time warning him. The last thing Ben needs is a massive fight in his hotel, and the last thing any of us needs is to be arrested.' She brightened. 'I've got his driving licence too. I'll be able to give that back to him. It might help him get away if he's still using his own name.'

291

'I don't like the idea of you going alone though,' Helen said. 'Can you tell Ben, at least, that you're worried and he needs to keep a watch on Glynn?'

'If I see him. Though Glynn won't hurt me,' Leah assured her. 'He knows he owes me his liberty, and maybe now even his life. Besides, he . . . .' She trailed off, flushing slightly.

'He loves you,' Helen supplied. 'Well of course he does. Just promise me you won't get sucked back into that life, alright? From what you've told me he can be very charming and persuasive when he wants to be.'

'I must have a leaning towards that sort,' Leah agreed with a little smile, seeming easier in her mind now she'd shared her story. 'Look at Adam.'

'Speaking of whom, I'd really feel much happier if you had him there with you.'

But Leah shook her head. 'Absolutely not. You saw the way he came home after their last encounter, he's a liability to himself. Glynn poses no danger, don't worry.'

'Alright.' Helen realised she'd get nowhere, and subsided. 'Now do you want to keep stripping the skin of your throat, or should we go downstairs and get some tonic water for that?' She nodded at Leah's glass.

'Now I've told you all my sordid little secrets, we can sit where we like. Thanks for listening, Hels.'

'I have some news of my own,' Helen told her as they left her room and made their way towards the stairs.

Leah stopped. 'The job?'

'I can start as early as September, if the contract suits.' Helen examined her feelings and found them oddly flat. 'I don't feel the slightest bit excited *or* nervous though. Isn't that strange?'

'It's a big change,' Leah said, starting down the stairs, 'but seeing the details will make it seem more real. We can thrash it all out together downstairs, and maybe we'll discover whether that's what you want after all.'

'Of course it's what I want.' Helen hurried after her. 'I'm just a bit overwhelmed at the moment, that's all. Especially now you've told me this.'

The lounge was full, so they took one of the last spots in the lobby, and Helen couldn't remember seeing the place so busy during the off season. Normally it didn't get like this until at least Easter.

'It'll all be a bit different at The Pearson,' Leah said, evidently noting the same. 'At least, until you've had a chance to work your magic.'

'I can hardly claim the credit for Rex bringing Daisy and Freddie here,' Helen protested, laughing.

'No, but you can claim it for the fact that, despite everything, they went back and told their friends what a wonderful place it is.'

'Despite everything,' Helen repeated. 'That's probably the biggest understatement I've ever heard.'

'So about The Pearson then,' Leah said, accepting a fresh drink from Jeremy Bickle with a smile of thanks. 'Will I be able to come and stay there, too?'

'I assume so. I'll still only be an employee though, don't forget. If Pagett puts his foot down, or whoever he sells it to — '

'Which he will.'

'Which he will. I'd have to abide by the rules, I'm sure they'll be laid out in the contract.'

'You still don't sound terribly enthusiastic.'

'I'm not,' Helen confessed. 'If it weren't for all of

you skedaddling off and leaving me to it, I'd never have thought about moving away.'

'And Alfie?'

'Alfie will be happy with Beth.' Helen heard the words emerge with a calm she could be proud of, belying the swift rush of regret.

'You haven't heard, then?'

'Heard what?' Helen felt a strange gnawing sensation in the pit of her stomach as she looked at the smile spreading across Leah's face. 'What is it?'

'While I was waiting for you to finish talking to David, I saw Sam Douglas. He's here for a few days, apparently, staying at the Sandy Cove.'

'Yes,' Helen said, trying to keep the impatience out of her voice. 'He's brought the final two paintings for upstairs, though I've not seen them yet. What of it?'

'He told me the Nancarrow wedding's off. Mutual, apparently, so you don't have to feel bad that you're happy about it.'

'Off?' Helen's eyes fixed on her friend, searching for some sign of uncertainty, but there was none. 'For good?'

'For *your* good, I'd have thought.' Leah laughed and leaned across to prod Helen's knee. 'Where's that smile then? I'd have told you sooner, only I was a bit preoccupied with that stupid telegram.'

Helen couldn't think of a single thing to say, though she knew her feelings were clear on her face, even if she didn't express them in a smile. But there would be time for thinking about Alfie later, when she was alone and could give all her attention to the implications of Leah's news. Her practical side took over.

'Look, since Sam's back, why not take *him* with you to the Summerleaze?'

Leah looked tempted but unsure. 'What if he's obliged to go to the police with anything he finds out about Glynn? I don't know how these things work, and it'd be impossible to ask without giving the game away.'

'You don't have to tell him that, do you?'

'Well he'll want to know why I need a lift, but don't want him to come in.'

'Alright,' Helen said, glad to have another focus for her thoughts, for a while at least. 'Let me have a discreet word instead. I'll see if I can find out what he has to disclose and what he hasn't.'

'How, and when?'

'When he comes over with the paintings. I don't know how yet, but you know me, I'll find a way.'

'You will too, won't you?' Leah smiled. 'I'm going to find Adam, and make sure he won't be anywhere around tomorrow evening. Come and find me when you've spoken to Sam.' She finished her drink and stood up. 'And don't take too long thinking about the Alfie situation,' she added with a wicked glint in her eyes. 'You don't want to miss a second chance, do you?'

* * *

Despite Leah's words, Helen put all thoughts of Alfie, and of the Pearson job, firmly out of her mind and went to see if Sam had arrived yet. With nothing to do at Sandy Cove, he had taken advantage of Adam's open invitation to spend his time at Fox Bay, and it was around dinnertime when Helen found him making his way to the dining room.

His face broke into a beaming smile when he saw

295

her. 'Ah, Mrs Fox.'

'Helen,' she reminded him. 'I understand you've brought the last two paintings?'

'I have. Would you like to see them now? Or are you happy to wait until after dinner?'

Despite the leading manner of his question, she chose to go with him right away to the sitting room, where he uncovered the two paintings he'd brought with him. She could tell immediately that they were exactly what she and Adam had hoped for, but used the time looking at them to try and think of a way to bring the subject around to his obligations to the law.

'I must say these will suit the lounge and small sitting room perfectly,' she said. 'Do you yourself have a preference for which room they go in?'

He considered. 'The lounge I think, the light from the window falls better in there.'

'Do you always paint countryside scenes?' Helen didn't know yet where this conversation would lead, but it felt faintly useful, so she went along with it.

'I *am* usually inspired by natural beauty, rather than man-made,' he said slowly, as if he'd never really thought about it before, 'but somehow farms and their buildings always seem more natural than not. As if they've grown out of the ground rather than been placed upon it. If you see what I mean.' He gave a little, self-conscious laugh. 'That sounds horribly pretentious.'

'Not at all. So you weren't tempted to stay on and sketch those glamorous hotels in Liverpool? Leah says they were stunning inside.' Now she understood why her instincts had guided her in this direction. 'You were keen to return to Cornwall?'

'Absolutely. I loathe big cities.'

'Is that why you're never tempted to return to the life of an officially appointed officer of the law?'

'That's the long and short of it, aye. Besides, there's rather too much corruption for my liking.'

'Yet you're still obliged to tell them if you find out someone's broken the law?'

He turned and looked at her carefully, and she reminded herself that beneath the pleasant, easy-going exterior lay a razor-sharp mind. 'You told us you couldn't condone any action Adam chose to take against Glynn and his cohort,' she reminded him. 'I think it's admirable. It must be a difficult balance to strike.'

'I also *neglected* to write certain notes down when Adam first came to see me in Truro,' Sam pointed out in a level voice, 'so as to ensure only the relevant details were traceable.' He cleared his throat. 'Mrs Fox, I think you're fishing, and before I sample the bait I'd like to know a little more about the net, if I may?'

Helen's admiration increased, though she felt a mild panic that she'd gone too far, too fast. He seemed to sense it and sat down in one of the armchairs, indicating the sofa for her.

She took it, and faced him squarely, determined not to appear weak or uncertain. 'Do I have your word that your pen, metaphorically speaking, is also laid down now?'

'No, I'm afraid you don't. But let me ask you one or two questions, then you can ask me that one again.'

Helen nodded. 'Go on.'

'Are you about to inform me of a death, or a serious threat to life?'

'Yes.'

297

He winced. 'Did you, or anyone you know, contribute to said death or serious threat to life?'

'No.'

He relaxed a little. 'Are you in possession of knowledge that might result in death or serious threat to life?'

Helen hesitated. 'I do hope not,' she said at length. 'But if it does, it might actually be your fault.'

Now Sam looked nonplussed. 'Alright, ask me again.'

'Is your pen laid down?'

He regarded her for a moment, then clearly came to a decision. 'I have no pen, metaphorical or otherwise. I might find one though,' he added in a warning tone, 'if I discover you haven't been truthful.'

Helen wondered if she should leave out the information about the false identification, but accepted that that would count as not being truthful, so she told him everything. 'So we'd both be hugely grateful if you'd escort her to the Summerleaze, and see she comes home again safely,' she finished.

Sam was silent for a minute, and she could see him chewing over what she'd told him. 'So you're saying that the threat would be down to me refusing to accompany her on this visit.'

'She'll probably be fine,' Helen said, 'but . . . well, yes. Would you?'

'And she just wants me to sit in the car and wait?'

'You must be used to that,' Helen said, venturing a little smile. 'It's tomorrow night. Would you go? We'd be *so* grateful.'

'Why didn't she ask me herself?'

Helen shrugged. 'She doesn't think she needs anyone. I'd just prefer it if she had someone with her, but

298

she refused to entertain the idea of telling Adam that Glynn's back.'

Sam pursed his lips, then nodded, stood up, and straightened his waistcoat. 'Alright. Tell her I'll be ready at five-thirty.'

* * *

Her duty done, and feeling much better about Leah's trip to Bude tomorrow, Helen went up to her room and drew a deep bath. While she waited for it to fill, she picked up the picture of Harry that she'd kept with her since she'd moved here.

'I know you'd tell me to chase every bit of happiness I'm offered,' she said, 'but am I being an idiot falling for someone like Alfie Nancarrow? You and he couldn't be less alike.'

But, now she thought about it, she realised that wasn't quite true. She traced the outline of Harry's face; as Kay had pointed out, handsome as a movie star. Alfie was attractive in a less obvious way, but Helen realised they both had the same kindness around the eyes, the same ready smile, and the same infectious sense of the absurd. It was only that, while Harry had been outwardly charming and confident, Alfie's was a quieter warmth, and he only shared his quick wit rarely, and with very few people. He'd always shared it with her.

Now he was no longer promised to Beth, what did that mean for what he'd said on Christmas Eve? She had it by heart.

'*It wasn't until after Bertie's accident, when I saw the fiercest Fox of all rise up, that I knew I was doomed.*'

She'd laughed at the description, unable to help it,

299

even then. But was he still doomed? Was she? He'd finished by telling her to go home and get warm, and she had. She'd woken on Christmas morning feeling a deep happiness, and spent the day pondering the feelings she had never suspected in herself, but that his words had uncovered, and she had realised that their friendship had grown and changed, and that she loved him in return. Hopelessly. The next thing she'd heard, he was engaged to wed his sister-in-law.

She'd wanted to believe she had put her own feelings aside out of a sense of loyalty and honour; Beth had loved him longer, therefore she deserved him more. But the truth was simply that she hadn't even recognised them for what they were until Alfie himself had shown her his own. Standing there with snow gathering on those ridiculously thick eyelashes, and on his hatless head, telling her he'd been unable to stop thinking about her since August . . . How could she have been so stupid?

Helen turned off the tap and tested the water before dropping her robe and sliding into the blissful, fragrant warmth. She rested her head back against the bath, feeling the lapping of hot water as she moved, dampening the hair that had come loose from its pins, and rising to cover her chin. It flowed away again immediately, and she found herself waiting before moving her knees again, just to feel that embracing warmth on deliberately chilled skin. But she soon sank lower so the water covered her properly; why would anyone want to deny themselves true comfort when it was there for the taking? It was an insult to those who had no choice.

Abruptly she sat up straight, and the water streamed off her heat-pink skin. Why indeed? She stared at the wall opposite, following threads of thought: back over what had happened, forward through what might come, unaware of anything else until her eyes started to sting, and then she slowly lay back down again. Tomorrow she was going to be busy all day, but as soon as the evening staff took over she was going to visit Alfie Nancarrow. And this time she'd say exactly what she should have said on Christmas Eve.

19

Sam reversed his Crossley Tourer into a space in the small parking area at the back of the Summerleaze. 'If you're not out in twenty minutes, I'm coming in.'

Leah didn't know whether to be grateful or frustrated. 'I'm perfectly safe with Glynn.' Her eyes narrowed. 'Unless you're secretly hoping for an excuse to make a citizen's arrest?'

'I promise you I'm not,' he said grimly. 'If all this came out, and it turned out I'd aided his escape to start with, I'd find myself in hot water up to my neck. Not to mention now being party to that deception with Wilf Stanley's body.'

'Helen shouldn't have put you in this position,' Leah admitted, 'but it is good of you to come.'

'I promised. And I'm still not entirely sure you're doing the right thing, seeing him alone in his room.'

'Don't worry about me,' Leah said with a little laugh. 'I'm tougher than I look.'

Sam eyed her for a moment, then nodded. 'I believe you are, yes.'

'Then have faith.' Leah smiled, then lifted an eyebrow. 'Well?'

'Well what?'

'I might be tough, but I'm still a lady. Aren't you going to open my door for me?'

Sam sighed. 'Fickle.' He climbed out and went around to her door, helping her out with an exaggerated flourish. 'My lady.'

'Thank you, sir.'

302

Leah grinned as she left him tutting loudly after her, and went around to the front of the hotel. She patted the driving licence in her pocket, and used the time to think of other ways she could help Glynn reach safety. There wasn't a lot of money she could lay her hands on, but she was sure Adam would be only too glad to cover any shortfall, once he knew what it would be for; anything that removed Glynn from Leah's life could only be a good thing, in his eyes.

Inside, she didn't bother looking around for Ben, and instead went straight over to the reception desk. 'I'm meeting a Mr Bitterson.' An odd feeling swept over her as she remembered saying exactly the same thing when she'd arrived in Liverpool. Had all that only been last month?

'Oh, it's *you*!' A woman's voice cut through the receptionist's query about her name. 'I knew I recognised the photograph, but couldn't quite place you.'

Leah turned in surprise, to see Lily Trevanion, as smartly turned-out as ever; coolly beautiful, and with a warm, welcoming smile. She'd met her once or twice, briefly, but they'd never spoken properly. 'Hello, Miss Trevanion, it's nice to see you again. What photograph is this?'

'One that Ben took. I was having a little look over some of them in case I could use any for the *Summerleaze Siren*, and saw the one of you and Daisy Conrad.'

From the corner of her eye Leah saw the receptionist give a little start, and she couldn't help smiling; Daisy's name usually had that effect. '*Summerleaze Siren*? I take it that's the name of your magazine. Adam's idea originally, you know, intended for Fox Bay, but very well suited to your hotel too.'

Lily's expression indicated she wasn't keen on being

303

pulled off her conversational track.

'Lovely cottage. Daisy's?'

So Ben had told her, at last. Good thing too; there were too many secrets around lately, it would be good to drop this one. 'Yes,' she said. 'Well, a rental anyway. Daisy's moving there to write, and we were helping her with her things on that day.'

'Do you know her well then?'

'Quite well, yes.' Leah was growing distracted again now, and saw that the receptionist had given up the idea of breaking into such a high-level conversation. Instead he wrote a room number on a piece of paper and pushed it across the polished desk for Leah to pick up when she was ready.

Leah gave Lily an apologetic smile, relieved she wouldn't have to say her false name aloud. 'So sorry, Miss Trevanion, I'm late for a meeting. I hope we'll have chance to chat soon, I'd like to know how Ben's getting on.'

'Oh, he's getting on marvellously,' Lily said, and even through her distraction Leah realised the young woman's smile was now maintained through effort and professionalism. 'I'll be sure to tell him you asked.'

As Leah hurried towards the lift she saw Lily's expression change, and realised, with a sinking feeling, that the woman had still had no idea that Ben and Daisy had become close, never mind that Daisy was now living just a few miles down the coast. She hoped Ben wouldn't find himself on the sharp side of that formidable tongue, but just at the moment she was more concerned with finding a way for Glynn to stay safe. And dead.

The room was on one of the uppermost floors, though it was difficult to keep track of precisely where, once she stepped out of the lift and into a corridor identical to so many of the others. She thought it was at the back though. She checked the number again, and knocked at the correct door.

In case anyone was listening, she stayed in character for the time being. 'Mr Bitterson? It's Millicent.'

Glynn didn't reply, but she heard movement from the other side of the door, and then it opened. Before she could do more than begin to glance up, her smile ready, his hand clamped her arm in a fierce grip, and he pulled her into the room. The door was closed and locked behind her, and she turned to demand an explanation for the urgency . . . And froze.

'Hello, Mrs Scripps.' Leonard Neville's smile was as wide as it was false. Leah took a half-step back, not trusting herself to speak. Her heart was hammering as she looked around the sparse room, and Neville shook his head.

'He's not here. That is, I assume you're looking for Jacob . . . I'm sorry, *Glynn*.' He put a hand into his pocket and Leah snatched a sharp, painful breath, but he withdrew a cigarette case, his smile turning into something like a smirk. 'I'm not going to shoot you, my dear. Not in a hotel room.'

Leah remained silent, still not sure whether she ought to continue as Millicent, or accept that he knew who they both were. He put her out of her misery at last.

'Is it alright if I call you Leah, or would you prefer Mrs Marshall?'

Leah found her own voice as the shock wore off, and with it her old confidence. 'Mrs Marshall will do, thank you. What do you want?'

'Cigarette?' He offered the case, and she took one,

glad to see her fingers had stopped shaking. He lit it for her, then his own, taking his time until Leah felt like repeating her question. But she held her peace for the moment.

'I'm booked in at your place from Friday,' Neville said, in a maddeningly conversational tone that jarred with Leah's tightening nerves. 'I was lucky enough to get a cancellation.'

'How nice.'

'Hmm.' Neville blew smoke from his nose as he said it, and went to the window to pull back the curtain slightly. 'Who's the man with you?'

'Man?'

'The one in the car,' Neville said, with exaggerated patience.

It was on the tip of Leah's tongue to ask, *what car?* But she realised he'd more than likely been watching for her arrival, and witnessed the theatrical nonsense they'd believed had been private.

'He just gave me a lift,' she said instead.

'Ah. You're not *so* devoted to your missing husband after all, then. That's a shame.'

His tone had hardened, and she realised the only reason he hadn't yet hurt her, was because the one he really wanted was Glynn. As long as he believed she and Glynn were close, she was of some value.

'Of course I'm devoted to him.' She took a quick puff of her cigarette. 'That gentleman was good enough to offer to drive me here tonight. Fox Bay isn't just around the corner, you know.'

'Oh, I do know,' Neville assured her. 'I went there first. I had no idea it would be full at this time of the year, but they very kindly recommended this place.' He let his eyes rove the plain ceiling and stark walls.

'Not a patch on your pile, though. So why does he think you're here? What did you tell him?'

Leah lowered her eyes. 'I think he believes it's some kind of . . . of assignation, but is too polite to say it.'

'And he worries for your safety?' Neville gave her a knowing look. 'Be truthful for one moment, Mrs Marshall, he thinks you're a woman of loose morals, doesn't he?'

Leah could scarcely believe he'd given her this gift. She nodded. 'I believe he does, yes.'

'Is he hoping for . . . a reward, of some kind?' His meaning was clear from the amused tilt of his head, and Leah scowled.

'How dare you? He's engaged to the hotel's owner! He was simply being kind!'

'Of course.' Neville shrugged. 'And I assume your gallant driver knows to come and find you, if you're not back by a certain time?'

'Of course.'

'Very wise, too. What was it you said in Liverpool, about a woman alone in the city? Even if you are meeting who you assume is your husband. And,' he added, 'happen to be an extremely accomplished con artist in your own right.'

'Are you going to tell me why you're here?' Leah adopted a bored tone. 'Or can I go now that you've made your point?'

'I've nowhere near *made my point*,' Neville said, and as he ground out his newly lit cigarette in the black ceramic ashtray she realised, for the first time, that he was barely holding a bubbling rage in check. The smooth tones and sardonic smile had hidden it well, but they were slipping now. 'Your husband and his friend made a fool out of me. They lied and tried to

307

steal my money, and they used you to do it. I've spoken to Freeman, or whatever his real name is, and now I need to have the same chat with Marshall.'

'Spoken to him!' Leah couldn't suppress the short laugh, but her insides were curling into knots again. 'I've seen words have a disturbing effect on people, but never seen them take a man's legs off. You think I'd give up Glynn, just so you can push *him* in front of a train, too?'

'So you know about that?' Neville shrugged. 'Well, we did chat first. How do you think I knew where to find you?'

'I don't even know where Glynn is,' Leah said. 'I only know the police think he's dead, thanks to the driving licence you left on Wilf Stanley.'

'I didn't leave that,' Neville said dismissively. 'Why would I? And more to the point, how would I have got it? No, that would have been Freeman, or rather Stanley, getting ready to set your husband up to take the fall for something else instead. So I wouldn't go wasting any tears over that nark, if I were you.'

'The fact remains, I truly don't know where Glynn is. Now if you'll excuse me, I'm going.'

'No, you're not.' Neville moved easily towards the door and blocked it. 'We haven't finished our chat, yet.'

Leah's hands felt clammy, and she tried to resist wiping them on her coat. 'What more is there to say?'

'Oh, plenty.' Neville gestured to the window. 'We might be longer than you were expecting, so go and give your driver a little wave, to show him all's well. If I think for one minute you're making any kind of signal, trust me, he'll never see you again. At least,' he added, 'he'd not recognise you if he did.'

Leah had no doubt he meant what he said; the memory of Wilf Stanley's mutilated body on the cold mortuary table was something she'd never forget. It brought with it the associated smells of the formaldehyde and blood, and she felt her stomach roiling; she'd seen and smelled worse during her time as a nurse, but this had been different. Sickeningly final, and personal.

She pulled the curtain back again, and saw the pale shape of Sam's face through the windscreen of his car, staring upwards. His attention must have been caught before, by the movement of the curtain and nothing more than a shadowy figure in the window; knowing Sam he'd have immediately guessed this was the room where Leah was, and was no doubt poised to come up if he felt it was necessary. She toyed briefly with the idea of defying Neville's instructions, but Sam was too far away; these corridors were all the same, and Sam might become just as disorientated as she'd been. It wasn't worth it.

So she gave him a cheery wave, and saw his hand rise from the steering wheel to wave back. Neville had noted it too, and gave a satisfied grunt. 'Now we're going to talk, and, as much as you've proved you're good at it, you're *not* going to lie. If I think you've been useful, I'm going to let you walk out.'

'And if not?' She could feel panic rising again; even if she could bring herself to give up Glynn's hiding place, she had no idea where it could be.

Neville shrugged. 'Let's just cross that bridge when we come to it, shall we?'

He drew her away from the window slowly, so as not to raise any alarm below, and as she left the comforting sight of the outside world, and Sam Douglas's reassuring presence, Leah suddenly felt very lonely, and very, very frightened.

★ ★ ★

Helen sneaked a look at the clock, and swallowed a sigh. Kay and Adam were glowering at one other, each of them convinced they had the right argument, while David merely looked uncomfortable. Hardly any wonder, Helen thought, knowing Adam and Kay's history. Adam absolutely refused to budge on his decision to sell to Hartcliffe, and Kay was needling him ever closer to revealing a truth which would send her, first through the ceiling, and then to the telephone to Jeanette. Both would be disastrous.

She wished she could just leave them all to it. It was dark now, which meant Alfie would have finished work for the day, would have had time to change and eat his evening meal, and so wouldn't feel rushed or hurried if she turned up at the farmhouse door. She glanced at the telephone, but this wasn't something to talk about over a wire.

'Well isn't it, Helen?'

'What?' She came back to reality. Kay was looking at her with both eyebrows raised. That was never a good sign. 'I'm sorry,' she said, 'you'll have to say that again.'

'I said it was high time Adam settled down on his own, instead of hanging around like an unwanted stray.'

Helen looked at Adam, who was clearly itching to say something about unwanted strays himself. 'It's thanks to Adam that we have this place at all,' she reminded her sister-in-law.

310

'And thanks to him you almost lost it to begin with.'

It was an old argument, and Helen was twitching with impatience to be away to Higher Valley. 'Look, as long as Ben will still have his share, whenever he wants it, it's up to Adam to do what he likes with his. Has anyone seen Leah come back yet?'

The others looked blank at this sudden change of direction, but Kay's mouth tightened. 'That woman's a dreadful influence too,' she said to Adam, who groaned and glanced Heavenward in a plea for patience. Then Helen's words seemed to register.

'Back from where? I didn't know she'd gone out.'

'Just into Bude,' Helen said airily. 'Sam Douglas gave her a lift in to visit Ben.' She felt the first tug of worry, then guilt, as she realised how long they'd been out; she'd been so focused on Alfie, and then this infuriating stalemate, that she'd barely given it a thought.

Adam looked put out. 'She should have waited, I'd have taken her. I'd like to have seen him myself, see how he's getting on with that camera.'

'We needed to talk, Adam,' Kay said, her voice tight.

'No, *David* and I did,' Adam told her. 'He's the one with the money. And the family connections,' he added, with unnecessary pettiness.

Helen had reached the limit of her endurance. 'I suggest you put away your toys for tonight, children. If you insist on pursuing this squabble you can tell me what you've decided tomorrow.'

'I'm going to Bristol tomorrow,' Adam said. 'I'm getting some finer details squared away, with Simon and Jeanette.'

'You'll be back by Saturday I hope?' Helen grew even more cross now. 'It's changeover day, and

311

without Bertie and Ben I'm going to need — '

'I will be!' Adam held up a hand. 'Don't worry, I'll be back around lunchtime.'

'Good.' Helen went out into the lobby in time to see Leah coming through the revolving door, Sam just behind her. She breathed a quick sigh of relief, but Leah's face was taut and wary as she looked around to thank Sam. A quick signal from him brought Helen to the office, bidding a silent farewell to thoughts of talking to Alfie as she went.

'What happened?' She closed the door behind her, and then locked it as well in case Adam had also spotted Leah's return. 'What did Glynn want?'

'It wasn't him,' Leah said heavily. 'That's the second time I've gone somewhere expecting to see him, and seen someone else instead. Only this one was, unfortunately, very much alive.'

'Who was it?' Helen asked, dismayed to see Leah looking so shaken.

'Leonard Neville.'

It took a moment for Helen to attribute the name to the story Leah had told her of what had happened in Liverpool. 'So *he's* the one I sent to the Summerleaze? What's he doing in Cornwall?'

'Wilf told him about Glynn and me before Neville killed him.' Leah explained everything, including being made to wave to Sam and abandon his protection, before being questioned over and over. And the threats. 'They made me feel sick, Hels. I don't know how I can have been so arrogant to think I could just walk in alone and — '

'It's not arrogance,' Sam said quickly. 'It's courage, and confidence. You did everything perfectly, you weren't to know you were being duped. And besides,

312

you're here, aren't you?'

'He didn't hurt you?' Helen asked, looking her over for any sign she was hiding something.

'Surprisingly, no. He was furious though, at the way he'd been tricked. Not that I can blame him for that, but you'd think his desire for revenge would have been satisfied by what he did to Wilf Stanley.'

Helen shuddered. 'It doesn't bear thinking about.'

'He came down to the lobby with me, to make sure I left without speaking to anyone. Ben saw us, I think, but I didn't get the chance to say anything, or signal to him.' Leah sighed. 'I hope he doesn't think it was some assignation with a stranger behind Adam's back.'

'We'll telephone and tell him.'

'Don't, it's not fair to involve him. Besides, Neville told me he's booked into here from the day after tomorrow.'

'Oh no he isn't,' Helen said firmly. 'I'm going to cancel it right now.'

'No.' Leah looked at Sam, who nodded. 'I'd be happier having him here, where Sam can keep an eye on him.'

'But why would he stay at all, now he's accepted you don't know where Glynn is?'

'For the same reason he didn't do to me what he did to Wilf.' Leah took a quick breath. 'He says he has a proposition for me. A job. And that if I agree to do it, he'll leave Glynn alone.'

Helen tensed. 'What sort of job? The kind of thing you used to do?'

'Presumably. I don't have any details yet.'

'Any job for this man won't be like it was with Glynn,' Helen said, growing more worried. 'He's not

313

going to look after you the same way.'

'I'll be watching out for her,' Sam put in. 'I'll do a better job this time, too.'

'You did exactly what you were supposed to do,' Leah assured him. 'Anything else and it might all have ended very differently.'

Sam looked unconvinced, but nodded. 'Whatever it is he's got planned, it won't succeed. We just need to catch him red-handed in whatever it is he's up to.'

'That's very good of you,' Helen said, feeling a little more relieved, but still not happy. 'You won't let her get into any dangerous situations, will you?'

'I doubt I could stop her,' Sam began, but, seeing Helen's face, he relented. 'I'll do my very best.'

'It's Adam I'm concerned about,' Leah added. 'We'll need a firm hand on him to stop him flying at Neville when he gets here.'

'It's probably best if you don't say anything to him tonight then,' Helen cautioned, 'he's on a short fuse already. We can talk to him when he gets back from Bristol.'

'There is one other thing,' Leah said, and now she wouldn't meet Helen's eyes.

Helen frowned. 'Go on.'

'Neville wanted to know who Sam was, and why he was waiting for me. I already knew he was coming here by then, and I wanted him to think I'm alone now, without Glynn or anyone else on my side. An easy target. So . . . I told him *you* and Sam are engaged.'

'Engaged?' Helen stared. She felt her skin heating up as she looked at Sam, who was regarding her with equal embarrassment. 'I'm so sorry,' she said, 'she should never have said that. Leah! How *could* you?'

'I had to say something quickly, and it was the first

314

thing I could think of!'

'So,' Sam said briskly, 'whenever Mr Neville is around, we'll have to remember to use our first names. The odd endearment too, perhaps, if the situation calls for it.'

'And you'll need to swap that,' Leah nodded at Helen's wedding ring, 'with an engagement one. I'd lend you the one I used in Liverpool, but he'll recognise it.'

'I wouldn't wear that revolting great thing anyway, not if you paid me,' Helen said with a little grimace of distaste. 'I've still got my own, thank you.'

'And a little peck on the cheek now and again wouldn't go amiss.' Leah gave them both her most winning smile. 'I'm sure two attractive people like you will be able to convince Neville you're in love.'

Helen gave her a look. 'That'll do, thank you. Sam, could you leave us alone for a few minutes please?'

He withdrew, and Leah sent a grateful smile after him before closing the door behind him and re-taking her seat. 'I'm really sorry, Hels, it was all I could think of to throw Neville off the scent.'

Helen waved the apology away. 'How long is Neville staying?'

'I'm not sure, but it won't be long. Apparently he just has to wait for some information from higher up, before he can bring me into whatever it is he's got up his sleeve.'

'The thing is, I'd sort of decided to . . . In the light of what you said about . . . .' Helen took a deep breath. 'I was going to talk to Alfie.'

'But that's marvellous!' Leah sat up straight. 'Well why should this stop you?'

'Because, should the miracle occur, I can hardly explain to him that I'm going home to pretend to be

315

engaged to someone else, can I? And I don't want him involved in any of this, so I'll have to wait 'til it's over. Which means I don't know whether to accept that job either, because if Alfie and I *do* have a future, I won't want to move away after all.'

'How long do you have, before you have to sign the contract?'

'Until the end of the month. Less the time it takes to post it back, of course, and it's not even here yet.'

'Oh, I'm sure the Neville thing will be sorted long before then,' Leah said. 'Bound to be.' The breezy tone vanished as she looked around the cramped little office, with its too-big desk covered with paperwork. 'I don't mind telling you,' she said quietly, 'there was a time in Neville's room tonight that I really thought I wasn't going to see this place, or you, ever again.'

It was on the tip of Helen's tongue to tease away the sudden melancholy, by reminding her friend how much she'd always loved the thrill of danger. Looking at Leah's face though, she realised that, while there was undoubtedly a time when that would have been accepted with comfortable, shared laughter, it wasn't tonight.

20

Caernoweth Air Base

'Are you two going back home this weekend?' Tory's question was directed at both Bertie and Gwenna, as the three of them made their way to the canteen for lunch. Tomorrow was Friday, and marked a week since they'd arrived; Bertie could hardly believe it had only been that long. So much had happened, so many new people had come into her life as if they'd always been there, and Fox Bay seemed a million miles away.

'No,' Gwenna said, 'but I'll have to go back next weekend, to help Mum with the end-of-month stock-taking.'

'How about you, Bertie?'

'I hadn't thought about it,' Bertie confessed. 'It's a bit soon so I think I'll stay here this time, but if you two aren't going to be here next weekend, I might go back then. You?'

'Nowhere *to* go,' Tory said, though cheerfully enough, 'so I'm glad you'll both be here.' Then she brightened. 'Oh! Maybe I could come back to Treth-kellis with you on the twenty-eighth?' She grabbed Bertie's arm. 'It'd be wonderful, don't you think?'

'I don't think there are any rooms,' Bertie cautioned, but she couldn't help thinking it would be fun, and give her a chance to seal a friendship that was making tentative hops off the ground but hadn't yet left it completely. 'I suppose you could bunk in with me, though.'

317

Gwenna's face darkened, and she looked as if she wished she could take back her own plans, but it was too late now. 'Bunk in?' She pulled a face. 'You're not children!'

'Well you two share a dorm,' Bertie pointed out, 'what's the difference?'

Gwenna shrugged, and Bertie knew that, while Gwenna had been friendliness itself when it came to her prosthesis, and was softening in other areas too, there was a long way to go to make up for 'stealing' her instructor. 'Are you really needed at home?' she asked. 'Why don't you come, too? I'm sure Fiona would put you up in her room if there isn't another one. She still has the spare bed in there from when she befriended a girl she rescued at sea.'

Both girls' faces turned to her with interest, and the slight awkwardness was forgotten as she told them about the waif, Amy, and all that had happened at Christmas. It was the first time she'd mentioned the Hollywood visit too, and when she slipped in that Daisy had actually moved to Trethkellis she felt herself grow several feet in stature at the looks on their faces. Even Gwenna's.

'That settles it,' Tory said, 'I'm definitely coming to stay. How about you, Gwenna?'

Gwenna looked torn, but eventually she shook her head. 'They're expecting me,' she said. 'And it's a long job, stocktaking. Perhaps another time.'

'Oh no, look at the time.' Bertie had once again been talking so much that the lunch break was almost over, and her meal was almost cold. 'You two go on,' she mumbled, around a mouthful of mashed turnip, 'I'll catch you up.'

'Don't be late, or you'll be locked out of the session,'

Tory reminded her, standing up. She and Gwenna left, along with the rest of their cohort, and Bertie shovelled down as much as she could before her time ran out and she was forced to push her plate aside. She hurried out of the canteen and began to make her way back to the training room, determined not to miss a whole afternoon's training.

'Fox!'

She turned to see Tommy Ash waving to her, and waved back. 'I can't stop, I've got to get back before Bowden closes the door.'

'Just a minute!' He jogged over. 'Singleton was looking for you, did she find you?'

Bertie shook her head, and cast another desperate glance over at the training room, where Bowden was standing in the doorway, his pocket watch in his hand. 'I'll be late!'

'Ah, there you are.' Jude sauntered into sight from around the back of the hangar. She followed Bertie's gaze, and grinned. 'Never mind him.' She waved cheerily at Bowden, who pointed at his watch, and then at Bertie. 'I was going to ask you if —'

'Please, I have to go . . . .' Bertie gave a wail as Bowden stepped back and shut the door. 'Now look!'

'I told you, never mind,' Jude said, and started to walk away. 'Come with me.'

'Where?' Bertie followed, cursing her wish to impress her friends.

'I thought it might be time, and the perfect weather,' Jude added, glancing up at the clear sky, 'to show you a little bit of Caernoweth from the air.'

Bertie's heart gave a jolt hard enough to stop her in her tracks. 'A flight? Already?'

'As a passenger only,' Jude cautioned, but her smile

319

widened to match Bertie's. 'Yes, a flight. I'll give Bowden *ostriches*, if he had his way you'd stay ostriches forever. You can borrow Joey's wings for today.'

'I don't have my coat, or a scarf,' Bertie stammered, hurrying after her. 'They're in the classroom.'

'Borrow my coat,' Tommy offered, shucking it off. 'Just hunch down inside, it'll keep you warm enough. Singleton will have everything else you need.'

Bertie took the coat and pulled it on, and broke into laughter as she tried to fasten the buttons. 'My fingers are shaking too much!'

Tommy made her stand still, and did the buttons up for her, before yanking at the collar so it stood up around Bertie's ears. 'You look . . . warm,' he said, grinning. 'If a bit ridiculous.'

'Thank you, kind sir.' Bertie looked down at herself, then up at Tommy, and was touched at the pleasure he was taking in her excitement. Xander would have been just the same, she knew, and she wished she could have seen them larking about together.

'Well come on then!' Jude reappeared and gestured to her. 'It'll be dark by the time you get organised. Ash, let the girl get on with it, for crying out loud!'

'Well, you heard her,' Tommy said, tweaking her collar once more. 'Get on with it!'

Bertie allowed Jude to strap her helmet in place, and accepted a tatty-looking scarf, which she wound around her neck. She thought fleetingly of the white silk, but there was no time to dwell on the way she'd expected this to happen; it was happening now, as difficult as it was to believe.

'Pay close attention to everything I do,' Jude said, as they approached the Camel. 'The adaptations to this plane were made quite recently, this wasn't a purpose-built trainer, like most. We've had to reduce the size of the fuel tank, but then training flights are much shorter than the ones I used to do. And the armaments have been removed, so you'll see no bomb release handle, front or back. The forward cockpit is moved up, and the rear one doesn't have a lot of leg-room. Right, up you get.'

Jude helped her to settle in the seat at the back, where she saw the same instrument layout in front of her that she'd seen yesterday in the cockpit, but instead of the blades of the propeller, she was looking at the back of Jude's head. She fastened the safety belt across her waist and tried to peer into the front cockpit to see what Jude was doing, but wasn't able to see much without leaning forward, and the safety belt limited her movement.

'Checking the pressure gauge,' Jude called back, and Bertie felt her stomach alternately squeezing and twisting, and a fire licking along her veins as Jude, satisfied with the reading, gave a thumbs-up to the propeller-swinger.

There was a choking, spluttering sound, and the plane juddered beneath Bertie and all around her, as the propeller caught, reversed, and spun into life; the noise made all further communication impossible, but Bertie, stretching as far as she could in her seat, saw Jude's hand drop to her left side and move the fuel mixture lever forward. The irregularity of the engine sound evened out a little, but it increased with the surge of power, and, after a moment, the plane began to move.

Bertie held her breath, trying to remember the instructions and diagrams Bowden had painstakingly taken them through, but it was all a jumble of words

321

like *steerable tailskid*, and *rudder pressure*, and she eventually gave up and let herself sink into the experience.

Jude brought the Camel around so it was facing into the wind, the engine noise stepped up again as she increased the power, and the plane surged forward. The bumpy ground beneath the wheels set Bertie's teeth clacking, but she knew that, when they hit roughly fifty miles per hour, all that would cease, and they would be airborne.

She almost didn't notice that moment, having waited for it for so long. It was only by noticing Jude's head dip slightly to the left, to check the wheel, that she realised the bumping sensation was different now; it was purely vibration from the engine. They climbed steadily, and it seemed even the roar of the engine and the jagged propeller sounds had softened, although they couldn't have.

Bertie's eyes streamed but she couldn't raise the goggles to wipe them; the way the wind was tearing at her she'd be lucky to keep hold of them. They began to bank to the left, and Bertie's amazed eyes found the ground below them speeding by much faster than it seemed they were moving. She saw the Caernoweth Fort Hotel, with its ancient and crumbling outer wall, and felt she could almost reach out and pick up the scattered boulders and rocks and replace them.

The Camel straightened again, and banked the other way, and Bertie's breath stopped entirely, as the cliffside vanished and in its place were white-topped waves, which in turn gave way to a heaving grey mass, as if someone were waving a great dappled cloth, sending ripples across it for as far as the eye could see. Here and there tiny white flashes showed the places where rocks lay just beneath the surface, breaking up the waves as they rolled towards the shore. The air grew suddenly colder, almost icy, and Bertie gulped at it through her scarf as the plane banked still more steeply.

The plane seemed to be labouring more now, and Bertie saw Jude's hand moving from control stick to fuel control lever, but she couldn't see the fine adjustments the instructor was making. The engine faltered, and in the sudden silence Bertie's indescribable joy turned to gut-freezing terror. Her mind was filled with images of Xander, out over this very same stretch of coast, never to return. She closed her eyes, willing the sudden nausea down, and only breathing again as the spluttering roar returned, coughed, then evened out again.

The plane tilted back onto a level path, and Bertie realised it had only been a split second, but it had seemed to last minutes. She saw Jude's hand come off the control stick again, this time to give her a thumbs-up signal before sketching a brief salute against her flying helmet. Bertie imagined that clever, impish face, grinning behind the scarf and goggles, and she found herself laughing, partly in half-hysterical relief, and partly in renewed excitement. When she'd rolled out of bed this morning, grumbling to herself about the early start, she'd never dreamed she'd be doing this before teatime.

The ferociously roiling sea spread out beneath them, but now there was no fear, only a longing to be the one at the controls. The one charged with taking this incredible machine from its prison on the ground and setting it free among the clouds.

'I'm always chasing rainbows . . . .' The song rose to her lips, and her memory added a lower voice blended

323

with her own; her father, gone for ten years this very week. She closed her eyes again and saw his laughing face, and remembered his quiet pleasure when Fiona had demanded the song of him, time and time again. She'd been right about something else as well: up here she did feel closer to him; this moment had fused his memory in place, and he was now forever bound up in this sensation of freedom and weightless joy.

All too soon, Jude began banking around to bring them back to shore, and down to the airfield once again. Bertie resolved to draw every single moment of sensation out of their final few minutes, and made herself feel the hardness of the cane seat beneath her, the tug of the wind at the collar of Tommy's coat, and the sting of it on her skin.

They began to lose altitude steadily, and Jude used the blip switch in short bursts as they came in over the field; it was unnerving, hearing the engine cut out completely, even for the split second it took, and knowing it was deliberate. But it was necessary in order to make the descent swifter, and Bertie tried to memorise the way Jude was doing it now.

The nose began to come up as they approached the ground, and the tail dropped, and a moment later they made contact again in a perfect three-point land-ing. There was no bone-shaking bounce, no judder, just a bump and then a long, gradual slowing down, as Jude brought the plane off the runway and taxied to a stop behind the hangar.

Bertie sat utterly still, her father's voice and that song still playing in her mind, and the feeling of fly-ing coursing through her body. Jude also remained motionless, and Bertie wondered what thoughts were going through her mind; her glory days as a fighter pilot? Her first pupil? Her last one? There was no way of knowing, but for that minute they were each lost in their own worlds.

Eventually the airfield came to life around them, and Jude twisted in her seat and lifted off her goggles. 'Well? Still want to do it?'

Bertie nodded, not trusting herself to speak at that moment; tears were still ridiculously close. Jude studied her for a minute without saying any more, then banged her hand against the fuselage.

'Good. Come on then, you've still got lessons to attend.'

'But Bowden — '

'He'll do as he's told.' Jude hoisted herself out and lent Bertie a hand to clamber from her cockpit. 'You've paid for this training, he's got no right to deny you and he knows it.'

'Jude?'

'Hmm?' Jude was busily removing her outer wear, and Bertie did likewise.

'Women aren't allowed to fly fighter planes, so why did you say what you did, about me learning?'

'Oh, we're allowed to fly them,' Jude said, 'just not in combat. We'd be permitted, for instance, to transport fighter planes from airfield to airfield. *Very* exciting,' she added dryly, 'still, better than nothing.'

'But the war's over anyway,' Bertie said, 'and there won't be any need for fighter planes, so why is it even offered here as training?'

Jude's face was expressionless, but there was a sudden tightness to her movements as she took Tommy's coat from Bertie. 'War's never over, lass. You'd do yourself a favour by remembering that. And by being prepared.'

'Could you prepare me?' The words were out before Bertie had time to think about them, let alone bite them back.

Jude folded Tommy's coat over her arm, and her eyes crinkled at last into a satisfied smile. 'Come on, Fox. Back to your lessons.'

★ ★ ★

On Friday morning, Beth took her order book down to the hotel, as usual. Alfie had taken the boys to look at a tractor for sale; the first time he'd even considered one . . . It seemed he was preparing them for his departure already, although he still hadn't said when he was going, or whether it was permanent or just to give them some breathing space.

It was still a source of sadness that he wouldn't be at Higher Valley every day, but at the same time perhaps it would give her time to ease him from the front of her mind to where he really belonged; somewhere distant and happy. And Jory and Jowan were both thrilled at the thought of driving a tractor, which had made both Beth and Alfie smile.

Beth approached the hotel from the back, as always, but nowadays it was only so she could stop for a brief chat with Miss Tremar. Since the day she had come to speak to Helen about the girl Amy stealing her food, she had realised that, not only should she not regard herself as staff, to be banished to the back rooms, but that Helen had never thought of her as such, either. Since then she had come to the office, like any other business partner might, and they had discussed the hotel's needs in just as businesslike a manner.

Helen expected her at this time every week, and until

today she had always been ready — she knew Beth's time was no more expendable than her own — but Mr Bannacott met her in the lobby, and he apologised and asked her to take a seat.

'Mrs Fox will be here shortly,' he said, 'she's been held up for a few minutes. Can I fetch you a pot of tea?'

Beth shook her head and took a seat, enjoying the rare opportunity to relax and look around. Helen was at the reception desk, presumably taking over from the regular young man, who was nowhere to be seen, and was checking in a tall, bland-looking man, smiling at him, and pointing out various things on a map she'd handed him. He was clearly an important guest, but as far as Beth was concerned he could be the biggest toff in the county and she still wouldn't recognise him.

Her gaze shifted away and fell, surprised, on Sam Douglas, who was trotting down the stairs as if he'd lived there all his life. She smiled and was about to rise and go to speak to him, but remained seated as she saw Helen's face turn to him and light up with pleasure. He slid familiarly behind the reception desk and put an arm around her shoulder, then dropped a kiss on her temple. Helen's light laughter carried across the lobby and she gave Sam a playful push.

'Not while I'm working, darling!'

Beth smiled to see Sam's abashed expression, and the look of adoration Helen gave him as he touched her face gently and retreated. It was about time the woman had someone to look like that about . . . though Beth couldn't suppress a swell of envy; they looked so glamorous together.

The newly arrived guest signed the book and

returned the pen to the stand, and a bell boy appeared at his elbow to take his bags.

'Room four,' Helen told him, and handed him the key. When the honoured guest, whoever he was, had followed the boy to the lift, Mr Bannacott spoke to her, and she looked over towards Beth. 'Come in, Mrs Nancarrow, I'm sorry to have kept you.'

'Someone important, is he?' Beth nodded in the direction the guest had taken, as she followed Helen into the office. 'I'd not know him if he was the prime minister.'

'He's certainly not that,' Helen said, but didn't elaborate. 'Now, as you know, we're coming up towards what's going to be a heavy summer, orders-wise. Are you going to be able to manage?'

'Well you might need to increase some of your other orders,' Beth confessed, 'though we can supply what we always have. But extra might be a little bit more difficult, since we're losing Alfie soon.'

Helen lowered her pen. 'Losing him?'

'Down to Porthstennack. Priddy Farm, where he used to work. He's going to help out an old friend who recently lost his wife.'

'For . . . for good?'

'I don't know,' Beth said honestly. 'I suppose it all depends on how long Keir needs him.'

'When is he going? Just so I know when to increase any other orders,' Helen added.

'I'm not certain. Nor's he, I don't think. As soon as the lads are happy to do without him, I reckon.'

Helen nodded. 'I see.' She opened her own notebook, dismissing the subject and turning it back onto business, with an abruptness that might have seemed rude in another person. As she ran a finger down one column, Beth noticed the ring on her finger, and that envy bubbled up again, but she was still glad, nevertheless. Sam was a good man; charming, gentle-natured, and most of all kind. He and Helen would make a wonderful marriage.

★ ★ ★

When she arrived back at the farmhouse she saw Alfie and the boys had already returned. Still dressed in their going-to-town clothes, they were seated at the kitchen table doing sums on a scrap of paper.

'Good tractor then?' she asked, hanging up her coat. 'I take it you're working out if we can afford it?'

'I reckon we can,' Alfie said, turning the paper and pushing it towards her. 'It's a Fordson, but priced fairly enough. That's what we'll get from Fox Bay over the summer, and that there,' he pointed, 'is what we'd have to pay out each month on hire purchase.'

'You said *we*,' Jowan said, and exchanged a glance with Beth. 'You're not changing your mind, are you?'

There was an odd silence, then Alfie shook his head. 'No. I love it here, you know I do, but . . . I have to leave.'

He really did seem torn, but Beth knew that was because of the farm itself, not because of any second thoughts about a future with her. Through selling the land for the golf resort, he'd shaped Higher Valley into a smaller, more efficient, and solvent business, it was true, but it was more than that; his family had owned this land for generations. He belonged here.

'I hope you'll feel you can come back,' she said. 'Anytime, once we're . . . you know.'

He nodded. 'How did it go at the hotel?' he asked,

neatly changing the subject. 'I know they're busier than ever this year.'

'They are, and we've talked about what we can provide.' Beth indicated her notebook, which she'd put on the dresser. 'If we can afford that tractor though, we'll be able to do a lot more. Oh, and you'll never guess what else?'

'You're right enough there.' Alfie smiled. 'Knowing that place it might be anything.'

'Helen Fox has found herself a new man.'

Alfie's smile remained fixed. 'Who? Not Adam Coleridge?'

'Sam Douglas. Jo told us about him that night Bertie was here, remember?'

'The detective?' His voice cracked, and he cleared it with a cough. 'Oh yes, I know the one. Never met him though. Good for them.' He brought the scribbled workings around in front of him again, and pretended to study them, but Beth was gifted with the insight of someone who loved him, and she saw it all clearly now.

'Go and get changed then, lads,' she said briskly. 'There's still work to be done.'

Alfie took the opportunity of sudden activity, to stand up and go to the sink. He poured a cup of water, and drank it down, then fetched his boots while Beth sat silently at the table. When the boys had gone upstairs, she followed Alfie out into the yard where he was leaning on the gate where he always stood to chat, or just to think. She knew what he'd be thinking about now.

'Have you told her?' she asked. He straightened as she spoke, but didn't reply, and she went to stand next to him. 'Does she know?' she persisted, keeping her voice gentle.

Eventually he nodded. 'I know she doesn't feel the same, so it shouldn't come as a shock that she's found someone else.'

'But it still does.' She put a hand on his back and rubbed gently as if he were one of her sorrowing sons. 'I'm sorry, Alfie, I had no idea. I thought it was Leah.'

'Leah?' He turned to her in surprise. 'What on earth made you think that?'

'Well, you've always got along so well. And she's the . . . the glamorous one. The pretty one. The — '

'The obvious one?' Alfie shook his head. 'No. It's never been her.'

'Always Helen?' Beth tried not to sound accusatory or bitter.

'No, not always her, either.' He put his hands on her shoulders and looked at her with an intensity that told her he was telling the truth. 'I'd have been more than just content to make a life with you, I'd have been happy. You must know that. You weren't a substitute, Beth, you were my comfort and my friend.'

'But she was your love.' Beth smiled. 'Your poetry.'

'Eventually, yes.' His answering smile was rueful. 'It was slow coming, but I have it now, so I'm like you. I know I'm not a lost cause no matter what.'

Beth turned back to the gate and rested her elbows on it, cupping her chin. She waited until she felt him move to stand beside her again, then said, quietly, 'She was wearing an engagement ring.'

'Well, no sense in hanging around at our time of life.'

Beth glanced sideways at him, but his matter-of-fact words didn't seem to be masking anything, there was only acceptance. She didn't know whether to be relieved or exasperated; he could still fight for what he truly wanted, and she could have sworn Helen had reacted with something more than surprise, when she'd learned he was leaving. She wanted to say so, but it was nothing more than a feeling, not anything she could put into words. It wouldn't do to raise his hopes, just in case she'd read it all wrong.

'This Sam bloke,' he said, after a few minutes of silence, 'I've never met him. What's he like?'

'Very nice looking,' Beth said promptly, without thinking, then glanced up to see him scowling across the yard. 'In a completely different way from you,' she added, hurriedly. 'He's charming, Scottish, and a wonderful artist.'

'*And* a detective,' Alfie mused. He gave her a wry smile. 'I never stood a chance, did I?'

332

21

Adam made his way across the busy lobby to the reception desk, where Martin and Guy had just booked in the last of a new group of guests. 'Is Leah about?'

'I thought she'd gone to Bristol with you.' Martin peered around Adam as if he expected to see her standing behind him. 'I've not seen her since Thursday evening.'

Adam tensed, but forced himself to relax again; Leah was safe here and surrounded by people who cared for her. Not to mention a private detective, who seemed to be becoming part of the furniture at Fox Bay, he mused, as he saw Sam Douglas hovering near the lounge room doors talking to Helen. He picked up his overnight bag, and was almost at the stairs when he heard a voice shout across the lobby.

'Uncle Adam! Wait!'

Helen had turned too, at that voice, and both she and Adam smiled to see Ben hurrying across the floor, carrying a large folder. 'Darling!' she called. 'What on earth are you doing here on a Saturday? Aren't you *busy* at the Summerleaze?'

'Don't look like that, Mum.' Ben grinned, diverting his steps to go over and give her a kiss on the cheek.

'Like what?'

'As if you're hoping that's the case,' he said with mock severity. 'It's wicked of you!'

Helen laughed. 'What brings you here?'

333

'I came to talk to Adam,' Ben said. 'Although it concerns you too. Is the sitting room free?'

Adam went over and pushed open the door to check. 'Empty.'

Ben turned to Sam. 'You too, Mr Douglas.'

'Should I get Leah?' Helen asked, but Ben shook his head.

'No. Not yet, at least.'

Perturbed by the way the young man constantly checked the lobby, Adam found himself looking around too, before he closed the door behind them all, but there was nothing amiss that he could see. Ben seemed to be gathering his thoughts before speaking them — they were clearly troubling him; the easy smiles out in the lobby had given way to a taut nervousness now they were alone.

'I saw Leah on Wednesday night, at the hotel,' he began, 'but I didn't get the chance to speak to her, and — '

'I thought that was the whole point of her going there,' Adam broke in, but Helen shushed him. He frowned and subsided, sensing trouble, and threw a suddenly suspicious look at Sam; he was the one who'd taken Leah to the Summerleaze; was Ben about to reveal something sordid?

'She went to one of our guests' rooms,' Ben went on, 'and stayed there for almost an hour, according to Lily. When she came out, she was with the guest, and it looked as though he was hurrying her to the door before she could come over and say anything.'

Adam was more than tense now, he was beginning to feel sick. Why hadn't the lad come to him alone to tell him this? Then he realised that, though Sam was looking warily at him, there was no guilt there, and

334

Helen didn't even look the slightest bit surprised. His confusion deepened.

'I know Leah would never do anything to betray you, Uncle Adam,' Ben assured him, 'but there was something . . . off, about this man. So, while he was out I went to his room and had a look around.' He opened the folder he'd brought with him, and withdrew some photographs. 'What do you make of these?'

He put the photographs on the coffee table, and the other three crowded around to look at them. They were pictures of papers, mostly handwriting, with a few hastily drawn diagrams peppered with arrows, and a series of numbers. At the top of each of the sheets, the word *Kojote* was printed and underlined. The photographs were dark and under-developed.

'I was in a hurry when I took them,' Ben said apologetically, 'and I didn't get around to processing them until last night, so they're a bit rushed, but you can still just about see what's there.'

'I can't read the . . . Ah.' Sam picked one up. 'It's not English anyway.'

'I think it's German,' Ben said. 'I don't know what those diagrams are.'

Adam frowned and took one of the photographs with a diagram over to the window. He held it up, the niggling familiarity of the image pushing aside, for the moment, the question of what Leah had been doing for an hour alone with the man. He turned the page this way and that, and then froze.

'What's the name of the guest?'

'He booked in as Jacob Bitterson.'

'Glynn?' Adam lowered the photograph and stared at Sam. 'Did you know this?'

'It's not Glynn,' Sam said, 'it's Leonard Neville. He

335

used the Bitterson name to lure Leah to the Summer-leaze, and it worked.'

For a second Adam's mind wouldn't accept what he'd heard, then a chill swept over him as he contemplated how much danger Leah had really been in. 'I only went in once,' he said at length, 'but this diagram looks like part of the ground floor of the Empire Park Hotel, in Liverpool.'

Sam took it from him, and nodded. 'It is. There's the staircase, and the ballroom.'

'What's going on, Sam? Where's Leah now?'

'She's well. She's keeping out of sight for a while,' Helen said. 'I'm sorry, Adam, I was going to talk to you about this when you got back, but Ben beat me to it.'

'But if this happened before I went to Bristol — '

Helen looked pointedly at the photograph Adam had unknowingly crumpled. 'She knew you'd be off to Bude to confront Neville, before she'd get the chance to talk you out of it. She wanted time to think about how best to proceed.'

'With what?' Adam smoothed out the photograph as best he could, and put it back with the others.

'Neville wants her to do a job for him,' Sam said. 'If she does it, he'll leave Glynn alone.'

'And what is it he wants her to do?'

Helen shrugged. 'We don't know yet, neither does Leah. Evidently Neville is still pulling it all together and clearing her involvement with his team.'

'She can't do it,' Adam muttered. 'The man's a shark.'

'Who's a shark?' David closed the door behind him; they'd all been too preoccupied to pay attention to the quieter click as it had opened.

336

'No one,' Helen said quickly. 'Can you give us five minutes?'

'What's this?' David's attention had fallen on the photographs strewn across the table, and he stepped closer. Before Sam could gather them up he'd seen the word at the top of the pages, and paled. 'Kojote?' he whispered, and raised wide eyes to his sister. 'Dear god, Hels, what are you involved in?'

Sam frowned. 'You've heard of that word?'

'What is it?' Helen asked. From the look on her face she was growing as frightened as Adam felt. 'David? Can you read the rest?'

David screwed up his eyes, but soon gave up. 'Just the odd word. It's not just because it's come out too dark, I'm not fluent anyway.'

'But you know that word,' Sam pressed. 'What is it?'

'It's a code name. Coyote. We've . . . *they've*,' he amended, with a grimace, 'been after him for years.'

'David worked for the War Office,' Helen explained, seeing Sam's blank expression. 'David, are you saying Neville is a *spy*?'

'I'm saying Kojote is,' he said, 'I don't know the name Neville, who is he?'

'Leonard Neville's a new guest,' Adam said, shooting Helen a look to stop her explaining anything about Leah's Liverpool activities. 'He's staying here under the name Bitterson.'

'You can be sure neither one is his real name,' David said grimly.

'But there aren't any spies now, are there?' Helen looked confused now. 'The war's over.'

David shook his head. 'There have always been spies in peacetime, just as in war, and there always

337

will be.'

'What *did* you do in your job?' Sam asked, eyeing him with a new curiosity.

'I was hardly more than an office boy,' David confessed, 'but the office in question was the Committee of Imperial Defence.' A touch of pride entered his voice. 'One of our reports was actually responsible for starting the Secret Intelligence Service, you know.'

They all stared at the photographs. Ben looked both horrified, and excited that he'd been the one to bring this to light, but Helen's face was as pale as her brother's, and Sam looked at Adam with a shared realisation that they, and Leah, had been playing with a fire far hotter and more explosive than they'd dreamed. It was like swimming back to shore and learning you'd been treading water above an active volcano.

Helen broke the heavy silence. 'What do we do?'

'We do exactly what he wants us to do,' Adam said grimly. 'We have to keep him here for as long as we can, so David can get on to his old office and tell them what we've got cornered here.'

'I need to know everything, first,' David said, 'they'll want every minute detail, to pass on to Foreign Intelligence.'

'We can't give you that,' Adam put in quickly. 'I'm not risking Leah getting into trouble for what she's been doing.'

'Why?' David asked, momentarily distracted by fascination. 'What *has* she been doing?'

'Never mind that,' Helen said firmly. 'If he's really working for the Germans, I think it's a safe assumption that the 'job' he has in mind for Leah is recruitment.'

'You're probably right.' David picked up the papers. 'I might not be fluent, but there are certain words we

338

saw a lot in our department, and this was one of them.' He pointed. '*Flüchten*. It means *defect*, as in *abscond*. He might be looking for a replacement for someone they've lost to our side.'

'He'll have seen she's a valuable asset, as a bit of a chameleon,' Sam agreed. 'No doubt he feels that, with her husband out of the picture, she'll be fair game to win over.'

David nodded. 'He's probably talking about it to his handler even now, convincing them she's right for them. They'll have to do a lot of checking into her background.'

Adam tightened up at that. 'But if he manages all that before we have the SIS on our side, we'll lose them both.'

'Then we'll have to try and delay things for a while, get Leah to hesitate, or maybe say she thinks she knows where Glynn is.'

'She'd only have to hold this Neville character off long enough for me to convince the War Office to hand it over to Foreign Intelligence,' David said. 'And that won't take long; they're desperate to get their hands on him.'

'You can telephone from my office,' Helen said, but David shook his head.

'I don't trust the telephone here, there could be something in place to intercept the call.'

'What on earth are you talking about?' Helen looked mystified, but Sam was nodding.

'They've been doing it for years. It's possible to tap the wire and record conversations, and if Neville's been able to get into your office overnight, there's a risk he's already done it. I'll get it checked,' he added, in response to Helen's look of dismay.

'In the meantime, we're wasting precious travelling hours.' David picked up the photographs. 'I can always stop somewhere along the way and call ahead though. Can I take these with me, Ben?'

'Of course. I'm sorry they're so dark.'

'Don't worry. I assume you still have the negatives?'

'Not with me, no. They're back at the Summerleaze.'

'Never mind. The office should still be able to decipher these.' David put the photographs back into their folder, looking so much younger and brighter than he had five minutes ago that Adam was poignantly reminded of their childhood. 'I'll leave right away. Not a word to Kay about this, mind,' he added.

'What do I tell her?' Helen asked, standing up.

David gave her a swift grin. 'Tell her I've gone to see Clare,' he said. 'She'll be angry enough to hope I stay gone for weeks.'

★ ★ ★

Adam made his way upstairs, his head still spinning to think that, while he'd been sitting in Simon Hill's office discussing figures and projections, over stewed tea, Fox Bay had been thrumming with all this activity and deception. Helen had briefly explained about the necessary misleading of Neville with regard to herself and Sam, so at least he was prepared for that whenever Neville was around . . . . It occurred to him, though, that he still had no idea what the man looked like, and with a full hotel he'd be hard pressed to tell him from any other guest.

He knocked at Leah's door. 'It's me,' he called in a low voice, aware that Kay was in Bertie's room just

340

down the hall. The last thing he wanted was to bring her out of the woodwork just at the moment.

Leah opened the door, and he relaxed a little as he saw her wide, welcoming smile. 'You're back, good. I have to talk to you.'

'I know,' Adam said, following her inside. 'I've heard.'

'Heard what?'

He told her how he'd barely got in the door before Ben had called to him, and then explained all that had happened downstairs. Her eyes widened as he told her David's news about the Coyote, but she was clearly relieved to see she wouldn't have to explain why she'd lied about her trip to the Summerleaze.

'I'm sorry,' she said, taking his hands. 'You do understand though?'

'I do, but that doesn't mean I have to be happy about it.' He drew her close and kissed her forehead. 'Have you been skulking around up here ever since?'

'More or less. The thing is, all he knows is that I live here, he doesn't know how close I am to the family, and I don't want him to.'

'Do you think they'd be in danger if he did?'

She shook her head. 'Not really, although I suppose, if he were to doubt me in any way . . . No, the main thing is that I don't want him to think I have people to step in and help me. I want him to think I'd be ready to drop my so-called lonely life here, and do whatever he demands of me, to save Glynn.'

'Do you think you'll be able to hold him off long enough?'

'I suppose it depends how long it is before he comes looking for me and puts his proposal.' Leah pursed her lips. 'You do realise that if I refuse, he's going to

341

have to silence me before I blow the whistle on him?'

Adam went cold, why hadn't he even thought of that? 'But you won't refuse,' he said, 'so you'll be safe as long as he believes you're interested.'

Leah crossed to the table by the window and sat down. Adam joined her, and waited while she stared out over the cliffs to the sea beyond. He knew she wasn't taking in the view, and he waited to see where her thoughts had taken her. His heart shifted a little as he watched different expressions touch her features: concentration, a dawning notion, then clarity, and finally excitement. His spirits sank, and he knew for good and all now that she was made for a life exactly like the one Neville was offering. Not that she would consider such an offer, but it had shown her how much more there was to life than Fox Bay. And him.

'Let's beat him to it,' she said, turning shining eyes on him. 'Let's get there before he does!'

'I'm not . . . What do you mean?'

Leah jumped up and began pacing. Her movements were controlled, but her voice was rich with the exhilaration he had seen on her face. 'I go to *him*. I tell him I know who he is, and that I don't want some silly job he might have lined up for me, I want to be what *he* is.'

'What difference would that make?'

'It would put the timing back in my hands, to begin with,' Leah said. 'He'd also have to keep a low profile, knowing I could tell people, but also that I probably won't, *if* he considers recruiting me.'

'He'd be in a pretty difficult position alright,' Adam mused. 'Talk about torn.'

'Exactly! I'd be in control, at least for a while, which should give David time to get what he wants from his old office. Who'd have thought?' She grinned. 'Boring old David Marlowe, helping uncover a spy!'

'He was never boring,' Adam protested, 'he just, sort of, started to fade into the background after prep school. We were best pals until then.'

'He'll be rewarded now, that's for sure. He might even get his old job back.'

But Adam couldn't share Leah's enthusiasm just yet, there were too many questions. 'How will we explain you suddenly knowing who he is, when you had no idea the other night?'

Leah paused in her pacing, and stared into space, her hands on her hips and her fingers tapping. As much as Adam loved looking at her in that attitude, able to study her without her knowing, he loved even more that he knew her astonishing mind was whirring away, picking up ideas and casting them away faster than he could come up with even one. He was amazed he had ever once considered her nothing more than a diversion from his supposed higher feelings for Helen.

'Got it!' Leah clapped her hands together, making him jump. 'We make sure someone else recognises him, someone unconnected with me, and I can say I heard it from them.'

'I could do it.' Adam heard his own words and couldn't believe it. Now she was making *him* eager to be part of this madness. 'He doesn't know we know one another the way we do.'

'Not you, no. As far as anyone's concerned you're just part of the management, and not likely to be involved in anything like that.' A slow smile spread across her face. 'We'll ask Kurt to do it.'

'Strommer?' Adam shook his head, perplexed. 'What can he do that would convince Neville he's a

343

spy too?'

'Well, he'll know he's German of course, from the hotel literature. That'll give him a head start. And a sous-chef occupies a position where he's practically invisible, yet he'd be perfectly placed to observe any clandestine goings-on, and also,' her smile turned wicked, 'to . . . administer anything, to any meal, should his superiors require it.'

Adam suppressed a shudder. 'That's almost too believable,' he admitted. 'Go on then, tell me how it would work.'

Leah sat down again, took a deep breath, and began outlining her plan.

★ ★ ★

Sam left Helen and Ben alone in the sitting room, and Helen eyed her son shrewdly. He had made no move to return to his own hotel, and something about the way he'd avoided her question about the place earlier was starting to niggle, now that the other business was out of the way for the moment.

'Won't Lily be expecting you back?' she probed. 'Not that I'm not delighted to see you, of course.'

'I'm not much bothered if she is,' he said, in a heavier voice than she was used to hearing.

'What does that mean?' Helen sat opposite him. 'You've worked well together so far.'

'We still do. But,' he sighed, 'she's found out about Daisy and me.'

'Ah.' Helen rose to pour a drink, but he raised a hand to stop her as she picked up a second glass.

'Not for me, thanks. I might be unwilling, but I do still have to drive back to Bude in a minute.'

344

'You'd better tell me what's going on then,' Helen said. 'How did Lily find out about Daisy?'

'Leah told her. It wasn't her fault; she assumed Lily knew, once the story about the photograph came out.'

'Photograph?'

Ben told her about the moving-in-day picture he'd taken, and how Lily had found it. 'So now she knows Daisy is a permanent fixture, and that she and I don't have a future. Since then she's been behaving like a spoiled brat.' He ran his hands through his hair and sank lower into his chair; he didn't look like a man eager to return to his home, that was for sure.

'You still have a job to do, darling,' Helen said gently. 'Come on, you can't just play truant because your assistant manager's making life difficult.'

'It's more than that,' Ben confessed. He dragged himself upright again, and looked as if he wished he hadn't refused a drink. 'I can't stand that place, Mum. It's awful.'

Helen felt for him, but couldn't help smiling. 'You've been there less than three weeks,' she pointed out. 'Give it a chance.'

'I mean it. The staff move around more like prison warders than service staff, and Lily won't allow any kind of contact with them, beyond issuing orders.'

'Lily won't? Ben, you're the manager. It's not up to Lily.'

'I don't feel like it.' Ben looked down at his feet. 'That's why I'm leaving. Going to London.'

'What?' Helen's spirits plummeted. 'Why London?'

'I'll never feel at home at the Summerleaze. It's the wrong kind of place for me.'

'And what's the right kind?' Helen asked, hoping she knew the answer already.

345

'I know you'll think I'm being pathetic,' Ben said, on a heavy sigh. 'And you'll say I'm near-sighted, and lacking ambition, but the sort of place I want to manage is more traditional, more . . . intimate, I suppose. Stylish but friendly. Like here.'

'*Like* here? Or here?'

'I don't want to go back to being an invisible, night-shift manager,' Ben said, avoiding the direct question, his lowered eyes not seeing the smile that had settled on Helen's face. 'I don't want some unnecessary job that was invented for me.'

'Ben,' Helen said, leaning forward to touch his hand. 'Look at me. You can be the full-time, main manager of Fox Bay. *I'm* moving on, and I can't think of anyone I'd feel happier handing the reins to. It's yours, after all.'

He raised his face to hers, frowning. 'Moving on?'

'I have a job somewhere else. It's hard to explain, but so many of my family and . . . and my loved ones are leaving, or have left already. It's felt as if things were, sort of, falling into fragments around me.' Helen waved a hand, unable to put into words how adrift she'd been feeling. 'All of you have either found your feet in the wider world or will be doing so, soon, so I decided it was time I explored what was out there, too, and I found a job. An hotel Pagetts are building in Truro.'

'The Pearson?' Ben looked as if he were still taking in what she was saying. 'Will you live there?'

'For the most part, yes. But this will always be my home, and I'll come back often. But the point is will *you* come back, and claim your inheritance early? I'll sign it over to you if that will help.'

'No.' Ben's eyes were wide and excited, belying the

346

blunt response. 'I mean, yes! I'll come back, and I'll manage it, but you mustn't sign it over, I'm not having you feel like a guest again, not now. It's yours. But I'll be happier than you can imagine to come and work for you.'

Helen bit back a laugh of relief, and kept her expression sober. 'Good. I'll publish the advertisement next week, and expect your application in the post.' She grinned at the suddenly uncertain look on Ben's face. 'You never used to be so gullible, darling.'

Ben snorted, and went to pour himself a drink after all. 'I think I'll sleep here tonight,' he said, 'it's not as if I have to worry about a good reference, now, is it?'

★ ★ ★

Helen enjoyed the chance to chat to him, something they'd rarely done even when he still lived at home, but after a while she noted it was almost dinnertime, and excused herself to finish writing up the Higher Valley order. She picked up the scribbled notes, ready to enter them neatly into the ledger, but even as she began copying her mind wandered, and all she could hear was Beth telling her Alfie was leaving. She soon abandoned them, and instead went to the shelves to find Harry's old, tattered atlas, which she opened at the larger-scale West Country section. She placed one finger on Truro, and traced a line to Porthstennack with another, and stared in surprise as she realised it was only around twenty miles. She checked again but there was no mistake, and she smiled; down there they'd be unknown, unfettered by other relationships or complications . . . there might still be a chance for them.

347

In fact, the more she thought about it, the clearer it became: if one of them stayed in Trethkellis, and the other moved away, there would be no hope at all. Despite any promises they might make, with two busy lives it would be impossible; one of them would have to give up their job and their home to be with the other — which would inevitably lead to resentment — otherwise they'd simply drift, no matter how deeply they felt for one another. If one went, the other must go too, so this was perfect. Fate had smilingly approved; Helen had done the right thing applying for the Pearson job after all.

The railway ran neatly between the two, with midway stops at Stithians and Rame. Helen closed her eyes and imagined meeting him at the station, both all dressed up in their Sunday best, and Alfie looking as uncomfortable as ever in a smart shirt and tie. In her mind's eye she walked towards him, on an unknown little branch-line platform somewhere, and saw his smile turn from shy and uncertain to wide and happy; she felt his hands on her face, and saw the blue of his eyes darken as they came closer to hers, his lips barely touching hers, as he breathed her name before the kiss became firm and inescapable . . .

'Mrs Fox!'

She jumped, and felt the flush on her cheeks, but the door was still closed; Martin had not witnessed her daydreaming. 'What is it?' she called.

'The post.' He popped his head around the door. 'Came a bit later than usual, but I've already taken out anything for Mr Coleridge.'

'Thank you.' Helen held out her hand, noting immediately that one envelope was thicker than the others, and realising it must be her contract.

With her new hope for a future with Alfie Nancar-row still at the forefront of her mind, she opened it and spread it on the desk in front of her, one hand already reaching for a pen with which to sign it, to make it final. Then she could go to Alfie with a plan instead of a wish.

For a moment, the words swam in front of her eyes, making no sense, and she had to stop and begin again, after making sure hers was the name on the envelope. Then she dropped the pen and put her face into her hands; Fate was no longer smiling, but had taken another look at her dreams, and stamped all over them.

22

Leah had kept out of everyone's way all weekend. She had taken her meals in her room, and had not seen any sign of Leonard Neville, but wasn't sure if that was down to her efforts, or his intention, and now that she was ready to begin her newest charade she could feel that familiar low thrum of excitement in her blood.

She looked at the clock and made her way down-stairs, praying it would all come together as she'd planned. Neville was taking his seat in the dining room, and Leah glanced around, ensuring her room number was on the table directly opposite. She delib-erately chose the seat that left her facing him, and as she saw him she assumed an expression of shock, then gradual, determined calm. Finally she allowed her eyes to linger on his in a provocative stare that clearly said, *Well? If you want to talk to me, here I am.*

He looked away, shaking out his napkin, and spread it across his lap, and she did the same. She gave her order to the waiter, and now and again she let her eyes linger challengingly on Neville, though the sight of him made her flesh creep. She ate steadily, vaguely aware of the movements of others, and perturbed to note how quickly Neville was getting through his meal. Suddenly worried her opportunity was passing her by, she raised a finger to a passing waiter, and manufactured a huge smile.

'I'd be so glad if you could have the chef brought to my table, so I can thank him.'

The waiter disappeared, and Leah wanted to take a sip of water to ease her suddenly dry throat, but feared it might slip; she'd never been so nervous, not even in Liverpool when things had started to go wrong. So much depended on this, it would be too obviously staged if she had to do it again at a later date.

'Madam,' a light, cheerful voice said in her ear, and she silently praised the chef for his breezy acting. From the corner of her eye she saw Neville's attention naturally swivel to the new arrival, as had everyone else's.

'I wanted to thank you for a delicious meal,' she said, 'and to pass my compliments to you directly. It was perfection itself.'

Kurt Strommer played his part well. He bowed low, and as he rose again his gaze fell naturally on the table opposite. Leah heard him snatch a sharp breath, and whisper, 'Der Kojote,' before whipping around and hurrying back to the kitchen. She was tempted to look at Neville, but had to assume he'd at least seen Kurt mouth the word, even if he hadn't heard it. She twisted to look after the chef in surprise, but made no sign that she had connected the strange word with the guest opposite.

She saw a lady at a nearby table looking at her with raised eyebrows, and she laughed. 'Artists,' she said with a little roll of her eyes, and the woman smiled back and sketched a little salute of agreement. Leah returned to her meal and studiously avoided looking at Neville again.

★ ★ ★

Later she went to the kitchen and signalled to Kurt to meet her outside. After a few minutes he joined her

351

by the back door, and they walked a short way down the path.

'Did he hear you?' she asked, offering him a cigarette.

He took it, and cupped his hands around the end as she lit it for him, then drew deeply on it, and she could see he was shaken. 'I don't know,' he said, 'but he saw me, for sure.'

'What did he do?'

'Like this.' Kurt's mouth dropped open for a second, then his jaw clamped shut and he mimed eating quickly.

Leah gave him a tight smile. 'You were brilliant. Remind me to recommend you for the local drama society.'

Kurt nodded. 'And now I go away?'

'For a while.' Leah took an envelope from her pocket. 'There's your next month's wages in advance, you shouldn't need to be away longer than that. Will you go home?'

'Maybe.' He shrugged. 'Maybe I should like to visit Austria instead. There are many places I have not yet seen.'

'Thank you, Kurt. None of us knows how many lives you might have saved if this all goes to plan.' Leah stretched up to kiss his cheek.

'I will do it again for you, if you like,' he said with a wink, and Leah laughed.

'That won't be necessary, thank goodness! Make sure he doesn't see you now, alright? The taxi will be waiting on the main road in twenty minutes.'

She went back indoors and slipped up the stairs, unseen, to where Adam waited in her room.

'How did it go?'

352

'Like clockwork.'

'How long will you leave it?'

Leah fell backwards across her bed, exhausted from the tension. 'Until tomorrow. Long enough for him to have ascertained that Kurt has left. That's down to you, you know what you have to do?'

'Make a song and dance about how unreliable he is, and announce that I'm telephoning Harry Batten to take over.'

'Great.' Leah groaned. 'I can't bear all this waiting around! I'd rather be down there talking to him than up here thinking about it.'

'Come down then, watch me do my party piece.'

'You can't do it tonight,' Leah said, 'it's too soon. He has to have not turned up to start the lunch service, before you'd be likely to go looking for a substitute. Breakfast is an annoyance but not a disaster, but missing lunch would result in his marching orders, and you'd need Harry by dinner. When did you actually call him?'

'When you were having your bath, after we talked on Saturday.' Adam sat down next to her, and she pulled herself upright and nestled against his side as his arm came around her. 'David should be back tomorrow. He stopped off at his home in Exeter and telephoned Helen from there.'

'Good. The more information I can throw at Neville, the better.'

'Have *you* spoken to Helen at all?'

'You've seen her more than I have,' Leah pointed out. 'I've been skulking, remember? Why, is she alright?'

'She's being very secretive. Do you know something I don't?'

Leah hesitated, then decided he had a right to know. She told him about Helen's new job, and why she'd felt the need to move on now that everyone around her was doing the same. 'She feels as if the heart is going out of Fox Bay,' she finished, a little sadly. 'You losing a quarter share to Hartcliffe hasn't helped.'

'And are you one of those who's *moving on*?' he asked, his voice low and serious.

She twisted to look up at him. 'Why do you ask?'

'That Liverpool business, and now seeing you so keen to throw yourself into this, with Neville. You still miss it all, don't you?'

She nodded, there was no sense lying. 'But I know I can't go on with it forever,' she said. 'What I really want is a life of my own. Not leeching off the kindness of friends, or living someone else's, even if it's someone I've made up. I want a home, and I'm curious to see what my life is like once everything else is stripped away.'

'Would there be room in it for a slightly decrepit, shop-soiled old reprobate?'

Despite the humour in his words, there was an echo in his voice. A faint emptiness lined with hope, and she felt a warmth spread through her at the knowledge that she was the one he needed.

'I might find a dusty corner,' she allowed, letting her fingers walk up his waistcoat to the open collar of his shirt. 'Provided he doesn't take up too much room, or get in my way.'

He huffed a soft laugh, and dragged her back down so they were lying widthways across the bed, and she draped her arm across his waist and curled in close. Only one more hurdle to get over, and her own life could begin, with Adam by her side.

The following morning David returned from his short trip to London. He sent Fiona to fetch Leah, who hurried down to the sitting room to where Helen and Adam waited.

'Sam's on his way,' Adam said, reaching for her hand. 'Neville heard me demanding to know where our chef was, but you'd have been proud of me, darling, I didn't ham it up in the least.'

Leah grinned as she took the last remaining chair. 'Good for you.' She was feeling that fizzing sensation again, and noticed her foot was dancing up and down where she had one leg crossed over the other. She stopped it, with a conscious effort, as Sam came in.

'You've managed to keep Kay at bay, then?' David said, as Sam closed the door. He looked at Helen, who seemed distant, even though things were reaching a head now. 'Hels?'

'Hmm? Sorry. Yes, Fiona's been doing sterling work keeping your wife occupied with all the little things she'll need to know if she buys into the place.'

'She's still talking about that?'

'Yes, but she won't be running it, Ben will.' Helen smiled at last. 'He's coming home this weekend, to take over from me. But I'll explain that later.' She waved at David. 'Go on, what happened?'

'Right, well that business in Liverpool had been set up, but not by the police. By the Secret Intelligence Service. They used the police because they didn't want their man . . . what was his name, Leah?'

'Wilf Stanley.'

David nodded. 'They couldn't bring someone like him into their confidence, but he'd be likely to accept

355

police involvement, and respond to a deal offered by them. The officers themselves weren't even told the full extent, just that the government needed them to bring in this man under a genuine charge, at which point they'd take over.

'And I scuppered that,' Leah said. 'I gave him the chance to get away.'

'Well you've made up for it since, interesting him enough to bring him here to recruit you. Anyway, it was Adam who made you withdraw from the deal.'

'I wouldn't do a thing differently,' Adam broke in, scowling. 'Leah's safety was infinitely more important!'

David ignored him and turned to Leah. 'It's vital we catch Neville actually *in the act* of recruiting you, otherwise we'll have no cause to hold him while he's investigated. So by all means speak to him, get him on the hook, as it were, but make sure you keep him dangling while *you* weigh things up, which will give him time to do the same.' He turned to Helen. 'You'll have to make sure there's a room near Neville's. Next door, if at all possible, for me to move into.'

'You? But you don't even work for the War Office anymore, let alone the Intelligence services.'

'They're sending an agent down, but they don't want to spook Coyote by introducing someone new right next door to him. He doesn't know we're onto him, but he knows the hotel's full, and he's not remained undiscovered this long without being alert.' He started to look self-consciously pleased now. 'So, since this is going to be very straightforward they've given me temporary power of arrest. And a Webley revolver, thank goodness.'

Helen paled. 'I'm not sure I like the idea of guns in

356

the hotel.'

'You can be sure they're already here,' David pointed out. 'We'll need them too, if we're going to be bringing him in.'

'How soon will your other agent get here?' Leah asked, feeling her nerves stretch even further, but eager to begin her role in Neville's capture.

'I'll receive a telegram when he's on his way. I have permission to engage Mr Douglas too,' he added, 'so I'll brief you afterwards, Sam.'

Helen still looked unsure. 'Those first-floor rooms are fully booked for months. How will we justify removing guests at a moment's notice?'

'You'll just have to manufacture a fault,' David said, a little impatiently. 'Adam, you can apply your rather sneaky mind to that one.'

'*Sneaky?*' Adam's eyes widened.

'Very.'

Leah had never seen Helen's mild brother so assertive, but it seemed to be doing him good. 'We'll think of something,' she assured him, over Adam's mutinous muttering. She glanced at Helen again, who had once more subsided into her own thoughts. It had been a few days since they'd been able to talk, and she made up her mind to put that right as soon as they'd finished here.

David opened his briefcase and took out some papers. 'Translations taken from the photographs Ben took . . . .' He looked around. 'Where is Ben? It's thanks to him we discovered the Coyote in the first place.'

'He's still at the Summerleaze for now,' Adam said. 'I'm sure he'll be pleased to have helped.'

'There's a chap we've been trying to bring onto our

357

side,' David said, again directing his words to Leah, 'who Der Kojote will definitely have heard of, but, in all likelihood, never seen. The man's code name is Gürteltier, which means armadillo.'

'Doesn't sound nearly as dashing as Coyote,' Adam said, and Leah heard the grin in his voice. 'Sounds like something you'd be called, David.'

'The armadillo is well known for sleeping,' David said, narrowing his eyes. 'But I wouldn't expect you to make the necessary leap of logic.'

For old friends, the two men certainly seemed to enjoy needling one another, but Adam was definitely being more provocative, and Leah dug him in the ribs.

'Stop it!'

'A sleeper,' David went on, rather pointedly shifting his attention back to the others, 'is an agent who integrates him or herself into a false life until the moment they're required. A chef being the perfect . . . cover, if you'll pardon the pun. And particularly at a place like this, so close to the sea and with its own beach. So, if Leah says that Strommer told her he was Gürteltier, he'd be likely to believe her. D'you see? It's just one more layer of credibility.'

'Understood.' Leah practised the name under her breath a few times. 'Right.'

'And you could throw in the name, Erich Raeder, too,' David instructed. 'Current head of the *Reichsmarine*. Likely to be in the chain of command of someone working from the coast, like Strommer.'

'Erich Raeder.' Leah committed the name to memory. 'Anything else?'

'Strommer won't have had time to tell you much,' David cautioned, 'so don't go in there all guns blazing and getting those names just right. You need to

358

stumble over them a bit, perhaps get one slightly wrong, but it'll be clear you know enough to be either threat or saviour.' He paused, thinking. 'And make sure you find a good reason to explain why you had him brought to your table,' he added, 'that's something else that will ring an alarm bell with him, once you make your move.'

'You're very good at this,' Helen said, coming out of herself and giving her brother a look of surprised admiration.

David's smile was a thin one. 'Just because my wife doesn't rate me, doesn't mean I'm the drip she thinks I am. I was good at my job.' There was real regret on his face now. 'I know I've been all breezy about it, but this little foray back into that world has reminded me how much I've missed it.'

'You know,' Adam said, looking at him carefully, 'you'd make quite a good spy yourself. Why don't you suggest it?'

'Are you mocking me?'

'Certainly not. You and old Neville out there have that, sort of, nondescript thing in common.'

'Adam,' Helen warned, but Adam held up his hands.

'Believe it or not, I was offering a compliment. David *would* make an excellent agent. Almost unnoticeable, but with that sharp brain of his taking everything in. And with the added bonus that he already knows the job, and has signed the Official Secrets Act.'

David looked unsure whether he ought to take Adam's earnest response at face value, and Leah could hardly blame him, but she knew Adam better, and she sensed he was being sincere. It seemed David had come to the same conclusion; he gave Adam a wary half-smile, and turned back to Leah.

359

'Are you ready?'

'Absolutely.'

David held out a hand. 'Good luck. Remember what I said: reel him in slowly, just give us the chance to get our backup chap in place.'

Leah shook his hand, amused at the brisk, *you're dismissed*, tone in his voice. 'I just want a word with Helen,' she said gently, disengaging her hand from his.

'Oh. Of course. Sam, I'll meet you in the lounge after lunch. Meantime, I'd better go and find Kay, I suppose.'

The comical reluctance in those last few words brought a ripple of laughter, and he gave them all that same little smile, perhaps proud to have played his part in the unfolding drama, but Leah suspected it was more the sense of easy friendship that now pervaded the little group.

Helen stood up and embraced him. 'You've been wonderful, thank you.'

'I'll be around whenever you need me,' Sam said to Leah. 'Don't worry if you can't see me right away, I'll be there somewhere.'

'And I'd better get out and be the face of Fox Bay for a while,' Adam put in. He looked pointedly at Helen before he slipped out, Sam at his back, leaving Leah and Helen alone again.

'You've told him I'm leaving, then?' Helen said, pouring herself and Leah a drink. She looked poised to say more, but Leah cut her off before she could deliver her opinion.

'I'm sorry, I know I should have left it to you, but I was cornered. He already knew you were up to something, and . . . Anyway, it led on to a conversation

360

about our own future.'

Helen's expression changed from introspective to interested, as she handed Leah her drink. 'Oh? And what was the verdict?'

Leah smiled. 'I don't know where we'll live, or what we'll be doing, but I think we're going to be alright.'

'Good.' Helen raised her glass in salute. 'It's about time. With Ben back, at least we'll keep the hotel mostly in the family.'

'You've been looking a bit strange this morning,' Leah said. 'That's what I wanted to talk to you about. Is it Alfie?'

'He's leaving.' Helen told her what Beth had said about Keir Garvey's farm in Porthstennack. 'She doesn't seem to know if it's for good, but I rather suspect it will be.'

'Oh, Hels, I'm so sorry. Why does life have to be so complicated?'

'I keep reliving that moment in the churchyard, over and over. Why didn't I just tell him there and then?'

'Don't keep blaming yourself for that, you did the right thing not just throwing yourself into something you weren't sure of. That could have been the worst kind of mistake.' She gave Helen an encouraging smile. 'Perhaps fate will find a way to bring you together later, down in Cornwall, away from complicated family things and — '

'He's in the lounge.' Sam spoke even as he shoved open the door, and Helen looked at Leah nervously, but kept her voice brisk.

'Looks like you're on. We'll talk later.'

Leah emptied her glass too quickly, blinked to clear her watering eyes of the fumes, and then stood up and straightened her skirt. She took a deep breath and blew it out slowly, until the shakiness in it steadied. 'Wish me luck.'

* * *

She found Neville in the lounge, enjoying a pre-lunch snifter. He was seated alone, near the window, but glanced up as the door swung open. Leah knew that any hesitation would render everything she was about to do useless, so she marched straight across to him and sat down opposite.

'I know who you are, and what you're doing here.'

Neville froze in the act of raising his cigar to his lips, and just stared at her. Leah sat back and waited. Her heart was skipping uncomfortably, but she felt that old excitement zipping through her limbs, sparking her brain and keeping it alive to everything around her.

Eventually he spoke, as she knew he must. 'What exactly is it that you think you know?'

She couldn't help admiring his calm, but he was a professional. It was time to show the side of her she wanted him to believe, and she dropped the brisk attitude and leaned forward again, letting her eyes dart left and right, and especially towards the bar.

'I had to come and see you because ... Look, I want to be part of it.'

'I don't know what you —'

'*Kojote!*' Leah hissed, carefully watching Neville's face, which remained expressionless. 'Kurt told me.'

There was an agonisingly long pause, then Neville rose to his feet. He glanced out of the window. 'The gazebo,' he said in a low voice. 'Don't follow me out of this room until someone else has left first.'

Leah waited, and after a group of two couples had decided it was time for their lunch, she trailed them out into the lobby, casting glances around to make sure Sam was there. She saw him in one of the seats where he had a clear view of the lounge door, but it would be next to impossible for him to follow her, unseen, out to the gazebo. Something Neville had clearly considered. This was probably the most dangerous part for Leah, she realised, having already revealed what she knew about him.

She prayed he wasn't carrying any weapons and, finding courage in the fact that it was still daylight, at least, she slipped out through the side door, into the cloisters, and around to the tennis courts. Neville was waiting in the gazebo, still puffing on that infernal cigar. She climbed the steps, but kept her distance, fighting the urge to look behind her to check Sam hadn't risked following her anyway.

'Kurt Strommer knew you,' she said, determined to take control of the conversation from the start. 'We've been . . . close, I suppose you'd say. That was why I wanted to bring him out at dinner, to let him have some of the glory that Gough bloke normally gets, since he does most of the hard work. Anyway,' she went on, waving the apparently inconsequential detail away, 'when I asked him what had frightened him so much, he told me everything.'

'And where is he now, this storyteller?'

'Stop pretending!' Leah said in exasperated tones. 'I told you, I want to be part of it. What do I have to do?'

'I said, where is he?' Neville demanded, his voice harder now, the lazy amusement gone. He dropped his cigar, and Leah watched with relief as he ground it beneath a tooled leather shoe; there was something about its glowing tip that had unnerved her, she could imagine all too vividly what it might feel like pressed against her skin if this discussion took a dangerous turn.

'He's gone,' she said.

'I know he's gone, I heard the manager complaining about it. I want to know *where*.'

'I don't know where! I suppose he realised he'd shown himself, and once he saw I wasn't taking his side, he had to leave.'

'But he was happy to tell you his secrets,' Neville pointed out. 'Why would he do that?'

'I told you, we've been close in the past. Intimate, even. He was one of the reasons I stayed here so often, which is why he was hoping for a different response, I think.'

'And *I* think you'd better tell me everything he told you,' Neville said, leaning back against one of the pillars that supported the high, arched roof. 'All of it, mind.'

Leah furrowed her brow. 'He said he was working for the British Secret Intelligence Service,' she began slowly. 'I asked if that meant he was a spy, and he said yes, and that he'd been placed here at the coast to intercept coded messages during the war. He's been waiting all this time, to be called up to London for re-assignment. He said he was instructed to go about his life normally until he received word.'

'Did he mention another name, by which his people knew him? A code name, perhaps?'

'Gertle, something,' Leah said, frowning harder. 'He said it meant *armadillo*, and they used it because he's . . . sleeping?'

'Gürteltier?' Neville said, in a soft, disbelieving voice. He turned away and stared at the deserted tennis courts, and Leah remained silent, sensing with relief that she'd begun chipping away at his mistrust. After a moment, Neville swung back.

'This man began as an agent for his own homeland,' he said, 'hence the German code name. The British must have turned him.'

'He recognised you right away,' Leah ventured, 'they must be keeping him up to date. But he seemed frightened of you, and I couldn't work out why, if you were both acting for the same government.'

'Then you'll know we're not,' Neville said. 'He'll have a new name by now, but I never learned what that was. I must get word back that he's been turned.'

'No wonder he was frightened then, he must have known you'd recognise him, and that it was all up.'

'But I didn't recognise him. I've only heard of him, never seen him.' For a moment he'd been distracted by the startling news, but he abruptly came back. 'You said you wanted to be part of it. Why say that to me, and not to him?'

Leah turned away, but not before she let him see the knot of painful memory on her face. 'The British army killed someone very close to me,' she said. 'Before Glynn, and all the things we did, there was his brother Daniel who died in the war. They said he was buried in a tunnel collapse.'

'All the more reason to hate the Germans, I'd have thought.'

'They *lied* to me!' Leah swung back, satisfied to see him react to the hatred that blazed from her eyes. 'I later heard a rumour that it was a cover-up, after some ghastly miscalculation by the brass hats. Daniel and

365

three of his fellow sappers were blown up on purpose, to stop the truth from getting out and the officers facing charges.' She pointed to the low wall that ran around St Adhwynn's church, separating it from the hotel's land. 'There's a grave marker just down there.'

'Only a marker?'

'His body was never recovered. After the war there were memoirs published, of course; no names, but we knew because of the dates. When Kurt confessed his identity to me I asked him if he knew of it. He said he'd heard there'd been a cover-up to protect some high-ranking officer, but that he hadn't known my Daniel was one of those who'd been killed. I vowed that I would never support such a corrupt government.'

'Corrupt, indeed,' Neville hissed suddenly, startling her. 'You have no notion just *how* corrupt!'

'So if there's a chance of me working to bring them down, I want to take it. Please!'

'Are you sure you know what you're asking?'

'What was the job you wanted me for?' she countered. 'Whatever it is, I'll do it, to prove to you I trust you, and that I'll be loyal.' She allowed tears to shine in her eyes, and lowered her voice to a whisper. 'Only please, give me a chance to avenge Daniel.'

Neville fell silent, studying her, and she could see he wanted to confess that what she had asked of him was the very thing he'd hinted at, when they'd met at the Summerleaze. And now he believed they'd lost another valuable sleeper, it could only strengthen her cause.

But he kept his thoughts to himself. 'Did you tell anyone about our meeting in Bude?'

'Who would I tell? I've got no friends here.'

'The man who gave you a lift? Affianced to the owner, didn't you say?'

'I told you, he assumed it was an assignation,' she said, lowering her eyes. 'I didn't disabuse him of that notion on the way home. Neither he nor Mrs Fox are people I could talk to about my . . . other activities.'

Neville took out a cigarette and tapped it thoughtfully against its box. 'If Gürteltier has indeed been turned, as you suggest, we're going to need a replacement.' He spoke as if he were merely musing aloud, and Leah tensed, but remained silent, hoping she was right in her assumption that he lacked the authority to approach her here and now.

'Go back inside,' he said, after a moment. 'Don't speak to anyone about what your chef friend said, or what we've discussed. If you do, you won't see another daybreak. Don't for one minute think I don't mean it,' he added, his voice hard.

Leah nodded, though a chill crept through her as she looked at him; it would be the easiest thing in the world for him to make good on that promise. She turned away and stumbled down the steps, wiping at her eyes as she went, and ran back across the grass to the cloisters, where she found Sam chatting to a guest. They exchanged a brief glance, and she gave him the tiniest nod. The bait had been laid out, and all she could do now was wait.

23

Bertie enjoyed Tory's rather slapdash approach to driving. She found herself flinching from the snapping hedgerows, but laughing at the same time, as Tory negotiated the narrow lanes between Caernoweth and Trethkellis, nattering away non-stop.

The moment their last lesson had ended, a little earlier on a Friday, Tory had brought her M-Type Midget around to the front of the air base, her bags already stowed in the back beneath the canvas. Gwenna had watched, with poorly concealed envy, as Bertie had added her bag and the two of them had driven off the base to begin their weekend at Fox Bay; despite feeling bad for leaving her behind, Bertie couldn't deny she was looking forward to showing her home off to her new friend, and vice versa.

They arrived at around six o'clock, to find Fiona in a state of great excitement. 'What are *you* doing back? Never mind,' she rushed on, before Bertie could answer. 'You've missed *the* most exciting thing, but the best is still to come!' Her attention fell on Tory. 'Hello, I'm Fiona.'

Tory put out her hand. 'Tory Gilbert, Bertie's friend. She talks about you all the time.'

Bertie gave her a sidelong look; the first and only mention had been when she'd told the story about Amy and Daisy Conrad, but Fiona looked pleased, so she kept quiet. 'What's been happening?' she asked instead.

'I'll tell you when you're settled in . . . oh.'

'What?'

'Well, you know how busy we are at the moment,' Fiona began, but Bertie shook her head.

'It's alright, Tory can sleep in my room.'

'No, that's what I was going to say. Aunt Kay is in your room. We didn't know you were coming back,' she added quickly, seeing Bertie's frown.

'Well you didn't wait long, did you?'

'It wasn't my fault,' Fiona protested, 'she turned up out of the blue.'

'Why isn't she staying with Uncle David, in Granny's room?' Bertie held up a hand. 'No, don't tell me, they're not speaking. Again.'

'They are,' Fiona allowed, 'but it's not anything we ought to hear.'

Tory giggled, and Bertie's irritation faded; it *was* rather funny. 'Where's Mum?'

'I'll see if I can find her. Then I'll come and tell you everything Aunt Leah's been doing.'

'I might have known it would be her.' Bertie grinned, relaxing properly now. 'I thought all that business was over?'

'Far from it! It's top secret, but now you're here you'll have to know all about it in case you ruin things.'

Tory was looking from one to the other as if she suspected she was being teased, and Bertie grabbed her sleeve and pulled her towards the sitting room. 'Whatever she's talking about,' she said, 'you can bet your last shilling it's real.'

Fiona returned after ten minutes, when Bertie had given Tory a brief description of Leah and her little 'games'. She had just finished telling her what little she knew about the Liverpool trip, and Tory was looking flabbergasted.

'Mum says she'll turf Aunty Kay out of your room,' Fiona said. 'Uncle David is going to be livid, because now she'll have to move in with him. Although at the moment —'

'Can't she have Ben's room?'

'Oh of course, that's another thing you don't know. Ben's coming back this afternoon!'

'To live? He's decided he likes working nights now, does he? Or have he and Lily had the inevitable falling out?'

'Haven't a clue,' Fiona admitted. 'Mum's so excited you're here for a visit, she said she'll be in to see you in a minute. She's just talking to Adam about something. He's sold half his shares, you know, which means his old business partner will own a quarter of the hotel. Oh, there's *so* much to tell you!'

'How long have you been gone,' Tory asked Bertie, amused, 'two weeks, or two years?'

Fiona continued, ticking things off on her fingers. 'Harry Batten's taken over from Kurt Strommer, just for a few weeks, but he's going to be doing it permanently soon, when Nicholas leaves and Kurt takes over as head chef. And the *big* news,' she lowered her voice until it was barely a whisper, and Bertie had to lean in close, 'is that there's a spy staying here, and Leah's going to help the government catch him!'

She told them everything, in a babbling gush of excitement. 'Guy told the couple who *were* in the room next door to him that there was a leak,' she finished, 'and moved them to a different hotel, at our expense and with a full refund on top. Uncle David's moved in there instead, and he's keeping a close watch on this Mr Bitterson. Or Neville, as Adam keeps calling him. Leah gets really cross when he does that.'

'I'll bet. She's much better at that sort of stuff than he is.'

Fiona grinned. 'Aunt Kay spends all day flirting with Bitterson, you know, and he's pretending to be interested, but he keeps trying to slip out without her hanging onto his coat tails.'

Any further discussion of Kay, and her unrequited interest in Mr Bitterson, was quashed as their mother came in, a few unopened letters in her hand. She embraced Bertie warmly, greeted Tory with a friendly handshake, and handed Bertie the letters.

'I was going to send these on this weekend, but you've beaten me to it.' She pointed to one of them. 'This one has a Brighton postmark; I've been so keen to know what she says.'

'Who's 'she'?' Tory asked.

Bertie took a deep breath. 'Xander's sister, Lynette.'

'Oh! I hope she's had a change of heart.'

Bertie looked at the letter thoughtfully. If it were simply a polite note thanking her for attending Xander's funeral, it would feel as if she were being pushed aside all over again, and she wasn't sure she wanted to see it. But with her mother hanging over her eagerly, and Tory all but jumping up and down, she couldn't really put it off.

The letter was no brief acknowledgement. It was three pages long, and smudged in places, with many crossings out, and corrections, but as she skimmed through it she caught the words, *forgive*, and *talk*, and Lynette had signed it, *your friend always*, and that was enough for now.

Helen had been watching her anxiously but was visibly relieved by Bertie's reaction. She dismissed Fiona back to work, overruling her protests with a reminder that they were too busy for half days, and that she was no more entitled to them than any other member of staff, but as the girl turned dejectedly to the door, their mother relented.

'Your job, this afternoon, is to instruct your sister and Tory on all we have to do, and not do, in order to maintain this latest pretence of Leah's. I don't have the time myself, and it's important that we all know what we're doing.' She gave Tory an apologetic look. 'You'll have to forgive us, but I'm sure Bertie has explained we're well used to aiding my friend in her little deceptions.'

'I can help Ben unpack all his things too, if that helps?' Fiona gestured at the pile of boxes Ben had left in the corner by the window.

'If he asks you for help, then by all means, it's been there quite long enough. Right then,' Helen straightened her shoulders, and gave them all a grim smile, 'wish me luck, I'm going to tell your Aunt Kay to pack her things and move into Fleur's old room.'

'Will she hate that?' Tory asked, puzzled, and Bertie laughed.

'It's alright now, but just wait until Uncle David has to move back in with her.'

★ ★ ★

Later that evening, when Bertie and Tory had settled their things into Bertie's room, they went back downstairs to find Ben had arrived with Daisy. Fiona had told them all she knew of his return, but she hadn't been able to explain anything more than that he was taking over as the hotel's general manager.

'Mum must be getting tired of it,' she'd said, but

Bertie hadn't shared that view; that wasn't their mother's way at all. Was she secretly ill? She didn't want to ask Ben, in front of the others, and wasn't sure she wanted to hear the answer anyway, but she needed to know what had prompted this sudden decision, whatever the reason.

Tory was having trouble keeping her eyes off Daisy, she could see. She was perhaps particularly fascinated because Daisy was dressed to fade into the background and it clearly wasn't working. The bright red hair was wrapped in a plain green scarf, and dull-coloured trousers and a shapeless coat hid the famous curves, but, once the carefree laugh had caught the attention of people nearby, nothing could disguise the dazzling smile and huge green eyes.

While Ben was introducing himself to Tory, Bertie spoke in a low voice to Daisy. 'Would you mind taking Tory off for a quick tour, while I talk to Ben?'

'Not at all,' Daisy said. 'I think there's some stuff he needs to tell you too.' She held out her hand to the star-struck visitor. 'Come on, Tory, these two have a couple things to catch up on, so why don't I show you around? The bar's usually a good place to start.'

Tory took the proffered hand, and shot Bertie an amazed look that made Bertie grin despite her worry. As soon as the door had closed behind them, Bertie pulled Ben away from where he was carefully moving his sabrage sword out of the way so he could open the topmost of his boxes.

'You'd better tell me everything,' she said. 'Is Mum sick? Is that why she's not working anymore?'

'Not working?' Ben's expression cleared. 'Ah, she hasn't told you then. You'd better sit down.'

Bertie sat, more worried than ever, but her fears

373

eased as Ben told her about their mother's new job in Truro. 'It'll be strange for a while,' he said, 'but she was very keen that we should understand she still thinks of this as her home, even if she's working elsewhere.'

'But living there too.'

'Well yes, but only in the same way as you are.'

That made her feel better, since she herself couldn't imagine letting go of Fox Bay altogether. It was comforting to feel anchored to something, even as she explored the world a little further.

'I wonder why Mum hasn't told Fiona?' Bertie mused.

'Maybe she was waiting to be sure I came back, to make it all less of a shock for her.' He shrugged. 'Anyway, the thing is, I *am* back, and bloody glad of it. What about all this stuff with Leah then? Could you credit it?'

'Life would be so dull without her,' Bertie agreed with a little laugh. 'I suppose we'll all have to get used to that though, she's sure to spend less time here once Mum's gone.'

'That's true.' His expression sobered for a moment, then he shook it off. 'Come on, I haven't heard anything about your training yet. Tell me all.'

Bertie did. And as she described the sense of closeness she felt to their father, during her first flight with Jude, she saw his eyes soften and grow a little brighter, just as she knew hers did. They spent some time talking about him then, wondering how he'd react to their mother's new plans, and Ben taking over the day-to-day running of Fox Bay. Eventually, inevitably, they moved on to Adam's latest news.

'Could you buy those shares he's selling instead?'

Bertie asked. 'That would give you and Mum three-quarters between you, and keep it more or less in the family.'

'I'd like to, but I don't know what I'd use for money.'

'You could sell the Bugatti, to begin with . . . .' Bertie saw the look on his face and held up a hand. 'Just a thought!'

The door opened and Leah came in, her face breaking into a broad smile as she saw the two of them together. 'This is quite like old times,' she said, giving each of them a hug. 'I suppose you've been told what's going on?'

'I'm so glad I came home this weekend after all,' Bertie said. 'What's going to happen?'

'Nothing very much, despite what you'll no doubt have heard from Fiona. All I have to do is make sure Mr Neville makes an offer of recruitment, within earshot of your uncle David. He tells me there will be at least one other agent in place by tomorrow evening, so it will probably all go ahead then.'

'Another agent?' Ben looked perturbed. 'I thought it was all going to be straightforward.'

'It is,' she assured him. 'But once David moves in and makes the arrest, he's going to need someone on hand to take him away. Sam's going to be there too, in case of any last-minute slips, but it'll all be over in five minutes.' She lowered her voice. 'David's been armed, of course, but we have to assume Neville is, too, so Sam's going to try and search the room tonight while he's downstairs.'

'So he'll take away any weapons he finds?' Bertie relaxed a bit. 'That's good.'

'Well no, he can't remove anything,' Leah said, 'that will alert Neville. But he can make sure it's not usable, at least.'

'That sounds horribly risky. What if he doesn't manage to find anything, or there's more than one and he misses something?'

'Neville's got no reason to believe anyone else suspects him,' Leah pointed out. 'As far as he's concerned I'm the one who approached *him*, and I don't have any allies here now that Kurt's gone, so if you see me around between now and then you *must* ignore me. Alright?'

'Understood,' Bertie said, smiling. 'I honestly never know whether to say we're strangers, best friends, or out to poison each other, anyway!'

'Well this is the last time,' Leah said firmly. Nevertheless Bertie suspected, from her expression, that she already had regrets. She thought of her own unexpectedly fierce new ambitions; there were some people who would forever be searching for the next thing to take their breath away and remind them they were alive, and she and Leah would always be among them. It remained to be seen how that squared with Leah settling down to domestic comfort, but Bertie didn't give much for Adam's chances of a quiet life.

★ ★ ★

Billy Lang's Pure Blues band played in the lounge; quiet tunes for now, though with a steady percussive beat. They would grow louder and livelier later, and it wouldn't be long before the dancing started. Adam found it hard to stay away from Leah, who persisted in her appearance as someone with no friends; sitting alone in the lobby and shunning advances from the several gentlemen who offered their company. Instead

376

he sat here with Sam, his nerves tightening by the minute, his eyes scanning the room for the appearance of the man calling himself Bitterson. Sam had already made a point of introducing himself yesterday, in order for him to naturally bring about today's meeting.

'I'll engage him in conversation,' he said, as they brought their drinks over to sit down, 'and introduce you as a fellow businessman as well as a hotel manager. After a few minutes I'll make my excuses, and you just have to keep him here while I search his room. But,' he stressed, 'don't — '

'Don't make it obvious, I know.' Adam nodded. 'Don't worry, I've learned quite a lot from Leah over the past few months.'

Sam grinned. 'She's quite an actress, isn't she? I wonder she doesn't take off to America to try her luck.'

'Don't,' Adam pleaded. 'I don't think it'd take much to persuade her to try. And with her looks, she'd make it too.'

'You wouldn't like that?'

'No, I would not!' Adam took a drink and placed his glass on the table. 'I mean, would you? If you were hoping to keep someone close by?'

A light flush touched Sam's skin. 'I suppose not.'

'Is there anyone?' Adam asked, interested now.

'Anyone besides the fair Helen, you mean?' Sam smiled at the look on Adam's face. 'Oddly enough there *is* someone who's caught my eye since I've been spending time around Fox Bay.'

'Not Leah? Not that you'd tell me if it was, I suppose.'

'What do you take me for, man?' Sam shook his head. 'No, it's not Leah, and it's not Helen.'

'Not Kay?' Adam asked, alarmed. 'Because, let me tell you, she's not worth the — '

'Not her either.' Sam looked uncharacteristically shy, and shifted in his seat. 'Someone else. Someone who was, until recently, engaged, but who now appears to be . . . unshackled in that department.'

Adam frowned, thinking, then caught Sam looking out of the window, up towards Higher Valley. '*Beth Nancarrow?*'

'Don't say it like that!' Sam's face darkened. 'She's a very pretty woman. More importantly she's an honest and kind one. And she's spent far too many years running around after those men of hers, it's time she had someone running around after her.' His flush deepened and he took a huge slug of his drink. 'That didn't sound quite as I intended, but you know what I mean.'

Adam laughed. 'Give her some time to get over Alfie, and she couldn't help but fall for your Scottish charms.'

'Time, I can give her.' Sam smiled, and raised his glass. 'Slainte.'

'Cheers. Oh, here he is.' Adam nodded discreetly towards the door. 'And Kay hasn't fastened herself to him yet, either, so finish that up quick and go and meet him.'

Sam downed his usual small whisky, and crossed to the bar, where Adam heard him greet Neville . . . *Bitterson*, he reminded himself, with something approaching ferocity. Christ, if he got that wrong it would be all up. He wished he'd never even heard the name Neville. How on earth did Leah do this?

The two men came over, and Sam smiled at Bitterson. 'Jacob, this is Mr Adam Coleridge. You'll know him as manager here, but he's a businessman like you. Adam, Jacob Bitterson is the gentleman I took Mrs Marshall to meet the other night.'

Adam rose to shake the man's hand, and hoped his own wasn't sweating. 'Glad to meet you, Mr Bitterson. Why don't you sit down?'

'Thank you.' Neville hung his jacket on the back of the vacant chair and settled down. 'Wonderful ambience in this lounge, isn't there?'

Adam took the bull by the horns. 'That lady you mentioned?' he said to Sam. 'That's the pretty one who asked you for a lift into Bude?'

'That's the one. My fiancée wasn't too pleased, I must say.' Sam gave a hearty, all-boys-together laugh. 'Still, she couldn't argue, when a guest needed assistance, could she? Anyway, Mr Bitterson here's a big noise on the stock market, so I'm told.'

He soon eased the conversation onto the Great Crash, and the two businessmen fell to discussing the ups and downs of high-stakes investments. Adam began to relax in this familiar conversational territory, and even to forget its real purpose, so he received a nasty jolt back to reality when Sam excused himself.

'I must catch Helen for a few minutes before she retires for the evening. I won't be long.'

He made his exit, in order to search Neville's room, and Adam suddenly felt his words dry up. It baffled him to think he'd been capable, for so many years, of charming the birds from the trees, and the savings from their investors, but tonight, when it mattered more than ever, he was unable to string a coherent sentence together without someone there to help.

Thankfully, Neville didn't appear to notice the faltering in his speech, and looked around him with

379

contentment. 'Nice place,' he observed. 'Much nicer than that square box in Bude. Are you on speaking terms with all your regular guests?'

'Some of them. Why do you ask?' Did he sound defensive? He took a drink to hide it, if so.

'You and Mr Douglas seem friendly, that's all.'

'Ah, yes. He's engaged to Mrs Fox, you know.'

'Yes, so he said.' Neville gave him an odd smile, which Adam couldn't interpret. 'So did Mrs Marshall. Have you met, by the way?'

'Only to nod to. She keeps to herself.' Adam forced himself to put down his glass, worried he'd become loose-lipped if he drank much more. He wished he could get the subject back onto business; the man would get bored and wander off in a minute, and Sam would barely have had time yet to get up to the first floor. 'How long are you staying?'

'As long as it takes,' Neville said, with an irritatingly deliberate air of mystery. He sat upright. 'I say, that girl over there . . . .'

Adam twisted in his seat. Bertie, Daisy, and a girl he'd never seen before, were crossing the lounge to an empty booth at the far end. 'Which one?'

'In the green. Isn't it that film star, Daisy what's-her-name?'

'Conrad? Yes, that's her.' Adam smiled inwardly. If investments weren't going to keep the conversation going, this would. 'I understand she's recently moved into the area. She was here with Freddie Wishart at Christmas, you know.'

Neville frowned, then his brow cleared. 'Oh,' he breathed. 'So *that's* how.'

'How what?'

'Nothing. It's just . . . I heard she was leaving the

business, and I couldn't understand where my source got her information. I've just realised.'

Adam tensed, worried he'd shone a light on something best kept hidden. 'Oh?'

'The minx!' Neville looked torn between admiration and annoyance as he took a slim box from his pocket. 'Cigar?'

Adam accepted. It seemed admiration had won, and he took it as a sign that this news had even gone in Leah's favour; he supposed it must show her to be resourceful, and not without the sort of guile Neville and his ilk would find useful.

Besides, with Daisy Conrad in the room there was little chance Neville would become bored enough to leave, so Adam settled back into his seat. He thought he'd be able to relax now, but his thoughts kept turning to tomorrow and to Leah's potentially dangerous role in the arrest of the man opposite. It could so easily go wrong, and if Neville suspected Leah at any point . . .

Adam could only hope Sam had found, and disabled, any firearm the man might have stashed away in his room.

381

24

By Saturday evening, the agent sent down from London was *in situ*, waiting to escort Der Kojote back to London following his arrest. But, to Leah's consternation, Neville had not approached her again; she would have to take the bull by the horns and force the issue tonight.

So, as soon as Neville was safely ensconced in the dining room, David and Sam took up their positions in the room next to his. Sam had drilled two small holes in the wall behind the mirror, and David was to witness, and take notes, while Sam was to remain alert to the slightest hint that Leah needed help. He'd taken charge of the Webley that the SIS had given David, and Leah had to admit she privately felt much safer with that arrangement.

'When you're ready,' David had said while briefing her, 'say the word *shoes*, so we know you're happy to carry on with this. If you even suspect things might be slipping from your control, say *brandy*. We'll be ready to pull you out.'

'I disabled the firing pin of the pistol I found hidden in his *en suite*,' Sam put in. 'You can't tell just from looking at it, so unless he's tried to fire it he won't know.'

Leah nodded, relieved. 'What will you do when you've heard him make the offer?'

'Don't worry,' David said, 'we'll wait until you've left his room. Let him lay out any details he needs to, and then the third code word we'll be listening out

382

for is *coffee*. Alright? That's when we'll know you're on your way out, and we can move in as soon as you're safely away.'

★ ★ ★

'Shoes, coffee, shoes, coffee,' Leah muttered now, as she dressed. 'Come on, Leah, you've done this a hundred times!'

It never hurt to look as appealing as possible when engaging Neville, so she made doubly sure her make-up was immaculate, and that her hair was curled just-so, but slipped her feet into flat shoes; always in the back of her mind, at times like these, was the thought that she might have to run somewhere. Her dress was loose-fitting, for the same reason, but elegantly styled; grey to match her eyes, and hanging neatly to a dropped waist with a flat silk bow, and a skirt with stylishly concealed folds.

Down in the dining room she spotted Neville at his usual table, and instructed the waiter to escort her directly to him. 'Mr Bitterson! Do you mind if I join you?' she asked, gratified by the appreciative look he gave her as he rose to his feet.

'By all means, Mrs Marshall.' He gestured to the chair opposite, and she waited while the waiter quickly set an extra place. Once she was seated, and the waiter had taken their orders and left, an uneasy silence fell between them.

Eventually Neville spoke, in a low voice. 'I've considered your proposal — '

'Hush. Not here.' Leah flicked her gaze around them. 'We'll talk after dinner. For now, I just think it's helpful if we appear to at least know one another.

383

Don't you?'

'Very well.'

'Your room?'

'Of course.' Neville poured water into their glasses, from the elegant carafe on the table. 'We'll speak of other things for now, shall we? Such as the *astonishing* coincidence that Miss Daisy Conrad is apparently a regular guest.'

Leah caught the gleam in his eye before it vanished, and grinned. 'I see you've rumbled me.'

'I have indeed.' He looked pleased with himself, and Leah spent the rest of the meal carefully and subtly stoking that little flash of self-congratulation. Now and again she let him see her shrewd side as well, and watched his eyes narrow as he filed it away against what he'd already decided.

She was enjoying herself so much she barely noticed the time creeping by, and as the dining room began to empty she realised it was almost time to bring this, her most dangerous but exhilarating game to date, to a close. Poor Sam and David would be getting cramp, waiting by their listening-holes, and probably calling her every name under the sun as their own tension mounted.

When the meal was over she followed Neville up to the first floor, and as she passed the room where Sam and David waited, she stopped to adjust the buckle on her Mary Janes, resting her hand on the door for balance. 'New shoes,' she explained, as Neville turned to see why she wasn't directly behind him.

He inclined his head and waited for her to catch up, then let them into his room. She tried to still the trembling sensation in her stomach, but the rush of adrenalin matched the fear, giving her a heady sense of invincibility.

'Look,' she said, adopting a weary air. 'You've had plenty of time to think about whether or not you're willing to take me on, to teach me how I can be of use to you. What else can I do?'

'It's not me who's needed convincing,' he said, 'I'm one of the smallest cogs in this particular machinery.'

Leah doubted that; hadn't David said the department had been after the Coyote for years? 'What was that job you were offering?' she pressed. 'Why don't I do it for you, and if I'm successful, you consider recruiting me, and if not, I'll vanish from your life and never bother you again.'

'If you're *not* successful, you'll certainly vanish.' Neville gave her a tight little smile.

Leah's eyes met his, and she hoped there was no visible sign of the sudden fear she felt. 'Then tell me what it is.'

'In good time.' Neville seated himself at the table in the corner, and Leah joined him, trying not to look anywhere near the mirror. Neville poured them both a drink. 'I've used the time between our last talk, and now, to look into your claims,' he said. 'I can't verify there having been a cover-up involving senior military personnel, not as you describe, anyway, although there's no doubt they occur. But I have verified your relationship with your husband's brother, and his death in service at Arras.'

'Meaning what?'

'Meaning you're likely correct in your understanding of what happened to him, and even if you're not, your mistrust is justified.' He sat forward, suddenly earnest. 'The corruption is *rank*, Mrs Marshall! And it goes to the very highest position in government.' He regained his calm and returned to his former position, relaxed in his chair, playing with the whisky tumbler on the table.

'The job?' she prompted. Seeing him like that had unnerved her, not least because, for the first time, she saw passion and belief in a cause on that bland face. He truly felt he was in the right, and who could say he wasn't? She clamped down on that thought, and drew on the emotion he'd displayed. 'Just tell me! I'll do it.'

Neville eyed her, and now he looked cold again. Impersonal. 'When Freeman, or Wilf Stanley, that is, told me what you really were, I wanted to kill you. I wanted to do to you and your husband exactly what I did to him, and watch as the train rolled over you. I was so ... angry. Humiliated. It's as well for your husband that he's chosen to make himself disappear, because if I see him again ... well. You understand, of course.'

Leah remained silent, sensing apologies were not what he wanted. Instead she nodded, accepting, and Neville went on. 'But the more I thought about it, the more I decided it wasn't because of the way you had deceived me that angered me, only the fact of it. You made me believe a lie, and no one has ever fooled me so completely. Yours is a very special gift, Mrs Marshall.'

'Thank you.' *Just ask me!*

But he remained irritatingly enigmatic. 'We have, as I've said, been checking your background most carefully.'

'So then,' she said briskly, 'you'll know I live in Wales but spend time here regularly. And now you know the real reason why,' she said, looking out of the window, to where St Adhwynn's Church lay shrouded in

386

darkness. 'You'll know I was a nurse during the war, and that my mother's sister now owns the home in which I grew up, which is another reason I spend so much time here. What else do you know?'

'What else is there to know?' He hadn't disputed any of her claims, which she took as a good sign.

'Nothing much. I don't know how deeply you've investigated my current circumstances, but I can assure you I have no ties to Cornwall, or even to Wales. My aunt is quite happy living alone, so I'm free to travel anywhere you might put me to use.'

'Our trail does end with the death of your mother, and the job you recently left. Why did you leave that job?'

'It was in my mind to return to nursing,' Leah said truthfully. 'Mr Neville, the job?'

'I have to make a telephone call first.'

Leah lowered her head, tightening her lips against a hiss of frustration. 'A telephone call,' she repeated, in a soft, scathing tone. 'You truly are a small cog. How disappointing for us both.'

He bristled at that, but wouldn't be drawn. 'Would you be so good as to wait outside?'

'Why? You're talking about me, aren't you?'

'Outside please, Mrs Marshall.'

Leah pulled Neville's door closed behind her and waited, frustrated beyond belief, in the corridor. The door to the next room jerked open, and David's head popped out.

'He can't make any calls,' he murmured, looking worried, 'which he'll find out any moment now.'

'What?' she hissed.

'Guy has cut his room off at the switchboard end. We didn't want Neville dialling out of the hotel for help, if he suspected anything. I don't know what we'll do now, we can't go through all this again.' He looked around hopelessly, as if he expected to find an answer printed on the walls.

'I could let him use my telephone,' Leah suggested.

'No, we need to be able to hear him actually recruit you, or we won't have a leg to stand on and his lawyers will make a proper show of us. Besides, we can't let him see you have a third-floor room, with the family.' He chewed his lip, as they heard footsteps crossing Neville's floor. 'Right, get him to the private sitting room,' he whispered. 'We'll follow as soon as it's safe.'

He pushed the door shut without latching it, and Leah leaned against the wall a bare second before Neville opened his own door. She looked at him hopefully, dropping the disdain in favour of a humbler approach.

'All done?'

'The telephone isn't working. Which is your room?'

'There isn't a telephone in there,' Leah said. 'My room's a far plainer one than this. But,' she added, 'the Fox family have a private sitting room downstairs, you could use the one in there.'

'I can't just wander into the family's private rooms,' Neville protested.

'Everyone knows that ghastly woman who's related to Mrs Fox has been draped all over you for days,' Leah said, waving his protest away. 'What's her name?'

'Mrs Marlowe?'

'Yes, her. If anyone sees you in there, you can just say you're looking for her, and they'd believe it just like that.' She snapped her fingers.

He hesitated, then nodded. 'Good. Alright.'

'What's the telephone call about? If it concerns me,'

she added, seeing him about to ignore her, 'I believe I have the right to know.'

He hesitated. 'I've been waiting for confirmation of what we discussed out in the gazebo,' he said after a moment. 'If it's approved, I'll have the authority to make you an offer.'

'And if not?'

'There is more than one way to cross a bridge,' he said blandly, 'but in all cases, we must reach one first. Just let me fetch my jacket.'

Leah was about to ask why he needed it, but as he slipped it on she saw him check the pocket, then pat it, and was unable to suppress a shiver of fear; he'd been carrying that jacket last night in the bar. Did that mean he'd had a second weapon with him all the time? From a simple, and relatively safe, exercise, this was becoming uncomfortably risky. She tested the word under her breath, for the first time: *brandy* . . .

★ ★ ★

Helen had, so far, been unable to put out of her mind what might or might not be happening upstairs in Neville's room; she couldn't bury the notion that Leah was putting her life at risk tonight. Adam had been of the same mind. He'd been hard to convince into his role as guardian of the rest of the family instead, but had eventually given in to David's insistence that he leave Leah alone. He had gathered everyone together in a corner of the lounge, where they waited for a signal from David or Sam that it was over, and that Neville was safely in the custody of the waiting agent.

Helen, however, had insisted on going about her normal duties, in order to maintain an appearance of

389

normality to the guests. The last thing they wanted was a string of difficult questions, and curious would-be sleuths trying to unravel any mystery they might infer from the answers.

She finished a distracted, post-dinner meeting with Nicholas Gough, and, rather than join the others in the lounge, she stepped outside to snatch a breath of air and calm her nerves. Since it was a mild evening she walked slowly along the pathway between the back of the kitchen and the sitting room, and midway there she heard a surprised voice coming from the shadows outside the combined pools of light from the hotel.

'Helen, is that you?'

'Alfie?' For a moment she wondered if her deeper wishes were playing tricks, but he emerged into the light, as real as the building at her back. 'What are you doing lurking in the dark?' She tried for a humorous tone, but he must have sensed it was forced.

'I didn't scare you, did I? That's why I spoke first instead of just — '

'No, it's not you.' Helen looked around, but there was little to see except the wall that ran around the kitchen garden across the way, and ahead there was only the field, with the path that led down from Higher Valley Farm. 'What can I do for you?'

He gave a soft laugh. 'That sounds very formal.'

'I'm sorry,' Helen said. 'It's only . . . There's something going on tonight, and I'm just waiting for it all to be over.'

'What's happening?'

Helen looked reflexively upwards, at Leonard Neville's room. 'I don't think it's fair to involve you, but it'll be over soon.' She smiled at the mystified expression on his face. 'Don't mind me, I'm just being daft.'

'You're never . . . Well, alright, but not very often.' He took another step closer, and she didn't move back. His familiar height was a comforting thing this close, and it meant she didn't have to look up at him; she focused her gaze instead on the frayed top button of his waistcoat.

'I heard you were leaving,' she said, to keep some sense of reality.

'It's true I've been considering it,' he said carefully. 'Would it . . . inconvenience you, or the hotel, at all?'

'Would that make any difference?' Helen countered.

The silence stretched, and then Alfie gave a low chuckle, and Helen was startled by the wave of affection that swept over her; she not only wanted to hear that sound every day, for the rest of her life, she wanted to be its cause and its fuel.

But the affection was gently eased aside by a flare of heat as she felt his hand on her cheek. Utterly unprepared, she heard her own small gasp, and then wanted to laugh; she might have been in one of Rex Kelly's films. She half-expected music to start up from nowhere, and for Alfie to sweep her into a waltz . . . The unlikely image brought the laugh closer to the surface, and she looked up at him, ready to share her amusement.

The sparse light made his dark blue eyes look black, and his brows fierce above them, but his smile was the kindest thing she had ever seen. It was at once tender and hopeful; how could she have doubted her feelings for him, and how could he doubt them now? The humour once more made way for something deeper, and her words dried up.

'Can we talk indoors?' he asked. 'I think we might

391

both have things to say, before any decisions are made.'

Helen nodded. To remove any doubt before she ruined things again, she stretched up and placed a kiss beside his mouth; he turned his head slightly and captured her lips before she could withdraw, returning the gentle pressure.

Her hands caught at his waist as she almost lost her balance, and then he was pulling her close, his hands moving to caress the back of her neck beneath the fall of her hair. Even after the kiss broke, she stayed pressed against him while the cool evening wind brushed her hot face, and his hands splayed on her back as if he feared that same wind might blow her away.

She laid her head on his chest, feeling the quick rise and fall that she knew would be echoed in her own shallow breathing, and after a moment she moved back to look up at him. She'd always acknowledged his attractiveness, so different from Harry's, and maybe it was a reaction to what had just happened, but she still wondered at her good fortune to have found two men whose kindness, and generosity of spirit, were matched by features she could never tire of looking at.

She smiled up at him. 'Well that seems to have cleared up one or two questions.'

'It's certainly helped a bit with the decision-making,' he said in thoughtful tones. His eyes no longer seemed black and unfathomable in the semi-dark, and they lengthened now in another smile. 'I know I've told you this, but I love you — '

'You haven't, actually,' Helen pointed out.

'What?'

'You never actually told me you loved me. Just that you were doomed.'

There was a short silence, then Alfie laughed, and

Helen felt her entire body absorb the sound like an embrace. She lifted her hands to bring that laughing mouth onto hers, but was startled as he suddenly pulled away. His focus was on her left hand, and he caught it and brought it down so he could look more closely. She followed his gaze and saw, as he had, the sparkle of the sparse light as it caught the diamonds in her engagement ring.

'This is pretty.' His voice was flat. 'Beth was right, then.'

'Right about what?'

'You and this detective bloke.'

'How did *she* know?' Helen realised that was the wrong thing to say, but Alfie had already taken a step back.

'Look, it's alright,' he said, 'I knew about it, and I'm in no position to complain. But I can't be the reason you and he don't marry.'

'You won't be. The reason we won't marry is because we're not engaged!' Helen looked down at the ring again. 'This is the one Harry gave me. I never wear it while I'm working, and tonight it's just for show. It's to do with what's happening here.' Helen once more cut that subject short. 'If you knew, or thought you did, why did you come here tonight? Did you think you might have changed my mind?'

'I think I hoped you might change mine,' he confessed. 'I don't *want* to leave Higher Valley again, I was born there. But I felt foolish after saying what I did. Knowing you were just down the road would have been — '

'I've been kicking myself ever since that night,' Helen said. 'I wanted you then, but I didn't know it. And I felt Beth was more deserving.'

'Which you took pains to explain to me,' he pointed out, and now the hesitant humour was back in his voice. 'The thing is, Jory told us tonight that he's taking up work with Sally Penneck's father, at the family tannery. He's finally making something of himself, which has pleased Beth no end, but if I went to stay at Priddy now, even for a little while at this time of year, it'd put her and Jowan in a tough position. She'd have to hire in.'

'So you're staying at Higher Valley after all?'

'I wanted to come and see you first. To put things right between us, so I could at least stop avoiding you, and your hotel.' He gave a little laugh. 'No matter how foolish I felt about what I said, I still miss that way you have of making me feel like I'm the most interesting person you've spoken to all day.'

'Our guests can be *very* dull.' Helen's heart was singing now.

'Ah, now I remember,' he grinned, 'you're the evil Helen, while the nice one goes around smiling at everyone and being the perfect hostess.'

'Evil's more fun, after all.'

'You appearing out here tonight . . . It's like fate and the devil got together to make me forget all my good intentions and make the same mistake all over again.'

'See? Evil *is* more fun.' The wind gusted, and Helen shivered. 'I'm glad you listened,' she added softly, and brushed his face with her fingers. 'Come indoors, we can talk properly there. The sitting room should be empty, everyone's in the lounge.'

'Just for the record,' Alfie said, taking her hand as they walked, '*would* I have changed your mind?'

'Let's see,' Helen mused. 'On one hand we have

a suave, good-looking detective, with a lovely accent and a huge artistic talent. On the other, a muddy farmer with scruffy hair, dirt under his nails, and the rattliest van in Cornwall. Hmm.'

'It's a difficult one,' he agreed. 'But can your detective do this?' He stopped and pressed her gently against the wall, and this time the kiss was deeper, more demanding, and Helen returned it with a hunger she hadn't felt in over a decade. Even through his coat, her roving hands felt the strength of long days spent in the fields, but the fingers that cupped her face held her as if she were a butterfly in his palm. The contrast was intoxicating and exciting, and when the kiss ended they remained close, not quite ready to break apart yet, their hands linked at their sides.

Alfie's lips curved against her cheek. 'Well?'

She felt the warmth of his breath on her chilled skin, and pressed her face closer again, sealing it between them. 'What detective?' she said, and felt his smile widen.

'Then that's settled, at least.' He tugged her away from the wall, where she'd have been happy to stay all night. 'I thought you were cold?'

'Not anymore.'

'Well I fancy a nip of something warming.' He drew her onwards. 'You can tell me what on earth's going on down here now. Life with you Foxes is never dull, is it?'

'It should be over by now,' Helen said, looking up again towards Neville's room. To her relief, the light was now off, but when her gaze lowered to the sitting room window, she frowned. 'Someone's in there.'

Alfie squinted. 'Isn't it that girl from the Summerleaze?'

'Lily?' She looked closer. 'Yes. Wait here just for a minute, I'll find out what she wants then send her on her way.'

She pushed open the French window, and stepped inside, only realising as she crossed the threshold that Lily Trevanion wasn't alone; her heart slipped as she saw Mr Neville, standing with Leah at the other end of the room near the fireplace. It certainly didn't look as if he were in any kind of compromised position yet, but what were they doing down here?

'Come in, Mrs Fox,' Neville said. 'This young lady is looking for someone. Perhaps you might be able to help her?'

'Mr Bitterson just needs to use the telephone for a private call, Mrs Fox,' Leah put in. 'Mrs Marlowe did say it would be quite alright.'

Helen came in, reluctant, but understanding Leah's eagerness to be rid of Lily so she could complete her part in all this. If she could help by speeding it along, she'd be only too glad to do so, before her nerves reached snapping point.

'Miss Trevanion,' she said, smiling at the younger woman. 'How can I help you?'

'Where's Ben?'

'He's probably in the office. Shall I take you?'

'No. You can give him these.' Lily flung a folder on the table. 'And you can tell him he can forget any pay he's owed!'

'I know you, don't I?' Neville said, evidently looking closely at her for the first time. 'Aren't you on the staff at the Summerleaze?'

'Assistant manager,' she snapped. 'And not likely to be that either, for much longer, thanks to Ben Fox!'

'I'll tell him you've called in,' Helen promised,

holding out one hand to guide Lily from the room. 'Would you like to take those with you, or leave them for him to look at?' She moved to pick up the folder, but tensed as Neville got there first and opened it.

'Photographs,' he murmured. 'That one looks like the film star you have staying here, Mrs Fox.'

Lily snorted. 'Damned right it is, and that's not all!' She glared at Helen. 'Look at the others.' She tried to take the folder back, but Neville jerked it out of her reach, and continued flicking through. Finally he raised his head and looked directly at Helen, expressionless, but with a muscle jumping in his jaw.

Helen went cold, and gestured again to Lily. 'I'll get Ben to come and see you,' she insisted, trying not to sound either desperate or guilty. 'It's best if you go, now.'

'Don't worry, I'm going. Your son's a sneak, Mrs Fox, and what he's been doing is illegal. He'll be lucky not to get a visit from the police, for what he's done.'

'Actually I think those must have belonged to Kurt Strommer,' Leah said calmly, looking over Neville's shoulder. 'Did you, or this Ben person, perhaps get them from *his* room?'

Helen prayed for the girl to follow Leah's lead, and just for one hopeful second, even Neville looked as if he expected her to confirm it. It would make the most sense to him, after all.

But Lily looked from one to the other as if they were mad. 'I was looking in his darkroom for photographs of Daisy Conrad, so I could confront him with his lies. I found some negatives, and took them to a studio in town to get them developed. I don't know what these are, Mrs Fox, but they're clearly a guest's private documents.'

Helen realised, with a sick feeling of dismay, that all the while Lily had been speaking, Neville had been watching Leah.

'You're no more a loner here than you were a grieving widow in Liverpool, are you?' he said softly. 'You're just a nasty little swindler, doing what you do best.'

★ ★ ★

There was no time for *brandy*. Neville pushed Leah aside, and before she could do more than recover her balance he had tugged an ugly-looking handgun from his pocket. With his free hand he pulled the hammer up and back, and as it clicked into place, Leah's breath stopped. She'd seen this type of gun before; Lugers had been regularly confiscated from wounded prisoners of war. She also knew, as Neville thumbed the safety catch up, that the chambered round was ready to fire. He'd had a second weapon all along.

Lily uttered a low cry of horror, and backed away, her frozen gaze never leaving the semi-automatic pistol pointed at Leah's head.

'You!' Neville barked over his shoulder at her. 'Do you drive?'

Bright tears flew from Lily's eyes with the vigour of her nod, but she remained speechless.

'Fetch my car,' Neville said. 'Green Siddeley, parked at the end of the row.' He pulled out his keys and threw them to Lily, whose shaking fingers failed to catch them and she scrabbled on the carpet. 'Not that way!' he hissed, as she took a step towards the door. 'The window.'

Lily turned to obey, but gave a breathless shriek as a tall figure appeared in the opening, grabbed her arm, and pulled her roughly aside. She stumbled against the side of the window and then over its ledge, sprawling on the grass outside, and in the same instant that Leah recognised the figure as Alfie, Neville straightened his arm and brought the Luger around to rest over Alfie's heart.

Helen's anguished cry tore through the room, and Leah was aware of the blur of movement as her friend flew towards Alfie, who was all too clearly outlined in the window. Her heart seized in sudden panic as she realised Helen had put herself in the path of Neville's bullet, but there was nothing she could do; her eyes were on Neville's finger as it tightened on the trigger, knowing she'd never reach him in time to deflect his aim.

That split second seemed to last minutes, until Leah gradually registered there had been only a dry click as the trigger was depressed, and that both Helen and Alfie remained on their feet, unharmed. Neville pocketed the gun in disgust, and Leah breathed again. Thank god for Sam after all . . .

But behind Alfie, outside the open window, chaos was erupting. Two dark-clad figures lunged forward out of the shadows and grabbed his arms, dragging him backwards to an accompaniment of his outraged shouts. Helen flung herself on his assailants, tugging at them as they tried to force Alfie's hands behind his back, and Leah took a few steps forward to help, but stopped in shock as she came up against the point of a blade: Ben's sabrage sword.

Neville used it to push her back into the room, where she could only watch in horror as Alfie was subjected to a barrage of blows. He responded with equal ferocity, landing several hits of his own, before a well-placed pistol butt to the diaphragm drove the breath from him and he sank, gasping, to his knees. He was finally subdued by a blow from the same gun to the back of his head and he slumped, still conscious but clearly dizzy and disorientated, as his attackers moved into the spill of light from the sitting room.

Leah sucked in a shocked breath of her own as she realised one of them was Sam, and that he clearly still had no idea who he had just helped to bring down. The other was the agent from London, who produced a set of handcuffs and yanked Alfie's arms behind his back.

Neville pressed the tip of the sword to Leah's chest, and gave her a wide grin. 'Oh dear, they've got the wrong man. Let's see how long it takes them to work that out, shall we?'

'The others know what you look like,' Leah reminded him furiously, trying not to think about how badly Alfie might be hurt.

Neville came around to stand behind her, and the blade was now lying across her throat. 'Which means we won't have long before they come crashing in here,' he said grimly. He began to draw her away from the window, presumably to give himself time to think, but stopped as a voice sounded outside.

'Wait, this isn't him!' It was Sam, and he sounded aghast.

'And that's not Leah, either, look.' David's voice joined him now. 'They're still in there!'

'Not a word, Mrs Marshall,' Neville whispered, his breath hot and damp against Leah's cheek. 'We're going out, you're going to take me to your car — '

'I don't drive,' she said, 'and even if I did, do you think I carry the keys with me everywhere I go?'

'You've got a bit of an impudent tone, for someone within inches of getting their throat cut.'

'It'd take some sawing,' Leah said, forcing a mocking note into her tight voice.

'What?'

'It's a sabrage sword. It works better when the edge is blunted. You could stick me with it,' she offered, feeling reckless and a little hysterical, 'but if you're planning to slice my jugular you'll have to allow time for a few goes at it.'

'As you wish.' Neville brought the short blade down so it jabbed into her back, and her insides shrivelled, but she felt the shift in advantage now; in this position, a single shot from a trained marksman would kill him before he had time to push the blade an inch, let alone through her body. He had clearly realised the same, and uttered a curse.

'Stand there.' He kept the tip of the blade levelled at her as he took out the Luger again, and awkwardly slid the loaded magazine out. He examined it briefly, and grunted. 'Misfire.'

Leah hoped she was making a good show of the dismay she should be feeling, as, the gun pressed against her temple and the short blade once more at her back, she stepped over the threshold of the window. Thank goodness Sam had done something more complex to the Luger than simply removing the ammunition; she was ready to bet there was a fresh magazine in that pocket, and it would have only taken seconds to re-load. She just had to get Neville in range so the agent had a clear shot . . .

David and the agent both had their own guns levelled at the French windows as Leah and Neville emerged, and, even knowing that the one pressed against her skin was disabled, Leah felt sick with fear. Helen was crouching beside Alfie, her face white, her hand clasping his. She looked up, and Leah tried to send her a reassuring look, but had the feeling it had only appeared on her face as a grimace.

'Put down your firearms, and get me my keys,' Neville called out, pushing the barrel of the Luger harder against her head. 'Do that, and I'll let her go once I'm away.'

Leah couldn't shake the fear that, even if the professional agent were a superb shot, and might be expected to hit the right target, David was just . . . Helen's brother. Sam could have taken Neville down, knowing the Luger wasn't the mortal threat it seemed, but he had disappeared. She thought fleetingly about shouting out to the others that they were safe to shoot, but she'd seen what even the butt end of a gun could do; she'd be unconscious and still at Neville's mercy before a single word was out, let alone have time to convince them to fire.

'Uncock your weapons and throw them over there.' Neville nodded towards the kitchen garden, and after a moment's hesitation David and the agent reluctantly lobbed the two government-issued Webleys over the high wall. 'Keys?'

David stepped forward, holding the keys he'd taken off Lily. 'The green Siddeley, correct?'

'That's the one.'

'Why don't I fetch it for you?'

'Why?'

David sighed. 'Look, we all know you've got us over a barrel, I just don't want you involving any other innocents you might come across, out there in the car park.'

Leah could sense Neville hesitating, as he weighed up the chances of escape, against the suspicion he was being tricked. The gun grinding against her temple was sending sharp pains through her head, making her feel distracted and faint, and it was hard to stay focused.

'Where's Mr Douglas?' Neville demanded. 'I heard him out here too, where's he gone?'

'He's taken that poor Trevanion girl away to safety,' David said, his voice tight and angry. 'Do you want me to fetch your car or not?'

Leah felt Neville nod. He pulled her back against the wall to wait, and she took slow breaths to steady her heart as David went to bring the Siddeley around. Once or twice she felt the hard metal barrel of the gun slip, but she kept remembering how easily Alfie had been brought down with a single blow. She might wake up anywhere if that happened . . . Or not at all.

Alfie was mumbling something, and Helen was trying to get him to lie still. Her face was a mask of utter fury as she looked at Neville, and if the sword hadn't scraped the skin of her back at that moment, Leah might have taken her chances and tried to fight her way free; she felt somehow complicit in what had happened to Alfie, standing so still like this.

She felt a bead of blood oozing beneath the blade, and soaking into her dress, and kept deadly still. After a few minutes, the lights of an approaching car lit up the grass, and the low murmur of a well-tuned engine rumbled towards them. Neville pushed Leah ahead of him, into its path, and it stopped a scant three feet away.

'Leave the engine running!'

Leah grunted in pain, as Neville shoved her into

403

the side of the car, and she hit her head on the edge of the roof. At least he had now cast the sabrage sword aside to lie harmlessly on the grass. Helen gave a little cry at the sight of it, and Leah turned to tell her she was alright, but Neville pushed her into the car, cutting off her words.

'Move across.' He stood back as Leah crawled into the passenger seat, but as her hand reached for the door handle on the other side, Neville spotted her intention. He leaned in and grabbed her hair to drag her back, then slid behind the wheel, the barrel of the Luger now never more than a few inches from the side of her face again, and she tried not to look directly at it. It was a terrifying sight.

David and the agent were recovering their weapons from the kitchen garden, but it was taking far too long, and Leah knew that once Neville was away from the hotel it would all be up for her. He couldn't let her live now; reprisal would be swift and final. His own life depended on getting far away, while Leah's, and the lives of those she loved, depended on him instead being apprehended.

There was nothing for it now except to somehow find a way to seize control. Even as Neville briefly switched the gun into his right hand while he shifted into gear, Leah felt her limbs tightening, readying themselves for something she hadn't even planned yet. But the Luger was already back in Neville's left hand as the car moved forward in an ungainly leap, and pressed against Leah's temple. She felt the car slide on the damp grass, and for a single, horrifying second she thought they were going to drive over Alfie and Helen, but Neville pulled the wheel sharply back to the right, avoiding them by only a couple of feet.

As he did so the gun's barrel dropped a fraction, and Leah knew she must act now or die. She ducked her head and simultaneously brought her right arm blindly up and around, connecting with Neville's wrist, and sending the primed gun spinning into the back seat.

The roar ripped through the car like overhead thunder, and Leah was momentarily deafened by it, as the car slewed around and came to a slamming halt. The jolt sent her crashing against the passenger dashboard compartment, and then backwards, and a violent pain shot up through her neck as her head and shoulders jerked under the impact.

She saw Neville starting to turn towards her, his face white and stunned, and before she could fully register what had happened she had pushed open her door, and flung herself onto the damp grass, scrambling away from the stationary car before Neville could reach across and grab her.

'Stop! I'll shoot!'

For a heart-freezing second, she almost did, but then realised the shout wasn't directed at her, and it wasn't Neville's voice. She flipped onto her back, still crabbing backwards, and blinking away the blood oozing into her left eye, and saw Sam climbing from the back of the car, the Luger trained on the fleeing figure of Leonard Neville. He had almost made it into the trees, but when Sam raised the Luger and fired into the air he stumbled to a stop, his hands raised.

Sam kept the gun trained on him, but Neville had accepted his fate now, and, as he turned to face his captor, his gaze fell on Leah. She climbed to her feet and wiped sticky blood from her eye, and to her surprise she saw he had an oddly regretful smile on his face.

'Such a waste,' he called, 'you'd have made a bloody good one. Something tells me you'd have enjoyed it, too.'

'What the hell were you playing at?' Sam growled at her. 'You could have killed us both, that bullet missed me by an inch!' He pushed Neville ahead of him as he passed Leah on his way back to the sitting room.

'I thought it was . . . that you'd . . . .' Leah shook her head. Reaction was setting in now, and she couldn't quite gather her thoughts properly.

'Are you alright?' he asked her more gently, and she started to nod, then shook her head, wincing at the pain that shot through it.

'I have no idea,' she said, 'but I couldn't half do with a brandy.'

* * *

With the window now firmly closed, Helen drew the sitting room curtain tightly against the night, and took stock of the motley group in her sitting room. It didn't make for a restful scene, and part of her still felt as if she were outside kneeling on the grass, watching that awful car lurching towards her and Alfie, and knowing there was nothing they could do about it.

Leah sat down beside Alfie on the sofa, and tipped his head forward so she could see the back of his head. 'That'll need cleaning, and you'll have a nasty headache for a while. How's the rest of you?'

'About as good as you, by the looks of it.' He gave her a faint grin, and Helen wished she could share the wry humour. Both he and Leah were streaked with blood; Leah's smeared down half her face, and Alfie

406

on the back of his neck, and every time either of them moved, they winced. Alfie's hand was wrapped across his ribs, and Leah kept rolling her head to ease the pain in her neck, and plucking her dress away from a cut in the middle of her back. Both were going to be horribly bruised in a few hours, but at least they were alive.

Sam pulled the curtain aside and peered out. 'You'd think the sound of a gun would keep the guests indoors,' he grumbled, 'not send them running outside to investigate.'

'Are you saying you wouldn't do the same?' Helen pulled him away from the curtain and closed it again. 'Just leave them to it, Sam. They'll get cold and bored in a minute, there's nothing to see now.'

'Where's Neville?' Leah asked, pressing two fingers to Alfie's right side, and making him grimace as she checked for broken ribs.

'On his way back up to London,' Sam said. 'Your brother's gone with them,' he added to Helen, 'he asked me to tell you he hoped to be back in a day or two, but will need to be de-briefed. He'll telephone, the first chance he gets.'

'Would you fetch a bowl of warm water and some cloths?' Leah asked him, once more examining the back of Alfie's head. 'I need to get this cut cleaned up, before it dries and we end up having to shave his hair off.'

'What about you?' Helen asked, as Sam left the room. 'How are you feeling?'

'Shaken,' Leah admitted. 'Still in shock, I think, but physically just a bit bashed about. Nothing serious, or broken.'

'What on earth happened back there?'

Leah explained about the second gun, that Neville had evidently kept with him while the spare remained in the *en suite*. 'Neville was right, this one was only a misfire, but when it didn't go off I thought it was the one Sam had tampered with.'

'I can't believe how lucky you were, Helen,' Alfie said, and now he sounded as shaken as Helen felt. He reached for her hand. 'You could have been killed, getting in the way like that.'

'I'd do it again.' She couldn't speak any further for a moment. She didn't think she'd ever forget seeing that vile thing pointed at Alfie's heart, and she pictured, all too clearly, how it might have been different. The thought of losing him right in front of her eyes, as she had lost Harry, was unbearable and terrifying.

'I suppose the unfired round'll be somewhere on the floor of his car.' Leah rubbed her forehead without thinking, then flinched and lowered her hand again. 'Sam was already in the back seat, waiting for a chance to make his move, but I had no idea of that either. I could have *killed* him!'

'But you didn't,' Helen said gently. 'It's all over now.'

'Whatever it was,' Alfie added pointedly, and she was able to smile at that.

'I suppose I can tell you what it was about, now you've almost died because of it.'

'Because of me,' Leah said. 'I can't believe I brought all this to your door, Hels.'

'It wasn't your fault,' Helen protested. 'You left! You tried to keep us out of it.'

Before she could say anything further, the door was flung open and Adam came in, his blond hair sticking up, his face tight.

'Leah!' He crossed to her, and she rose to her feet to prove she wasn't badly hurt, but the blood running down her face ruined the calming effect. 'What happened?' he asked, pulling her close. 'We heard the shot, and everyone panicked. Now Sam and Ben are trying to corral everyone in the lobby and explain what it was about.'

'But I sent Sam for water,' Leah mumbled against his shoulder.

'It's on its way, don't worry.' Adam led her back to the sofa, where he did his best to clean the blood with a handkerchief before his attention slid to the sofa's other occupant. 'Christ, Alfie! What happened to you?'

'Mistaken identity,' Alfie said, and shifted to allow them more room. Helen noted, with a frown, that he closed his eyes briefly as he did so. 'Sam's got a good right hook, as it turns out,' he added.

'He's mortified,' Helen said, 'they just saw the back of you dragging poor Lily out, and assumed you were Neville, and she was Leah.'

A knock indicated that someone had brought the things Leah had asked for, and Helen opened the door, expecting to see one of the evening housekeeping staff. 'Fiona?'

Her younger daughter brought the tray in, her eyes going from Leah to Alfie, and then to Helen. 'What happened?'

'I'll tell you later,' Helen said, and brought a small table over to the sofa. 'Why on earth have you brought this?'

'How else was I going to be allowed in?' Fiona put the tray down on the table. 'Besides . . . .' She hesitated, and Leah leaned over to dip a cloth into the

409

bowl of warm water.

'Did you want to help?' she asked, and Fiona nodded.

'Sam said there were some minor injuries to clean up, and I thought this might be a good place to start learning.'

'Learning?' Helen looked at the girl, who'd become a young woman without her really noticing, and recognised the same determined tilt to her chin as Ben and Bertie. She smiled, and some of the awfulness of the night receded. 'You want to become a nurse?'

'I started to think about it after Christmas, when I couldn't help either Daisy or Amy.' Fiona flushed, as she got to what was obviously the deciding factor. 'And, since Danny is *determined* to follow his father's footsteps into the police force,' she rolled her eyes, 'it occurred to me there might be some use in knowing how to patch people up.'

'Not to mention it would make you extremely useful at the lifeboat station,' Helen pointed out, and Fiona's face broke into a grin that brought the impish little girl back for a moment.

'That too. So, can I?' She gestured to the clean cloths, and Leah nodded.

'Watch how I do Alfie's, then you can do mine.'

When Leah had finished cleaning Alfie's head, Helen felt free to perch on the arm of the sofa closest to him and take his hand in hers again.

'Are you still sure you want to be part of this mad family?' she asked with a little smile.

'Not on your life. How soon can I leave?'

She laughed, which turned to a murmur of approval as she heard Fiona firmly telling a worriedly hovering Adam to go and find something useful to do. 'You're in my light,' she complained. 'Go and help Ben, or something!'

'He's doing perfectly well without help,' Sam said, coming back in. 'You must be glad to be able to leave the hotel in such good hands when you go, Helen.'

'Leave?' Alfie looked at her, startled, as did Fiona.

'You're going away?' Fiona's smile fell away, and she stopped dabbing at Leah's brow.

'It's true I'm turning my job over to Ben,' Helen said, 'I've been offered a new position at — '

'But this is your home!' Fiona cried.

'Truro really isn't so far away,' Leah told her comfortingly. 'And the trains are getting better all the time.'

'Truro?' Alfie braced his hands ready to push himself to his feet, but stopped with a hiss, his hand going to his side. Sam looked as if he wanted to apologise yet again, for the rough treatment, but now wasn't the time.

'Pagetts have offered her a wonderful job as manager at The Pearson,' Adam said, as if daring Alfie to try and throw a spanner in the works. 'She'd be mad not to take it.'

Alfie looked up at her, puzzled and disappointed. 'Why didn't you say anything?'

'Because I'm not going anywhere.'

It was Leah's turn to look surprised. 'But you said you wanted something new.'

'You can't give up an opportunity like that,' Alfie said. 'Look, I'll tell Keir I'm coming to work at Priddy Farm after all. I can travel from Porthstennack to Truro easily enough.'

'You're not fit to take up that sort of work yet,' Leah said quickly. 'At a rough count I'd say you've got at

411

least three cracked ribs there.'

Helen put a hand on his shoulder to prevent any further movement. 'I'm not taking the job at The Pearson, because the job isn't at The Pearson. I only assumed it was.'

It had only been a week ago that she'd looked at the information that had arrived with the contract, and thought it spelled the end of everything. With both her and Alfie leaving, everything might have worked; it gave her hope, at least. But the details of the job had thrown her into turmoil again, and she'd been tearing herself in two trying to decide which she should give up: her exciting new future, or her chance at a life with this man who, against all expectation, she loved beyond measure. Now Alfie had told her his own news, there was no need to choose after all.

She smiled around at them all, and curled her fingers around Alfie's. 'I'm going to be the new, the *first*, manager of the Harry Fox Golf Resort, Trethkellis.'

25

Easter weekend had always swelled the numbers at Fox Bay, as the weather became kinder and brought with it the artists, who preferred to visit before the summer rush, and again at the onset of winter. Helen and Adam had exchanged words about the cheaper rate they still enjoyed, and Adam had ventured the opinion that perhaps it was time to prioritise higher paying guests, but Helen insisted their regular, loyal visitors were accommodated first. Adam had eventually acquiesced, in the face of her assertion that loyalty was worth more than what might be a temporary surge in popularity, so, in the early evening of Good Friday, Helen helped Guy section off part of the dining room for the group who'd arrived that day in high spirits, as always . . .

She moved around the room slowly, remembering her first night here, and her first encounter with the lively group, Leah included.

'A lot of water under the bridge, these past years,' she said with a smile, as she pushed the last chair into place. 'Are you still enjoying your new role?'

'It feels as if the job were created just for me.' Guy picked at something on the snowy cloth, but Helen still never knew if any of those bits were real, or if he felt compelled to make the final tweaks to everything. 'I gather you've heard from Fleur too?'

Helen laughed. 'I had the feeling she wouldn't stay

over there forever, but I really thought she'd give it more than four months!'

'Fox Bay has always been in her blood,' Guy said. He'd naturally been delighted at the news that his old friend was returning, but his impatience to see her was showing now too. 'I'm surprised she wasn't back by February.'

'I'm sure it's not just the hotel she misses.' Helen noted his quiet pleasure, with another smile of her own. 'Right, that's me done for the day, I'm off to put my feet up. If Leah arrives, tell her I'm in the sitting room.'

'What time is she due back? I'll look out for her.'

'Not for another hour or so, but I'm quite likely to doze off, we've been that busy.'

Helen found the sitting room blissfully empty, and pulled open the French window a crack, to let in the sound of the April evening as she sat and enjoyed the peace. It was a rare treat lately, to just rest and think, and her mind turned, with pleasure, to her children; youngsters no longer, but each one with very clear ideas of what they wanted from life, and how to go about getting it.

Bertie's tentative reunion with Lynette had been a great relief and joy to them both, and Lynette had promised to return to Fox Bay soon. There was no chance of a similar reunion for Bertie and Jowan, however, and she now knew why, but it was nice to know that Bertie was coming home alone this time; Helen looked forward to the chance to talk properly. It was impossible to miss the new glow that surrounded her elder daughter these days, and she wanted to know whether it was the training that had put it there, or someone she'd met down at Caernoweth.

Fiona had heard back yesterday from the hospital in Bude, where she planned to do some voluntary work for a while to see if she really wanted to take on the training. Of course she would; Helen could tell already that she was raring to go.

Ben was three weeks into his new role at Fox Bay, and it was as if he'd been in charge all his life. Although, now she came to think of it, he'd been a bit secretive lately, and she hoped he hadn't gone back to those card games —

'Good evening, Mrs Fox.'

The low voice made her jump, instinctively still on edge after what had happened, but a warmth spread through her as she saw Alfie at the window. 'Come in,' she said, 'don't just hang around out there.'

'I can't,' he said regretfully. 'I'm all over muck and grass.'

'I don't care.' Helen went over to put her arms around him, mindful that it had only been three weeks, and his ribs were still tender. He returned her careful embrace, and she breathed in the fresh scent of the open air that clung to him, burying her face in his neck, and resting her lips against the warm skin beneath the open collar of his shirt. The solid strength of him filled her arms, and her heart, and she wished it were winter, so he had an excuse to stop work for the day.

'Did you come down for anything in particular?'

'Only this,' he said, kissing her forehead. 'Oh, and this.' He pressed something into her hand, and she looked down to see a bent coin, around an inch across and embossed with an image of a pilchard, and ingots of metal. She turned it over to see the words *Cornish Penny* on the other side, and the image of a pumping

415

engine.

'I found it up by the farmhouse,' he said. 'Eighteen eleven, see? Supposed to bring you luck, and I know how much store you set by that kind of thing. Magpies and all that.'

Helen knew exactly where the coin had come from but she had the feeling Fiona wouldn't begrudge her keeping it. 'See a penny, pick it up,' she murmured, smiling. She'd told Fiona she didn't think a token worked the same way, but she'd been proved wrong then, too. 'I've never felt luckier,' she said, folding her fingers over it. 'Thank you.'

'I'd best be off,' Alfie said regretfully. 'Jo's waiting for me up the path a bit.' He put a hand on either side of her face, and kissed her so softly she almost fell into him when he moved away. 'What time's Bertie's train in tomorrow?' he asked.

'Ten-thirty.'

'I'll be down by ten, in Cornwall's rattliest van.' He started away, then came back and kissed her again, leaving her laughing as he dragged himself away with a groan. 'Stop it, woman, you'll be the ruin of me!'

'Ten o'clock,' she called after him, and when he looked back she raised the coin and kissed it.

His face broke into his familiar, sunny grin, and with a mixture of affection, and pleasure at his easy grace, she watched him cross the field until he was out of sight. Then she told herself off for the thoughts she was having, and tucked the coin into her pocket as she turned to go back indoors.

'He's perfect for you, isn't he?'

'Daisy!' Helen pushed away her embarrassment and embraced the girl, who'd come in silently and remained quiet until Alfie had gone. 'What brings you over this evening? I thought Ben was coming to you.'

'He did.' Daisy smiled. 'We thought it'd be nice to see you though. He'll be joining us in just a minute or two, he has a couple things to do first. Is Adam around? Ben wants to speak with him.'

'Not yet, but give them half an hour or so. They're just on their way back from Truro. Shall I pour you both a drink?'

'Please. Adam and that Sam guy hit it off pretty well, didn't they?'

Helen nodded. 'Did you know he's writing to Beth Nancarrow?'

'No!' Daisy looked delighted. 'Is she writing back?'

'So Alfie says. Early days, of course.'

'Well for what it's worth, I liked him a lot. It's nice Adam and Leah can go visit him like this.'

For a couple of minutes they chatted about Leah, who Helen admitted she was a little worried about. 'I don't know what she's going to do now,' she said. 'She's been talking for a while about going back into nursing, but I'm not sure her heart's still in it.'

'How's she getting on with her driving?'

'That's helping,' Helen admitted, 'but . . . Ah, here's Ben now.'

Helen was happy to note the comfortable ease between her son and Daisy. No more awkwardness, or shy blushes, and Ben no longer looked star-struck and awed at the slightest attention she paid him; they were simply a young couple just starting out on a life together, and it warmed Helen's heart. Daisy was a sweet girl and would do Ben no end of good.

'How's the cottage coming along?' she asked. 'Is your writing room finished now?'

Daisy nodded. 'Not winning the Academy Award

was a relief in the end,' she confessed, 'I feel so much freer now to just up and leave Good Boy, like I planned.'

'Daisy's thinking about pitching her next film to a British company this time,' Ben said, his eyes proud on her as she nodded enthusiastically.

'Either British Lion, or maybe British International,' she said. 'They're making some great stuff over here; I'd love to be part of it.'

'Do you have an idea already?'

'Well I had that half an idea about writing the story of what happened at Christmas,' she said, 'and the more I think about it, the more I think it could be a great story. But I'd have to embellish it somewhat, and I wondered how you felt about that.'

'Embellish away,' Helen said, 'I'm sure you'll come up with something wonderful, after all *Dangerous Ladies* is going to be a hit, I'm sure of it.'

'Stone Valley Pictures thinks so, I'm getting a good advance payment.' Daisy looked uncomfortable, and added, 'It's not just because it's my father's studio — '

'Darling, you don't have to tell us that,' Helen said. 'Rex Kelly knew it was a great picture even before he knew you'd written it.'

Ben seemed to sense Daisy's desire to change the subject, and Helen saw him searching his mind for a new topic. 'I gather Aunt Kay and Uncle David have finally parted company for good,' he said at last. 'I bet she's absolutely fuming, especially now he's the big hero of the hour.'

'Her choice in the end,' Helen pointed out. 'I think she really thought that, faced with a choice of a big pay-out, or a job, David would choose the money.'

'Just goes to show she never really knew him that

well at all,' Ben said. 'He'll be so much happier back in his old department.'

'Oh, the job wasn't in his old department.' Helen assumed a secretive air. 'It's with the intelligence service.'

'He's going to be a *spy*?' Ben instantly, predictably, reverted to twelve-year-old boy, and Helen laughed.

'Sorry to disappoint you, but not everyone who works there's a spy. David's going to be an office clerk, just as he was before, but I don't think I've seen him so happy since we were children.'

'And Adam's still planning on holding on to his quarter-share of the hotel?'

'Absolutely, he'd never have let that go. He was devastated enough to lose the other quarter to Hartcliffe.' Helen grimaced and moved away from that unsavoury thought. 'I think he's feeling restless now, though. The renovations he planned are almost all done, bar the new lifts. After that he'll be on the prowl for his next project.'

'Speak of the devil.' Ben turned as Adam came in, and raised his glass in greeting. 'How was the trip?'

'Very good. Sam's an interesting chap when you really get chatting.'

'Lots of stories to tell,' Leah added, as she followed him in. 'And Adam even let me drive his precious Lagonda part of the way back.'

'I'm still shaking,' Adam said with a shudder. 'I'll take a whisky please, Hels, and make it a large one.'

Leah aimed a punch at his arm, and he grinned. 'Nice to see you two youngsters,' he said. 'You staying, or just off?'

'Actually, I have something to tell you,' Ben said, 'so I'm glad you and Leah are back.'

'Go on.'

'Well.' Ben shot a glance at Daisy, who nodded encouragement. 'I've been on the telephone for the past half an hour, to an investment company.'

Helen started, and looked at Adam. It had the ring of an awful memory about it, but Adam looked as blank as she felt, so he couldn't have been offering the boy advice. Thank goodness.

'Hartcliffe,' Ben clarified. 'Well, not the office, that wasn't open today, but . . . Well, I couldn't hold off until Tuesday.' He took a short, shallow breath and spoke in a rush. 'So, I found the manager's home telephone number in Adam's book, interrupted his Friday night dinner, and it's official as of ten minutes ago. I now own their quarter-share in Fox Bay Hotel.'

There was stunned silence.

'But . . . How?' Helen asked, her eyes wide. 'Where did the money come from?'

'Don't worry,' he said, 'I haven't been gambling again.'

Helen assumed an innocent look. 'I never thought you —'

'Yes you did!' he laughed. 'I told Bertie not to say anything about that, but you knew all along didn't you? Anyway, that's over.' He reached out and took Daisy's hand. 'I sold the Bugatti, on Bertie's advice, and Daisy realised I was serious about buying Hartcliffe's share back, so she offered to lend me the rest.'

'*Lend*,' Daisy emphasised, 'he's going to pay back every penny, he swears it. And I'll make sure he does, too.'

'I'll bet.' Leah clinked her glass against Daisy's, and put on a heavy New York accent as she winked at Helen. 'Tough broad. I like her.'

'She offered me some of the advance she got from Stone Valley for *Dangerous Ladies*,' Ben said, as the chuckles died down, 'so I called Simon Hill, and we discussed a fair price. He was never interested in the place to start with, and couldn't understand why Jeanette had been so keen to acquire it.'

'He knew the value though,' Adam said. 'He'd not have let it go for a song, that's for sure, no matter what he thought of it.'

'I'll say,' Ben agreed. 'It was tough negotiating.'

'And now it's yours,' Helen said wonderingly, 'which means you'll own three-quarters, when you inherit my share as well.'

'Keeping it in the family, Mum.' The pride in Ben's voice brought tears to the back of Helen's throat.

'All except my part,' Adam said, but Helen and Ben both turned to him at once.

'Still family,' Helen said.

'Same thing,' Ben said, at the same time.

Adam nodded. 'I'm glad,' he said, and to disguise how touched he was, he gestured to both of them with his whisky tumbler and a warning finger. 'Because I'm all out of noble gestures. I'm not handing you my last share as well!'

Leah rose on tiptoe to kiss him. 'You're *so* giving, that's why I love you.'

Helen laughed and picked up the telephone, and called for supper for six in the sitting room.

'Six?' Adam looked around.

'Fiona's been at the station, she'll be back by now, and getting out of her wet clothes. At least I hope so, though it'd make a change.' She turned back to Ben. 'I was worried Hartcliffe, or Jeanette at least, might have wanted to play a part in the hotel's future.

421

I couldn't have borne that. How did she react?'

Ben shrugged. 'I have no idea. I only spoke to Simon, and he doesn't need her permission, or her signature, to sign it over to me. The paperwork will be here first thing on Tuesday, after the Easter holiday.'

'She'll be spitting,' Adam said with a grin. 'Now the business with the tax audit's out of the way she'll have no reason to demand it stays on Hartcliffe's portfolio.'

'Gobbledegook,' Leah said, rolling her eyes. 'All that matters to me is that she doesn't get to come down here anymore and pull your strings.'

Fiona came in, not yet changed, and was surprised to see everyone there. But she was clearly relieved that it meant Helen had to be more indulgent than usual, and not make a fuss about her damp clothes.

'What are you all looking so perky about?' she asked everyone, after giving Daisy a hug. 'You look as if you've found Blackbeard's treasure.'

When Ben told her his news she was thrilled, but when she heard Daisy's plan to write about the traumatic event they'd shared at the excavation site, her eyes shone. 'Let me help you, *please*? I'd like nothing better! I'll . . . I'll sharpen your pencils, bring you coffee . . . Anything!'

'It's a deal!' Daisy laughed. 'Another thing I'm going to need to look for though, at some point, is an agent.'

'But you're already famous!'

'Perhaps, but not for much longer. The public won't have any cause to remember me once I stop making movies. Which is fine, as far as it goes, but I don't know the British film industry. Or business at all. And I don't have the . . . .' she clicked her fingers, searching for the words, 'the . . . *know-how*, or the confidence to talk up a great deal, you know?' She sighed. 'I need someone who can go in there to those big acquisitions meetings, full of charm and persuasion and really *sell* me . . .'

She fell silent as she saw everyone was looking at Adam, whose smile had been growing wider with every word she'd spoken. He cleared his throat and stepped forward, his hand outstretched.

'Miss Conrad,' he said smoothly. 'Welcome to the brand new Fox Bay Talent Agency.'

* * *

Supper was a cheerful, noisy affair, with everyone talking over each other, suggesting ideas for Daisy's new film, and for the magazine idea Ben planned to bring back to the hotel. The excitement of everything at once coming together, yet at the same time expanding so suddenly, was intoxicating, and there was so much to discuss.

'Bertie's going to go wild tomorrow when she gets here.' Fiona grinned, picking the tomato out of her sandwich. 'Not to mention what Granny Fleur will think of it all! Bags I get to tell Guy, too!'

Helen had been watching Leah closely throughout all the hubbub, as she saw that the slight nervousness she'd noticed earlier had returned. She leaned closer and lowered her voice. 'What aren't you telling me?'

Leah started, and looked about to deny it, then pressed her lips together and moved to speak directly into Helen's ear. 'Sam had an interesting . . . proposition, when we were there today.'

Despite her efforts at discretion, the room fell silent. With all eyes on her, she gave up and addressed herself to everyone.

'He saw how things went in Liverpool, of course,' she said, 'and he knew damned well I was enjoying that business with Neville. Most of it, at any rate,' she added, rubbing absently at the small scar at her hairline.

'He's offered you a job,' Helen guessed, not sure if she was appalled, terrified, or thrilled.

'He wants to spend more time on his painting,' Leah said, 'and on Beth, of course. At least he hopes so, and it's certainly looking promising in that direction. And . . . well yes, he thinks I'd make an excellent investigator.'

'Of course you will,' Adam said warmly, raising his glass to her.

'So you're moving to Truro?' Helen was unable to keep the disappointment from her voice.

'No,' Leah said, breaking into a smile at last, 'that's the beauty of it, Sam's been looking at setting up a studio and offices in Trethkellis. He's offered me more than a job, Hels, he's offering a partnership. We'd be Douglas and Coleridge!'

'Well that's . . . .' Helen's eyes widened. 'Douglas and *Coleridge*?'

'Oh yes, that was the other thing,' Leah said, with an attempt at an airy wave of her hand. 'I knew I'd forgotten something. Adam kept on asking, and I *eventually* caved in.'

'After how long?'

'Oh, ten seconds at least,' Adam said, laughing. He leaned across and met Leah's lips with his own, and Fiona started to give an unladylike cheer, then stopped.

'Not to pour cold water or anything,' she ventured,

424

'but aren't you already married?'

'Widowed,' Leah reminded her, 'with the certificate to prove it. And my husband has reassured me I will remain so.'

'He's gone for good, then?'

'America, just as he wanted. He won't cause trouble for me.' Leah's smile was surprisingly tender. 'Whatever else he might be, he's never wanted that.'

'I'm so glad I got home in time tonight,' Fiona said, 'I wouldn't have missed all this for anything!'

'Well, I've got one or two things to see to in the office,' Ben said, 'then I'm taking Daisy home.'

They said their goodbyes, and Adam went with them so he could discuss Daisy's plans with her, while Fiona was at last despatched to her room to change. Helen and Leah relaxed into the silence, and Leah closed her eyes in bliss.

'Such an awful lot going on,' she murmured. 'It's a bit overwhelming, isn't it? Sometimes it does me good to remember there's a huge, wide world out there, with things going on that make even our dramas look like nothing.'

'Hmm.' Helen looked tiredly at the clock again. 'Put the radio on, we'll just catch the eight-forty-five bulletin. That'll remind us that, despite it all, we're really very small fry in the great scheme of things.'

The radio crackled to life, and Leah tweaked the tuning until the BBC announcer's voice drifted out of the set and filled the room.

'Good evening, today is Good Friday. There is no news.'

425

EPILOGUE

28th July 1930

Bertie looked out of the window as the train rolled slowly through the Cornish countryside. Her twenty-second birthday party had been quieter, but every bit as much fun as her twenty-first, and it was perfect that it had fallen on a Saturday too; once they'd passed their first instruments test, the trainees were no longer required to study at weekends. It meant she had been able to invite both Tory and Gwenna back to Fox Bay with her this time, and as they'd all squashed into Bertie's room together she had finally made up for not sharing their dorm at the airfield. It was a warm and welcoming feeling, and last night she'd even toyed with the idea of asking if they'd mind her moving in with them now. But something in the back of her mind had silenced the idea before she'd voiced it. Just in case.

Still, it had been wonderful to have them at her birthday celebration, and today's leisurely trip back to Caernoweth would leave them well rested, and with time to prepare for their first flights next week . . . Bertie felt a twist of excitement and nerves at the thought, and wondered if Jude Singleton had received her note, written in haste on Friday, and left in Jude's pigeon-hole five minutes before they'd left. Before Bertie had time to change her mind —

'Your brother's a bit of dish,' Gwenna remarked, breaking into her thoughts. 'Daisy is so lucky.'

'He's the lucky one,' Bertie said. 'She's so good for him, but I can't believe she's as batty about him as he is about her.'

'I can.'

'You have a fiancé,' Tory reminded her. 'I, on the other hand —'

'He's not free!' Bertie flicked her rolled up train ticket across the gap between them, and Tory grinned.

'I'm not talking about Ben.'

'Who, then?'

Tory stared fixedly out of the window, as if the field they were passing held some deep fascination for her, but her reflection gave away her smile. 'Not telling.'

'You will, in the end,' Bertie predicted cheerfully. 'You always do.'

'What, like you and Tommy Ash?'

Bertie could feel the flush creeping up her cheeks. 'What about him?'

'You two are absolutely meant for one another!' Tory insisted, turning back. '*And* you both know it.'

'Rubbish! It's not that long since Jowan and I broke up.'

'At least four months,' Tory protested. 'Wouldn't you say it's long enough, Gwen?'

'Gwen-na,' the dark-haired girl said automatically, coming back from whatever thoughts had her attention. 'What?'

'Don't you think four months is long enough to stop mooning over a defunct relationship, and cast your net a bit wider?'

Gwenna shrugged. 'I'm not sure I'd get over it that quickly if Peter and I broke it off.'

'You just said you fancied Bertie's brother!'

'I did not. I just said he was attractive, and that I

427

could see why Daisy Conrad thinks so. That doesn't mean I don't adore Peter.'

'It was a lovely party though, Bertie,' Tory said, shaking her head and returning to the original subject. 'Your mum's fiancé used to work on my grandparents' farm, you know, before Keir Garvey took it over.'

'Really?'

Tory nodded. 'He even remembered me and my brothers. I saw him when he came back after Mr Garvey's wife died, but never once imagined him marrying into a family like yours.'

Bertie chose not to probe too deeply into the *family like yours* comment; if it had been Gwenna she might have done, but Tory wouldn't have meant anything snide by it. 'I knew he was from down here,' she said instead, 'but it really is a small world, isn't it?'

'My mother used to have a secret yen for him, but he was married back when she knew him.'

'Mine's not been this happy for years.' Bertie felt a gentle swell of pleasure as she remembered her mother at the party, sneaking what she'd thought were secret glances at Alfie, as if she still couldn't quite believe her good fortune.

'I love your little sister,' Tory went on, 'and your Aunt Leah's a scream.'

Bertie smiled. 'She certainly is.'

Leah had entertained everyone, as usual, with her array of accents and mannerisms, and her tales of what she and her husband had got up to in the old days, before the war. A proper pair of rogues they'd been, which had appealed to Tory and, more surprisingly, to Gwenna as well, who had really seemed to open up on this trip. Now though, she seemed to be withdrawing into herself again.

428

'Are you alright?' Bertie asked her. 'Not worried about your flight, are you?'

'Not in the least. I'm more than ready.'

'Are you still annoyed you didn't get Singleton?'

Gwenna turned to look squarely at her. 'I'm more annoyed that you did, to be honest.'

Bertie couldn't help bristling at that. 'I don't know why.'

'Because it's such a waste!' Gwenna became more animated. 'You've said time and again you want to train to fly civilian planes. Here's me wanting to learn the real thing, and — '

'Hang on!' Tory broke in; even her good nature was clearly tried by that comment. 'The *real thing*?'

'Oh, you know what I mean!'

'No, I don't.'

'Stop it, both of you,' Bertie broke in, not wanting to spoil what had been an enjoyable break. 'We all want the same thing, don't we? To become pilots. So let's not fight over the kinds of planes we want to fly, for goodness sake!'

'Well, you asked,' Gwenna said. 'I just think I should have had the chance to fly with a real fighter pilot, in a real fighter plane.'

'You will,' Tory said, 'if you're allowed to switch over after basic.'

'Fat chance. You've heard Bowden.' Gwenna's voice deepened. 'Ladies, you may leave early; the remainder of the afternoon will be spent looking at evasive manoeuvres in limited light conditions.'

Tory looked at Bertie, and the two of them couldn't help laughing at the accuracy of the impersonation of the gruff instructor. Gwenna started to frown, then seemed to realise the good naturedness behind the laughter.

'It's still going to be a struggle,' she said, allowing her own smile to creep back.

'A struggle, but not impossible, not if you really want it.' Bertie shifted her attention away again, to the trees flashing past the window. 'Would you be happier if I did?'

'Did what?'

'Want to become a fi . . . I mean, fly military planes.'

Gwenna leaned forward, her gaze sharp. 'Wait a minute, Miss Fox. Just wait a bloody minute! *What* were you going to say?'

Bertie coloured again, but this time it had nothing to do with any fledgling romance. 'I've no idea what you mean.'

'You were going to say you wanted to become a *fighter pilot*. Not just fly the planes.' Gwenna sat back again, her eyes wide. 'You actually want to, don't you?'

'Don't be silly. It's not allowed.'

'Don't give me that!' Gwenna and Tory looked at one another, and Bertie watched them, queasy with anxiety; after all her efforts to fit in, to be the same, had she ruined everything after all? Her mind went back to the girls at the motorcycle race track, when her shyness had come across as superiority and had immediately closed off any avenue to potential friend-ship. Her heart sank. She'd done it again.

'Look,' she began, 'I didn't say I *wanted* to, I said would you be happier if — '

'But you do want to, don't you?' Tory pressed.

'Of course she does,' Gwenna added. 'You only have to look at her in class to know that. And I thought I was obsessive about note-taking.'

Bertie turned away, miserable now, but determined

430

not to let her disappointment show. Well, maybe she didn't need to fit into a group after all; she'd managed perfectly well in her bike race without the other girls, she could manage here. She still had Lynette, and one or two casual friends from the telephone exchange.

But as much as she told herself it didn't matter, part of her wanted to snatch back the note she'd left in Jude's pigeon-hole and put the whole thing out of her mind. Only Jude would have read the real meaning behind it, after all.

Dear Jude.
   Please teach me everything. I won't let you down.
   BF.

'Well?'

Bertie looked up to see Tory's eyes on her. 'Well what?'

'Just admit it, go on.'

'Admit it?'

Gwenna nodded. 'Out loud. I dare you.'

'If you do, I'll tell you who I was talking about before,' Tory added with a cryptic little wink. 'The one who isn't your brother.'

Bertie was surprised to see they were smiling now, and her hopes began to inch higher again. She looked from one to the other, and, encouraged when they nodded to her, she took a deep breath.

'I want to be a fighter pilot.' She saw them exchange triumphant looks, recognised her own excitement reflected in them, and, with a flash of certainty she found the courage to go further. 'No. I *will* be a fighter pi — '

'Martin Berry!' Tory sang out, and Gwenna's and

431

Bertie's eyes met in a moment of shared bemusement. The silence stretched, with Bertie's life-changing pronouncement battling Tory's, and then Bertie's suspended breath broke free in a shout of laughter. The rich, joyful kind, that loosened every last thread of tension within her. The kind she hadn't felt since Xander.

After a moment Gwenna joined in, then Tory, and, as the train rattled steadily onward, Bertie gave herself over to the giddy realisation that the world really was open to them all. Huge, exciting, inviting.

Behind her, Fox Bay shrank into the landscape; ahead of her, Caernoweth Airfield waited; and above her, its vastness promising true freedom and adventure, the sky beckoned.

Acknowledgements

I'm enormously grateful to everyone who's made this series possible, and the making of it so much fun. **Burgh Island Hotel**, and the **RNLI** in particular, who indulged me without complaint as I asked a lot of questions and poked around, notebook in hand!

My thanks to **Martin Pengelly**, too, for helping me out with one or two questions I had about the aircraft of the era.

Continued gratitude to my online writing groups, and especially to **TSAG**, the **Author Support Network**, the **Savvies** and the **Book Connectors**. Thank you to **Deborah Smith**, who generously runs a couple of wonderful, supportive groups for writers and readers, and is always super-quick to share news on behalf of the writers in the groups.

Huge thanks to the fab **Eleanor Russell**, my editor at Piatkus, who has always been at my elbow with encouragement and advice, and is an unfailingly calm 'voice' in my inbox!

My final thanks go to everyone who has expressed interest in the shenanigans of the Foxes and their friends; you make it so easy to keep sharing them with you! I'm sad to leave these characters behind, but thank you for coming along, and for your continued support. I hope you'll come with me, wherever I go next!